Miracles
across the Bridge

To: Kelsey

From: Eva-Lyn

Enjoy reading and tell
your friends about it.

Miracles
across the Bridge

E. Vallin Suede

ARCHWAY
PUBLISHING

Archway Publishing books may be ordered through booksellers or by contacting:

Archway Publishing
1663 Liberty Drive
Bloomington, IN 47403
www.archwaypublishing.com
1 (888) 242-5904

All Scripture quotations are taken from the King James Version.

ISBN: 978-1-4808-8560-8 (sc)
ISBN: 978-1-4808-8558-5 (hc)
ISBN: 978-1-4808-8559-2 (e)

Library of Congress Control Number: 2020901892

Print information available on the last page.

Archway Publishing rev. date: 02/28/2020

One

It came to pass; the flames had risen from the land and sent a message that was interpreted as, "Here I am, the answer to a prayer." The interpretation was not ignored. The right person was at the right place and at the right time to interpret the message, and thus the parcel of land in the middle of the Buek River that had remained uninhabited for a number of years was reclaimed and renamed. This became the place where battered and abused women would find refuge and solace. Here was their Promised Land, across the bridge on the Isle of Hope, where miracles happened.

It was no accident that the inaugural ceremony for the opening of the new community coincided with International Women's Day. This was a day when the whole world showed respect, love, and appreciation toward women and also celebrated their political, social, and economic achievements. The organizers of the celebrations put extraordinary efforts into making the event a success. The aviation displays were awesome. Skywriting planes flew noiselessly by until they reached the area over the Isle of Hope, where they made some slow, peculiar, back-and-forth moves, leaving everyone speculating what exactly was happening. (These were special aircrafts with the ability to expel smoke to create writing in the sky and make it readable to onlookers on the ground.) When the word *Hope* became visible, the planes disappeared across the clear blue sky. Immediately there was a thunderous roar from the crowd as they gazed delightfully at such an achievement. It was a reminder of the annual Puca Luca Navy Air Show, and on this day, the best of the country's female aviators from the Puca Luca Defense Force had total freedom of the skies.

Then the banner planes appeared one after the other, each with a different message. The messages were written in white, purple, and green—the colors of the International Women's Day flag. The first had the word *HOPE* (Help Other People Escape), and another one had *HERS* (Hope, Empowerment, and Rehabilitation Services). Others carried messages such as "Respect Our Women" and "Women, Respect Yourselves."

Helicopters flew by and dropped several thousand flyers that explained the concept across the bridge and the reason for such a development. Back on the ground, minivans, pickup trucks, cars, and anything that had wheels went by with loudspeakers affixed to their roofs blaring the song "Across the Bridge." Immediately the crowd broke out in chorus on hearing this, and the march began across the bridge to the HERS complex, where a reception would be held to honor outstanding citizens who fought for women's empowerment and independence. Many women displayed leadership qualities and had the strength and courage to advocate for other women and children who found themselves in situations in which they lacked these qualities.

As the golden rays of the evening sun cast its last beam upon the blue sky, the day's events culminated in the controlled fireworks that exploded from the decks of the coast guard vessels anchored in nearby waters. Each burst spelled the word *Hope*. The indescribable beauty of the variegated lights of the fireworks mesmerized the thousands of spectators and well-wishers who lined the route. *Oohs* and *aahs* emanated from the people who had withstood the entire day's activities and were privileged to view this rather unusual, interesting, and awesome phenomenon.

Women needed protection, and if the people who pledged to love and protect them till death could not do so, and neither could their elected representatives, then an alternative had to be found. But the sad situation was that it was too late for the many women who were lying in cemeteries, gone too soon, killed by the hands of their husbands or boyfriends without any justifiable reasons. It was also too late for many of those who were alive because they were already physically and emotionally disfigured. These women placed little blame on their perpetrators but blamed their mothers, who'd forced them into marriages instead of encouraging them to get educations. The girls felt enormous pressure to get married and have children. And no doubt the mothers felt guilty at one time or another for telling their daughters that they shouldn't die old, single, and miserable, and that it was better to wear out than to rust out. A new breed of female emerged from this group, the anuptaphobics, who feared staying single and repeatedly made the same mistakes over and over again. These were women who had forfeited their lives by returning to their abusers even when there was definitely a way out, but they simply did not have the will to stay away. Joseph Conrad, a nineteenth-century Polish author, once said, "Being a woman is a terribly difficult task, since it consists of primarily dealing with men." But how many viewed it this way?

Someone had the foresight to recognize that it was time to reach the women who could be helped, and thank goodness that the opportunity existed for them to redefine themselves, get an education, and become independent. They realized that they could write their lives' scripts with happy endings. From that group emerged a different breed: the androphobics, those who had a fear of men. Whether they were once married and divorced or never married, they felt comfortable that they could become successful and independent without men. They ignored the stereotypes of being referred to as old maids, social deviants, and pitiable. They were under no obligation to justify their reasons for being single. They had the right to be looked at as normal and not be discriminated against.

The mastermind behind this rescue mission was a young woman named Ionnia Dunn-Ryte. She had witnessed the suffering of her own mother at the hands of a drunken batterer and abuser who'd called his only daughter a mistake, wished she had not existed, and made attempts to get her out of the way. Because of his actions, coupled with her frail physical condition, Ionnia was not expected to live. To compound the situation, she had a grandmother who also made attempts on her life. But Ionnia had survived for a reason. At an early age, when other little girls were playing hide-and-seek, hopscotch, and other children's games, this little one was passionate that she would make a difference in women's lives. It took some time for her dreams to materialize, but they finally did. When she was asked why she was so passionate about helping women, she quoted William Blake, an eighteenth-century poet who once said, "Can I see another's woe and not seek for kind relief?"

But on this day, International Women's Day, the ceremonious opening of the gates to the new complex and the cutting of the ribbons signaled the fulfillment of a promise that had been only a vision a few years ago and had nearly never happened. Early morning fireworks had started, but not the ones scheduled for that evening. At the crack of dawn, thugs with guns and Molotov cocktails attacked the guards at the foot of the bridge. But as luck or fate would have it, the devices malfunctioned, and the alert guards were able to apprehend the saboteurs before any structural damage could be done to the bridge. However, at a little distance away, others had already set fire to motor vehicle tires, which sent flames and black smoke twenty feet up in the air and which could be seen from miles away. Ms. Dunn-Ryte and her team were alert and well prepared for the femicidal maniacs and their supporters who would stop at nothing in their efforts to infiltrate and destroy the safe haven provided for the women whom they had battered, intimidated, and abused for many years. In the past, the bullies would have hunt the women down like wolves, but this new arrangement would make it difficult, if not impossible, for them to hurt their victims, and this angered them. The bullies could not grasp the idea that what they were doing to women was wrong, so they attacked the rescue concept as one of insanity, cultlike, and geared toward brainwashing women. The mentality of these men in response to women being rescued was synonymous to what the nineteenth-century philosopher Friedrich Nietzsche would describe as "Those who were seen dancing, were thought to be insane by those who couldn't hear the music."

This minor setback would not prevent the ceremony from taking place, and neither would it dampen the spirit of anyone who knew of or anticipated the tremendous benefit this project would be for women who needed help.

Ionnia Dunn-Ryte, formerly Quane, was known as the Lioness and the Intercessor. She exhibited all the traits of a lioness within her, and she would stop at nothing to protect the helpless. She was the protector of the indefensible. She had endured hardships unequaled to anything one can envisage, and then there she was: successful, wealthy, powerful, and beautiful, but still a very modest human being. To quote from Paul Cezanne, a nineteenth-century French poet, "The awareness of our strength makes us modest."

Was she belligerent, was she resilient, did she have self-confidence, or was it just luck that enabled her to eventually fulfill her purpose and witness the miracles that took place? She did not accept all the praise for this reality but would repeatedly say that she owed a great deal to an entrepreneur, Beatrice Zeme, who had a deep passion for Ionnia's mission and who made it possible by bequeathing all her worldly possessions to her. That was why Ionnia named the thoroughfare that led to the complex the Zeme Highway. Beatrice was only one of many individuals who deserved recognition for Ionnia's success.

Ms. Dunn-Ryte epitomized the essence of hope in her effort to overcome the poverty, neglect, abuse, scorn, and despair as she grew up in a world filled with hate. Her triumphs through her tragedies were difficult to comprehend, but she maintained her equilibrium, kept her feet on the ground, and soared toward greater heights even though others tried hard to break her wings. Her life sometimes seemed as though she was a bird in a tree that had the branches cut from underneath it, but she depended on the strength of her wings to propel her forward. Ionnia was truly a force to be reckoned with.

Two

Ionnia Dunn-Ryte's very arduous and eventful journey began some decades ago on August 15 when her mother, Loretty Quane, née Dulvert, gave birth to her in the town of Dartsdam on the island of Puca Luca. This extraordinary female went through some of the worst tragedies imaginable, but she survived for a purpose. Combined with what she witnessed in other people's lives as she grew up, she was propelled to fulfill that purpose. Her experience surely helped shape the course of her life.

Her mother, Loretty, who was the firstborn of Agnes Dunn and Cyril Dulvert, had married Lensley Quane, a small farmer, eight years before Ionnia was born. The couple had moved to Dartsdam, away from the rest of the family who, for some unknown reason, showed Loretty resentment and disrespect.

As Loretty's marriage hit rock bottom and she became disillusioned, someone once asked her what was it that she was expecting in a marriage. Her response was, "I thought my life would be one of prosperity and advancement, but it didn't turn out that way."

She enjoyed her marriage for a short while as long as she remained submissive to her husband, who would constantly remind her, "If you misbehave, you will be punished. In case you have forgotten, let me remind you that you took a vow to love, honor, and obey me."

Loretty tried her best to please her husband because she saw firsthand what other women went through when they rebelled against their husbands' controlling and manipulative hold.

Life had its ups and downs, but things got significantly worse after Loretty had her first four boys and then got pregnant for the fifth time. She questioned whether it was a reward from God that she had a child every year, or whether she was being punished for something. At the end of the first trimester of the last pregnancy, they discovered that Loretty was going to have a girl, and that infuriated her husband. "You cheating bitch! How dare you be unfaithful to me!" Lensley Quane bellowed. "A strong man like me can only father male children. This female is not mine." He called his wife all the derogatory names with which he was familiar, as well as some he made up. He repeated over and over that he didn't want a girl in the family. "They are more difficult to raise, and before you know it, they start breeding like rabbits. Look at Kerl Woodlot's daughter," he said. "See how many children she had at the age of twenty? And look at Felix Coote's daughter, Velline: she had her first one at twelve."

She was about to ask him whether the selfish bastards who'd gotten the girls pregnant shouldn't take some of the blame, and she was also tempted to ask him what he thought about his own mother, Ethel, who'd had six children for six different men, but she kept her mouth shut. Loretty had never seen her husband behave in this manner before, so to avoid upsetting him further, she calmly said, "What do you want me to do?"

"My mother knows someone who can whip up a potion for you, and in no time everything will disappear."

"Is that why your mother spends so much of her time in the bushes gathering shrubs, and why she is always brewing concoctions in her backyard? Are you saying that I should abort our child? I have been carrying her for months, and I will do no such thing. The nerve of you."

"You wouldn't be the only one to do that. Remember Beryl Nye?"

Loretty countered, "And you remember what happened to her, and the old quack who played both doctor and God with her life?"

Loretty vowed to keep the baby girl that she'd always wanted, and when Lensley Quane realized that he didn't have the power to do anything about it, he took to the bottle. His drunkenness escalated to the point where he neglected his farm and the rest of the family. He became a different man, and at times he appeared to be demonized. He referred to his daughter as a mistake and refused to let his wife give birth in the main dwelling, which they occupied with the four boys, Chad, Roger, Kyle, and Tyrone, each one a year older than the next. Chad was the eldest and was of superior intelligence for his age. He'd apparently inherited this from Zaccheus Mann, a distant relative of his mother's.

Ideas flooded Loretty's head as to how to make her husband change his mind and love her like she thought he used to. She abhorred the confrontations and detested the physical and emotional abuse meted out to her and her children. She hated to see her children cover their ears and scream when Lensley Quane unleashed his wrath on her. She loathed and despised him, but she always hoped he would change.

Ionnia was born in a small wattle-and-daub, thatched-roof, farm shed back in the days when Dartsdam had little modern amenities, most of which were only available to the privileged few. It was inside this shed that Lensley Quane had stored farm supplies back in the days when he had been a successful farmer. It was in this place that he'd tended to his sick farm animals, mostly sheep and goats, and nurtured them back to health.

It was close to 6:00 p.m., and Loretty had just finished eating dinner, some steamed vegetables and sweet potatoes. She began to experience labor pains. "Oh, God," she cried as she held her belly with both hands and pleadingly looked at her husband.

"Don't look at me."

"I think I'm going to have the baby soon."

He said, "Nonsense. I think you've had too much to eat."

"Well, can you at least go to the corner and call Miss Earlene for me?"

The contractions were very mild but regular. Loretty took a bath and began the preparation for her daughter's arrival.

Lensley made no effort to get help for his wife, instead walking away and drinking some of the cheap beer he had hoarded in the kitchen. When he finished gulping down the first bottle of beer, he tossed the empty bottle at Loretty, who barely managed to get out of the way.

"You are going to regret this someday," she said as she wiped her forehead with the back of her hand.

Somewhere around 6:30, Lensley saddled up his donkey and disappeared. Loretty felt as though her entire world was crashing down, so she turned to her young boys for help, two of whom stood there with frightened curious expressions.

"Chad, run as fast as you can to the clinic over in Farnsworth and ask Nurse Veetley to come over. Hopefully you can make it before sundown, and before your sister makes her entrance into the world."

Loretty didn't want to take any chances staying in the house in case Lensley returned and hurt her and her unborn child. She'd carried her daughter for nine months and was determined to have a normal delivery. Loretty came up with a plan to head for the shed at the back of the house, where a nearby ditch would fill up with water whenever it rained. She knew that this was the last place Lensley Quane would look for his family, if he looked at all.

While Chad was gone, Loretty gathered a few items, some of which she gave to Roger and Kyle, and some she carried herself. Tyrone held on to her skirt, crying all the way as all four of them headed toward the hut. The contractions were coming on fast—much too fast for comfort. "I could really use some brandy at this time," she said. Instead, she gritted her teeth, bit her lip, sat down on a tree stump, raised her head toward the sky, and prayed.

Nurse Veetley had delivered most of the babies in Dartsdam and surrounding communities, and she was a revered and outstanding churchgoing citizen who cared deeply about all of her patients, big and small. She had three children of her own who were grown and away with professions and families of their own: Carolyn, a journalist; Cynthia, a pharmacist; and Franklyn, an Anglican priest. Since her arrival in Farnsworth almost twenty years prior, no one had seen or heard of a husband, although she would sometimes make reference to someone in the Puca Luca coast guard who she said had been stationed in another island for most of his life and then moved to a foreign country. She never discussed her past, and if Loretty's neighbor, Myra Biddis, knew anything about her, she kept mum about it. Nurse Veetley was an outstanding citizen and had never been accused of any neglect or malpractice; that certainly couldn't be said for some of her cohorts.

Myra Biddis was known in the entire village of Dartsdam and the surrounding areas for being very nosy and inquisitive. She had a lot of time on her hands, and she had sacks upon sacks of scandal and gossip about almost everybody—the living and the dead, the rich and the broke, the beautiful and the ugly, and those who had been unfaithful to their spouses. What Myra didn't know about someone wasn't worth knowing.

Chad was familiar with the route to the clinic because Loretty took him and his brothers there to be immunized, as well as for preventive care and treatment of minor problems. As he negotiated the narrow dirt and gravel road at full speed, his shirt unbuttoned and blew in the evening breeze. He slipped on the gravel, staggered, and fell down not far from Myra Biddis's house. He almost fell in the nearby ditch, and if that had happened, there was no way that he could survive; his little body probably wouldn't have been found till the following day.

Chad screamed at first when he fell, and then his screams became louder when he saw the raw flesh and the blood on his little knee. One could hear the echo from almost two miles away. But this was about being more frightened than hurt. When he looked down at his knees again and the teardrops started mixing with the blood, it appeared to be more hurt than it actually was. He felt a stinging sensation when the raw flesh came in contact with the salty tears. He had had bumps and bruises before, but none as extensive as this. Chad had no intention of turning back. He loved his mother and didn't want it to be his fault if anything were to happen to her and his siblings, born and unborn.

Myra heard the wailing and got up from her veranda, looking toward the direction of the sounds. By that time, Chad had resumed his journey, limping as he tried to make it at a slower speed. Myra stopped him and asked, "Who are you running away from, son?" She feared the worst, knowing the temperament of his father, Lensley Quane.

Chad stuttered and told her of his mission.

Despite all the unsavory qualities that were bestowed on Myra, she was a remarkable woman who was not hesitant in giving of herself to helping others. She took out a handkerchief from her skirt pocket, dried Chad's tears, wiped his knees, applied some ointment, and bandaged them. She led him safely across a grassy path and then told him, "Run along."

Myra's husband, Clifton, was on his way home from work, and he offered to take Chad to Nurse Veetley's. He thought of taking the boy in his car, which probably would be a little faster, but he decided instead to take him on his bicycle. Clifton had an old car with a broken radiator, and it couldn't shift into third gear. When he turned the key in the ignition, the engine made a nasty sound similar to those made by old, tobacco-smoking men when they coughed up phlegm.

Myra headed to Loretty's to offer any assistance that she may need. She knew that her friend would need some help with the other three boys, so she took with her some necessary equipment and supplies. She passed by Miss Earlene's house to ask her to accompany her to Loretty's, but Earlene wasn't home.

Nurse Veetley was having supper when Chad arrived scared and bruised. Clifton Biddis carefully assisted the little lad off the bicycle, and as Chad limped toward the nurse's residence, he shouted, "Nurse, nurse! My momma is having a baby, and my poppa doesn't want her to have my baby sister in the house. She wants you to come right away."

"So where is she?" Nurse Veetley refused to go where her imagination was leading her as to where Loretty was in a time like this. Instead, she offered a silent prayer for her safety. Turning to Mr. Biddis, she asked, "Is Loretty at your house?"

But Chad didn't wait for the older adult to answer. He said, "She may be in the hut, where my poppa used to keep the goats." Then he started to cry.

"It will be all right," Nurse Veetley said comfortingly, and she handed Chad a small cup of warm goat's milk. By then, she had stopped asking questions and had begun to attend to Chad's wounds. When she was satisfied that Chad was going to be okay, she grabbed her bag, put Chad in her horse-drawn carriage, and headed over to his house. Chad offered to help Nurse Veetley pull the horse's reins, and he was fascinated how obedient the horse was.

"After I have supper, I'll stop by later to see If I can be of any help," Clifton assured them before they left.

"As a matter of fact, you can do me another favor," Nurse Veetley said. "You know where my assistant, Felicity Edge, lives? Stop by her house and tell her please to join me later."

"Do you mind if I ask Duke to do so? I want to go over to Miss Loretty's and fix that shed. I know of its condition."

"Not at all, Mr. Biddis. On behalf of Loretty and the family, thank you very much."

Loretty had already tried to make herself and the other three boys comfortable in the hut. This structure was only twelve feet by fourteen feet with earthen floor covered with grass in some places. In one corner stood a few small burlap bags of coffee beans, and there were some containers of corn, which Lensley had never bothered to sell and by now had been contaminated by weavils. Ventilation was very poor except for the holes in the thatched roof, which caused massive leaks whenever it rained; this was one night when she prayed that it wouldn't. There were concerns about Loretty and the baby getting a draught, so later on, Clifton Biddis, a carpenter and cabinet maker, brought over a tarpaulin and covered the roof to avoid any such incident in the event of inclement weather. There was the additional problem of landslide and a ditch which overflowed.

"Be careful where you put down the kerosene lamp or the lantern. If one of these should overturn, the entire hut would go up in flames before you can snap your fingers. This is the last thing we want to see happen," Loretty said in between contractions.

Clifton got busy. He erected a wooden post in one corner of the hut and hung a lantern on it. He also erected two small tables from pieces of wood and a board he'd retrieved from his work shed. "This will come in very convenient for the nurse to set up her equipment."

Lensley had not returned home, and so Myra seized the opportunity to snoop around in Loretty's house. She was appalled at the scant furnishings and inadequate facilities with which Loretty had made herself content. What she used as a living room had two small chairs and a sideboard with a few pieces of china, as well as a small clock that Loretty and Chad would take turns using a small hand tool to wind it up so that it wouldn't stop working. Myra drew a deep breath and said, "Loretty, you sure put up a good front."

One bedroom of the Quane house was for the couple, another was for the children, and a third was unfinished.

During the short period of time that Loretty was alone with the three boys, she had slowly and carefully managed to screen off a portion of the shed with one of the sheets they'd brought over. Then she put the boys to rest in a makeshift bed made of straw and hay. On the opposite side, she and Myra prepared a space for her to lie down. The boys complained of itching in their new bed, and Myra Biddis made them more comfortable with the use of sheets and piles of old clothes she had retrieved from the Loretty's main house.

"Perhaps I could take them back to the house and stay with them."

"That's a good idea. Thank you, Myra. But they might be too much trouble for you," Loretty said. "You haven't been around children this young for a long while."

"Please, can I stay?" Chad pleaded with the women.

Ionnia Quane, weighing five pounds ten ounces, arrived shortly after 10:00 p.m. As was customary, the nurse gave the baby a little slap to make her cry. Ionnia's cry was feeble, and her appearance was a little cause for concern. Her APGAR score was a seven. Nurse Veetley did the best she could under the adverse circumstances. Chad helped as much as possible before joining his brothers on the bed of straw. He felt proud of himself, and ever since that night, he decided that he wanted to be a doctor. He worked hard at achieving this goal.

Nurse Veetley could not stay all night with the family because she had to go to Northfield to deliver Julie Enderone's twin boys. Felicity, her assistant who had arrived earlier, made herself comfortable on a mahogany rocking chair in the corner of the hut, and she frequently checked on the mother and baby.

The next morning, Loretty's sister, Twyleith Gober, was told about the arrival in the world of her niece and the circumstances surrounding her birth, so she hurried over to the house. When she arrived at her sister's home around 8:00 a.m., Lensley was back from his overnight drinking spree. Twyleith fixed something for everyone to eat, but she was furious. She confronted her brother-in-law with an old frying pan. "Loretty and all the kids need to move back into the main house for safety, health, and hygiene reasons. I won't be telling you this again."

"Are you threatening me on my own property? Well, let me tell you this: I'd rather leave than have that woman move in with her little bitch. The boys can come and stay with me, but not that little bastard—she is not my child. I can't look at her, and I can't have her around me. Wake up and smell the coffee, Twyleith."

Twyleith looked with rage and dismay at the potbellied savage standing in front of her, his face contorted with the overnight hangover of liquor. She grabbed a fork that had fallen to the floor. "Get out of my way, you animal, because the only thing you might smell today is the contents of your nasty, big gut splashing all over this house."

The verbal confrontation continued for a little while until Lensley cursed under his breath and said, "All right, I'll go."

"Go to hell!" Twyleith hollered. "That's where you belong. You are going to pay for treating my sister the way you do."

"Your sister and her bastard are the ones who should go to hell—and you can join them. Just leave my boys out of this. I will take care of them."

"Over my dead body," Twyleith said. "You can no longer take care of your sorry ass, much less four children. What do you have in mind? There's no way any of your tramps are going to put their hands on my nephews."

Lensley stormed out of her way after taking whatever money was in the house. He did not care whether Loretty and the children had any because he didn't care about their survival.

The bell at the small Anglican church on top of the hill chimed twelve times, signaling to everyone that it was now the middle of the day. Twyleith and Felicity wrapped Ionnia and Loretty in blankets, placed the mother on an old door that Clifton had brought over, and slowly carried them back to the main house. Twyleith then left to purchase groceries and other necessities for her sister. Twyleith's situation was much different than her sister's. She had married a man who knew how to work hard, take care of his family, and accept them for who they were. Although his job took him out of town for extended periods of time, whenever he came home, he treated his wife like they were newlyweds and always brought home gifts for his two children.

Loretty gave Chad a huge hug and loads of kisses. "I'm proud of you, son, and no doubt your sister will show her gratitude in due course."

Just then, Ionnia let out a small whimpering sound.

"See? She already has." Loretty forced a smile.

"Did I really do well, Momma?" Chad asked as he looked down at his knee. "This doesn't hurt that much now."

Ionnia had such a delicate constitution that she was not expected to survive. This was a direct result of Loretty's privations during pregnancy caused mainly by poverty, neglect, and abuse. The baby was jaundiced and malnourished. Felicity turned to Loretty and said, "I'll have to take you and the baby to the clinic for further observation. I need to have Nurse Veetley and Dr. Crandon take a look at the both of you. Your blood pressure has elevated, and the situation with the baby doesn't look good."

Loretty felt a feeling of sadness overcome her, but she knew this was best for the both of them. "Am I going to lose her? I'm sure Lensley would be delighted. And God knows he doesn't deserve that satisfaction."

"Dr. Crandon is one of the best, and he will make sure your little one survives."

Twyleith said, "Don't worry, sis. We are all talking to the man upstairs. He has brought her this far for a purpose, and I'm sure she will live to fulfill that purpose. We may not be around when it happens, but it certainly will."

"Amen to that," Myra said. "For those who believe."

The best mode of transportation suitable for this journey to the clinic was mule-drawn carriage or a motor car, but neither was available at this time.

"My father has two strong donkeys. I'll ask him to lend a hand," Myra chimed in.

Lionell Stovern agreed without hesitation, saddled up the bigger jackass, and took the mother and baby to the clinic. Myra rode behind on the other donkey and carried clothes and other necessities for her friend.

Loretty spent three days at the clinic, but she had to leave Ionnia there in the capable hands of Nurse Veetley, Dr. Crandon, and the rest of the staff for what they thought would be a few more days but ended up being two weeks. While at the clinic, Loretty attended mandatory family planning lectures and read as much literature as she could get her hands on.

During a one-on-one visit with Loretty, Dr. Crandon advised her, "If I were you, I would think of having tubal ligation. Here are some additional information with the different options." He handed Loretty some brochures.

Loretty was quite certain that she did not want any more children by Lensley Quane, but in the meantime she toyed around with the possibility of having at least one child with someone she hoped to meet one day—someone who would respect and appreciate her. She opted for the reversible tubal ligation method. "I think I will come back in two months to have this procedure done," she told the doctor.

While Loretty was away at the clinic, her mother, Agnes Dunn, stayed with the boys and took care of them while her sisters, Twyleith and Darlene Dunn (nicknamed Dee Dee), visited as often as possible. The adults saw the pain in the children's eyes of missing their mother and sister and not knowing what was happening to them. The two older ones would say repeatedly, "We miss our momma and our baby sister. Are they coming back?" They said it with such emphasis that one could see how much they meant it. Chad refused to eat for a full day, and Roger refused to talk after a while. For the two younger boys, it was playtime as usual, but Kyle seemed to frequently get himself into trouble. He had an anger problem and behaved as if he should always have his own way. Not only did he throw temper tantrums, but he would also throw anything and everything that was in his way, and he couldn't care less with whom the objects came in contact. A number of family members raised concerns about him and feared that he may turn out to be like his father or his uncle Harry.

On the doctor's advice, Loretty returned home without her baby, and this caused a lot of rumors around the community. Each person had a different version of things. One rumor was that the baby had died. Another was that Loretty had given away the baby.

One neighbor, Lena Woodson, had the nerve to confront Loretty. "Tell the truth, Loretty. You gave away your only daughter like a puppy, didn't you? How dare you!"

"If you see the truth on a slice of bread you would eat it without noticing," Loretty said to Lena. "Pay attention to your own life and leave me alone. At least I carried my baby for nine months and delivered her safely. Where is yours?"

Not everyone knew whether Lena had had miscarried, had an abortion, or given up her baby for adoption. When she got pregnant as a teenager, she was sent away to Buek Ridge, and after two years, she returned home without a child.

Myra responded to Lena, "Can't you see that Loretty's baby girl is here for a reason? Look at all what this mother has been through."

Three

The hours went by slowly, and with each passing day, Loretty's focus was on her baby girl. Eager to know what was happening, she decided to pay a visit to the clinic. Halfway through the journey, she ran into one of the health aides, Sally Bettle. "I was on my way to your house, Miss Loretty," Sally said as she handed her an envelope.

Loretty's hands trembled. The earth seemed to sway from under her feet, and she clutched the nearest tree for support. She hesitated for a while before opening the envelope. She didn't know what to expect. The note was from Dr. Crandon. She breathed a sigh of relief when she saw the elegantly handwritten words. "Your miracle baby is well enough to be taken home." She made an immediate decision to return home to tell the others the good news and make the necessary preparations for her daughter's return.

Sally stood there surprisingly silent, waiting for Loretty to say something. She finally broke the silence. "Are you all right, Miss Loretty?"

"I'm fine. Tell Dr. Crandon and Nurse Veetely that I will be there first thing tomorrow morning." This was a happy but scary moment for her. She welcomed the good news but feared the repercussions from the adult male in the home, whenever he returned.

On the early morning of August 31, before the hot summer sun peeked over the hills, Loretty took Chad and Roger with her to the clinic to take her precious gift home. Kyle and Tyrone stayed with their grandma, Agnes Dunn.

Loretty wanted to show off her little bundle of joy to the neighbors, so she opted to walk the entire mile journey from the clinic to her house rather than take up Nurse Veetley's offer to ride in her horse-drawn carriage. They walked very slowly and enjoyed the joyful twitter of the birds, the buzzing of the bees, the lowing of the cows, the bleating of the sheep, the different sounds of the other animals, and the extraordinary scent of the late summer flowers. Mother sang to her baby, picked wildflowers, and sat under a cedar tree to give the boys some time to play with Ionnia.

"She is so quiet, Momma," Roger said. "Are you sure she is okay? She is so tiny, she looks like a string bean."

Roger began tickling Ionnia gently, either to make her smile or to make her cry.

"Son, be careful not to tickle the soles of her feet."

"Why?"

"Because according to folktales, doing so will prevent her from speaking at an early age—and if she did speak, she would stutter."

"You mean she would stutter like Mr. Montaggle?" Chad asked.

"You know Mr. Montaggle?" Loretty asked her son. "He seldom comes out of his house."

"He is my friend's father, and one day his son, Newton, got in trouble at school for beating up some boys who were making fun of his hair cut. When Mr. Montaggle got there, he could hardly get his words out."

"Did his son stutter too?"

"No, Momma."

Ionnia seemed to enjoy Roger's attention, as evidenced by the little sounds she made to assure him that she was alive and well. But before long, she fell asleep again. The nickname String Bean stuck with her as she grew up. She was always tall, thin, and athletic. Chad looked at her proudly, knowing that he had a big part to play in her being here.

The peace and quiet which they were enjoying didn't last long. As they walked past the huge star apple tree by an old, overgrown burial ground, there was a loud crackling sound, and a tree limb came crashing down. They had to scatter quickly to avoid being hit.

"Run, boys!" Loretty yelled at her two sons.

Was someone up in the tree? Had Lensley Quane set it up to get rid of Loretty and the baby? Loretty didn't let go of her baby girl or the few sprigs of flowers which the boys had picked by the wayside and stuck behind her ears. Was this a bad omen, or was this a sign that they were able to escape dangerous situations?

In the nearby fields, one could hear the merry voices of villagers who were tending to their animals and their tobacco crops. The women cooked food, and the aroma permeated the early morning air. It made Loretty and the boys very hungry. They could certainly have something to eat, but Loretty was not going to ask; they would wait until they got home.

The workers must have heard the loud crash. Soon thereafter, a number of them gravitated toward the group, and before long there was close to a dozen people gathering by Loretty, staring at her and her children, especially at the new baby girl.

"Are you hurt, Miss Loretty?" Myrtle Faheesy asked.

As the women wiped their hands in their aprons and focused their eyes on the infant, they asked, "Can we hold her?"

"She is too delicate to leave my hands at this time. I'd rather hold her myself. But you can take a peek," Loretty assured them as she carefully removed the little flannel blanket from around the baby.

"Is her name Precious, or Sunshine?" Valdorine Jessop asked in a mean, mocking, sarcastic tone.

"No, it's Blossom," someone else said.

"My sister's name is Ionnia," Chad chimed in. "And I am Doctor Chad."

"So you are the little doctor we have been hearing about?"

"Yes, ma'am," he said with a wide grin, exposing his missing front teeth.

Valdorine turned to Loretty, pointed to the bundle, and said, "I suppose this little one will be your favorite?"

"I don't have time to show favoritism," Loretty said sternly. "My main focus is to raise my five children on the limited resources I have and to give them the best education available."

Over in another field, other workers saw the gathering and became curious to know if something was being given away, so they hurried on down, not wanting to be left out of anything. By now the crowd had swelled to around thirty people including the inquisitive, and the gossipers. Some of those who had joined the group claimed they had the gift of correctly determining which parent a baby resembled at this time, or whom he or she would grow up to resemble. They didn't verbalize their opinions on this issue to Loretty and instead whispered among themselves.

In the end, everyone was polite enough in wishing Loretty and her family well, whether they meant it or not, including those who frequented the local drinking saloons with Lensley.

"What hypocrites," she said when the group had dispersed.

Loretty felt the need to nurse her baby, so she and the boys walked for a few more furlongs. She then sat down on an old, broken-down tomb a few yards away from the side of the road. When Loretty looked at the tombstone, she could barely make out the name, but as she brushed aside the rotten foliage, she recognized it: Vivienne Brackleigh. This was a young woman who, in her early years, had been molested by her father. When Vivienne had begun to reject his advances, he'd beaten in her head with a hammer until there was nothing left to recognize.

Ionnia yawned and stretched and then gave a hearty tug at her mother's breast.

"Did we do that too?" Roger asked.

When they arrived home, friends and relatives who had gathered extended a warm, loving welcome. Loretty hoped Lensley would not be home, and she was happy when she realized that her wish had come true. "Thank God. At least I can be happy for a while. But will the problems resurface even though I prayed that he would change? Why has God forsaken me? Is He going to let me live to see my children grow up, or is He going to let me exit this world early at the hands of this monster of a husband? Am I praying to the wrong God?"

"Maybe the reason is that you don't have plenty money to put in the collection plate on Sundays," Kerl Moulton said. "Perhaps we need to offer a little bribe from time to time. Who knows? He may like it."

"Kerl, stop the blaspheming," Myra scolded.

Lensley came home drunk as usual, ignored everyone, and headed for the incomplete section of the house located around the back. Loretty braced up her courage and approached him. "Don't you want to see your daughter?" She started to beg him to talk things over. He suddenly turned toward her as if he was going to push her in the brick wall. Loretty lost her balance and almost hit her head on a piece of steel.

Agnes had followed Loretty to make sure she was okay. "I swear if you put your hands on my daughter again, I will chop them off," she warned her son-in-law.

"I didn't touch her. I am having a headache, so allow me go to sleep." After looking at Agnes with a peculiar stare, he said, "Don't try anything stupid now."

"I don't have to. I can see that you are already dancing to the music that the devil is playing in your head." Agnes turned to her daughter and pleaded with her to come to her house, but she refused.

Lensley staggered to the hammock at the back of the house, where Kyle and Tyrone were playing with their marbles. When they saw him, they ran to their mother, but not before Kyle hit him in Lensley's head with some of the marbles.

As the weeks went by, Ionnia showed signs of great improvement, and she appeared to have put on some weight. However, this was short-lived, and she had to be rushed back to the clinic for some unexplained symptoms. She had stopped breastfeeding, and Loretty tried some of the formulas she'd gotten from the clinic, but the baby wasn't tolerating this. She couldn't stop vomiting, and she had an unusual stare as if she was begging for help. She was severely dehydrated and was immediately rushed to Whickam County General hospital, where she remained for five weeks under the care of one of Puca Luca's renowned pediatricians, Dr. Cyndia Etherton.

Loretty received a lot of unsolicited assistance from friends and relatives; her husband contributed nothing. Lensley Quane came and went as he pleased, and he always expected something to eat when he came home. There was peace in the Quane household for a few weeks, and Loretty liked this, but she hated to know that this was the calm before the storm. This was not the type of peace she wanted. She wanted it to be peaceful all the time. She wanted her husband to accept their daughter.

Just when they were enjoying a little solace, the sot returned. He did not inquire about the children, and according to him, he didn't care. He was relieved when he didn't see the baby girl and always wished that she was dead. Finally, one day when he returned home in another state of happy intoxication, he broke the silence and asked, "So where do you want the grave, or did you bury her already?"

Loretty was startled. She looked at him with disdain and asked, "Whose grave? Are you talking about your mother, the murderer?"

"Don't you talk about my mother like that! You know whom I am talking about."

"Do you realize how your behavior is impacting the whole family? You were never like this before. You need help. Admit it."

"Don't annoy me, woman. *You* caused this problem."

Loretty was used to seeing that angry look in his eyes, but she was afraid of what he would do next. She attempted to put on her shoes in the event she had to run. Lensley thought she was going to throw the shoes at him, and his anger turned to a violent rage. "I swear I will kill you if you throw those shoes at me!"

"I wouldn't dare defile my shoes," she shot back. "It is of much more value than you."

Ionnia was brought home from the hospital in a small ambulance, accompanied by two community health aides. As usual, her father was absent. Someone must have tipped him off that the baby was coming home, and three weeks went by before he returned home. Loretty tried her best not to do anything to annoy him when he returned. She was tired of him slapping her around and telling her that she deserved what she got. She was in no shape to be subjected to any physical or emotional abuse at this time. She didn't ask him any questions, and she didn't care where he stayed during his absence. One thing was certain: wherever or with whomever he was staying, it appeared as if he wasn't being fed.

Loretty continued doing her chores, hanging the clothes on the line. Being ignored aggravated Lensley even more. He spoke to the boys, who were playing outside, and gave each of them a piece of candy. Then he turned to Loretty and said in his loudest voice, "Go fix me some food, woman. I'm hungry."

He stumbled onto the veranda past the bassinet where Ionnia lay comfortably asleep, took one look at her, and said, "Everything was okay until you had to come along and spoil it, you bastard."

Loretty was familiar with that tone of voice, and she smelled danger. *I know how dangerous he can be when he speaks like this*, she said to herself. She glanced over her shoulder and didn't wait to see what Lensley was going to do to her baby. *Please, God, don't let him throw my baby over the rails*. With that fear engulfing her, and with fire in her belly, she made a mad rush toward the house, grabbed the frail body of her daughter, and held her closely to her heart. Ionnia stretched, yawned, and then smiled up at her mother, oblivious of her impending danger and giving a look on her face which could be interpreted as, "I am here to stay." Loretty held Ionnia on her side, and without any fuss, she proceeded to fix Lensley some food—food which he had not provided, and food which had been donated courtesy of the Whickam County Department of Health. Loretty's salty tears flowed copiously and fell on the utensil with which she was preparing the ration. "I wish it was something more lethal than my tears getting into this man's food. Oh, how I despise Lensley Quane. Am I insane for staying and putting up with this?"

"Hurry up, woman." He moved toward her. "Do you need me to get rid of what you have on your side so that you can move a little faster?"

"Murderer! The apple doesn't fall far from the tree," Loretty mumbled under her breath.

"What did you just say?"

"This is your child you are talking about," she cried as she looked lovingly into her daughter's eyes and then scornfully at the man who had once pledged his love for her. It made her sick. "When will you come to your senses?"

"The day when the real father puts his name on the birth certificate, and you finally get your ass out of here."

Loretty shoved the plate of steamed chicken wings and sweet potato in front of Lensley and then walked away. She looked back at him and said, "Choke on it."

A few weeks later, Twyleith reminded Loretty, "It is about time for Ionnia's birth to be registered. You do know what they say about not registering a child after ninety days?"

"I am too scared to discuss this with that scum I call a husband. He is sure to go berserk if he's asked to put his name on the birth certificate."

"But it has to be done. She cannot exist without a name."

"How do you suggest I go about it?"

"I will ask Harold and Pastor Brathwaite to speak to Lensley for you."

Twyleith kept her word, and the two men met with Lensley Quane for almost two hours. He was very reluctant at first, but he finally agreed to be present at the registrar's office at the small post office in Farnsworth.

"Loretty, the bishop and I will make sure Lensley doesn't decide to pull a fast one, and we will also make sure he shows up sober," Harold assured her.

The day went by without incident. Lensley kept his word and was the first one to arrive. He did put his name as the father of baby Ionnia, but a few days later, he began to have regrets. He was at one of his watering holes and babbled to his buddies in his usual drunken stupor. "I did something wrong, and I will have to live with for the rest of my life."

"What did you do now?" asked Jasper Hookings, the owner of the bar. "We didn't know that you had a conscience."

"Yes, tell us about it," Arthur Felcopper begged him.

"You wouldn't guess what Loretty, that bald-headed brother-in-law of hers, and the bishop coerced me into doing."

"What, did you marry her a second time? Many people renew their vows after finding love again following turbulent times in their lives."

"Marry someone when you are still married? You idiot—that would be bigamy."

The men burst out in roars of laughter and could barely control themselves. It took them almost ten minutes to settle down.

"This calls for a round of drinks," Herschel Dinkleworth said. "Jasper, serve people what they want. It's on me."

"Now, tell us what happened," Jasper urged Lensley.

"I signed the birth certificate for the girl. I made a mistake. I should not have listened to them."

"Then why did you do it?"

"I guess I was scared when the bishop threatened me with the wrath of God and fire from hell."

A few of Quane's buddies looked at each other and asked, "Since when you are afraid of either God or the devil?"

"Maybe I have a heart after all."

"Yeah, the one that pumps the blood that circulates throughout your body. Or is it liquor going through those veins? Whatever it is, go home, Lensley, and show some respect for your family. You did the right thing," Arthur Felcopper said as he held Lensley by his elbow and hauled him out of the bar. "You will sleep better tonight."

"It's funny that you should mention the word 'sleeping'. You all are guilty of sleeping with my wife," he accused them as he stumbled out of the bar.

"She is a good woman," Arthur called out. "You don't deserve her. If she were like other people, you would really have a problem."

Four

The community of Dartsdam derived its name after Lurline Darts, wife of the Honorable Norman Whickam, the first governor of Puca Luca who, in the early eighteenth century, had set up residence in that area. Lurline's great-grandfather, Shafton Darts, was influential in the erection of the first dam to harness and store water from the Shafton River, mostly for irrigation purposes. Dartsdam sits atop the Shafton Mountains in the county of Whickam, and it was here that Lurline recovered from a long-lasting, suspicious, and unexplainable ailment that almost caused her untimely death. The media claimed they did a study that showed that this area was among the top ten healthiest places in Puca Luca to live. But as the years went by, while other areas of Puca Luca were moving forward, the larger area of Dartsdam was like a forgotten place. Up until recently, there was a marked difference between a group of people who were considered well off and those who struggled to make ends meet. Then there were those in between. There were the privileged few and many ordinary folks, and if one was to draw a comparison, the difference in lifestyle between these two groups of people was like night and day.

On the hilltops where once stood the opulent residence of Governor Whickam, nestled among lush gardens, sat the elegant mansions where the more affluent people continue to reside. These were businesspeople, investors, politicians, clergymen, and retirees from various other professions. Those folks were no strangers to the conveniences of life, and at one point in time, they'd tried to distance themselves from the poor and the middle-class folks who lived in the distance and on the slopes. They wanted to rename their section Dartsdale, stating that Dartsdam sounded more like a damned place. They literally and figuratively looked down on people who were not like them and described them as social inferiors, even those who worked as gardeners, chauffeurs, and household helpers.

Many years ago, when a salt mine was discovered in the vicinity, people moved from different areas of Puca Luca to Dartsdam and surrounding areas in order to obtain employment. But when the salt supply was depleted and the operation ceased, some of the investors and operators moved out, and some stayed behind to reside among the wealthy on top of the hill. Some of the names synonymous with wealth included, DelAyoren, Whickam, Oop, Ernakki, Byroo, Locksley, Flaze, Rusk, and O'Kook.

During the operation of the salt mine, the other residents below had just begun to enjoy some semblance of independence and self-sufficiency and regarded themselves as middle class. They were beginning to emerge from their unfinished two- or three-bedroom, thatched-roof structures and had begun to erect stronger, more modern dwellings with tile or aluminum roofs.

Materials used to construct these homes were in abundance in Dartsdam and surrounding towns and villages. Cedar, mahogany, and lignum vitae trees were everywhere, and from these a large amount of lumber was produced. The DelAyorens owned and operated a lumberyard and sawmill a few miles away, and they employed both natives and outsiders to run this lucrative operation. Thatch, which grew wild on almost everyone's property, was another resource that could not be overlooked. And apart from thatch being used as roofing material, a majority of women earned a livelihood using this product to make baskets, hats, and floor mats.

Dartsdam also thrived on its agricultural resources; the largest and most profitable crops being tobacco and pineapple. Most of the agricultural properties were owned by wealthy land owners who engaged in the business of sharecropping. This was a system in which landowners allowed tenants to work their land for a share of the crop produced, usually 50 percent. There were the farmers who owned land but lacked the resources, so they were not obligated to share 50 percent of their crop. Sharecropping was of great benefit to both farmer and landowner, but it was in the best interest of the farmers to do their best in making the harvest a large one. Farmers who were not functionally literate sought the intervention of the school principal or the justice of the peace to work out the specific agreements as to expenses for seed, irrigation, fertilizer, and pesticides, to name a few.

There were two distinct entrances to the community, one for the rich and the other for the middle class and the poor. During the rainy season, one set of residents had to slowly meander through waterlogged and muddy roads to access their homes, whereas the other set was privileged to have paved roads which they paid for with their own money. It was also quite an unbelievable experience going through certain areas of Dartsdam during the dry season. The amount of dust was similar to what one read about in desert areas.

Some of the middle-class and underprivileged residents of this rural community survived for many years without telephone, electricity, running water, and other basic amenities. Some relied on rainwater caught in huge oil drums, which they bought from the factory owners. Others depended on their supply of water from a nearby spring, and they would carry the water in aluminum buckets on their heads to their homes. Sometimes fights broke out at the spring when the more controlling and bullying set of people demanded first preference. The more humble people were afraid of them and would prefer to fetch water at the crack of dawn, just as the sun was peeping through the trees.

The hilltop residents constructed underground wells. Another alternative was to erect huge aluminum and steel reservoirs to ensure a constant supply of water. During the very dry season, when the underground sources were depleted and the wells ran dry, the rich bought water from adjoining municipalities and had it delivered in oversized tankers, which would be emptied out and stored in the reservoirs.

The wealthy enjoyed the comforts of washing machines. The underprivileged washed clothes by the river using the traditional scrubbing board, large wash pans, or washtubs, and they caustic bar soap that sometimes got too harsh for the hands of the young women, who ended up with severe allergic conditions.

The luxurious homes on top of the hill were powered by electricity provided through the installation of huge standby generators. Their food was cooked on electric or propane stoves by servants. Others cooked their food on wood stoves, coal stoves, or kerosene stoves, and they settled for kerosene lamps, lanterns, and candles at nights. Those not at the top of the hill constructed firepits in outdoor kitchens and would ensure there was ample supply of firewood at all times. Over these pits, they would erect stands to hang and smoke their salted meats, which they stored for months at a time.

The happiest occasions for people who didn't live in luxury were the Christmas and New Year celebrations, which were always observed and celebrated in the village square or at the churchyard. The men played Christmas carols on their accordions and harmonicas, the women operated turntables with 33 and 45 rpm records, and the children sang along. They were encouraged to enter singing competitions and awarded prizes. The under-six age group would get balloons and toys, and the older children received storybooks and school supplies.

The snobs up yonder celebrated the season in a different style. Some of the estate homes had elaborate ballrooms where the wives entertained politicians, investors, judges, bishops, and other dignitaries of their ilk. The guests were all bedecked in diamonds, elegant gowns, and tuxedoes, but that did not prevent them from getting rowdy and out of control. Although the wealthy turned up their noses on those below, they used them as hired help in their homes, who occupied outer dwellings on the premises built specifically for servants. It was in one of these living quarters at the home of Lynette and Neville Flaze that Lena Woodson was raped by one of the rowdy, inebriated millionaire guests. Lawrence Byroo, who owned a soft drink factory, staggered in the back of the premises and apparently couldn't find his way back to the party. That was when he pushed open the door to the small, one-bedroom cottage where Lena, a sixteen-year-old young lady, was lying across the little single bed waiting for her mother to finish her duties in the main house. By the time Byroo was finished with Lena, he had probably sobered up. He threw a large wad of cash in her face and said, "Shut your mouth. I don't know you, and you don't know me." However, someone had seen them and revealed the secret years afterward.

People who did not gain employment with the snobs assisted each other in the true sense of a unified community, and as time went by, those who had saved their money moved to the nearby village of Farnsworth, which was rapidly developing. It didn't take long for Farnsworth to get overpopulated, and as the years went by, these residents petitioned the government to do something about the conditions in Dartsdam and to stop the exodus to other communities. Politicians found their way to the area during election time and made all different kinds of promises that never materialized. One business-man and philanthropist turned politician, Basil Oop, not only empa-thized with the conditions but pledged to right the wrongs, and he eventually did something about it. He condemned the government's insensitivity to the plight of the citizens and brought in the news media, which continuously reported on the conditions until those in authority relented and did something.

Basil was resolute in his efforts to bring about change. He never relied solely on the allocation of funds from the government. Instead, he solicited funds from his wealthy counterparts and urged them to share their wealth, which they reluctantly did because they were proud to see their names in the newspapers. Basil Oop was called a Robin Hood and labeled a socialist, but he was not deterred by any of these labels—in fact, he was proud of it. Sometimes he would jokingly say, "Jesus was also a socialist." He kept reminding villagers that there was a solution to their situation and that it would only last until most residents of Whickam County become self-sufficient.

Basil came up with a plan for people who lacked financial means to further assist them with skills to make them employable. They pooled their meager resources together in a partnership situation to become mini entrepreneurs. The group was led by his wife, Isabelle, who encouraged them to contribute small amounts of money, which would be lent to someone to start a small business enterprise. Not everyone would be a businessperson, but all would benefit from the profits once the businesses began to thrive.

Basil Oop was encouraged by his mother to run for election as a commissioner for the county of Whickam, a seat made vacant by the death of Nathaniel Lifurdy, the oldest politician who was known to serve anywhere in Puca Luca. Basil was elected and lived up to his promises, which was a rarity for politicians.

New roads were constructed, and a new housing development was established during this stage of growth. A limestone quarry was discovered on lands which Basil Oop bought from the family of the late Henry Muggerdon. Had the Muggerdon family known that they were owners of the mine, they would not have sold the land. One of Muggerdon's sons approached Oop to buy back the land for three times the amount Oop had paid for it, but he was laughed at. Commissioner Oop knew that in no time, he could make ten times the amount he'd paid for the land. First he had to conduct tests to determine the type of limestone and what markets were out there for this product. Mining of the quarry brought additional employment and wealth to Dartsdam, and Oop did not selfishly keep the profits to himself. He distributed the wealth. First, he established scholarships for children whose parents endeavored to provide their children with a good education but who were barely scraping by. The Basil Oop Health and Education Foundation was born. Many benefitted from this and had to sign a bond to give back to their communities once they had achieved some level of success.

Basil continued to encourage his wealthy friends to pledge to the fund, and they complied. They were cognizant of the fact that if they invested in the education of the youths of the country and in the overall health of the people, they would reap the benefits later. Improvements were made to schools in Whickam County, and adult literacy classes were established for those who lacked formal educa-tion and wanted to improve themselves. The foundation was also responsible for making physical improvements to Farnsworth Health Clinic, and it provided the opportunity for more qualified staff to be employed. The clinic, which was fully equipped, resembled a mini hospital, and when the first ambulance arrived, there was much fanfare. Basil Oop was like a god to the people. Electric lights and running water were made available throughout the area, and as time went by, more residents were able to afford these modern amenities, and more and better jobs were available.

With the new developments, there emerged another distinct class of people: the Dartsdam middle class. Many of these folks had made a determination not to remain at the same socioeconomic level for-ever, and they made a commitment to help others, whereas the more selfish ones competed against their neighbors. Some began to regret having hastily moved to Farnsworth and other areas, and when they witnessed the transformation of Dartsdam, they desperately wanted to return. They approached the people to whom they had leased their properties, offering them extra sums of money to purchase their crops and for them to terminate the lease.

With the massive improvements, a different breed of people moved to Dartsdam. There were the con men, the prostitutes, and those seeking prime agricultural lands (which they used to cultivate marijuana). This crop flourished for a while, and the business was a lucrative one. Some helpless residents expressed concerns, but others, including cops, were easily bribed and looked the other way. People flaunted their newfound wealth. They built big houses and drove newer model expensive cars. They spent money without discretion. The situation was almost out of control.

Finally, the superintendent of police in charge of Whickam County intervened and dispatched some of the county's most fearless men and women to stop the growth and trade of marijuana. No one could forget the predawn activity that took place one Good Friday at a small, makeshift airstrip in Dartsdam behind the limestone quarry. The police were tipped off by one of their informants that a shipment of weed was supposed to leave on one of the most sacred Christian holidays.

Around twenty men and women dressed in black and armed with various types of weapons positioned themselves inconspicuously and waited for the helicopter to arrive. The tension mounted, and adrenaline rushed through the men and women as the sound of the helicopter grew louder and louder until it finally landed. The group had been briefed by the commanding officer to wait until he gave the okay before they made their move.

A young, trigger-happy constable, Barnsworth Lamb, decided to play hero and ignore the commands of his superiors. The adrenaline-laden constable dashed from his position with his rifle drawn as he headed toward the helicopter. He fired the first shots. The pilot, caught by surprise, attempted a sudden takeoff, performed some peculiar maneuvers, and (whether intentionally or accidently) beheaded Lamb with the helicopter blades.

Before the machine could become airborne, the officers emerged from their positions and made sure it went nowhere. A barrage of shots went off, and the helicopter was immediately brought down.

Both pilots were killed after being riddled with hundreds of bullets. Barnsworth Lamb's head was found some twenty yards away from the rest of his body. At this gruesome scene, a considerable amount of money was recovered from inside the helicopter, and the local police had to hire part-time help to count it. The law enforcement personnel set fire to the building that housed what was estimated at nearly two tons of weed and several gallons of hash oil. Since that time, all such crops were destroyed either by fire or with pesticides and were never again grown in Dartsdam and surrounding areas. The news reporter Carolyn Veetley, who covered the story for the *Whickam Daily Mirror,* received the coveted award of Correspondent of the Year.

Marijuana farmers who were engaged in this type of activity were never prosecuted, but after a while their lifestyle changed drastically because they were no longer able to afford the extravagances. It was the fastest rise and fall one had ever witnessed. This was enough punishment for them. As the saying went, nothing lasts forever, but it appeared as if these people thought that life in the fast lane would. When some of them could no longer maintain the extravagant lifestyle, they committed suicide; others left the area as hastily as they'd come.

Five

Lonnia's young years went by miserably and slowly, but she never relinquished her will to live. She fought a good fight with the help of the only parent who cared, her mother. After a while, it could be said that her father was married to the bottle rather than to her mother, who did the best to raise her five children. Lensley's indulgence became so extreme that he no longer paid attention to his farm and his animals, the means by which he'd supported his family in the past. His father, Walton, had pity for the emaciated goats and sheep, so he took them to his farm in Redwood Vale. No one knew whether he gave his son any money, but later it became obvious that he didn't. Although it was humiliating to talk to Walton about money, Loretty was hurting for money to take care of her children, so one day she approached him and asked, "What arrangement you had with your son with regard to the money when you sold the animals? I need to know because my children and I helped take care of them, and I need money to feed my kids."

Walton let out a big, mocking laugh. "You certainly did a good job taking care of those animals. And to answer your question, I haven't given Lensley a dime. You may not know how much money your husband owes me. These meager animals are not even enough to repay me."

"Well, can you at least help your grandchildren?"

"I'll think about it. How are they, by the way?

Lensley's hatred, rage, and anger escalated into more neglect, emotional, financial, and physical abuse of his wife and children. He even turned against the four boys, whom he'd previously adored. His mother, who was his biggest supporter, believed the lies that he fed her about Loretty, and as a result she treated her daughter-in-law and her granddaughter like the pariah of the community.

"Whore," Ethel Twipple said with disdain and bitter contempt whenever she looked at Loretty. If and when she brought over food to her son's house, she gathered her four grandsons and shared what she had with them; not once did she offer to give any to Loretty or Ionnia.

Then the unexpected happened. When Ionnia was around four years old, Ethel brought over a basket of fruits: pineapple, mango, pomegranate, and papaya. She put the basket down on the front step of the house and said to Loretty, "This is for your little bastard. No one else is to have any. You can say that I am making up for past misdeeds. It's time to put the past behind me."

A stunned Loretty stood speechless by the clothes line, where she was about to hang her children's clothes. She became suspicious of Ethel Twipple's generosity and was angry at the way in which she spoke to her about Ionnia. Loretty's first thoughts were to tear the clothesline down and wrap the cord around Ethel's neck. Ethel was a short, petite person, and Loretty was the total opposite. She was sure she could overpower her easily, but she exercised a lot of restraint.

Ethel stood there making hand gestures, as if waiting for Loretty to thank her.

"What has caused this change of heart?" Loretty asked her mother-in-law.

"It's time, Loretty. It's time for something to happen, and if you don't want the fruits, I can understand. I haven't exactly treated you like a daughter-in-law, but better late than never."

Loretty couldn't stand there any longer and listen to Ethel trying to prove herself as the good soul. "No, no, leave it. You sound genuine, and I don't want to be the bad one here. Thanks. They look beautiful, and I am sure they are delicious."

"I hope things get back to the way they used to be." But the semblance of genuineness didn't last long. As Ethel was leaving, she pulled down some of the wet clothes off the line and stomped on them.

This woman has a death wish, Loretty said to herself as she rerinsed the clothes. By doing so, she left the basket of fruits unattended, and half an hour later, the fruits turned black and began to give off a pungent odor. Her first thought was that the smell was emanating from the fertilizer plant, but that was too faraway. "Sweet loving God, what has Ethel Twipple done to these fruits? This is scary. I can't believe that someone, especially a grandmother, would want to hurt an innocent child. What a scum. I really should have strangled her with that clothesline." Loretty sweated profusely, her body shook, and the tears flowed down her face. She dried her tears and began searching her thoughts for other reasons that might have caused the discoloration and the odor from the fruits. "Maybe it's the pesticides. A number of farmers have continued to use substances that were banned by the Department of Agriculture, and everyone knows that they care about profits more than the health of the consumers." But Loretty could not justify the situation by herself much longer, and she wanted witnesses. "Will anyone believe me? Which one of the neighbors should I tell?"

She looked in several directions and finally saw two of her church sisters; Verniss and Myrtle, who were on their way to the post office and had stopped to wait for Myra. Loretty beckoned to them to come over, and as they approached the house, they put their handkerchiefs over their noses.

"What is that smell? Did your latrine break down?" Myrtle asked.

Loretty told them what happened.

They promised, "We will soon find out what's wrong with the fruits."

Verniss claimed that she was a born-again Christian who had the gift of the Holy Ghost, and for almost five minutes, she exploded in some incomprehensible utterances, which was commonly referred to as speaking in tongues. Then she declared that she had received a message.

"Tell us what the Holy Ghost said to you," Myra implored.

Verniss looked at each of the women and said, "Your suspicion was right, Loretty—and Ethel didn't act alone."

The women's handkerchiefs were not thick enough to ward off the smell, so they grabbed their skirts and covered their noses as they took the container of fruits to a nearby open field. They watched as birds and other insects took one taste and then dropped dead instantly.

"Dear God," Myra said as she made the sign of the cross.

The others were flabbergasted. "Never before has anything like this occurred in Dartsdam."

Loretty sobbed uncontrollably as all four of them walked back to the house. Then she fainted and lost consciousness for a short while. When she revived, her first comments were, "Did Ethel want me to watch my little girl drop dead in front of me as she took a bite of one those fruits?"

"What are you going to do?" the women asked.

"I know that Ethel was a murderer, but I thought she would have stuck to brewing concoctions and mixing them with the castor oil, which she makes and gives to young girls so they miscarry," Myra said. "I never thought that she would go to this extreme, especially with her own flesh and blood."

"So you know about her illegal medical activity?" Loretty asked. "Let us pray for Ethel Twipple and hope she will confess to her crimes, say who her coconspirator is, and ask God for forgiveness."

"Someone should ambush her and shove her head in that iron pot of castor oil one evening," one of the women said angrily.

"Vengeance is mine, I will repay, saith the Lord. Do you remember that passage in the Bible?" Loretty asked.

"But you can't continue turning the other cheek. She has hurt you enough, and this has been taken to a new level."

"Every pond has its puddles, and every dog has its day," Loretty said.

Ethel Twipple was confronted in the village square by Myrtle, and Ethel denied having done anything to the fruits. "I bought them at Mr. Grinn's stall at the farmer's market in Farnsworth. I don't think I should be held responsible for what happened to them. I had one of the mangoes, and here I am standing in front of you. You are not looking at a ghost. And how dare you accuse me of attempted murder?" It was obvious that she wasn't ready to snitch on the culprits who had conspired with her to commit such a heinous act.

When word of the incident got out in the community, as well as the fact that Ethel was shifting the blame on Mr. Grinn, many customers discontinued their patronage for this well-respected grocer and instead began patronizing Mr. Kursock. It was sad how easily loyal customers began to point fingers accusing Mr. Grinn for being a part of the conspiracy. When the truth eventually came out, Mr. Grinn got his customers back, and many apologized for doubting him.

Harold Gober was the one who had hired a private investigator to find out the truth. It didn't take him long to discover who the real culprits really were. Glovene Hatford, a daughter of a longtime friend of Ethel Twipple's, worked with Bertram Inkst's family, who prospered in the lucrative racehorse industry. Glovene admitted to stealing some chemicals and a syringe from a small laboratory run by Bertram's nephew, Byron. Glovene had given it to Ethel Twipple and showed her how to inject the chemical in the fruits to give to Loretty for her little girl. Loretty didn't press charges for attempted murder, but now she had a valid reason for distancing herself from her mother-in-law.

When Bertram Inkst learned what had happened, he did the obvious: severely reprimand Glovene and then terminate her from her job. "I should have you put in prison," he said. "Just remember that there is more than one way to skin a cat."

Glovene didn't know what to expect. Every day, she looked over her shoulders.

Lensley pledged to avenge his mother's coconspirator, Glovene Hatford—not for trying to kill Ionnia, but for causing the community to think of his mother as a would-be murderer. He put all the blame on Glovene. He concocted a scheme with his paternal half brother Harry to befriend Glovene, gain her trust and love, and at the appropriate time unleash his wrath on her.

Lensley was close to his brother Harry, who was a violent person and a bully. Most people were scared of Harry, and the very mention of his name made them shudder.

Glovene was unaware of Harry's intentions, so she readily established a relationship with him. They relocated to the village of Eppon Harbor, the same area where Harry's mother, Hilda Morraine, lived. The relationship went well for the first three months, and everyone thought Harry was a changed man, but later all hell broke loose. Harry constantly beat Glovene with his belt, and on one occasion he held a sledge hammer to her head and threatened to bust it open. She sought refuge many times at his mother's house, but Harry always found his way inside. One day Harry grabbed Glovene, lifted her off the ground by her hair, and threatened to hang her from a tree for all to see. Another time he shoved her into a room, locked the door, and kicked her so hard her body broke the door to pieces; she rolled several yards and out into the open. She was hospitalized with multiple broken bones.

Harry hated his mother because he remembered the scoldings and the beatings he'd received from her to "keep him in line," but those beatings had not kept him out of trouble. He blamed his mother for getting his father fired from his job on the Muggerdon property. He unleashed his wrath on any woman who had a slight resemblance to his mother, and because Glovene was one of those whose features were similar to Hilda's, that was a constant reminder to Harry.

Glovene managed to escape to an undisclosed location where she knew Harry or Lensley wouldn't be looking for her. All that time that Harry was inflicting his wrath on her, she was unaware that she was pregnant. When she found out, she became concerned that her child would suffer some mental or physical disability. Within seven months, she gave birth to a son, Curtis, whom she called a miracle baby. When Curtis was a year old, Glovene got married to Gus Bedwin, who never asked any questions about the child's biological father but willingly adopted him and gave him his name. Gus was a model citizen who forgave Glovene for her past mistakes and gave her a taste of the good life; she no longer had to work. He also made sure that she received the best medical care from the army hospital. As a young man fresh out of engineering school, he had his sights set on becoming one of the finest officers in Puca Luca's military. He joined the Puca Luca Defense Force (PLDF) but met an untimely death at the hands of his fellow soldiers in what was described as friendly fire.

"I will get revenge on all those people who have made my life miserable and empty, no matter how long it takes," Glovene said in her anger and frustration. She blamed everyone but herself for what had become of her life. She blamed the PLDF for her husband's death, and for the small compensation she received as a result. She did not take responsibility for having stolen the chemicals she'd given to Ethel Twipple; rather, she blamed Bertram's son Wendell for their improper storage. She also blamed him for being careless, inattentive, and negligent. Wendell in turn blamed his cousin Byron for allowing Glovene to be familiar with the names of the chemicals and where they were stored.

Loretty had a good relationship with her sister-in-law, Bobeth McLight, Lensley's half sister, and was positive that if she were around, she would be one of the few people on whom she could depend for moral support. She also knew that she would not condone her brother's behavior. She was a remarkable woman who had never shown any resentment to Loretty and her children in the past, and she was sure she would never do that now. She would stand up to her mother and brother. When Loretty gave birth to one boy after another, it was Bobeth who would constantly tell her, "You need to have a girl. The boys need a sister to dote on. If not, they are going to end up playing with dolls. And you know what labels are stuck on them when that happens."

There was no sister-in-law nearby to comfort Loretty right now, and God knew her daughter needed her aunt. Bobeth was away in a foreign country, and no one knew when she would return home for a visit or to resume permanent residency. Loretty didn't want to ask Ethel for an address, so she dug into some old letters she kept into a shoebox and found an old address for Bobeth. She wrote to her and was careful not to include anything too personal at this time, because she wasn't sure whether that address was current, and she didn't want more people to know of her personal situation. It was common knowledge that some of the postal workers were famous for opening letters and skillfully resealing them without detection. This was how many people ended up without the money that relatives had sent for them at Christmastime, and also how many people's private affairs became public ridicule.

Loretty was overjoyed when she received a reply from Bobeth, who expressed how happy she was to hear from her to learn of the existence of her niece. She quickly replied and unloaded a lot of her troubles on her, but if she were to give her all the details, it would cost her every penny she owned to send the package by chartered air courier instead of ordinary airmail. Bobeth was flabbergasted upon learning of her brother's and mother's behavior. What Bobeth wrote in one of her letters came as a shock to Loretty. Bobeth was an abused and neglected woman, though probably not to the extreme as to Loretty's experience. She empathized with Loretty's situation and offered to help her relocate to Hampstead, where she had a past schoolmate and good friend, but Loretty declined the offer.

Loretty would read and reread her sister-in-law's letters, which contained many comforting words that gave her the strength to continue to nurture and protect her daughter. While Lensley was rummaging through Loretty's belongings and looking for money, he came upon one of the letters that Bobeth had written encouraging Loretty to leave her husband. This upset him more than ever. "Imagine my own flesh and blood turning against me. She will eventually find out what it is like to turn against family. This means there are three people I need to get rid of now, but I can't do it alone." He told his mother what Bobeth had written.

"Leave everything to me. I will remind her that blood is thicker than water." Ethel wrote to her daughter, and asked her, "How dare you take that whore's side?"

Bobeth shot back, "Mother, I'm shocked to hear you talk about Loretty this way. You used to love your daughter-in-law. How can you let Lensley turn your mind against her? And even if something went wrong, I don't think Loretty is to be blamed, and you should be able to forgive. Do you still go to church, Mother? If not, start going again and ask for forgiveness. You have committed numerous sinful acts in your lifetime, and I am ashamed of you."

Six

The more abusive Lensley Quane became, the more Loretty convinced herself that she wouldn't have any more children with him. She kept her appointment at the clinic for the tubal ligation procedure. She knew all too well that he had a habit of forcing himself on her. If she were to tell anyone that her husband raped her, they would laugh at her and ask, "How is it possible that a husband can rape his own wife?" At the final meeting with Doctor Crandon and Nurse Veetley, Loretty had a specific request that seemed to puzzle everyone. "Can I get the reversible procedure?" she asked.

"I know that you have had time to read the material and make an intelligent decision," the doctor said. "So tell me, what makes you want to go that route?"

Nurse Veetley shifted in her chair, straightened her glasses on her face, and looked at Loretty without saying a word.

"Just in case I should find a way out of the present situation and eventually marry someone else," she remarked.

"You are very optimistic about your future, and I applaud you for that. If that is what you really want, we will respect your choice and grant your wish."

Loretty withheld the information from her husband about the procedure, and she was confident that Nurse Veetley and her staff were careful about confidentiality issues. However, Henrietta Saddler, one of Theophelous Saddler's illegitimate children, was temporarily employed at the Clinic as a community health aide, and she somehow sneaked into Loretty's medical records and spread the word about her recent birth control procedure. The hospital staff was infuriated. "You make us all look bad," one of her coworkers said.

Henrietta was immediately terminated and prohibited from talking to anyone about this and any other situations at the clinic. Nurse Veetley made sure that all this was in writing and signed by Henrietta; if she broke the agreement, she would face serious consequences. But that did not prevent the other gossipers from chatting about Loretty's procedure. Henrietta was also compelled to tell everyone that she had made a mistake. She apologized to Nurse Veetley and to Loretty.

"Why would Loretty do this?" Lena Woodson asked. "God directed women to be fruitful and to multiply, and to me, that means that a woman should have as many children as God allows her to have."

"That husband of hers is the one who should have some procedure done," Myra Biddis chimed in. "He should be castrated. However, he has had so much alcohol in his body that by now, those little swimmers are drunk too and wouldn't know which way to turn to fertilize any eggs."

"And if he were to impregnate any woman, the baby would be born with what is called fetal alcohol syndrome."

Ethel Twipple got wind of the information and relayed this to her son. Lensley was beside himself when he heard what his wife had done, and when he got to his favorite saloon, he started talking about his wife in the usual derogatory manner. To anyone who would listen, he said, "This is her way of continuing to be the slut she's always been.

This is it—I am done with her. She will have to support those five children all by herself."

"As if you care," Norman Butts said to him.

"I hear you stopped supporting them a long time ago," Samuel Woodson reminded him. "Look at you. While everyone tries to maintain his farm, you let yours become overgrown with weeds and bushes. Where are your animals? And by the way, where do you get money to buy liquor and to support other women with whom you cheat on your wife?"

"I hear he steals from his family and cons other women out of money," someone else chimed in.

"Pathetic," Woodson said.

Loretty was a very fine seamstress who designed fine outfits for people and sewed school uniforms for most of the neighborhood children. Sometimes she would do this for free for those who couldn't afford to pay, and sometimes she would exchange her services for food and other necessary domestic supplies. She was never unfaithful to her husband even though she had the means, reason, and opportunity. She had taught her little daughter how to use a pair of scissors and a needle, and as soon as she mastered, this she was able to help her mother make buttonholes, tack on buttons, and baste the hems of garments. Ionnia's tiny, slender fingers held the scissors, needles, and other pieces of equipment carefully so as not to get hurt, but many times it happened. She had so many needle holes on her fingers that they looked like a sieve. Ionnia became fascinated with sewing, and as the years went by, she obsessed about becoming a fashion designer, taking special notice of what people wore. She ruled out becoming a fashion model, but she could probably be a famous designer like Mohaline Van Bruh, the international fashion designer who was the current chairperson of the Puca Luca fashion industry.

No matter how small the earnings, Loretty believed in saving some money whenever possible. She wanted to stash away some of the money in a place where she hoped Lensley would not find it because she knew that he would tear the place up until he gets his hands on something. She asked her sister Twyleith, to keep it for her. As predicted, Lensley turned the place upside down and didn't find Loretty's money, but he found the children's piggy bank, so he took a hammer to it and escaped with what little savings they had. That was the last thing anyone expected a father to do. If he hadn't found the piggy bank, Lensley would have taken whatever was of value and pawned it at Grant Lavid's pawn shop in Kerquat. Grant was a person who didn't care where the goods came from. He didn't care whether he got busted for possession of stolen goods, and when the rightful owners approached him regarding their properties and valuable possessions, he would threaten them with his shotgun unless they paid him an amount exceeding 100 percent of the actual value of the goods. People were afraid of him, so they guarded and protected their possessions from predators and parasites.

Lensley would disappear for weeks, and when he returned, he was stoned, drunk, and dangerously violent. He would demand sex from Loretty, and when she refused his advances, he would respond by saying, "See? I was right. You are giving it away." Then he would unleash his wrath on her and the children. He would beat the children with whatever he could get his hands on. At nights he woke the boys and made them sit at the edge of their bed for hours, as if forcing them to witness the abuse against their mother. The dreadful crashing of walls and doors, and their mother's sobs and screams, reverberated in their little heads and hearts. They ached so much for their mother and baby sister, but they were too helpless to do anything. The two youngest boys would always complain of being dizzy after the episodes, and Chad taught them how to curl up in a fetal position and cover their ears. While they rubbed their tired, sleepy little eyes and nodded their heads, Lensley told them how worthless their mother and sister were. They weren't too young to understand that their mother loved and cared for them and that he was the one who was no good. Thank goodness he did not spend enough time telling them this until they believed it, because they might have. When they got to school, they were always tired and inattentive; it was a miracle that they learned anything.

Roger was the only boy in the family who grew up with a passion to play musical instruments, and as soon as his teachers recognized this talent, they encouraged him. He was the drummer in his high school's band, and he played the drums with such emotion that one would think he was taking out his anger at someone. Apart from the drums, he practiced his music at home with other improvised instruments such as kitchen utensils. He made a guitar from a piece of old board, a few pieces of strings, and an old tin can. Ionnia sang along to the rhythms. She made up her own lyrics, which focused on her mother's issues. Judging from this, it was evident that even at this young age, she saw the need to right the injustices suffered by women and wished she could do something about it.

How did Lensley Quane's behavior affect his children? Despite empirical evidence that showed a substantial number of children who were exposed to violence and abuse grew up also to be violent and abusive, these children beat the statistics, which mystified everyone who was familiar with their circumstances. They grew up to be productive, progressive adults. That took a lot of therapy in self-assurance, self-esteem, resilience, and a defined goal in life which they all worked toward by ensuring they had a good education.

During one of his moments of tyranny, Lensley grabbed Loretty's sewing machine, threw it in a nearby avocado tree, and smashed it to pieces. How could the existence of a child turn someone into such a monster? What had having a daughter done to his manhood? Because of these actions, Loretty was without income for a while, and apart from seeking alternative sources of income, she again had to rely on friends, relatives, and her church community for support. She even approached her father to lend her money to purchase a new sewing machine, but he shrugged her off. He cared about some of his children but showed indifferences toward others. Whereas Cyril Dulvert showed preferences to Loretty's other four sisters and two of her brothers, her mother, Agnes Dunn, appeared to show equal affection to all her nine children. Others said that she loved Loretty in a special way because Loretty was the one who'd dropped out of school in the sixth grade to help raise the other eight children. Agnes wished she had the money to help her.

One would think that Loretty's siblings would appreciate what she did for them, but the only ones who expressed their gratitude were her younger brother Dwight and her sisters Twyleith and Dee Dee (or Double D, as she was affectionately called because of the size of her breasts; when she was in school, her schoolmates teased her and called her carrot, indicating that she was shaped like one).

Loretty constantly thought about the strange relationship with her father, but she could never figure it out. Whenever she asked her mother about it, she said, "Stop digging up bones. Some dead things are better unexhumed."

When one of Loretty's nephews, Dwight's son Phillip, saw how his aunt was struggling, he prepared advertisements from old pieces of cardboard and had these displayed at conspicuous places throughout the community. Karedo Bay Girls' Academy had a position for a housekeeper and someone to do laundry. Someone saw the advertisement, and Loretty was contacted to do some of the laundry work. Loretty had knowledge that some of the women who did laundry on premises would often get into fights and brawls, so before she accepted the position, she asked the supervisor, Carmen Dussle, "Could I take home the laundry to do at my home? It would be more convenient for me, and I could work my own hours."

"That shouldn't be any problem, Loretty," Ms. Dussle said.

Loretty and her children picked up the laundry early Monday morning, and in the absence of a washer and dryer, everyone at home assisted with the washing of the clothes, the ironing, the folding, and delivering the clothes back to the academy on Friday afternoon.

Loretty compensated her children for the help they gave her. They needed to start saving some money again. Loretty saved most of the money, but some of it she used to purchase an old sewing machine from Francene Wesley, who taught home economics at the school. Fran's husband fixed up the machine the best way he could, so Loretty was able once again to continue sewing for most of the neighborhood children. By this time, she had already lost some of her regular customers to Ms. Wesley and other seamstresses. Some folks continued to use Loretty's services, but that didn't help her much because those were the people who could barely afford to pay.

A thought came to Loretty in a dream. She approached old Arthur Felcopper, who owned a bakery in Dartsdam, and begged him for the unsold baked products. Felcopper didn't question Loretty too much, but because he knew of her situation, he promised that he would help—but not before he made known what he wanted from her in return.

"I may be poor and needy, but I still have my self-esteem. Do you really think I should earn a few pieces of stale bread on my back?" Loretty asked.

"I was only joking, and I am sorry for offending you. I can see that you are not like the other women in this community."

"What does this mean? And who are you talking about?"

The conversation ended abruptly, and both of them pledged that the subject would not come up again.

She put her creative culinary skills to be work and made bread pudding, which the children loved having as a Sunday treat. She made the best bread pudding in Dartsdam and would make money selling slices at school or at church fundraising events.

When Felcopper saw how resourceful Loretty was, he came up with an additional plan to help her. He sold Loretty the empty flour bags at a low price she could afford. "I'm sure you can put these to good use. And believe me, I don't have any ulterior motive for doing this," he assured her.

Loretty washed the bags, bleached and tie-dyed them, and used them to make window curtains, bedspreads, and pillowcases that were beautifully trimmed and decorated with plaid, stripes, or floral trimmings. She would sell some of the finished products on weekends at the market in Farnsworth, where she had a special display area. She received lots of commendations on her creativity. Loretty was a survivor, and in addition to the flour sacks she received from the baker, she bought empty chicken feed bags from Daryl Nooks, who owned a chicken farm in nearby Farnsworth. Dee Dee's boyfriend, Harvell Packston, worked at the farm and was able to buy the bags at a reduced cost, and he agreed to be compensated whenever Loretty's finished products were sold. Loretty used the material to make beautiful patchwork quilts and window curtains.

Not long afterward, Loretty had some competition. One of her church sisters stole her ideas. Otelle Ivonnis, affectionately called Aunt O, operated a store in Kerquat Square, entered into a partnership with Mr. Nooks, and began making quilts and matching curtains from the chicken feed bags. She improved on them in ways Loretty couldn't because she had more resources. Everyone thought the displays in her store were Loretty's, because Aunt O was a person who often tried to help other people in need, and the products were sold as quickly as they were made. Women bought the quilts to send to their children in boarding school. Loretty was devastated. She mentioned this to Ms. Wesley, who told her, "You were intuitive enough to come up with the idea, and I'm sure you will come up with something else."

When Aunt O was confronted, she took on a different attitude. "It's survival of the fittest." Now more than ever, Loretty was motivated to work for the benefit of her children, all of whom would get a good education.

Seven

It was common knowledge that children's success depends on parents' motivation, inspiration, and persuasion. As a result, many parents devoted a lot of time to giving their children a head start prior to enrolling them in school. Some hired private tutors, and some relied on older siblings, relatives, or retired teachers to give them a boost. It was an undeniable fact that early childhood education made good economic sense that had long-term benefits, and it also inspired children to be more competitive in the high school entrance examinations. This was encouraged throughout every social strata of the society, and it was proven that girls who received early childhood education grew up to be independent and opted to not get married and get taken advantage of like so many who thought that marriage was life's purpose.

Loretty could not afford the luxury of private tutors and didn't want anyone to take the credit for her children's success. She was her children's first teacher, and as soon as they could utter their first words, she introduced them to the three Rs. Even though she lacked the means to obtain adequate, up-to-date educational materials and did not get much financial assistance from her children's father after Ionnia was born, she improvised in some of the most creative ways one could imagine. She wrote the alphabet with sticks and stones in the dirt of the unpaved yard, which had to be meticulously swept by the bigger boys every morning. She collected small ends of colored chalk from school to write on old cardboard, and when she ran out of chalk, she used charcoal. Loretty made it a point of duty to retrieve old newspapers from other neighbors who could afford to buy them. She kept up with the news stories from other areas of Puca Luca and surrounding islands, but sometimes when she got the papers, the stories were no longer current. She enjoyed reading the comic strips to the boys, and Kyle had fun recreating the images. Loretty was not ashamed to pick up pieces of paper, empty soda cans, and bottles along the side of the road. She would read the labels to the children before taking these recyclables to Ken Dacy's grocery store in exchange for much-needed everyday items. Most important, Loretty taught the children to read the Bible. She was a strong believer in the Holy Scriptures, and had enough faith to believe that life would eventually get better.

Loretty continuously instilled in her children that a good education was of paramount importance and that this was the way of escaping poverty. Ionnia and her brothers grew up believing that, and they did their best to excel in school despite the many odds that presented themselves. It was almost magical how the family dealt with and overcame the obstacles they faced. Their coping skills were phenomenal and nothing short of miraculous.

Had Loretty not dropped out of school to raise her siblings, she would have had a profession and probably married the man of her dreams, Kingsley Muggerdon. She was a very smart woman, although some would say this was questionable because of the way she handed over her life to Lensley Quane and allowed him to abuse her the way he did. She presented herself in speech and demeanor so well that any stranger would believe she was college educated. She read whatever books and newspapers she could get her hands on but owned only three books: a bible, a hymnbook, and a dictionary. The other books she read were borrowed from friends and relatives or from the mobile library, which stopped at the village square in Kerquat every Friday afternoon.

When Ionnia was five, Loretty enrolled her daughter in Dartsdam Elementary School, which had an enrollment of 250 students. No one could miss the two buildings, which were painted brown with yellow trim, the same colors of the girls' uniforms. In order to get inside the larger building, which housed grade four classes and up, one had to walk up six stone steps without hand rails, and much to the surprise of everyone, there was never an accident. The inside of the schoolhouse was a large hall separated by huge movable partitions and blackboards in some locations. The smaller building had just one step and was designed to accommodate students from grades one to three. Ionnia was placed in the first grade in the smaller building. Loretty met with the principal, Miss Kat Bigsby, and asked her, "Could you place my daughter in the second grade, please? I was observing the first grade material, and my daughter is much more advanced."

"We will have to wait a week or two and see how she performs, and it all depends on the recommendation of her teacher, but I promise I will continue to pay regular visits to the classroom."

On that first Monday morning, Ionnia could feel butterflies flutter in her little stomach. A tear fell as she held firmly to her mother's hands and squeezed her eyes shut. She walked timidly to the back of the line, where thirty-four other children were waiting to be seated on the narrow wooden benches.

While Loretty lingered, Ionnia hesitated and then took her seat at the back of the class beside a girl named Bessie, who appeared to be around eight years old. At one time, Bessie's mother sold baked goods and lemonade at a small shack adjoining the school's premises. She never bothered to enroll Bessie in school when she should have done so, because she needed her to assist with the preparation and sale of her products. Not long afterward, she was investigated by the health department when it was rumored that the lemonade was made in the same tub in which the family washed their clothes and took their daily baths. No matter how this young entrepreneur tried to show everyone that she had separate containers for the lemonade, no one would patronize her, and eventually she had to shut down the operation. Bessie was constantly teased about this, and she took out her anger at everyone, even the innocent.

Loretty remained at school for almost an hour to make sure her daughter was okay. The principal visited the classroom, stayed for around fifteen minutes to observe the students, and then whispered something in the teacher's ears. Miss Connie Wingloss, the teacher, removed Ionnia from the back of the class and placed her in the front seat beside a boy named Ibrau, who was always talking about food and bragging how he helped to prepare food at home for his family.

"I thought we were going to be friends," Bessie said to Ionnia as she gathered up her belongings.

"Yes, we can still be friends." Ionnia could sense that Bessie needed her because everyone else was avoiding her, perhaps because of the aforementioned problem.

Ionnia was the youngest and the smallest student in the class, and she was among the few who had not repeated first grade. As the days and weeks went by, there was enough evidence that Ionnia's accomplishments and potential exceeded the teacher's expectations. She became Miss Wingloss's favorite student, and this caused many in the class not to like her. She wasn't picked to play games with most of the other students. Despite the odds, Ionnia exhibited resilience beyond the ordinary and always questioned herself as to how she was able to accomplish this feat. Whenever she talked about it, there was always and adult to say, "There is a time for everything," citing Ecclesiastes 3:1. Ibrau heard the saying very often, and he also reminded Ionnia of that particular Bible verse, but he couldn't properly pronounce the word *Ecclesiastes*; he would say, "Ease de elastics," and when he did, everyone except Ionnia would burst out laughing.

Miss Wingloss made learning fun, and Ionnia liked her. She was not particularly fond of rote learning because she realized that this method of learning caused the children to memorize but have no knowledge of what they were saying. However, there were some Bible verses and nursery rhymes that they had to memorize whether or not they understood them.

Loretty would have liked to go home and catch up on her projects, but instead she decided to hang around till lunchtime. She stopped by the small school garden and began pulling weeds from the vegetable plot. When Kyle's third grade teacher, Miss Lane saw her, she called out to her. "Mrs. Quane, can you come here a minute? Good morning, I'm so happy to see you."

Oh, no, what has my little boy done now? Loretty asked herself. She approached Miss Lane questioningly. Miss Lane immediately saw the fear in her eyes and said, "I'm glad I caught you. Do you have a few minutes?"

Loretty did not like the suspense, but as she glanced around the classroom, she saw that Kyle was engrossed in his work, and she was satisfied that he was not in any trouble. "Thank God," she whispered as she breathed a sigh of relief.

"Can you please help me to organize my classroom? We are having our annual inspections soon, and I need these charts displayed on the south wall before the children complete their math assignment. Also, if you could stay till after the social studies class, I would like you to help me distribute these reading materials among the students."

Loretty got to work immediately. "I feel like a real teacher's assistant," she said to Miss Lane. It was a bittersweet feeling, enrolling her last child in school and helping her son's teacher.

"Thank you very much. Feel free to come in and do this anytime. You can place the lunch bag on top of my cupboard."

When the lunch bell rang, Loretty went to get her daughter, and then she met the boys at the usual spot under the lignum vitae tree behind Mr. Bill's grocery store. She fed them with some sardine sandwiches and lemonade that she had taken with her. It was not possible every day for Loretty to bring them lunch, so they would have to participate in the free lunch program at the school. The school made sure that a well-balanced diet was served, and they could rely on the cook, Ms. Miriam McSteen, affectionately called Ms. Mirrie.

The boys were eager to hear about Ionnia's activities. The questions came fast and furious.

"I need to be in second grade."

"Don't you like your teacher?" Roger asked.

"Yes, I like her, and I like the children—except Bessie. It's the work. It's too easy."

"Just a few more weeks, and you will be right where you belong," her mother said.

"What about Bessie?" Tyrone asked.

"Miss Wingloss removed me from beside Bessie, and she has given me the evil eye because of that. But I have two more friends, Ibrau and Tammy."

After Loretty hugged and kissed her children, she bade them goodbye and left for home. She looked back several times to see if they were looking back at her, and she wondered what they were thinking at the moment.

As Ionnia watched her mother walk across the playground, she felt lonely and abandoned. She realized that this day had to come, but she never knew that she would feel this way. This was an entirely different situation than the one she was accustomed to when she attended Miss Leam's preschool, near her house. There, she could run home at recess or lunchtime. Here, she was on her own for an entire day, and she had to do her best to cope.

Earlier that day, when Ionnia watched other parents, especially fathers, accompanying their little girls to school, she thought of her own father, who hated and despised her. She wasn't too young to distinguish between love and hate, and she wasn't too young to know that one day she would overcome. She constantly reminded herself that she was special and was put on Earth for a reason. One of her

Sunday school songs, "Jesus Loves Me," appeared in her mental vision, and she took comfort in that.

Ten minutes before the bell rang for the start of the afternoon session, the children separated from each other and joined their friends in their favorite games. Ionnia's new friends, Tammy Gladson and Ibrau Kraun, ran to meet her, held her hands, and took her to play hopscotch until the sound of the second bell alerted them that it was time to file in the classroom to the tune of "Once again the bell has called us from the playground to our class." This song was written by a famous educator, Tom Poe, who maintained that children should have as much fun getting back to class as they had on the playground.

Loretty's children did not escape the teasing and bullying from other children. They were teased for wearing patched clothes with mismatched buttons, and they had one uniform each, which was mandatory to wear only on special days and special occasions. While other children in the neighborhood wore clothes bought from department stores or sent by relatives who lived in foreign countries, the Quane children wore clothes carefully and lovingly sewn by Loretty and Ionnia. As soon as the clothes got torn, the larger holes were covered with unmatched pieces of cloth, and the smaller holes were darned very creatively. But none of this deterred them; they were passionate about learning and were resolute in their desire to excel. They were pressured by their peers to engage in unbecoming behavior, but they stood their ground and would not participate.

Ionnia was ridiculed for her appearance. She was as thin as a string bean. She had high cheekbones and sometimes had a strange look on her face, as if she was always afraid of something or someone. She had dental problems like most of the children in Dartsdam and surrounding areas. This was mainly due to poor diet, the unavailability of good treated water supply, and the lack of funds to buy oral necessities. Four of Ionnia's front teeth were so decayed that she refused to open her mouth and answer questions in class. Although she had a melodious voice and loved to sing, at one time she had to refrain from doing so because of the condition of her teeth. Dr. Boskill, a renowned dentist, visited the schools in the county and provided much-needed dental care free of charge to all who needed it.

The children were mocked for walking barefooted to school. The only pair of shoes each one owned was kept in the patchwork book bag made by their mother. On their arrival at school, they put the shoes on, wore them for the day, took them off on their way home, and put them back in the book bags. If one boy outgrew the footwear, it was passed on to the younger as long as it was still in good shape. They were expected to keep a pair of shoes for as long as possible.

Chad and Ionnia were at a disadvantage. There wasn't any sibling to hand down any shoes to them. However, Chad had better luck. Harvell Packston's sister, Cyndia, had a son two years older than Chad, and they wore the same size shoes. Cyndia and her husband were well-to-do people who could afford everything in abundance, so she would give Loretty shoes as soon as they decided that they didn't want their son to wear them any longer.

Eight

"Starved for affection" was an understatement when it came to Loretty. Of late, her husband treated her like a lemon that was thrown away after the juice was squeezed out. They barely spoke, and when he came home heavily imbibed and wanted sex, if she refused she, would end up with some bruised or fractured body parts. There was nothing enjoyable about this act anymore. She simply lay there and let him help himself, all the time blocking this out of her mind and feeling sick to her stomach. Sometimes Loretty vomited so violently that she had to seek medical attention for chest and neck pains. On one occasion, they thought she had serious external injuries, and after undergoing a battery of tests. the medical social worker at Whickam County General Hospital suggested she get away for a little while from the toxic environment which was hazardous to her health. Despite this suggestion, Loretty returned home. She felt that if she were to leave, her husband would find her and probably kill her. She had seen and heard it happen to a number of women. She was also fearful that he would do something terrible to anyone who rescued her.

Lensley's extramarital affairs were was no secret, and everyone who knew about them wondered what attracted these women to him. Strange as it may seem, all his girlfriends said that they loved him.

One could certainly believe the saying "Love is blind." Although he had nothing to offer them at this moment in time, he claimed he was managing a business with his father, which he co-owned down in Black Cay, and he made promises to the women based on this. Whenever he disappeared, he would tell them that he was in that part of the country taking care of the business. They believed him up to the point at which he was unable to deliver. When confronted, he accused his father of ripping him off, and so some of them directed their anger at Walton Quane.

Loretty had vowed not to be confrontational with anyone, but when her husband's lovers taunted her and especially her children, it mortified everyone who loved and respected them, and some urged her to retaliate. It was obvious that a number of people had lost respect for Loretty because she'd made the decision to stay with her husband. "What she is saying is that it's okay to tolerate abuse," Buelah Pancippy remarked.

One of Loretty's rivals, Emily Brank, couldn't keep away from the family. She frequently walked past the Quane household and hurled insults at Loretty and her children. It was painful to endure, but Loretty did not lower herself to that level. It so happened that if she was outside when that woman passed by, she would quickly go inside. It became such a regular occurrence that Emily began telling people Loretty was afraid of her.

One afternoon when Loretty was on her way from purchasing sewing materials at Traverse McSam's haberdashery, she ran into Emily, and an altercation ensued. "It's one thing to attack an adult, but the children? Leave them out of this. If you interfere with my children again, you will live to regret it," she warned Emily. "You can have my husband; he has nothing. He is simply a broke, drunken, disgusting human being."

"Ha! Don't you know about the business he has over in Black Cay? Where do you think he is when he is not with you or me? When he leaves you, I will have all of that and also your precious little children, except the one that does not belong to him," she mocked Loretty.

Loretty reached in her basket, retrieved a newly purchased pair of scissors, and pointed it at her tormentor. "Good luck. If you live long enough to find out that this is all a lie, what will you say then? And how are you going to react when you find out about all the other idiots like you? Let's see who will have the last laugh."

"What you don't get is that you are the biggest idiot of them all," Emily taunted her.

A day or two after this confrontation, Chad and Roger couldn't keep still any longer. They gathered up the courage to approach their father, and they didn't care what the repercussions would be. "Please stop people from harassing us," they said. "Don't you love us anymore?"

"Stay out of big people's business," he warned them as he walked away.

With nothing positive from their father, the boys decided to take matters into their own hands. They wanted to punish someone for wreaking havoc in their lives. The path that Emily took to do her weekend shopping was familiar to the boys. They knew the ins and outs of the beaten path, could name all the trees that lined the route, and could tell what birds nested in them. One Friday night, at the onset of dusk, they hid in a tree and waited for their prey. As Emily leisurely walked toward the grocery store, they used their slingshots to pelt her with stones. She took her shoes off and tried to run as fast as she could, screaming at the top of her lungs. Emily's hobble skirt was so tight that it almost split to her waist during the escape. She didn't have a chance to notice who the culprits were. Her arms flopped like a fish in a creel as she threw her straw basket in the bushes. Emily ran into Delrine Montaggle and stuttered while telling her of the attack, but swore she had no idea who the attackers were.

"Slow down, Emily. You almost sound like my husband. This could be anybody. You know you have a lot of enemies. Have you also thought that it could even be a ghost?"

By now the boys had alighted from the tree and made their way safely home before anyone could miss them. They felt as pleased as a punch with what they were able to accomplish. No one suspected them, and it remained their secret.

At Delrine's mention of a ghost, Emily's countenance changed, and she looked like she was about to pass out. Near this area was the scene of one of the most deadly and brutal attacks that had ever been meted out to any human being in that part of the world. A young woman named Sylvia Kursock met her untimely death at the hands of her boyfriend, Lynton Stemp, and stories circulated in the community that she had been haunting the entire area ever since.

Lynton was an abusive, jealous, and possessive person who always wanted to know Sylvia's whereabouts. He told her what to wear and forbade her to socialize, especially with her male acquaintances. She made several attempts to bring the relationship to an end, but like most abused women, she went right back to the abuser. Their two children, Hirfa and Barry also suffered physical and emotional abuse at their father's hands.

One night after many days of begging, Lynton gave Sylvia permission to attend a birthday party for her aunt Daphnie. He showed up unannounced and saw her dancing with Daphnie's husband's cousin, Howard Denim. When Lynton saw Sylvia dancing with Howard, he became enraged. He humiliated the two in front of everyone, but he was no match for Howard, a former colonel in the Puca Luca army who stood six feet two inches tall. His physical appearance reminded everyone of Harry Quane.

"I will snap your neck with off with my bare hands!" Howard threatened Lynton.

Linton didn't like Howard's tone, and this set off his premeditated plan. He had sharpened a machete on both sides, and on his way to the party, he'd hidden it in a grassy spot under some brush. He meant to harm Sylvia that night. He grabbed her by her hair and said, "Come on. We are leaving." Now Sylvia's fate was sealed.

They both left, and as soon as they got to the spot where he had hidden the weapon, he stopped and headed toward it. "I need to heed nature's call," he said to her. "Wait right here."

When he emerged from the bushes, he caught Sylvia by surprise, and with the well-sharpened machete, he wasted no time in making its connection to Sylvia's body. No matter where she ran to escape Lynton, he cornered her and chopped off another piece of her body with the machete. For weeks, the neighbors, their dogs, and the vultures were picking up body parts all over the road and in the bushes. Whenever anyone saw a vulture hovering over a particular spot, they would hurry over to the scene, and sure enough there was another piece of Sylvia's body ready to be devoured by the vultures. Sylvia's right hand was never found.

For several days, the villagers searched for Lynton to give him a taste of his own medicine, but he didn't wait for them to do so. His body was found hanging from a tree later that week on his uncle's property. Most people began wearing pendants in the shape of a cross around their necks because they felt that made them immune to Sylvia's appearance and torment. Unfortunately, one person, Theophelus Saddler, did not own one.

Saddler was not one to easily get scared whenever a black cat ran in front of him, or when he heard strange animal sounds at nights. He dismissed these as old folktales. He described himself as a brave man, and whenever he heard dogs howling at nights, he would grab his shotgun and fire off a couple of rounds. He could be heard saying, "How dare you disturb me when I am trying to get some sleep?"

Saddler, another one of those men whose only way of communicating with his family was with violence, recalled an experience he had with Sylvia's ghost while on his way home one night. The full moon that was out that night cast indiscernible shadows on the ground as it shone through the leaves of the trees. Amid the shadows, what suddenly appeared before his eyes was a woman flagging down his horse-drawn carriage, begging for a ride. Who was this? The two horses must have also seen the apparition, because they suddenly leaped up in the air, and stood only on their hind legs, neighing as loudly as they could.

While Saddler was paying attention to stabilizing the horses, he felt a most unusual warmth on the saddle next to him. He looked in that direction and saw a beautiful dove staring at him and making some strange sounds as if begging for some help. The dove was missing its right wing. When Saddler's gaze shifted back to the road, there was no woman. Saddler tried to move his lips in an attempt to say something and make the dove go away, but no words would come out of his mouth. He pulled hard on the reins, and the horses lunged forward and galloped away faster than Saddler expected, indicating that they were frightened by something. He almost fell off the horse, but he held on as much as he could while all manner of sounds came from different parts of his body.

When he reached the crossroads around half a mile away, the horses stopped in the middle of the road, and no matter how hard Saddler pulled on the reins, the horses would not budge. It was as though their feet were stuck in cement. Saddler looked in the direction where the dove had been sitting, but it was no longer there. Suddenly he felt more heat, and he swore he heard what sounded like a woman crying.

When the sensation disappeared and he found his voice, Saddler cursed under his breath, dismounted, and led the horses around the back of Arthur Felcopper's bakery and bar. He tethered them to a post and hurried inside to have a stiff drink. By now he was sweating profusely and could hardly breathe. When the patrons inside the bar inquired what happened, he mumbled, "I just gave Sylvia a ride."

Now he had everyone's attention. They drew closer to him, looked at each other without saying a word, and stared at him in a manner as if to say, "Go on."

While leaning against the bar counter with a bottle or a glass in one hand, each man looked steadfastly at Saddler with suspicion. He told the story from the beginning, stopping only to steady his hands, wipe his forehead, and gulp down some brandy he'd poured from someone's glass. Then he told them, "My body suddenly grew so cold, and if I didn't know otherwise, I would think I was in the Arctic Circle. Immediately my body was filled with goose pimples and was insensitive to touch. My head became so heavy, I wondered if I were Atlas bearing the weight of the world."

"Drunks and children always tell the truth," someone whispered.

Saddler was widely known as a person who didn't fear God, man, or the devil, so seeing him this way made the men in the bar want to believe his story. What convinced them was where he alleged it to have happened. As he gulped down another double brandy on the rocks, his bar buddies clapped their hands and said, "Tell us everything. Don't leave anything out."

Since that scary episode, Saddler was a changed man. He was as humble as a lamb. He began treating his wife and children with respect, and he even started going to church.

"Imagine, it took a dead woman to get my husband to turn his life around," Saddler's wife said to her eldest daughter. "Everyone has a purpose in life, but it seemed that Sylvia has fulfilled her purpose in death."

Nine

Lensley Quane had a habit of finding fault with everything Ionnia did for him, just to take out his anger on her. One Friday afternoon, after consuming beer for most of the day, he tossed a pair of shoes at her and said, "Clean these. You may as well learn how to clean a man's shoes, because you will not amount to anything better than the whore your mother is."

This cut through her like a hot knife going through a slab of butter, but she said nothing. What came to her mind was the sixth commandment in Exodus 20:12, which said, "Honor thy father and thy mother." "This is not fair," she said. "How can anyone honor someone like this?"

She did the best she could with the shoes, but her father was not satisfied. He cursed under his breath and walked away. However, for a while it seemed that he wasn't going to reprimand her, so she continued doing her chores and let her guard down, believing that she was safe. Her brothers were somewhere around the other side of the house, but her mother was not. Loretty had been running multiple errands that afternoon, and she was not at home when this incident occurred. Loretty had gone to deliver some school uniforms she had just finished sewing for some folks in Dartsdam, and on her way home, she planned to stop at the butcher shop for soup bones to make her traditional Friday evening beef soup. She would kill more than two birds with one stone because she had also planned to make a stop in Kerquat square to borrow a few books from the bookmobile, which made its weekly stop at that location.

Ionnia was in for a big surprise. Lensley crept silently behind her with the shoes in one hand and his belt in the other. "Is this the best way you know how to clean shoes?" Then he swung the belt at her, hitting her all over her frail body. The first blow landed on her left arm, tore in her flesh, and left a deep cut. Being the athlete that she was, she sprinted toward the bushes to escape more of her father's wrath. Lensley was too drunk to see in which direction Ionnia had fled, so he kept swinging and swearing. "You serve no purpose! Get out of here—and take that whore of a mother with you."

Ionnia ran out of the house crying, "Murder!" at the top of her lungs. Her father took off in the direction of the sound but did not get very far. He fell headlong among some cactus plants that bordered his property and that of Julius Coote's.

Ionnia navigated her way through the thick, thorny bushes, and the apron she was still wearing ripped. She used pieces of the torn apron to carefully clean the wound left by her father's belt buckle, and then she dropped the bloody pieces of cloth along the way. *If people come searching for me, they will have an idea where to look*, she said to herself.

Ionnia glanced behind her several times to see whether her brothers had heard her screams and were coming after her, but then she said, "I know that if my father should see them, he would put the fear of God in them and try to stop them." What she didn't know was that he was lying helplessly among the prickly plants with no one to help him. Her brothers began running in different directions, calling out her name, but they got no answer.

When Loretty got home, she saw the scared looks on her sons' faces, and she immediately knew that something bad had happened. "What's wrong?" she queried. "Which one of you got into some sort of trouble now?" She looked at Kyle, expecting him to fess up, but this time he was not guilty of any wrongdoing.

"Poppa did something to her, and she ran away," Tyrone said.

Immediately Loretty's thoughts went back to Vivienne Brackleigh's tombstone. She did not share her thoughts and concerns with the boys. Fear gripped her, and forgetting that the boys were right there, she blurted out as loudly as she could, "What did he do to her?"

"He beat her with his belt," Kyle said. "And she may not come back."

Although this was a terrible act, Loretty felt relieved. She told the boys to sit on the bed because she swore she saw the devil standing in front of her and telling her what to do with the man who had once pledged his love for her before God, family, and friends.

After silent contemplation, Loretty sat beside her sons, pulled them close to her, and said, "We will find her. Before long, one of the neighbors will bring your sister home. She probably ran over to her friend Tammy's house. One of you run over there and get her, and let her know that everything will be all right."

The afternoon turned into evening, and Ionnia was still nowhere to be found. Loretty made inquiries from a number of the neighbors, but none of them had seen her daughter. The boys went to different locations but came back empty-handed. At this point, they began to get really scared, but they found it necessary to make light of the situation. "I hope Miss Sylvia hasn't taken her," Kyle said.

"She has no hands," Roger reminded his brother.

"Be serious, guys," Chad said to them.

"Surely, Ionnia does not want to come back here and share the same space with people who hate her," Tyrone said. "Maybe she needs to be rescued by someone who will care for her. I hope she has a guardian angel looking out for her. I am tired of that man we call Father."

"By the way, where is he?" Loretty asked. Not that she cared; she didn't want to see his disgusting face at this time.

"Over there, keeping the cactus company," Tyrone said.

"Good, let him stay there. I'm glad he is not in a position to ambush Ionnia and kill her. That poor child must be so scared, wherever she is."

Ionnia wandered along a path through Muggerdon's property, all the while tolerating her pain and stopping only briefly to pick edible berries, some of which she stored in her apron pocket. As though a guiding force was leading her to safety, she slid through a narrow opening between two huge rocks and navigated her way through a dark, dank, claustrophobic, bat-filled passageway that led into an undiscovered cave. She stopped, coughed a little, and said, "I feel like Columbus." A little glimmer of light broke through, and she caught her first glimpse of the jaw-dropping formations of the stalactites and stalagmites inside the cave. These she remembered clearly from one of her science classes. One of the stalagmites was shaped in the form of praying hands, and she interpreted this as something or someone sent there to protect her.

Ionnia followed the sound of dripping water, and it led her to an area where four small streamlets converged to form the most beautiful lake. The pristine water meandered around the rocks, and its circular motions looked like four huge eyes. She named this newly discovered place the Four Eyes Cave. Ionnia felt rather amused at the existence of her new surroundings. She positioned herself on top of a rock and dipped her feet in the water. It felt warm and soothing. She needed to wash the wound on her arm where her father's belt buckle had landed, but fearing of falling over in the lake, she decided to not bend over and scoop up the water. She put her creative skills to work. She took the laces from her sneakers, tied them together, and attached them to a piece of withe. She tied this makeshift rope to one of her sneakers and gently lowered it into the water. She was used to doing this with a bucket and rope at the well. She carefully guided the sneaker full of water to where she sat, and then she used some of the precious commodity to wash her wound. She tied the arm with another piece of her apron.

"I'm thirsty, but I can't drink the water from my shoes." She looked around for another rock nearer to the water, and she thought she heard a voice that said, "Over here."

"This couldn't be. No one followed me here." She peered in the direction from which she heard the sound and saw no one. Instead of thinking negatively and focusing her thoughts on beings from the spirit world, she said, "Everyone has a guardian angel, and mine must be here with me, but I wish he or she wasn't so invisible."

Ionnia saw a more comfortable-looking rock, and she walked over to it and sat down. There, she scooped up some water in her little hands and poured it down her throat to quench her thirst. But she was disappointed: the water had a pungent odor and tasted bad. She remembered the wild berries she had picked on her way into the cave and stashed in her pocket, so she reached for them and squeezed the juices in her mouth, which immediately replaced the bad taste of the water. Ionnia shifted on the rock, soaked her feet in the water, and felt an unexplainable calm feeling come over her. She felt relaxed, so she listened for another utterance from her guardian angel, but nothing happened. Instead, she heard an owl hooting in the distance; according to folktales, this was a sign of bad luck or death.

Farther down the cave, the lake changed into a waterfall. Ionnia did not want to climb down this unfamiliar path on the slippery rocks for fear she'd slip and fall. She was not a very good swimmer, even though she had been learning this activity for some time. So she sat down on another rock, listened to the sounds of the rushing stream, and watched the shapes formed by the ripples. *What undiscovered beauty?* she said to herself. She kept herself calm by saying a little prayer and reciting Bible verses, and again she thought of one of her Sunday school songs, "Jesus Loves Me." After that, she fell asleep.

Ionnia must have slept for a long while because when she woke up, the streak of light had vanished. *This must be midnight,* she said to herself. But she was able to see with the help of fireflies, peenie-wallies, and other unfamiliar insects that flew around the cave, blinking as they passed her by. Some of these little ones had perched on different parts of her body, and she tried to examine them closely. Then she started giving them names. Huge, menacing bats flew around by the dozens, but none hurt their new companion. The air quality in the cave seemed to have an effect on her, and she started coughing, wheezing, and sneezing.

Ionnia's arm no longer hurt, but now she was very hungry. She started salivating as she thought of the fresh beef soup that her mother regularly cooked on Friday evenings." "I wonder who got my share tonight, and how that person feels devouring it? Do they know that I am hungry and all alone?"

She tried not to think too much about this but instead concentrated on finding a more comfortable spot to lay her head. Despite the coldness of the ground she'd chosen for a bed and the hardness of the rock she'd chosen for her pillow, she stuffed her thumb in her mouth, said her prayers, and hoped she would be found by the right people. If not, she'd let destiny have its way. She lost track of time, and as she cried herself to sleep, she thought about her mother and her brothers. Fear gripped her, and for the first time she was afraid and questioned her existence.

At that moment, her guardian angel spoke to her a second time. "You are put on this earth for a purpose, and your time has not yet come."

"Who are you? Where are you? What is my purpose?" she asked as she looked around in different directions. "Show me a sign." But instead of receiving a verbal answer, a tree limb broke and fell in the water below. "I can't swim," she said. But as she looked at the broken tree limb, she realized that this was something to hold on to if she should lose her balance and fall in the water. Perhaps the hooting of the owl was not a bad omen after all.

Earlier, back at the house, Loretty paced the room where she and the boys were gathered. She too was waiting for natural or supernatural signs and clues that would give her assurance that her daughter was okay. She also anticipated the familiar sound of one of the neighbor's voices, but that didn't happen. She was devastated, and the boys told her, "It's okay, Momma. We will find Ionnia soon." Children were often called the flowers of the Earth, but these looked more like wilted flowers from the pits of hell as they expressed fear for their sister and hatred for their father.

The only person who was unremorseful and unmoved at the disappearance of Ionnia was Lensley. When he emerged from among the cactus plants, he was more concerned with the wounds on his body. After looking at Loretty, his first remark was, "You call yourself a wife. You wouldn't even try to put some ointments on my wounds. Instead, you are focusing on someone who shouldn't be here in the first place. One less mouth to feed." He said it in the cruelest manner one could imagine.

"I am not going to argue with you." The pain in Loretty's belly shot up to a level that, if it could be measured on a Richter scale, would read about 7.5. She looked at the bottle of kerosene oil she had just bought for her lamps and thought of pouring some on her husband's wounds, but she decided against it.

The boys saw the pain in their mother's eyes and decided to stand up to their father a second time. "Shut up, you bum," Chad yelled at him. "How dare you talk about our sister like that? Do you see the pain Momma is going through?"

Lensley ignored his son and continued his inaudible ramblings. The only thing that was decipherable was his intention to force old Coote to get rid of the cactus on his side of the property.

Everyone who got wind of what had transpired was left speechless, knowing that something like this could happen and that someone could get through this thick brush unharmed. Loretty quickly mobilized a neighborhood search party to find her daughter. The male folks used machetes to chop down shrubs so that the women and children could maneuver without difficulty. When they came upon pieces of Ionnia's apron with the blood on it, Loretty let out a long, wailing sound that could be heard a mile away. She was convinced that a wild hog had eaten her daughter. "I'm not prepared to bury a child at this time."

"No, no, don't go there. We will find her alive," Myra Biddis said as she comforted and embraced Loretty. "And moreover, we have not seen one wild hog in this area for the longest while, not since Amy Lude disappeared and it was speculated that she was eaten alive by one of them."

The sun had set, and there was a bright full moon in the starry, cloudless sky. Humidity was low and spirits were high. Some of the searchers brought out their flashlight and lanterns in the event of the appearance of any dark clouds to overshadow the full moon. They called out Ionnia's name several times but got no response. Arthur Felcopper brought out his bullhorn and called as loudly as he could, but all anyone could hear was the echo of his voice.

The group was getting hungry and tired, so they decided to call off the search for the night.

"Let's hold each other's hands and pray for our dear sister Loretty's child," Deacon Garnett Boot announced. When he finished praying, he told the group, "It's either a sixth sense or a voice from the Almighty, but I feel that this little girl is alive and well."

"Deacon, that's no sixth sense, that's the voice of the Almighty," someone shouted. "Shame on you. Have you stopped believing that you can hear God speaking to you?"

"Amen," shouted everyone except Molly Bullock, who whispered to herself, though everyone could hear. "What a bunch of schizophrenics, talking about hearing voices." Needless to say, she didn't get a response.

Loretty was sleep deprived, and it began to show. It was very difficult knowing that her daughter was out there at the mercy of the elements or, in a worst-case scenario, devoured by wild animals—and she couldn't do anything about it. She blamed herself for what had happened. Perhaps she should have taken her on her errands. She went to the window, pulled the curtains away a little, clasped her hands, looked toward the heavens, and said, "Show me a sign if my one and only daughter is safe, and if there is a guardian angel out there protecting her." Just then, a streak of light flashed across the night sky. "Thank you," she said. She breathed a sigh of relief and attempted to go to bed.

Lensley lay helplessly across the bed and snored away as if nothing had happened. His sounds were equivalent to those heard down by the saw mill. Loretty shook him violently. "Wake up. We need to discuss the search plans for tomorrow."

Lensley rolled over half awake, looked at Loretty with a peculiar grin, and in a sarcastic tone said, "You haven't found her? I think she is better off wherever she is."

Loretty recognized the tone with which Lensley asked the question, and she was convinced that there was no deep desire for any information regarding his daughter's safe return. *This man really hates his daughter.* The hot, salty tears flowed down her cheeks in torrents, and she could not control her emotions. "You savage. It is quite obvious you thoroughly enjoy the misery that you have put your family through. But then, I didn't expect anything better from you. I don't know why I bother to say anything to you." She looked around for something to throw at him but decided to save her strength for her children.

"Leave me alone," Lensley bellowed. "What do you want from me? Aren't you happy that the boo-boo is finally gone?"

"Perhaps you care after all. I can see you give her a pet name."

"Come to your senses, Loretty. A boo-boo is a mistake."

Loretty could hardly believe what she was hearing. The pounding headache which she had developed inhibited her from continuing to argue with Lensley. The more her husband tried to break her spirit, the less he succeeded because she never stopped trusting in a supernatural force, and her faith was stronger than ever. She went to lie down beside her tired boys in the other room. Chad, who was the only one awake, dried the tears from his mother's eyes with an old pillowcase, and they both settled down to try to sleep.

The silence in the room was broken when Kyle let out a loud scream followed by four words. "Come back, come back!" Obviously, he was dreaming. This woke everyone else, and Loretty shook Kyle to wake him up.

"What were you dreaming about, Kyle?"

"I dreamed that I saw my sister near the old well on Miss Earline's property, and she was waving goodbye. She was wet all over."

"I'm sure that part about waving goodbye was just a nightmare," Loretty said as she took him in her arms. The other boys gravitated toward their mother while she prayed for Ionnia's safety.

"Why didn't Poppa agree to help with the plans for the search?" Roger asked. "Doesn't he feel badly that he is the cause of all this?"

Loretty couldn't bring herself to tell them what their father had just said.

"Do you think she has fallen down the well?" Kyle asked.

"No, dear. She is safe, but we need to find her. Tomorrow we will search the well." With that said, they forced themselves to go back to sleep.

The search, which resumed early Saturday morning, began with just a few people, but as the day wore on, more and more people from near and far joined in. Although the police were concerned about the welfare of the child, they were contemplating what charges to file against Lensley Quane.

"This is criminal," Corporal Eli Stokman said. "I will find him and force him to get out here and find his daughter. Then I will decide how many charges to slap on him."

When the cops got to the house, Lensley was not there, and neither was there any sign of Ionnia. They had hoped that she had found her way back home, or that she was hiding somewhere nearby. They searched under every bed and in every old tar drum on the premises, but there was no sign of the little girl.

Back out in the wild, the search team scoured acres and acres of thick brush. As they went on, they peered up into the tall trees to see whether Ionnia had climbed any of them. She was agile and tomboyish, and she could climb a tree faster than the squirrels. They searched the nearby lakes and ponds and lowered boys with ropes tied around their waists down the empty well. At the same time, they kept their eyes open for any signs of Lensley Quane, but he knew better than to show his face. The crowd would certainly lynch him, just like they'd done to Buster Keenley when he'd attempted to steal one of Mr. Coote's prized bull.

Some of the children who accompanied their parents were old enough to understand the seriousness of what had happened, whereas some younger ones displayed a picnic-like attitude. The little boys used their catapults (or slingshots, as some called it) to shoot birds, and the little girls cleared away shrubs to skip, play hop-scotch and hide-and-seek. In between games, the girls made small fires and took turns roasting some of the birds killed by the boys.

A large area of the property was cleared out by some of the men, and a command post was established. The women made fires, on which they roasted corn and cooked whatever food each person brought.

"This is more like a county fair rather than a search-and-rescue operation," observed Twyleith. "It's heartening how people can come together in times like these."

The people were in constant prayer asking God for strength, especially to face the outcome were it not to work out the way they had hoped. Emotions ran high, and some called down the forces of evil on the man who caused the disappearance of the young girl. But Loretty held on to her strong belief that her little girl was okay, and she was able to convince quite a few people that God was on her side. Once again, the search had to be suspended till the break of dawn Sunday morning.

Pastor Brathwaite, who led the congregation of The Faith of the

Apostles Church, sent out messages to his members to resume the search for Ionnia. "We are aware that miracles can happen," and he quoted Philippians 4:13. "All things are possible through Christ who gives us strength."

By this time, the entire Whickam County had heard the news about the little girl who'd disappeared, as well as the fact that her father was the one responsible. People had begun to take out their anger and frustration on men whom others had suspected and accused of being abusive to their families.

The crowd grew bigger and bigger, and one of Puca Luca's most familiar faces, Samanthley Whitelace, a self-proclaimed prophetess from Ridgewood, was easily recognized. She claimed to possess extraordinary powers, and she claimed to have special abilities to set and remove curses. She also had immense knowledge of various herbs and roots used to cure many human illnesses and ailments, and this earned her the nickname the Root Mistress. A woman in her thirties, Samanthley was only five feet tall, and she weighed a little over a hundred pounds. No one could miss her presence because of the many trinkets and amulets she wore around her neck and wrists. This particular day, she wore a red scarf around her neck, which most people said was a sign of danger. She was petite and thin but athletic and strong. When she chanted her way to the head of the search team, Pastor Brathwaite was not too happy with this. Each time the man of the cloth suggested that the team take a certain path and conduct the search in a certain area, Samanthley led them the other way. She stopped periodically to mutter strange words, stating that she was calling on the spirits to lead them on the right path.

"Stop mixing the Lord's work with that of the devil," Pastor Brathwaite rebuked her at one point. "We do not need any evil spirits in our midst."

Samanthley ignored him and continued her chanting, dancing, and rubbing her trinkets. She stopped numerous times to spin around in circles and to make the sign of the cross. "Those among us who are unbelievers should step aside," she cautioned. "Your negativity is making it difficult for me to fulfill my mission."

"Pastor, do something. Don't let the devil take over," Earlene pleaded. "The more we give in to this, the less chance we have of finding the child alive."

While the crowd grew impatient, some shouted insults, accusations, and criticisms at Samanthley. "You abducted her!" someone shouted. "You know where she is, and you probably want to offer her as sacrifice later on. We hear how your type works and what you are capable of doing."

Samanthley ignored the insults and accusations being hurled at her. She went straight to the cave into which Ionnia had gone. The entrance was so small that only one person could go in at a time. It was amazing how anybody could get in through such a small space.

"This is as small as a rat's ass," Kemroy Gladson said.

"C'mon, Gladson. Be serious," Loretty said.

"It is important that an equal amount of men and women enter the cave," Samanthley explained.

Everyone looked at Loretty when she said, "I prefer to stay outside."

No one questioned her in that regard, and three men and two other women volunteered. Samanthley wiggled and slid her way in like a snake, and others had a difficult time entering, but their determination and resolve kept them going. It took them a long time to get to the spot where Ionnia was. Between bouts of coughing caused by the dank atmosphere, they managed to shout, "We are coming to get you, Ionnia."

Ionnia thought she heard her mother's voice and screamed for joy. "Momma, Momma! I'm over here!" But Loretty was not inside.

When the group got to Ionnia, she was unharmed. She was sitting on a rock, throwing wild berries in the water, and watching the ripples make various shapes. She kept mental images of those shapes, which in later years helped to piece together the big picture of problem solving. Ionnia seemed so comfortable, as if she owned the place. She looked at the six people who had come to get her. Her mother was not one of them, and suddenly she realized how much she longed for the safety of her mother's arms. At this time she had mixed feelings. She asked about her mother. "Why didn't Momma come with you? Doesn't she want me? Is she mad with me? Did my father hurt her too?"

Ionnia folded her arms around her chest, and appeared to be experiencing a chill. She took a few steps backward and nearly slipped into the water below. She quickly regained her balance and grabbed on to Samanthley's outstretched arms.

"C'mon, baby. Momma is waiting at the entrance. She wanted to be safe so that she can wrap her loving arms around you."

While the optimistic crowd waited outside, the group retraced its steps. It took the group a longer time to make their exit. They took turns carrying Ionnia on their backs as they crawled on their bellies like worms. Loretty was waiting at the mouth of the cave, and as soon as Ionnia saw her, she jumped in her arms. Loretty was overwhelmed and could not hold back the tears. She squeezed her daughter so tightly at first, but she released her grasp when she looked at her daughter's frail body. "Are you hungry? Are you hurting anywhere? Did the bats or the bugs bite?"

The nonmedical rescue team had already bombarded Ionnia with a lot of questions, but she was obviously too weak and tired to answer everything. She was also scared that her mother was going to scold her for running away. Ionnia's wounds that were inflicted by her father's belt buckle were almost healed. She attributed this miracle to the waters in the Four Eyes Cave. Ionnia dried her tears in her mother's skirt and said, "I'm okay."

Loretty looked at each member of the rescue team, gave them each a hug, and said, "Thank you." Samanthley received the biggest hug, and this did not please some of the people, who whispered under their breaths and walked away.

A number of people took turns trying to see inside the cave, and they emerged safely, but one young man, Franklin Ungers, went in and never returned. He either accidently fell in or was pushed in the lake. His swollen body was found washed up in the Shafton river several months after that.

As the six rescuers took their victory walk toward the command post, a thunderous applause erupted from the crowd. Loretty, Twyleith, and the boys held on to Ionnia, who waved at the crowd. She recognized some of her schoolmates, and some of them blew her kisses.

"Momma, all these people were looking for me?"

"They love you, dear."

Loretty led her daughter to an area where a two-member medical team was waiting to examine Ionnia. Afterward, they sat on a bench and ate some of the food the women had prepared. "We will have to take her to the clinic for additional observation," the medics told Loretty.

Pastor Brathwaite reached for his microphone, and after thanking God for the safe return of Sister Loretty's daughter, he made the following announcement. "Regular Sunday service will be held at this very venue today. Everyone please remain, whether or not you are a member of my congregation. And please partake of the wonderful meal which was prepared. It may appear that it's not enough, but remember Jesus's miracle of the five barley loaves and two fishes."

This was the biggest gathering since Pastor Brathwaite had started his ministry. Dozens of people heeded the altar call and surrendered their lives to God. This gave him a new idea to launch outdoor crusades to get new members in the church. Ever since then, he held annual open-air crusades and revival services at different locations, which brought in lots of people to the church—and of course lots of cash, with which he used to expand the physical structure of the church and to establish a day-care center and preschool on the church premises. Pastor Brathwaite made certain that Lensley Quane spent most of his time assisting in the construction of these facilities and remained sober while he did.

When Ionnia returned to school, she wrote an award-winning essay about her adventure. The main emphasis was about the structure of the cave and the healing components of the waters inside. This was published in the country's *Pupil's Own Magazine,* and it was read by parents and students of all age groups throughout Puca Luca and surrounding islands.

Ever since her unplanned adventure, some children referred to Ionnia as the Cave Girl, and some of the teachers who thought that was cute would frequently made reference to her by that name. She never retaliated, and as a result the name never stuck. She remembered her aunt Twyleith telling her that if she ignored something, it would go away.

Ionnia had numerous pen pals to whom she told a part of her life story. Their number one question was, "Where do you get the strength to survive?"

Her response was, "Because I have a purpose to fulfill."

Ten

The story about Ionnia's disappearance, search, and rescue appeared in major print and electronic news outlets in the region, and within a few months the main focus was the alleged healing waters of the Four Eyes Cave. The words on everyone's lips were, "Have you heard of the miracle water?" There was a contest on one of the evening radio shows asking listeners to give a name to the water if this commodity were to be bottled and sold. Some suggested that it should be named after the girl who discovered it, and others thought that it should be named after the property on which it was found, but none of those names stuck. Meanwhile, Muggerdon sat back and enjoyed every moment of this. His silence signified putting plans in place to cash in on the action somehow.

There were as many skeptics as there were believers about the healing qualities of the water. Curiosity got the better of them, and so to prove its authenticity, they would find ways to wiggle themselves inside the cave carrying small containers with which to collect samples of the water.

The news media relentlessly followed the story. They interviewed Ionnia until she became tired of them, and while sticking to her story, one time she politely told a reporter to leave her alone. They were always finding people who gave convincing testimonies as to the magical components of the waters after they collected it and used it for various purposes. Their identities were concealed in case Muggerdon wanted something from them in return. They reported stories of people being healed from lifelong ailments that doctors had tried unsuccessfully for years to cure. They reported on old, arthritic, or bedridden people who were seen walking briskly around after having been washed with the water.

Some infertile women reportedly got pregnant after drinking or bathing in the water, Other pregnant women weren't so lucky: after using the water, they had miscarriages, and this convinced others who had nowhere to turn to for an abortion to rely heavily on this product. Men used the waters as an aphrodisiac, and some young girls used it for weight loss.

Some people who were too skeptical or expecting too much too soon, when asked their opinion, shrugged and said, "No comment."

Then there were the unscrupulous con artists and scammers who collected bottles of water from domestic sources and sold them to unsuspecting consumers who saw no results; in some cases, their conditions deteriorated.

When Gus Muggerdon, grandson of the powerful Sam Muggerdon, got wind that people were profiting from his property, he installed a barbed-wire fence around the property and erected a "No Trespassing" sign.

"If the stories are true, I would like to prove the therapeutic value of the water for myself. We could make a fortune from this," he said.

He took this idea to his grandfather. "This is all poppycock," the grandfather said. "Very soon you are going to tell me that you believe in witchcraft, the tooth fairy, Santa Claus, and Jesus Christ."

Gus replied, "Pops, if you wish, we can hear it firsthand from the young girl who was found in the cave, or from some of the people who stole the water."

"I have a better idea." He was determined to get scientific evidence, so he hired scientists, chemists, and other medical personnel from the University of Krepston to conduct several tests to identify the chemical makeup of the water. He was one of the first subjects to participate in nonclinical trials to see whether people's testimonies were factual. He proved them right and indeed was cured of some of his ailments. After the completion of the lab tests, Muggerdon never shared his results of the chemical makeup with Gus or the public. He said only that the water had the potential to prevent and cure diseases. These compounds were rare and significant, and old Mugg kept these reports locked away in his iron safe to which only he knew the combination. He kept busy formulating a plan, and years later, he told Gus, "An amusement park and hotel will be built on this property, and the cave will be transformed into a tourist attraction and healing spa. From now on, if anyone is caught on the premises, I will deliver my own brand of justice. If I die before this plan materializes, make sure that it comes to fruition."

"I will always attribute our success to the girl, and someday, somehow, I hope to show our appreciation," Gus told his rich, heartless, miserly grandfather, who nodded in agreement. "These waters also had an astonishing impact on my grandfather's mental capacity," Gus opined.

The "No Trespassing" sign on the property continued to be ignored. People still found their way inside the Four Eyes Cave and collected bottles of water, which they kept for themselves or sold to people who really could use it.

The skeptics and the pessimists tried hard to persuade others into disbelief, but others reported positive memories from similar locations many years ago, and when they spoke, everyone listened. One such person; Alphonso Woodlot, a corpulent man in his seventies, a retired justice of the peace, and a government official, was well-known as the village historian. He was well respected and admired in all circles, and no one seemed to doubt anything he said.

Justice Woodlot (affectionately called Woodie) and others of his age group who were regarded as upper middle class would meet at the fire station each Friday afternoon, drink their favorite whiskey, and reminisce on the past.

"Justice, tell us whether you believe the stories about the so-called healing waters," Jack Laskind, the Whickam County fire chief, prompted.

"You know that I am not one to engage in unnecessary conversation and gossip, but the stories about the miracle waters could really be factual," he told his cohorts. "I have to say that I am a believer, and I know of a woman who benefitted from something like that in the past."

They were thirsty for the truth. "Who?" Blanford Bundle asked.

"My daughter Urcell, who is married to Desmond Deek."

The men, who had been standing with glasses in hand, pulled their chairs closer to the old man.

"It was many, many years ago, and I still remember clearly the pain and agony in my daughter's eyes, when after trying for years to get pregnant, her doctor told her to give up trying."

Samuel Sagoo hoisted his heavy frame on one of the tables they used for dominos and card games, looked Woodie in the eyes, and said, "That was terrible. How did that make her feel?"

Woody repositioned himself in his chair and continued. "This devastated my daughter so much that she had a mental breakdown. Urcell loved children and wanted some of her own. On her sixth wedding anniversary, her husband brought home a little two-year-old boy named Egbert, whom he claimed was abandoned by his teenage mother. Urcell seemed to be quite happy raising the boy. He was a spoiled child."

"Justice, get to the point about the water."

"There was an abandoned well in the community, and there were rumors going around that it contained miracle healing waters."

"What happened?" all the men asked in unison.

"Well, Urcell asked her husband to get her some."

"And did he?"

The justice lit a cigar and told the group that his son-in-law was hesitant at first, but when he saw the desperation in his wife's eyes, he relented. "'I do not want to disappointment you," Desmond said. 'As you well know, I am one of those skeptics who do not believe the stories. But I will try my best to get some for you. I hate to see you in this misery, but in the meantime, be happy with Egbert, because this thing with the water may not work out.'"

"And you know what they say about women who can't bear children?" Charles Brownshoe asked. "They call them mules."

"Charlie, don't be rude," Jack chided him.

Justice Woodlot's countenance changed when Charles made the comment, but he ignored him and went on to relate that it was an arduous task to obtain the water. He told how his son-in-law searched all over the neighborhood to find someone willing to do him the favor, and he was willing to pay a handsome price. He finally came across two seven-year-old boys whose parents could really use the money.

"'Look, Mr. Deek, you will have to pay a reasonable amount of money up front if this is so important to you,' the boys' parents said. 'How would you live with yourself if our boys get caught? What if they should disappear down that well?'

"'I will do everything possible to see that nothing happens to them. And if anything were to happen, I take full responsibility.'"

And so the story continued. One boy at a time was tied around the waist and let down with small metal tins, and before long he emerged with the precious commodity. The tins were not filled to the brim because, in Desmond's haste to get them out, some of the water spilled on the way up.

"'Please don't punish us for spilling the water, Mr. D. Perhaps Daddy can give you back some of the money,' they pleaded with Desmond."

Justice Woodlot paused. "Before I go any further, let me add that one of the boys had suffered with epilepsy, and the other one stuttered really badly. Since that day, when they accidently splashed themselves, not one of them ever had an ailment again."

"That's awesome."

"Anyhow, back to Urcell and Desmond. She drank the water every morning for seven days, and one month after consuming the last amount, she had all the signs and symptoms of someone who was pregnant. However, when she went to her doctor, he examined her and told her that she had a tumor."

"I bet Desmond started having feelings of regret?"

"Obviously, especially when this object inside of her began to get bigger and bigger as the months went by. After seven months, they decided that Urcell should have surgery to have the tumor removed. But Desmond had second thought. 'I will take you to see another doctor for a second opinion.'

"When that doctor finished his examination, he approached the couple, smiling from ear to ear. 'Congratulations, you will have a healthy baby boy in two months' time.'"

"Wow, isn't that a true success story?" the chief remarked.

"Did she really have a baby?" someone else inquired.

"Yes, Urcell gave birth to a baby boy they named Moses. I'm ashamed to say that the couple spent most of their time, effort, and love on the new addition to the family and neglected Egbert. Moses always got new clothes, whereas Egbert got secondhand ones purchased at thrift shops and at church rummage sales. Moses would be taken on trips with his parents, but Egbert was left with anyone who had time on their hands. My daughter and her husband began asking around if anyone wanted to adopt the little boy."

"Were they were willing to give Egbert up now that they had a child of their own?"

"Exactly, but no one took the child. Everyone cried shame at them."

"That was a very selfish thing to do."

"Then why didn't you take him?"

"After a while, I wished that I had taken him. But he turned out all right. I always inquired about him."

The historian went on to tell the group how, as Egbert grew older, he could sense the favoritism and the neglect, so he began to rebel against his parent, his teachers, and everybody around him. He did not mince his emotions when he was dissatisfied about something. He hated Moses and did bad, hurtful, things to him. Then he would cry his heart out while proclaiming his innocence. Egbert would be given a warning by Urcell and Desmond, but one day when Desmond's father visited the home, he threatened to beat Egbert senseless if he did not behave himself. That didn't faze the boy, and things got so uncontrollable that he was labeled as ungovernable. His first report card from school had the word *incorrigible* written in bold red letters.

One Father's Day, children were asked in Sunday School to say good things about their father, and when it was Egbert's turn, he shouted obscenities. This surprised the minister in such a way that he reprimanded the Deeks and compelled them to attend a parenting class that was held at the church every Tuesday night. Finally, they found someone who was willing to adopt Egbert; Police Inspector Vincent "Vinnie" Digginboss. He pledged to teach the boy to respect authority.

Vinnie was the most feared policeman in that part of Puca Luca, and his devotion to his job had some people referring to him as a hero. He was a little more than six feet tall and walked with a slight hunch. His uniform was always immaculate and crisp. He would stare at people from under his cap in such a manner that people would think they were about to be attacked by a raging bull or a bulldog. There was an expression of power about him. He had a deep voice, and when he spoke, little Egbert trembled. At one time, his quoted Rami, a thirteenth-century Persian poet and theologian, who said, "Raise your words, not your voice. It is the rain that grows flowers, not thunder." Vinnie frequently took him to lock-ups and jails to show him the results of disobedience and witness the consequences of criminal behavior. His favorite spot was the morgue, and Vinnie would point out some of the stiffs who were unfortunate enough to be caught in his line of fire. Despite these, Vinnie had a genuine love for the boy and always said that he wanted the best for him.

Vinnie's wife, Sheila, was also afraid of him, especially when he drank his favorite brandy. He never abused her physically, but he would do things which intimidated her to the point where she had to run to the closet and hide, like some people who were afraid of thunder and lightning. The only person who stood up to Inspector Digginboss was his housekeeper, Imogene Kopper. He knew she was serious whenever she referred to him as Speckie, and forthwith he would apologize to his wife for his behavior. After five years of marriage, Sheila left Vinnie, but she never divorced him. She didn't take the little boy either.

Inspector Digginboss had a soft side: his love for the sea, and as mentioned before, his love for Egbert. He owned a small boat, and on weekends or days off, he would go fishing and take Egbert with him. He exposed Egbert to the art of fishing, taught him the mechanisms of the boat, and sometimes allowed him to take control when Vinnie had had a little too much to drink.

Egbert was nauseous on the first few expeditions, but each week he got better thanks to a special herbal tea brewed by Imogene. The little boy's behavior improved tremendously, and he looked forward to these fishing trips with his new father. On one occasion, he caught a huge dolphin and was almost pulled overboard when he tried to haul it in the boat.

Just as Egbert was adjusting to his new life, tragedy struck, and Vinnie died.

"Let me guess. Someone had a beef with him and got him out of the way?"

"No, he was not shot by any of those whom he'd arrested and tortured, even though many would like it to have happened that way. Inspector Digginboss was killed one Friday night on his way back from a party given in honor of a retired circuit court judge, the

Honorable Villard Konningham. Vinnie apparently had overimbibed and was riding his motorcycle recklessly all over the road."

Not far from his home, Vinnie's motorcycle got out of control, hit a hydrant, became airborne, and went straight through the rear window of the car in front of him. The driver, Veronica O'Rigby, lost control of the car, hit a tree, and was pronounced dead at the scene.

Vinnie died at the hospital. Veronica's two sons were badly hurt. Fitzroy, who was sitting in the front seat, sustained some broken bones and a concussion. Anthony, who was seated behind his mom and was half asleep in the back seat of the car, suffered what doctors described as orthopedic decapitation. The impact of the motorcycle caused the boy's skull to be shoved forward and separated from his spine. He was pronounced dead at the hospital.

Imogene visited Fitzroy in the hospital, and when it was time for him to go home, there was no relative to take him, so she took him home hoping that some relative would come get him when they realized what had happened. Imogene contacted Sheila Digginboss to see whether she would take both Egbert and Fitzroy, but she had moved on with her life and said that she wanted to be a free woman and didn't want anything or anyone to be in her way. However, she reminded Imogene that she would help out financially whenever she could. "Where there's a will, there's a way," Imogene insisted.

"Where there's a will, I hope my name is in it," Sheila responded.

After the death of Inspector Digginboss, Imogene had to leave the government-subsidized residence provided by the police department for certain senior members of the police force, so once again Egbert had to change address, but this time he had a brother, Fitzroy. Both boys had formed a bond. Although Fitzroy suffered so much, he was a brilliant student. He was called Brains not just because he was brilliant but because he had a nevus, or a birthmark, on his right shoulder in the shape of a brain.

Eleven

When one recalls one's experience during one's school days, it is generally happy memories, but there were always situations and events that occur which one may wish to forget. One of the issues that plagued the Puca Luca school system at one time was bullying, or peer abuse as it was later called. Ionnia Quane was no stranger to this, and to make matters worse, the perpetrators of bullying were girls as well as boys. People unaffected by this situation will refer to the old cliché "Boys will always be boys, and girls will always be girls." The situation got out of control, and eventually it became cause for concern for some teachers and members of the school board. It was determined that if bullying in schools was not addressed, it would lead to social isolation of the victims, loss of self-esteem, and a reduced capacity to learn, and subsequently students would become school dropouts.

Ionnia did not escape the wrath of five female bullies: Vonnie Alvers, Jaylene Bullock, Amanda Bettle, Lenore Constantino, and Theresa Grantley. This group of girls considered themselves the most beautiful girls in Dartsdam Elementary, and Lenore was overheard one day saying to Amanda, "I can't believe God made me so pretty."

In the meantime, their morals and academic achievements left much to be desired. To quote an old French proverb, "Beauty unaccompanied by virtue is like a flower without fragrance."

These girls never let up with their taunting of Ionnia, the string bean or the cave girl who, quite unlike them, because of her intellectual curiosity excelled in almost everything she attempted. Maybe she should be called the miracle child. She was mocked and jeered her for her attire and her physical appearance. She was bow-legged and had a stern facial expression, fat lips, and thick, coarse hair. The girls concocted stories about Ionnia and her family, and they used paint, Crayons, pens, and pencils to write bad things about her. If it were allowed, they probably would have gotten their own billboard. They beat up on her, lied to the teachers about her, and escaped punishment. Ionnia's books were hidden so that her assignments would be late, but sometimes the teachers would ask her to come to the blackboard to work out the math problems. Some of the teachers sided with the girls and believed the odious and contemptible lies fed to them. Too often would Ionnia be punished for things she didn't do, most of which were not thoroughly investigated. At one time, Loretty contemplated homeschooling her, but she changed her mind when she thought what social isolation would do to her. "She needs to develop social and survival skills."

Ionnia's brothers and her friends, who sometimes came to her rescue, urged her to fight back, but most times she didn't. One of her teachers also urged her to fend for herself and cited a Swedish proverb: "God gives every bird his worm, but he does not always throw it in the nest."

"I don't have the physical strength to fight back, and moreover, I think it is unladylike to do so." She had nightmares and sleepless nights, but she steadfastly held on to the belief that whatever she was going through helped to strengthen her emotionally to fulfill her purpose in life. Ionnia cried a lot but always consoled herself by saying, "Nothing lasts forever. The journey through life's tunnel may be lengthy and rocky and appears to be dark at times, but there is always light at the end."

Loretty had to accompany her daughter to school many times, and she asked that her brothers walked home with her whenever possible. "There's safety in numbers," she would say. Ionnia had a few people on her side. Among them were one of her teachers, Ms. Lillian Finlaw, and her friends Ibrau Kraun, Beryl Osgrovel, Tammy Gladson, and Faye Hallamar.

Not only were bullying tactics exercised by the students, but some of the teachers were guilty of this too. They criticized Ms. Finlaw for believing Ionnia and not the other girls. The vindictive headmistress, Miss Kat Bigsby, threatened to give Ms. Finlaw bad grades on her annual evaluation so that if she were to resign from that school, she would have a difficult time finding a suitable job.

"These are decent girls from a good family," Ms. Finlaw's co-workers pointed out. "Why do you think they would be guilty of behaving in such the manner which you are describing and defending?"

"Because they have no self-esteem and no class," fifth grade teacher Ms. Roxanne Millwinkle said as she interrupted the conversation.

Someone must have heard the exchange and told the gang of five about it, because not long afterward, some rather disgusting things were written on a bathroom wall about Miss Millwinkle. The girls pointed the finger at Ionnia. The headmistress said that she had no problem believing the five girls because they sounded convincing. She expressed regret at having pushed for Ionnia to skip a grade, and she threatened to have her repeat the grade she was currently in.

A few more students came forward in Ionnia's defense, but no one in authority bothered to listen except Miss Millwinkle and Miss Finlaw. Ionnia was not believed no matter how much she denied the allegations and accusations. Just before the writing was discovered, a member of the school's janitorial team reported having overheard the girls threatening retribution on the person or persons who said that they had no class. He did not know their names, but he was able to identify them to Miss Bigsby, who told him to keep his mouth shut. "Their parents' generous contributions to this school help to pay your wages." Without investigating this matter thoroughly, Miss Bigsby suspended Ionnia from school for two weeks, and the five tormentors were allowed to continue with their education. They felt empowered.

Ms. Finlaw was upset and frustrated with the injustice. "I can't believe this could be happening and that Ms. Bigsby and other teachers would condone this behavior. I will be doing whatever I can to ensure that justice be served. Some heads certainly will roll when I'm done. You don't treat people like this just because they don't look like you."

The girls gloated about the fact that Ionnia was suspended, and they showed much delight in assuming that as a result, she would fail her midterm exams. But what they didn't know was that Miss Finlaw had been sending home enough material with Tammy to keep Ionnia occupied until she returned to school.

Mr. Isaac Finlaw, a prominent politician and a member of the Whickam County school board, was told of the situation by his daughter, who asked him to intervene, investigate, and do something about this and other bullying incidents that occurred in the county's schools. When news of this got to the principal and other members of staff, they realized that they had acted unjustly, that they weren't addressing the problem which had now reached epidemic proportion, and that their jobs could be in jeopardy. They put their spin on it, saying that Ionnia provoked the girls' actions, but this didn't sit well with some of the county's commissioners.

Theresa Grantley, who was the ringleader (or the lieutenant, as she preferred to be called), urged the girls to erase what was written about Ms. Millwinkle. As they were about to do so, they were stopped because the experts were called in to investigate and identify the handwriting. This turned out to be that of Amanda Bettle. The pen which was used had special characteristics, and it was traced back to Theresa Grantley. No one else in the school possessed a pen that used green ink. Ionnia passed all her subjects with nothing less than 100 percent.

A joint meeting of the school board and the PTA was called, and as a result of these investigations, Theresa and Amanda were expelled, and while Lenore, Jaylene, and Vonnie were suspended for the rest of the school term. The parents protested their daughters' harsh punishment and threatened to appeal this to the highest level of authority. But little did they know that their protest, instead of resulting in reversal of the decision, had an impact on the problems of bullying that the Ministry of Education had started to examine. This incident brought about new changes to rules relating to bullying at Dartsdam Elementary, all other schools throughout Whickam County, and the Puca Luca school system on a whole.

The headmistress, Miss Bigsby, was transferred to another school. Two teachers received reprimands for their unprofessional method of handling the matter, and two others resigned. Ms. Finlaw received a commendation from the PTA for pursuing the matter and exposing the bullying that went on in institutions of learning. Many people were so impressed with her investigative skills and said, "She would make a good detective." She was offered a position as a special victims' advocate with the Ministry of Youth and Justice, which she readily accepted, and they paid her a very handsome yearly salary. She later helped to draft legislation against bullying in schools, and she helped raise awareness for the need for psychological intervention for the bullies and their victims. A separate piece of legislation was enacted to protect the victims, and schools began to adopt a zero-tolerance policy toward bullying. Programs were instituted to teach social skills and self-esteem, and they also aimed at involving as many parents as possible.

Ms. Millwinkle wrote to the school board, "I came to Dartsdam for a fresh start, and I am so disappointed. I am tendering my resignation right away." She returned to the island of Buek Ridge and taught at its only high school, which had an enrollment of 150 students. Shortly thereafter, she married Garfield Trembley, who owned the island's largest chain of grocery stores, a fleet of delivery vans, and a fleet of cargo ships to transport merchandise to the surrounding islands.

Twelve

Prior to the full enactment of the new law against bullying, another set of students had to have a last stab at Ionnia. On her way from school one Friday afternoon, she was attacked by Hirfa Stemp and Nancy Reglon. These two were friends of Theresa Grantley and Amanda Bettle and pledged retaliation against Ionnia who, according to them, had caused their friends to be expelled from school. They were out for blood because Amanda and Theresa used to compensate them for doing their homework assignments for them, and now the spigot had dried up.

"Our friends shouldn't be expelled from school because of this cave girl. Now, where are we going to get our little allowance from? We are going to teach her a lesson. C'mon, Hirfa. You have to show some guts this afternoon," Nancy egged on her friend, who had begun to show signs that she wanted out of the plan. "This string bean can't hurt us," she added assuringly.

Based on the girls' behavior earlier that day, Ionnia had an intuition that something unpleasant was about to happen, so she tried to avoid them as much as possible. She ran back on the school premises and hid behind the canteen until she thought the pair had left. There was no one to accompany her home. Her brothers were not at school that day; attending school on Friday was not mandatory, so many students stayed away to help their parents with needed chores. Hirfa and Nancy were much bigger than Ionnia, and she thought of ways to take them on but she came up empty. She didn't want to involve her friends and relatives. Finally she said, "You can't be right for being wrong," so she left school alone.

The two were nowhere in sight, but as Ionnia approached the home of Claude and Doreen Dussle, Hirfa and Nancy, who had been hiding in nearby bushes, pushed her to the ground and started punching her with all their might. Her books were all over the road, and her only pair of shoes was tossed in the bushes.

Ionnia screamed at the top of her lungs with the hope of getting help from the neighbors.

Claude Dussle, the deacon at the Dolby Church of the Apostles, came out of his little shop behind his house. He was halfway to where the girls were unleashing their wrath on Ionnia when he looked away and said, "Had I known that it was this one, I would not have come out here."

Ionnia's spirit faded. "What have I done to this man? What does he know about me?"

Claude was a tall, broad-shouldered man in his late forties with a long, scraggly beard and huge eyes, and he spoke in a deep baritone voice. He was a sorry sight for a deacon. One would expect him to be more responsive, caring, and sympathetic because he was also district constable, appointed by the justice of the peace to keep law and order in Dartsdam and surrounding areas. How could he not help a child in distress?

Shortly after Claude made his brief appearance, the girls ran away. "Do you think he will report us?" Nancy asked Hirfa.

The deacon did not report the incident to the girls' parents or guardians, and neither did he try to reprimand them for their actions. However, word got around, someone did report him. Before long, all of Dartsdam knew what he had or hadn't done.

Bruised and hurt, Ionnia gathered her strength and ran away just in case Claude Dussle decided to hurt her too. She did not know what to think at this time, and she was terrified. Why did everyone hate her? Ionnia ran through the thicket of brush and found her shoes. While running away, she saw Dennis Felcopper, who insisted that she tell him what was wrong so that he could help. Deep inside, she was afraid of him, but she concealed the fear beautifully. Dennis was a heavyset who man was feared by almost everyone in the community. He was a retired government employee who was known as the Executioner. He worked at the country's gallows in Trevine for many years and was responsible for executing those people who were given the death sentence for murders they had committed. Dennis seemed to have enjoyed his job over the years, but he took early retirement when he had to put his brother Ezroy to death for killing his wife. It took a toll on him mentally, and since that time, he hadn't been the same.

Dennis had now taken on a new career: that of healing people through the use of herbs. He was nicknamed Dr. Root. Now Samanthley had a rival, as did the people who sold the miracle waters. This day in particular, Dennis was out collecting various plants, which he would brew and sell to people for different ailments. A lot of people believed they could be cured by drinking some of Dennis's potions or by taking long, hot baths with a few drops of his concoction. Dennis never revealed his secret; the only disclosure he made was when he announced that he had found a plant that looked like one called ibogaine, which could cure those addicted to alcohol and other drugs. If it were taken according to directions, then Puca Luca's drunks would no longer have the urge to drink. A lot of people were skeptical, but those who wanted help and believed in it tried it and kicked their drinking habit. He told no one what the ibogaine plant looked like or in what sections of Puca Luca it was found. When pressed for more information, all he told them was that it was a rare herb.

At a distance, Dennis could see Hirfa sitting at the edge of a pond and throwing pebbles in the muddy waters. She was probably feeling good about herself for what she had just done to Ionnia. By this time, Nancy had gone in a different direction to her house.

The evil side of Dennis emerged, and he forgot all about his role as a healer and helper. He silently crept up to Hirfa unnoticed, grabbed her by the neck from behind, and pushed her down an embankment and into the pond before she knew what was happening. When Ionnia saw that, she ran as fast as she could to her home and mentioned the first half of the incident to her mother, but not the latter.

Ever since her parents' tragic demise, Hirfa had resided with her paternal grandparents, Charley and Agatha Stemp, while her brother Barry lived with their maternal grandparents, Noel and Clementine Kursock. They were very protective of her, and at times they were accused of enabling her and condoning her wrongdoings. "She is just a child," they would say. "Children play tricks all the while. Give the orphan a break." But it was quite clear she had inherited some of her father's bad genes.

When Hirfa had not come home from school, her grandparents thought that she must be with her best friend Nancy. However, when Nancy was contacted, she told them the last time she'd seen Hirfa, though she never mentioned what the two of them had done to Ionnia. Hirfa's grandparents became concerned and started questioning other friends and acquaintances whether Hirfa was with them. Finally, Nancy told them about the incident and blamed Hirfa for everything. "I guess she feels guilty that you will scold her if you hear about the attack. Maybe she found her way into the cave."

As soon as Hirfa's disappearance was made widely known, a number of people began looking for her, but it was nothing like the magnitude of Ionnia's search party. There was no way Hirfa could have gotten over the barbed-wire fence on the other side of the Muggerdon property. They feared the worse. "I hope she didn't run away with one of the boys she was constantly seen with," her grandmother sobbed. "What happen if she gets pregnant? We are getting up in years. We couldn't raise a child now."

Felcopper was one of those who had assisted in the search for Hirfa, and he never uttered a word that he had seen her that evening. Neither did he lead them in the direction of the pond.

It was now early evening, and as was customary, the people in the area who had animals tied out in the bushes gathered them into their homes for the night. It so happened that two brothers, Paul and Terrence Ghitt, were doing their regular evening chores when they peered down into the pond and saw an unusual lump. Their first thought was that one of their goats had gotten loose and fallen in the pond. Terrence remembered where he had tethered the animals that morning and ran to see if all of them were okay. They were. So what was in the pond?

"It's the girl," Paul called out to his brother.

"Over here," they hollered to the group looking for Hirfa.

The stronger men in the group tied ropes to a nearby willow tree and let it down in the pond for Hirfa to hold on to while they dragged her out.

The pond in which Hirfa was pushed contained residue from runoff from a nearby garbage dump, and the bloody waters from the village abattoir also drained into the pond. Residents dumped hazardous waste such as car batteries and old medical waste from the nearby clinic. It also contained waste from a fertilizer plant a few miles away. Nobody wanted to dive into this pond to get the girl out. It was a miracle that she showed signs of survival. She held on to the rope and was pulled to safety. Her skin had bruises and looked bluish black. She didn't speak. Hirfa was taken to the nearby clinic suffering from severe chemical allergic reactions. Not long afterward, she became severely lethargic, and when she was able to mumble something, she complained of tingling in the toes and fingers. She had memory loss, visual and speech disorders, and lack of coordination. She lapsed into a coma, and biochemists and other specialists had to be called in from Whickam County General Hospital and from Trevine Memorial to analyze blood samples. Hirfa was diagnosed with methyl-mercury poisoning and succumbed to her symptoms two days later.

Hirfa's fall in the pond was ruled accidental, but to this day, many people suspected and blamed Nancy Reglon for pushing Hirfa in the pond even though she vehemently denied having anything to do with it, and even though there was no eyewitness to support their allegations.

During Hirfa's short lifetime, she and Nancy had frequent squabbles over the same boyfriend, Fernando Latley. Hirfa's brother suspected Nancy also and wanted to enact revenge, but he was fearful people would label him as a killer, and he did not want to be painted with the same brush as his late father, Lynton Stemp. Ionnia was also a suspect, but thanks to Dennis Felcopper, her alibi checked out. Hirfa's friends were furious.

Dennis Felcopper remained silent regarding his involvement in this girl's death. Putting people to death was his specialty. He mulled it over and over in his mind, and he even thought of turning himself in and confessing, but when he thought of his new life and what valuable contributions he was making by keeping other people alive, he shrugged his shoulders and said, "What the heck? I'll just ask God to forgive me one more time." One thing he did was avoid the area so as not to run into Hirfa's family, so he had a conscience after all.

The Reglons sold their property and moved to another part of Puca Luca. Nancy was sent to live with her aunt Vivette, who was a strict disciplinarian. When there was no other girl to be held culpable for the death of Hirfa Stemp, everyone turned their anger on the Dussles. The residents were convinced that if Claude and his wife had set an example and intervened appropriately as adults, the tragedy could have been averted. When the bishop learned of Claude's behavior, he stripped him of his responsibilities in the church, and Claude did not attend for a considerably length of time. The justice of the peace also suspended his law enforcement duties as a district constable. Where was the love that the deacon preached of on those Sundays when the pastor was absent? Was it a situation of "Do as I say and not as I do"?

Thirteen

Loretty was just about fed up with the environment at Dartsdam Elementary, and she felt powerless that she was not doing enough to bring about immediate changes. "I think a change of environment will do you good," she suggested to Ionnia. "How would you like to live in Redwood Vale?"

"You mean I could live with my grandma?" she asked excitedly.

"Not exactly. You could stay with your grandmother's neighbor."

"You mean Mrs. Bundle, who has that beautiful home opposite the railroad track?"

"Yes, dear. She used to take in boarders from near and far, but since she underwent major surgery a few years ago, she said that being a guardian for young people was too hectic for her. At this time, she has only one girl, who is around your age or maybe a year or two older. I promise you will get to see your grandma every day, and if you want, you can come home on weekends."

"Will you be all right, Momma? Poppa may stop the drinking when he does not see me around, and you will have the peace and quiet you were used to having in those pre-Ionnia days."

Loretty hung her head and appeared to be crying, but she was deep in thought. This was the first time Ionnia had spoken to her like this. What was Loretty thinking? They wrapped their arms around each other, and it didn't take long to find out what was on Ionnia's mind.

"Do you love me, Momma?"

"Of course I do. Why would you ask that?"

Ionnia said nothing else, and Loretty did not press her. She closed her eyes and thought for a while. *At least this is better than running away.*

Ionnia was enrolled at Redwood Vale Elementary School, but prior to being admitted to that institution, a battery of tests had to be administered. Among those was an IQ test, which revealed that Ionnia was a gifted student with a very high IQ. It was widely known that this elementary school had some of the best teachers, and parents from near and far tried hard to get their children enrolled. Loretty would be delighted to have her daughter's name added to the list of elites who attended the school. There was a long waiting list, but the Bundles had connections. Ionnia had a seat and a desk with her name on it. For six consecutive years, the school produced the winner of the all-island spelling bee. The school was also notable for successes in track and field, and it would recruit and lure athletes from distant rural schools. To be enrolled in this school and be a part of these competitive events would be good for Ionnia. Redwood Vale Elementary also had the most students who won academic scholarships to different prestigious high schools, both public and private.

Ionnia settled in comfortably with her grandmother's neighbor and friend, Claudia Bundle, as well as her husband, Nathaniel; their son, Darrell; their grandson, Cordell; and a new female boarder with whom Ionnia would share a room. Ionnia was hesitant at first to make friends with her new roommate, Olivine Deroniapp, but they eventually opened up to each other. They didn't have much in common and were from two distinct opposite social class. Olivine was a spoiled narcissist, whereas Ionnia was a humble person whose focus was getting an education.

Claudia honored Loretty's wish to send her daughter home on the weekends, and she arranged for her grandson, Cordell, to take her on Mr. Bundle's favorite mule named Anklestrap.

"I have never gone on a mule before," Ionnia told Cordell.

"It will be very safe." he assured her. "I can let you practice how to hold the reins and control the beast. You will love that."

The first weekend, Cordell took the shorter distance through the dusty mountain road, where he wouldn't have to compete for space with motorized vehicles. He placed Ionnia in front of him and placed his arms around her thin structure. Then she realized that Cordell was using this opportunity to fondle her.

"Stop it," she protested.

"Don't you like it? You ought to thank me for taking you home. Anyhow, I will not do it again. I'm sorry."

Ionnia was so naïve that she believed the young man. There was silence for another half mile, and she was afraid of making Cordell angry, so she told him that she accepted his apology. She was still a long way from home, and she could not walk that far on this dusty, rocky road.

"You cannot tell my grandparents about this, please," Cordell begged.

Ionnia kept her word to Cordell and did not mention this incident to anyone, not even her roommate Olivine, but it bothered her. She agonized over this so much, and her apparent change in demeanor became noticeable. She was not immersing herself in her books as usual, and at times she refused to eat.

"What's the matter, dear? If you are not feeling well, or if there is something you are not happy with, please let us know," Mrs. Bundle told her.

"I just miss my mother and brothers," Ionnia told her guardian.

"Oh. I thought you were having the puberty blues," Mrs. Bundle remarked.

Cordell's behavior in the home was that of an innocent teenage boy, and because he did not face any consequences for what he did to Ionnia, he thought everything was cool. At times, he stood as if expecting a pat on the shoulder.

Ionnia felt trapped because she was dependent on Cordell for the ride home; her family couldn't afford the money to pay her fare on the country bus. He let his ego convince him that she liked what happened and would not object to getting more. Was he really sorry about his inappropriate behavior, or did he simply say that to gain Ionnia's trust? Sometimes he would look at her with a peculiar smirk on his face, which angered the young girl. She had not observed any visible signs that he had bothered Olivine, but how exactly would it manifest itself, and how could Ionnia ask her?

Cordell was content that Ionnia had kept his secret. She was unaware that he had something more heinous up his sleeve. One Saturday morning, when they were around a mile from Ionnia's house, Cordell said to her, "One of my friends promised to leave something for me under a stone over there." He pointed toward a wooded area. "Come with me while I go to pick it up. This animal is so unpredictable, and I not want to leave you alone in case he gallops away with you." Cordell was a smooth talker and was very convincing, so it was a little difficult to imagine that he had anything else in mind. He alighted from his mount, and in the most careful and tender manner, as if he were handling butter, he took Ionnia off the mule and then tied the animal onto an almond tree.

Ionnia followed Cordell, very naïve and trusting. He held her hand and led her to a secluded spot under a weeping willow tree. Then his demeanor and appearance changed. He had the look of the devil in his eyes, and all he needed now was a pitchfork. Ionnia had not seen him like this before. *Is this what raging testosterone can do to a young man?* Before Ionnia had a chance to ask him if he was okay, Cordell threw her violently to the ground and tried to rape her. Ionnia kicked and screamed and pleaded with him, "Please don't do this to me!"

He became very angry and slapped her so hard that she could hardly see. Actually, she saw stars. The young girl gathered all her strength, just like when she was approaching the finish line when she ran the two-hundred-meter race a few months prior and won the coveted all-island track-and-field trophy. She fought back. She kicked him in his groin, and as he doubled over, he mumbled something inaudible. After realizing that Ionnia was not relenting, Cordell gave up and dragged her back to where the mule was tethered.

"You try to tell anyone about this, and I will deny it. I will say that you asked me to do it, you teaser."

She was afraid and furious. *What if people should believe him?* She thought to herself.

They mounted the mule and began the final leg of the journey. Cordell whipped the mule several times, as though he was taking out his rage on the poor, innocent creature. Around half a mile from her home, Cordell tossed Ionnia and her little brown grip off the mule and then pulled hard on the reins. As she lay helpless on the ground, the mule trampled on her, and then galloped off in a cloud of dust with Cordell in the saddle. She saw death staring at her like a kidnapped person looking down the barrel of a gun. She must have been there on the ground for close to half an hour before she was finally able to move. She tried to walk, but she hurt all over. She gathered her belongings and hobbled along the rest of the way, all the while thinking about why she being treated in this fashion. Had she jumped out of the frying pan and into the fire?

When her mother saw her, she held her in her arms and asked her, "What happened? Where is Cordell? Oh, my God, perhaps I didn't do the right thing." The tears flowed copiously.

"Cordell was chased out of the neighborhood by some bullies, and in his frantic attempt to get away, I fell off the mule," Ionnia lied.

Loretty kept questioning her. "So what happened to those boys? Did they hurt you? Did you get a good look at them?"

"They must be strangers because I don't know anyone from around here who fits that profile. The cowards ran away when they saw me on the ground. Maybe they didn't want to be identified and accused of beating up a girl."

Although she despised Cordell, she did not want her brothers or their friends to unleash their wrath on him if they should hear about this. But she believed in karma and the saying "Every dog has its day, and every cat its four o'clock." *Cordell's day will come,* she thought.

Although Ionnia showed her mother the visible bruises, she could not show her the invisible ones, especially the emotional scars and the internal wounds she may have sustained. Loretty was not convinced that it had happened the way Ionnia said it did, and she eventually said to her, "I don't want to say you are lying, but you are hiding something. I need to know the truth. Start over and go slowly. Don't leave anything out."

Ionnia couldn't hide the truth any longer. She broke down in tears and told her mother everything.

Loretty drew her daughter close to her, threw her arms around her, and said, "I'm so sorry, dear. Do you want to come back home?"

"Not now, Momma. School's great, Miss Claudia is so caring, and I like my roommate. Olivine comes from a rich family, and she offers to let me wear her watch sometimes, but I haven't accepted her offer. I hope you won't feel bad, but I feel safer there than here. Talk to Miss Claudia. I'm sure she and the rest of the family will deal with Cordell."

Following a warm soaking in a tub with different bushes and herbs, Ionnia was taken to the clinic, where she was seen by a pediatrician, Dr. Hillary DeNagle, who was doing a part of her internship at the clinic. Ionnia had sustained some internal injuries, and Dr. DeNagle informed her and her mother that the prognosis for motherhood when she grew up was not good. Coupled with this medical prognosis was the folktale that if a female was kicked or trampled by a mule, she would never be able to bear children. But was this an immediate concern for the young girl?

Instead of her speaking to the Bundles directly, Loretty thought it would be best if her mother did so. She and her sister Twyleith went to see their mother. "I'd like for you to talk to your friend about an incident involving Cordell and Ionnia, but please don't let this mar your friendship with Claudia," Loretty begged her.

When Loretty had finished explaining, they all walked over to Claudia's, who was stunned. "Oh, my God. Are we raising a monster? I feel I have let you down by not being able to protect your daughter. I promise you that this will never happen again. His father and grandfather will have the final word. I only hope he didn't try anything with my other girls in the past."

Loretty, Twyleith, and Ionnia followed Agnes Dunn back to her house, hoping to spend most of the rest of the day with her. After they left Claudia's house, Cordell's father came home, and Cordell was given a severe scolding from him and his grandparents. "We are disappointed in you. Do you know that we could have you turned over to the Juvenile Justice System and sent you away to a reform school? But we debated the issue and decided against it. Everyone deserves a second chance."

Darrell Bundle told his son, "And furthermore, you know of my political ambitions. I would hate to know that the word got out that my son is a violent rapist. What about the Deroniapps, whose daughter is a boarder in this house? What do you think they will say about your grandma? You will not be allowed to take Ionnia home anymore. You will apologize and stay away from her and Olivine, and some of your privileges will be taken away."

"I don't know what got into me," Cordell told his family. "I am deeply sorry, and it will never happen again. How can I make it up to her?"

"She is deathly afraid of you. Stay away from her. Maybe you are spending too much time with that boy Darnus Ashvern from Brownsbridge, knowing his reputation. Do you know what people are going to say?"

"What will they say, Dad?"

"The adage 'Show me your friends, and I'll tell you who you are.'"

Later that day, Darrell went to Agnes Dunn to apologize for his son's behavior. "We deeply regret what happened, but I assure you, your granddaughter will be all right here with us. I will personally see to it," he said. Then he begged her, "Please do not let this come between you and my mother."

"Maybe you can send him away to his mother," Twyleith suggested. "The more Ionnia sees him around, the more frightened and withdrawn she will become."

"Cordell's mother didn't want him fourteen years ago, so I don't think she would want to raise a testosterone-laden teenager at this time.

"What happened back then?" the curious Twyleith asked, and she listened keenly as Darrell related the story.

Fourteen years ago, when Darrell met Cordell's mother, eighteen-year-old Thelma Wreckitts, she was on the rebound, having recently escaped from an emotionally abusive relationship. She found refuge in the arms of an older man, and she felt safe. She trusted him.

She told Darrell, "I was young and vulnerable, and I was forced into the relationship by my mother."

Darrell concealed the relationship from his parents at first, but he couldn't do so for any length of time because Thelma got pregnant soon after they met.

"I am in no position to take care of a child," she told Darrell.

"What are you planning?" he asked.

"Just like what most young girls do."

"I won't have that. What about your parents?"

"I don't want them to be burdened with a grandchild. They have already raised their children and need to enjoy their lives now. What about yours? Your mother still takes care of other people's children."

Darrell asked his parents to raise the baby. Before agreeing to it, they suggested that the two get married, but neither of them wanted to be married at the time. However, Darrell put it to Thelma and gave her the option. "Whatever you want, I will go along with it."

"Darrell, even if you feel obligated to do so, I'd rather not. I am determined to get a profession and not be sidelined into a marriage. I can already see that it would not work out."

"Do you think I will not take care of you? Do you think I will not be faithful to you?"

"And what will you do with your current girlfriend? I did a little digging and heard about her."

Darrell did not pressure her any more but allowed her to choose her destiny. "If you change your mind, I'm right here," he assured her. As soon as she had the baby, she placed him in his grandmother's arms. She then went back to school to get her diploma as an accountant, and she established residence in Trevine, where she worked at one of the most distinguished five-star hotels that catered to the rich and famous.

Agnes, her daughters, and Ionnia accepted the explanations and apologies and decided to put this incident behind them, at least for now. Meanwhile, the disappointment that Darrell Bundle and his parents felt about Cordell was unbearable. They had a reputation to protect. "He is my only child, and I want him to have a great future. We have to help him identify ways in which he can expend his energies without taking it out on young, innocent girls."

"I know just the answer to the problem," Nathaniel Bundle said. "The boy is a very skillful rider, and he always expressed an interest in becoming a professional jockey, so I will encourage him to pursue this career."

"But he has no experience with horses, and I don't think it is the same as riding mules," his grandmother said.

"That can be easily worked out. He can talk to his friend Fenton Locksley, son of the famous Merton Locksley of the Jockey Club of Quigland Park. Merton owns several stables with dozens of thoroughbreds, and one or more of his horses always emerge as a winner at the weekly races held at the track on Wednesdays and Saturdays. I can picture Cordell as one of the top jockeys in the country."

"Oh, yes, he could be the next Luq Van Bruh, who was jockey of the year for six consecutive years."

"That's what I call turning lemons into lemonade," Claudia said gleefully. "I hope no one misinterprets this as rewarding bad behavior."

When the idea was put to him, Cordell was elated. "I'm confident that I can master the skills as quickly as possible. once I'm given the opportunity."

"But you will first finish high school, young man," his grandfather said to him as he poked him in his chest, indicating that he was very serious.

He discussed it with Fenton. who persuaded his father, the trainers, the exercisers, and others to give Cordell a try. "If you employ Cordell, he has the potential to make us rich," Fenton told them. "I know him. He is a talented youth and believes in anything to which he puts his mind."

After observing his son's enthusiasm about his friend, Merton Locksley acquiesced.

Cordell was ecstatic when Fenton gave him the news. His dream was realized, and he relocated to Quigland Park as soon as he finished high school.

Since the day Cordell and his mule assaulted Ionnia, she began traveling to Dartsdam on Saturdays in a horse-drawn carriage with Pillar Kaise, who delivered the mail to the small post office in Farnsworth and to individual residences of Dartsdam and surrounding areas. Ionnia looked forward to doing the mail route with Pillar, who compensated her for hopping off the carriage and running up to the houses with the mail. This saved Pillar a lot of time and energy because she suffered from a bad knee. No one really knew truth about her knee injury. If anyone asked how it happened, she would remark, "From praying."

Fourteen

Ionnia was bombarded with vast amounts of extra work, which she described as a piece of cake. While other students devoted their spare time and weekends to their books, Ionnia found time to help at the Redwood Vale Post Office on Friday afternoons. Her assignment was to sort the mail and place them in the alphabetized slots in the front section of the building. She loved this and was rewarded four dollars per month by the post mistress, Jennine DiPiper. She needed the money.

The post office was adjacent to a shabby little shop owned and operated by old Mr. Amos Giddeons, who stocked rare items, various odds and ends from small household appliances to groceries, and everything else a community needed that couldn't be found anywhere else.

Whenever Mr. Amos visited old junkyards to get merchandise to replenish his stock, he would leave his part-time hired help, Verness Arrineldie, in charge of the shop. Everyone knew her as Nessie. She was the mother of one of Ionnia's schoolmates, Merlette Arrineldie. They were not exactly best friends, but they were on the same athletic team. It would appear that Merle, as she was preferred to be called, had harbored some sort of resentment toward Ionnia because Ionnia would dominate most of the races and Merle would place second, except for the four-hundred-yard run. Prior to Ionnia coming to Redwood Vale Elementary, Merle would be always the one in first place, but now the gold medals stopped coming in. One would think that she would use those experiences to redefine herself and work harder to once again be the gold medal recipient.

Mr. Giddeons constantly complained that items such as candy and school supplies were disappearing from his store, and so he confronted the help. "Nessie, I am not accusing you of anything, but if you know who is doing this, you should let me know. No one steals from Amos Giddeons and get away with it. I've had to work too hard for what I have."

Merlette overheard the conversation and told the old man, "Maybe you should ask the girl who helps Miss Jennine in the post office. She comes over here sometimes with Miss Jennine's daughter and some of her other friends, and they seldom had any money to buy anything."

"We don't want to blame anyone unless we are absolutely sure, but I am going to find out soon. Then everybody will know who has been stealing from me," Mr. Giddeons said. He came up with a plan. He wanted to catch the thief, and because he had no video surveillance, he carefully rearranged the frequently stolen items in an inconspicuous area of the shop, and behind each arrangement he placed a rat trap. Before long, the culprit was exposed. Merle's right hand was caught in one of the traps, and the tips of her fingers were severely damaged. The secret was out, and the real thief was identified.

Amos Giddeons was sympathetic to Nessie. "I'm sorry for your pain. I will give you some money toward Merle's medical bills. I never meant to hurt you or your child. I simply wanted to scare the thief so that my stuff would stop disappearing and the culprit would be deterred. I didn't imagine that Merle was the one doing this."

"I had no idea either, Mr. Amos. I am very sorry, and I can understand if you don't want me to work for you any longer. And thank you, sir, for offering to help with the medical bills. You didn't have to do this." Nessie could not believe that her only child would do something like this.

But people who knew her husband would comment, "An apple doesn't fall far from the tree." Nessie's husband, Llewellyn Arrineldie, had allegedly defrauded a number of women while making empty promises of marrying them, and as a result he frequently moved from one island to the other to avoid prosecution and retaliation. It was also believed that he'd changed his name several times.

Word about the incident spread throughout the community like the fire that had razed the dry grass during the four-year drought ten years ago. There were some in the community, especially those who called themselves Christians, who blamed Nessie for what they called a poor upbringing. Then there were the others who blamed Amos Giddeons for having taken extreme measures.

When Merlette returned to school, her schoolmates were very cruel to her. They teased her and called her the Giddeon Rat. She was also severely reprimanded by the teachers. "We are disappointed that you did not learn the commandments, especially the eighth one, so as a consequence, you will have to write it a hundred times on the school's notice board, even if you have to hold the marker in your mouth."

Merlette had enormous difficulty carrying out the assigned task because she was unable to properly hold a pen or pencil in her right hand following the amputation of the two fingertips. Her mother approached the teacher with a plan. "I don't want it to look like I'm an enabler. This is most difficult for me, but if this will help, I will write the commandment on a piece of cardboard, and you can have Merlette hold it against her chest for an entire week during morning and evening prayers."

This was most humiliating to Merle, the star athlete. And worst of all, the friends to whom she gave the stolen goods had nothing else to do with her. She had no friends except for Thea and Ionnia, who forgave her for accusing them of theft. "Everybody makes mistakes," Ionnia told her, "and I'm sure you have learned your lesson from this."

"I'm sorry," Merle kept saying over and over.

The embarrassment was too much for Nessie to cope with, so she made a decision to take her daughter and relocate to a different area of Puca Luca.

"What about your property?" Mr. Giddeons asked Nessie. "If you are selling, could you give me first preference? I would really like to expand my business, and rather than move to another location and have to establish new clientele, I could do the upgrade right here."

"One of my husband's sisters is coming to stay here, but if I decide to sell, I will surely keep in mind your request," she said.

Merle was fitted with prosthetics at Whickam County General hospital by one of the most experienced orthopedists, Dr. Neil Blevick. It took a long time getting used to the new fingers, and she underwent extensive occupational and physical therapy. She was always seen wearing gloves, and she was overheard telling someone, "I feel like royalty." To this, some people mocked her and called her the Royal Rodent.

Ionnia had been friends with Jennine's daughter, Thea, who was about fifteen months older than her and who would pass on used books to her for free. Ionnia was very grateful for this gift, and she was able to spend her extra money on feminine essentials. She bought herself a second suitcase in which she stored her underwear, socks, ribbons, and other personal items. It also had a section in which she stored her diary and stamp collection and letters from friends and relatives.

Ionnia's academic achievement placed her in the category of an overachiever. She mastered the curriculum at Redwood Vale Elementary in less than no time, and she was the envy of most of the students because she consistently scored a hundred on all her tests and assignments. Ionnia was among the group of students selected to take high school level classes at Diamond Globe High School. This was a private, all-male institution, and 80 percent of the population came from the most affluent areas of Puca Luca. This school had a reputation of having almost 100 percent of their students enter universities at home and abroad, and many alumni held prestigious positions with the government. A number of them also became self-made entrepreneurs. Diamond Globe allowed students from neighboring schools to participate in high school–level classes, especially in math and science.

Agnes Dunn frequently brought over goodies to Claudia's house and would spend many evenings on Claudia's verandah drinking tea, sharing folktales, and reminiscing about their lives. Even though they both had a different set of stories to tell because they were from different cultural areas of Puca Luca, they shared a lot of cultural experiences in common with each other. One such afternoon, Ionnia's English teacher, Miss Maria Blender, joined them to discuss her potentials and her future career options. After she left, Ionnia overheard her grandmother telling Claudia how proud she was of her. This was no surprise; she already knew that because she would frequently tell her. But what was surprising, and what made her stop and eavesdrop, was when Agnes said, "I only wish her grandfather was equally proud." The conversation that followed made Ionnia almost want to puke.

"Why do you say that? He struts around like a proud peacock."

"Well, he must be proud about something else. It's not his granddaughter's achievement."

"Hmm, tell me about it."

"Do you remember when another teacher met with me to discuss Ionnia's achievement, and how she stressed the importance of the child having the required books and materials necessary for learning?"

"Yes, Miss Stolks was her name. Very caring lady."

"Well, I discussed this with Cyril and asked him for assistance in providing his granddaughter with school uniforms, shoes, books, and supplies."

"I'm sure he went to the bank immediately, or wherever he keeps his stash?"

"He laughed at me and said that I shouldn't waste my time and effort on her. He said that I should start looking around for a husband for her, and when she had him, see how quickly she pushed out children like rabbits."

"How can he say this about a beautiful, brilliant young girl who happens to be his granddaughter?"

"That was exactly what I asked him. I even went as far as to tell him that she needs to look more presentable now that she goes over to Diamond Globe twice per week for different classes. I added that when she becomes more successful, she may grow up to be this country's next finance minister."

"And what did he say?"

"He said, 'I will not lift a finger to help—she's your problem. Therefore if you feel so strongly about her future, you help her.'"

The teacup fell from Claudia's hands and crashed to the tile floor in what must have been close to a hundred pieces. "The fool and his money shall depart," Claudia said disappointingly.

"Speaking of money, he even mentioned about the inheritance my parents left me. And that's not all. He once asked me if I know how much I could get if I let one of those rich men have their way with my granddaughter. That led me to believe that he may have gotten some money from someone when he passed Loretty on to Walton Quane for his son."

When the women rose to clear the tea table and clean up the mess off the floor, Ionnia tiptoed to her room to avoid being seen. She choked back the tears. Her soul withered and died a thousand times. In a rather unhappy state of mind, she eased herself into bed and got under her covers. When Grandma came to wish her goodnight, she pretended to be asleep. She lay awake wondering why something like this could spring up just when she was about to reach out and touch happiness. She bit her lip so hard she could almost taste blood. She felt numb, and from then on, every time she saw her grandfather or heard his name, she shuddered. The intense loathing, contempt, and disdain that she felt for some of the adult males in her life were indescribable. She would definitely tell her mother about it.

C.D., the name by which her grandfather was widely known, got the nickname Bamboo because he was so tall and skinny. He had financial means and helped those he wanted to help. He owned numerous properties around the southwestern sections of Puca Luca, some of these parcels of real estate legitimately, and some through covert or illegal means. He bred mules, donkeys, and horses for sale. He was a successful peanut farmer, and he also owned many acres of walnuts. As a man of substance, C.D. lent money to others in need, but this was not an altruistic gesture because he bragged and boasted about it. He would embarrass the people to whom he lent the money if they didn't repay in a timely manner. These huge loans came with hefty interest rates and in some instances bizarre conditions, which the people were sometimes unable to tolerate. Consequently, C.D. would seize the properties or the animals of those who failed to repay him, and it was not unusual for him to demand someone's daughter for payment, which was common practice in those days. He would then send the daughters away to work with the more affluent people, who worked them like slaves. If anyone criticized his actions, he would simply respond with an angry chuckle. No wonder he was friends with Sam Muggerdon. As the saying went, birds of a feather flocked together.

Ionnia felt like a misfit at Diamond Globe High. She was unpopular because she refused the advances of the male students. Most of the other girls from Redwood Vale and other schools in surrounding areas who took classes at that school had intimate encounters with the boys. Someone informed the principals of these schools about the girls' behavior, and they launched an investigation. When the story was corroborated, several of the girls were withdrawn from the program, among them Olivine Deronniapp. It was as though Ionnia was wearing a placard on her forehead that read, "Accuse me," because the perpetrators falsely accused her of being the snitch. They taunted her and said, "You are just jealous because you are queer, ugly, and stupid, and no boy wants you."

She didn't have to put up a monumental defense this time because the so-called snitch was a reliable and credible eyewitness, the school's gym teacher, Jabez Fuzzlabber, known to everyone as Fuzzy. Ionnia shot back, "I don't care what you girls do and how little self-esteem you have. All I know is that I am lucky to have enough self-esteem not to be engaged in loveless, meaningless, one-night stands. And moreover, I'm not old enough for this sort of thing, but I'm not too young to realize that this would be nothing but an immoral and sinful behavior which the Bible spoke against. I do not believe in premarital sex. I am more concerned with getting an education rather than being popular."

"Whoa! What a speech," Caleen Dalmondie said sarcastically.

The headmaster of Diamond Globe also suspended some of the students who were involved. Among them was a sixth-former and promising athlete; Kenute Glenn, who was the favorite to be named head of the school's athletic program. Darnus Ashvern, who was the school's monitor for the first- and second formers, was also suspended.

Other officials from participating schools were outraged at the allegations and subsequent suspensions, and so were some parents, many of whom sued individual schools for failure to protect their daughters. They received no financial compensations, but because of their actions, significant changes resulted. The program was suspended for a while, but it was subsequently allowed to continue with new restrictions in place. Ionnia and a few less precocious girls excelled academically. She completed second-form courses at Diamond Globe and was therefore eligible to enroll in third-form whenever she got accepted at any high school.

Who's the stupid one now? she said to herself.

Fifteen

Although Diamond Globe high School allowed students from other schools to take classes at their campus, the governing body of the school would not yield to a request from the Ministry of Education to provide the students an opportunity to take their high school entrance examination at the school. On the first Friday in April each year, these students had to travel miles away to the town of Bethany to take the exam. This arrangement posed undue hardships to the have-nots. Those students who could afford it traveled by taxicabs and private cars, others traveled by public transport, and quite a few boys rode on the back of their fathers' motorcycles. Commuting by train was not the most convenient thing to do because the first train would arrive at Bethany 9:30 a.m., and the examination began half an hour earlier.

It wasn't hard to figure out why only two big country buses plied the route from Redwood Vale to Bethany. Licenses to operate the route depended on who knew whom. A few operators of fifteen-seater minibuses were given licenses to operate on Fridays and Saturdays. The students were aware that they had to share space with vendors taking fish and agricultural produce to the market. With the smell of fish, thyme, onions, vegetables, peppermint, and other provisions, along with the loud chatter of the passengers, one could swear one was in a village outdoor marketplace. The only thing that was missing was the animal carcasses hanging from large hooks.

Just past six o'clock on a crisp spring Friday morning, Ionnia donned one of her best outfits and left the house before any member of the Bundle household woke up. She had fixed her lunch the night previously, and she ate her breakfast on the way to the bus stop: some fruits and a hard-boiled egg. While on her way, she could hear the familiar tooting of the bus horns, and she ran as fast as she could to get to a spot where she would be picked up. What she didn't realize was that before the first rooster started crowing, some parents had taken their children to Green Bamboo Junction, which was two or three miles below Redwood Vale, to ensure they got seats on the bus. While Ionnia stood by the side of the road, the buses packed with students whizzed past her, their excitement and anticipation written all over their faces. Some children laughed at her when they saw how disappointed she was. She felt like screaming or hopping on the bus like the tomboy she was known to be. "There's got to be another bus that can take me to Bethany before it's too late," she consoled herself. Someone passed by and told her that the other forty-seater bus wouldn't arrive till 10:00 a.m.

Not long after that bus passed, a minibus came by, and it certainly was not in the best of shape. This was Ionnia's last hope. The minibus was rickety and smelly, the windows were broken out, and flies buzzed in and out as they saw fit. The door, which had been tied with rope, was opened slowly with a scary, creaky sound by a young man who didn't say much. She hopped inside the bus, which didn't have much room left, and as she squeezed her way inside, she saw the name Leonard Dulvert displayed in two different places. She stretched her slender hands across one of the seat backs and held on to a wooden bar that could use some much-needed repairs or perhaps should be replaced. She exercised much caution not to get splinters in her hand, so she took out her brand-new handkerchief and wrapped this around the bar. One woman looked at her and remarked, "What a snob."

Ionnia's uncle, Leanord Dulvert (Lennie for short), was driving the vehicle, and his seventeen-year-old son Max was responsible for collecting the fares. Ionnia was not close to this cousin and was not even sure he recognized her as his aunt Loretty's daughter. She may have seen him once or twice at her grandparents' home, helping his grandfather with the almonds and peanuts, but she had never engaged in any conversations with him. She didn't know who he was then; she thought he was just another one of Cyril Dulvert's hired help because he was treated as such, and other farmers always remarked, "His elevator didn't go to the top floor."

As was customary, the fares were collected halfway through the journey, and not at a bus station as happened in the big cities with the government-run transportation services. When it was Ionnia's turn to pay, she gave Max the two dollars she had, which was the regular fare on the bigger buses from Redwood Vale to Bethany. She had another two dollars for her return fare. She was unaware that it would be a little more expensive on a minibus, especially this one.

"Fifty cents more," Max said with a voice that sounded like he was eating hot potato.

"I'm sorry, I don't have any more," she said in such a polite way that she hoped he would overlook the situation.

She wasn't prepared for what would happen next.

"Poppa," he called out to his father, who had just begun to negotiate one of the most difficult corners of the journey in an area known as Croakers Mountain. Everyone knew that it wouldn't be wise for someone to be distracted at this time because this was the area where many vehicles went out of control and overturned down the steep embankments on both sides of the road, which did not have retaining walls. So many people perished in that area that some became convinced that after a while, many of these accidents were caused by drivers trying to avoid ghosts standing in the middle of the road. When Lennie did not respond, Max pushed on the buzzer so hard it was a miracle it didn't break. As soon as Lennie passed through Croakers Mountain and got to an area called Freedom Valley, he slammed on the brakes. The bags of produce and the empty fish pans on the top shelf of the bus shifted to one side, the bus slanted and rested on a tree, and passengers started falling over each other. Some started to scream, and others scrambled to gather the produce that were scattered all over the bus.

"Get a grip on yourself, boy. Are you crazy? What could be so urgent?" Lennie shouted at Max.

"This little girl doesn't have full fare," Max told his father as he pointed his finger in Ionnia's face. "We need to put her off."

"Please, Uncle Lennie," Ionnia begged. "I need to get to Bethany to take my exam. The two dollars is all I have."

"Why did you call me Uncle? I'm not related to you. Do you think that by calling me Uncle, I would have pity on you?"

"We are related, sir. You are my uncle. Your sister Loretty is my mother, and Cyril Dulvert is my grandfather."

"So you are Loretty's little mistake?"

Clearly word had gotten around, but Ionnia remained calm. She knew better than to get one of C.D's sons upset.

"Neither one of those two gave me any money to purchase my vehicle, so please get out right here, right now," Lennie hollered as he removed the rope and opened the door. "The rest of my passengers need to get where they want to go. And next time, tell your mamma to give you enough money for your fare."

Ionnia could not believe what was happening, and neither could some of the passengers.

"Shame on you, Lennie," one woman shouted. "Couldn't you at least leave her by the grocery store around the corner?"

"Shut up! Do you want to go with her?" he shouted back, and the veins in his forehead stood out like the ropes he used to keep his doors closed.

The contents were put back in place as best as possible. Lennie straightened up the bus, and off they went, leaving Ionnia by the wayside. One woman blew her a kiss and said, "It's going to be all right, sweetie. He will need your help one day."

Freedom Valley was one of the eeriest spots in Whickam County, and it was about a quarter of a mile from the nearest grocery shop and quite some distance away from the examination center. Ionnia thought for a while. "I could walk to the shop, but I couldn't walk that far to the exam center in Bethany. And even if I attempt to do so, I would not get to do the exam no matter what excuses I give, because by then it will have already started. Will I get another chance?" Her future flashed in front of her. "What have I done to deserve this treatment?"

This and other past experiences would have caused someone else to run to the top of Croakers Mountain and jump off the precipice, but not this girl. She was here for a purpose. Dozens of inspirational quotes came to the fore, among them this famous one from Richard David Bach, a twentieth-century American writer: "What the caterpillar calls the end of the world, the master calls a butterfly." With that, she seated herself comfortably on a slab of concrete under a fig tree where a building once stood, and she stared up at the clear blue sky dotted with only a few clouds. She sang whatever she could remember—nursery rhymes, church hymns, and school songs, one of which won the school a gold medal when she competed in the annual all-island singing competition. This gave her some much-needed comfort. "I have to get out of this lonely spot. I wonder when the next bus to Redwood Vale will come along? What will I tell Claudia, my grandma, my mother, and my teachers? How will they feel? What actions will they take?"

More clouds began to appear in the sky, and as Ionnia stared at them, she prayed that it wouldn't rain before the next bus came along. She found meaning in almost everything, and some of the formations of the clouds fascinated her. She fixed her eyes on one such cloud, and her interpretation was that of an angel holding a child in its arms. She remembered one famous scripture passage she'd learned in Sunday school, Matthew 19:14, when Jesus said to his disciples, "Suffer the little children to come unto me, and forbid them not for of such is the kingdom of Heaven." She occupied her time by shuffling her feet in the dry brush. Then she came upon a piece of paper that appeared to have been an old page from the Bible. She could make out Psalm 20: 4 which said, "May He grant you your heart's desire and fulfill all your plans." A sudden calm enveloped her, and she was no longer scared and afraid. "The building that once stood at this spot must have been a church."

Ionnia reached into her drawstring bag for her lunch, a peanut butter and jelly sandwich and a small bottle containing Kool-Aid. She placed these on the concrete slab and realized that she had company. Two tiny birds with yellow and red feathers joined her, and she smiled at them as if to say, "Welcome." They chirped back at her. They were the cutest things she had ever seen. She put some of the breadcrumbs on the concrete slab, put a few drops of Kool-Aid on a leaf, and watched the birds as they enjoyed their meal. The tiny little things seemed grateful, and to show their appreciation, they accommodated Ionnia with more sweet chirping sounds. Then there was more company. A larger bird flew overhead, hovered for a while, looked at Ionnia and the little ones, and must have been well pleased. Confident that the little ones were okay, she then flew away happily. The baby birds made no immediate attempt to leave their new friend.

"This must be their mother," Ionnia said. "And she must have realized that they are safe with me. Even a bird recognizes an innocent child when it sees one." When they finally flew away, she enjoyed the solitude.

Ionnia didn't have a watch, but she estimated the time of day to be around 10:00 a.m. At this point, she wished that she had taken the watch that Olivine had promised to lend her. In the distance, Ionnia could see a car coming slowly by. Those few minutes seemed like an eternity, and a number of things flashed through her mind. Should she climb the fig tree and hide? Should she run toward the bushes and hide? It wasn't long ago that it was reported in the papers that a young lady who was hitchhiking was abducted and never heard from again. She didn't want this to happen to her, so she opted to hide behind the fig tree.

The car came to a complete stop a few yards from where she was. Obviously, the driver had spotted her. A short, slim lady eased her way out of the car and came toward Ionnia. "What are you doing by yourself at this lonely spot?" she shouted. "Get over here this minute. Where is he?" She assumed that Ionnia was there with a boy.

"There is no one else here, ma'am. I was waiting on a bus to take me back to Redwood Vale."

"Call me Miss Enid. And get this straight: any young woman with a sense of decency or having half a brain would not be found hanging out here alone. How did you get here? There are no houses around."

Ionnia took a few timid strides toward the car, and the lady must have seen the fear in her eyes. Ionnia looked like someone waiting to be sentenced by a judge. She didn't want to be rude to Miss Enid, so she said nothing.

"You don't have to be afraid. I am not going to hurt you," she said as she strained her eyes in every direction, looking for another human being. At that moment, the mother bird swooped down on Miss Enid's hair, which was fixed in a bun. The bird must have mistaken the bun for a nest. Ionnia withheld her laughter, and there was a moment when neither person said a word, but when the bird flew away. Ionnia noticed an expression of kindness in the woman's eyes as she slowly removed the broad-rimmed glasses she was wearing and said, "Come in the car. I'm headed in your direction."

When Ionnia settled herself comfortably in the car, Miss Enid turned to her and said, "Now, tell me the real reason why you are here."

Ionnia told her what had transpired earlier that day, and Enid had some encouraging and inspiring words for her. Referring to Lennie Dulvert, Miss Enid quoted an old Yiddish proverb: "Everyone may be kneaded out of the same dough but not baked in the same oven."

She also told Ionnia that life was full of ups and downs and that hard, rough things and events are put in one's way, but not to stop one. She said Ionnia should continue to build on her courage and strength.

Ionnia listened attentively and absorbed every encouraging word. "Where did you learn all these proverbs and wise sayings, Miss Enid?"

"I read a lot, and so should everyone." Enid was not finished telling her new friend inspiring stories. She told her the story of the surfer and the ocean, who challenged wave after wave, grew stronger, developed more balance, and became more skillful every day. Then she referenced another quote: "A smooth ocean never makes a great surfer or a skillful sailor, and a struggle-free existence never makes a meaningful great life."

"You should go to the beach one day and observe one of these surfers for yourself," she urged Ionnia.

"Yes, ma'am."

"I can assure you that if I were on Lennie Dulvert's bus this morning, I would have paid the additional fifty cents for you. Some people just don't know how to treat others, much less to know the value of an education."

Miss Enid changed the subject by telling her young passenger that it was her first trip to Redwood Vale. "I am sure that you can honestly tell me something about the place," she said confidently.

"I really don't know much, ma'am, I am actually from Dartsdam. I attend school in Redwood Vale and go home on weekends." She gave her a brief history of the community and some of the prominent people who lived and had lived there, especially the famous architect Isaiah Redwood. Ionnia told her of some interesting places in and around Redwood Vale to visit. Ionnia was about to ask her where she would be staying, but she changed her mind.

The ride through Croakers Mountain was uneventful, and Ionnia felt compelled to see for herself what lay at the bottom of the precipice called Hollers Valley. She was able to distinguish between the mist and the smoke that rose slowly upward. She broke out in a cold sweat when she thought of the poor unfortunate people who had recently joined the dozens or even hundreds who'd perished in the pit of hell.

This area reminded one of Ezekiel's accounts in the Bible of the dry bones in the valley. Ionnia then focused her attention on the wild orchards and ferns that jutted from the crevices of the huge rocks at the foot of the mountain, and she wondered whether it was possible to retrieve some of these. She loved orchids and had once accompanied Olivine to the annual orchid show held in Knightsbridge.

After that leg of the journey was over, Miss Enid turned to Ionnia and said, "Look in the backseat, and you will find some reading material." There were motivational books, magazines, and comics books, and when Ionnia was flipping through the pages, she noticed that Miss Enid's last name was Arrineldie. Ionnia assumed that she was related to Nessie and Merle, but she did not ask.

Next stop was Redwood Vale. Ionnia got home close to noon, and Mrs. Bundle was very taken aback to see her. She piled on a lot of questions all at once, but when Ionnia did not answer immediately, Claudia immediately knew that something was wrong. "This is unlike you to not be excited about a test or an exam." Claudia stopped talking and gathered her thoughts. "No way you could take the exam and get home this early," she said to her young boarder. "Did you get cold feet? Are you okay, dear? Oh, my God, did you run into Cordell this morning?"

Ionnia stood there with a blank stare until Claudia stopped talking. "Calm down, Miss Claudia," Ionnia said. Then she related the early morning's incident to her.

Her eyes opened wide. "Oh, no, this is terrible. If you do not take this exam and pass it, your chances of getting into high school free of charge will be ruined. We have to put our heads together and come up with a plan that will give you an opportunity to take the exam at a later date. Anybody who is anybody will have to start pulling strings. I will get discuss this with Darrell. He has recently been elected one of Redwood Vale's commissioners, and he has a lot of influence. He was also placed on a committee by the Ministry of Education. As for Lennie Dulvert, he will meet his waterloo either by the devil or by the hand of God."

Agnes Dunn came over that afternoon to find out how her grand-daughter had done on her exam, and when Claudia told her about her son's despicable behavior, she said, "I'm appalled but not surprised. He is just like his father. All they care about is money."

Ionnia was not the only student deprived of an opportunity to take the exam that particular day, but for the other students from Dankoff and Perliddy Elementary Schools, their circumstances were different: they had been stricken with a sudden outbreak of chicken pox.

As soon as Darrell Bundle was informed of the situation, he immediately took action. He met with the principals of the different schools and the other members of the school board to work something out so that these students could get a second chance.

Redwood Vales's principal, Miss Kathleen DelRizzio, agreed that something should be done, so she organized a meeting with the other principals, the schools' PTAs, and the teachers' union. They petitioned the examination board and other officials from the Ministry of Education, and after numerous meetings, a decision was finally reached. The students would be allowed to retake the exam as soon as an independent committee could be formed to rewrite the tests.

This decision met with immense resistance among a number of people, especially the parents of those students who had already taken the exam. On the day of the exam, students and parents demonstrated at the examination center, hoping to interrupt the students' concentration and ultimately stop the procedure. This session was aborted, and another meeting with education officials was held. This time parents and teachers demanded that the first exam be declared null and void, and that a new one should be held for all students throughout Puca Luca.

A precedent had been set, and it received widespread national attention. One major news outlet conducted a poll that showed 90 percent of the country agreed with a retake of the exam. The Basil Oop Education Foundation sponsored and paid for an independent committee comprised of retired teachers and school inspectors to rewrite the tests for the new examination. When the news went out that all students would be able to resit the exam, another new set of issues came to the fore: transportation. It wasn't before long that some anonymous philanthropists donated enough money so that schools could charter buses and other modes of transportation to allow students to get to and from examination centers. This time Diamond Globe's principal relented and allowed his auditorium to be used as an examination center.

Ionnia passed the exam and was selected to attend Knoxford High school, one of the prestigious all-girls institutions in Puca Luca.

Sixteen

In keeping with the annual tradition that existed at Redwood Vale Elementary school, the top four students who attained 100 percent in the high school entrance exam to certain boarding schools in Puca Luca were expected to participate in an essay competition sponsored by major corporations, and the winner would be handsomely rewarded in addition to the scholarships. This year the students were given the option of choosing their own topics, and Ionnia chose to write about clouds. If Ionnia's class work was any indication of her literary ability, then this year she could emerge the winner of that competition. But her dreams were short-circuited, and her anticipation was short-lived. No one was prepared for what would come next.

The exam debacle caused many students to possess a deep-seated animosity toward Ionnia She was unaware of the magnitude of hostility that existed and how much some people wanted to retaliate and enact revenge upon her but, due to the anti-bullying law in place, could not do so on school premises. However, this did not deter a group of boys who wanted to vent their anger on her, so they covertly plotted a scheme where it would become difficult for them to get caught. The Thursday before the essay competition, while she was on her way from school, Ionnia stopped by the post office for the Bundles' and the Dunns' mail. She was ambushed by three boys who hit her body with stinging nettle. This was a plant that grew wild in that region. It had stinging hairs that could cause severe rash and irritation. If one did not seek immediate professional medical attention, one uses mud, saliva, and baking soda as alternative remedies.

Not satisfied with their vicious attack on this young, innocent girl, one of the boys hit Ionnia so hard with what appeared to be a baseball bat that he broke her right arm. She could hear the cracking sound that indicated that the bat may have also broken. As the boys ran away into the bushes, they could be heard yelling, "See if you can get the date changed for tomorrow's essay contest!"

Life's joys and dreams seemed to vanish slowly away as Ionnia fell semiunconscious on the narrow beaten path. If it weren't for the quick actions of a census taker, she would have lapsed into a state of unconsciousness. Veta McDode had parked her Jeep a little distance away while on her way to enumerate residents in homes accessible only by foot. She saw the boys running away, but she didn't get a glimpse of their faces. When later asked by investigators whether she could give an accurate description of the boys, she said that she could not. But one thing she was sure of: all three were wearing their khaki school uniforms. "I knew that they were up to some kind of mischief by the way they were running through thick patches of brush," she added.

Veta had heard Ionnia's wailing and cries for help, and she ran in that direction. She always carried a whistle as a measure of ensuring her safety, and she blew as hard as she could to alert other people in the community of impending danger. Not long after Veta reached the almost lifeless body of Ionnia, crowds of people gathered. Before long, almost twenty men women and children converged to witness the result of the brutal attack of this little girl who posed no threat to anyone. Some women sprang into action, making a paste from mud and saliva, and they carefully put it on the visibly affected areas of Ionnia's body where the stinging nettle had come in contact.

"Open your eyes. Say something, dear," Veta said to Ionnia as she gently shook her while making sure she didn't hurt her.

"This is Agnes's granddaughter, who lives with Claudia. Someone hurry and let them know what happened," one of the women said.

Ionnia let out a little groan and said, "Help me, please." Tears started running down her face.

"Okay, honey. You are going to get the help you need. But, tell me, did you see who did this to you?" Veta queried.

Ionnia waited a few seconds before whispering faintly, "No, ma'am." She did in fact catch a glimpse of the boys before they disappeared, and she recognized them as George Morette, the son of a bishop; Gladstone Bibb, son of a wealthy owner of a petrol station; and Jeffrey Dutte, grandson of Puca Luca's attorney general.

Six men from the community who had converged on the scene carefully lifted Ionnia and carried her to Veta's Jeep. Some women ran to give Agnes and Claudia the tragic news. They ran with their hands on their heads and bawled their eyes out as they went. One woman in particular, Minnie McHerring, knew exactly how to cry. She was one of many people who were on a few of the country's funeral directors' payroll to cry at funerals for the unidentified persons who had no one to mourn for them. Ionnia was transported to the hospital. Her grandmother and Claudia were outraged, and so was the entire community.

The county's weekly newspaper, *The Trumpet,* carried the story but refrained from making any inference that this attack was a deliberate attempt to prevent Ionnia from participating in the essay competition. The freelance reporter, Magda Ponce, referred to the attack as "a practical joke taken too far." This further enraged the community. Magda was a distant relative of Gladstone Bibb, so inquiring minds wanted to know whether she knew the truth and was covering up for her relative, or whether she was paid by someone to submit the story as she had. On the other hand, the editor was to be blamed. He should have had the source or sources properly investigated. The next week, a sportswriter reported on a baseball game between Diamond Globe and St. Jeele in which they lost to the out-of-town team because one of the star players was left out of the game due to some issue with a bat.

The essay competition was held on schedule the following day after the attack, and Thea DePiper's younger sister, Sherrene, was selected to take Ionnia's place. The invigilator of the exam reported how jittery and unfocused the three boys were in the room, and when the results were published, none of them did well enough to emerge the winner. This was a total disappointment for the principals of their respective high schools, as well as for the parents who had to foot all the expenses, but they could afford it.

Ionnia recuperated from her injury and returned to school. While she was away, her teacher placed a beautiful doll in her seat. By this time, the boys were preparing to go to different high schools. George would attend Diamond Globe High, Gladstone Bibb would go to a coed high school in Gravadee County, and Jeffrey would attend St. Jeele's High School for Boys in Trevine.

Ionnia had pen pals who either attended these schools or had relatives and friends who attended and were able to give her updates on these three miserable cowards. She said to herself, *I'm afraid that because of their connections to wealth, politics, and power, they will never be brought to face the consequences of their actions. For now, they will not be held accountable by authorities. That leaves the one other person, God, and if He doesn't punish them, then perhaps someone else should, no matter how long it takes.*

Would she be the one, or should she forgive and forget?

Despite their criminal behavior, based on their academic achievement and coupled with their parents' influence, she knew that they were destined to hold important positions in life. Ionnia vowed to embarrass them and bring them down by whatever means possible. "If they are not stopped, they will become serial abusers."

Agnes Dunn made another attempt with her husband to do some
investigations and bring the perpetrators to justice, but as usual he
did nothing about it. Claudia Bundle was upset with herself that she
was not able to protect Ionnia. "First it was Cordell, then Lennie, and
now these three boys."

When Mr. Bundle saw how devastated his wife was about the
situation, he offered her much-needed comfort. "It's not your fault,"
he insisted.

"I can't help but think that I have failed her."

Other members of the community tried to do their part in finding
the attackers, but all their efforts ended in futility. Bishop Morette,
who pretended to try to find the perpetrators, preached often about
forgiveness and reminded the congregation of Romans 12:19 from the
King James Bible: "Vengeance is mine, I will repay, saith the Lord."
But would Bishop Morette be able to accept God's vengeance on his
son if that were to happen to him?

Ionnia continued to participate in extracurricular activities. She was
an active member of the school's 4-H club, the debating club, and the
drama club. She also submitted articles to the school's newspaper, and
time she wrote a poem entitled "Three Evil Cowards."

> Three evil cowards, on a quiet eve,
> Went in search of a girl so young and naïve
> To enact harm on a girl so little,
> And to teach her a lesson with a bat and stinging
> nettle.
>
> Most people thought that this attack was a joke,
> Except a brother whose bat they broke.
> And members of the God Squad offered comfort
> To the young attackers, whose parents condoned and
> flaunted their worth.

The cowards were warned, "One day you will get exposure,
And the girl and her family will get closure.
You know it's a sin to uphold your silence
And seek to succeed without a conscience."

Too bad you didn't achieve the literary award;
That's payment enough for being a blackguard.
For the pleasure and pain you did impose,
Hell's fury is what I propose.

Ionnia won an award for this literary piece. The school's 4-H club presented her with opportunities, and she excelled in areas of home economics, fashion designing, speech, and communication. Apart from being the top athlete, she participated in numerous competitions, and for the short period of time she was enrolled at the school, she won the top award for her performance in needlework and design. As a member of the debating club, Ionnia won many awards at the district, county, and national levels. For these, the school received plaques and monetary awards. Ionnia received personal certificates, plaques, and other awards. She was almost running out of space to display these trophies.

Although Ionnia was unable to participate in track and field for a while, the moment she was able to do so, she regained her reputation as number one in the 100-yard sprint, high jump, long jump, and relay. At this early age, she wanted to prove to everyone that she was unstoppable. She pledged to utilize her disappointments as a motivational tool in order to excel in whatever she did.

While Ionnia worked hard at perfecting her academic skills and extracurricular activities, she found time to work on her hobbies: crochet, knitting, embroidery, and stamp collecting. She kept her stamps, but she sold many of the pieces of needlework to housewives in Dartsdam, Redwood Vale, and adjoining communities. This time she hoped that she would not meet the same fate as her mother. "Make sure you save your monies," the adults encouraged her. However, she felt a sense of pride at being able to purchase some of her needed personal items with her own money. She was not a spendthrift, so she kept back some of her savings for high school.

Seventeen

Ionnia was preparing for her return to Dartsdam to get ready for high school, and as she examined her plaques, certificates, and medals, her smile was as bright as some of the medals she possessed, and she was well pleased. But a little sadness came over her, and she said to herself, "I wish I didn't have to go back. I'm hoping that when my father sees all these awards, he will change his attitude toward me." After a brief pause, she continued packing. She handled her prizes in a delicate manner as if they were newborn babies. She wrapped the trophies and medals in crepe paper and packed them carefully in her little red valise.

As soon as she got home, she realized that nothing had changed. She came to the conclusion that it was incumbent upon her to be resilient and hopeful if she were to wake up from this nightmare. She stretched her patience to unbearable limits in the hope that change would come.

Ionnia's return to her home in Dartsdam seemed to reignite Lensley Quane's rage. He resumed the abuse on his family. His thunderous outrage would resonate through the neighborhood at various times of the day or night. He sounded like a bellowing bull, earning him the nickname Taurus.

The neighbors refused to intervene. "It's none of our business," some would say. Others would report the dispute to the authorities, who upon arrival would give Lensley a scolding and tell him not to let it happen again.

Abuse seemed to be an acceptable way of life, and as some women were overhead to say, "If the man doesn't beat you, he doesn't love you." But this had to come to an end one day.

Loretty refused to press charges on her husband; she was afraid to let go and move on. Her famous words were, "My children need a two-parent family. I only want to be there to protect my children, especially Ionnia. She is so fragile." Then she would add, "Those on the outside would argue that quality is better than quantity, and I can hardly blame them." Typical of battered spouses, Loretty had resigned herself to the discomfort of the hellish, familiar surroundings, and that made it difficult to break free rather than setting foot on new territory. She had hoped that one day this abuse would stop, but she did not know when or how. As an ardent member of her church, she depended on the prayers and support of her brothers and sisters in Christ. She prayed for a way out. In the meantime, she refused to liken her life to that of a garden where the blooms had fallen off and the weeds had taken over.

The boys could not understand why their father turned on them simply because Ionnia existed. The more their father resented Ionnia, the more they loved her. However, there came a time when her two younger brothers, Kyle and Tyrone, said things that could be interpreted differently. Were they simply trying to gain their father's love?

When Tyrone was two years old, he asked his mother, "Where did my sister come from? Can you send her back?"

Loretty replied, "When you are old enough, you will understand that it's not possible to do that. I trust that Chad, who will be the doctor in the family, will explain it to you then."

The lacerations, bruises, and swellings caused Loretty to be hospitalized on many different occasions, but she always returned to her home and to the man who battered and abused her.

During Loretty's stay in the hospital, the children stayed with relatives or with members of the church community. Loretty's mother, Agnes Dunn, was always to the rescue, but her father, Cyril Dulvert, leveled criticism at Agnes for having intervened in their daughter's domestic situation. "She is an adult—let her handle it," he said.

Ionnia looked forward to having her grandmother around because she felt safe in her company, as safe as when she was in her mother's womb. However, she could not return to her father's presence. Agnes Dunn and Twyleith could stand up to Lensley, but he would never hang around long enough to provoke a confrontation with them. Maybe he remembered how Twyleith had threatened him the day after Ionnia had been born. The women made sure that when they prepared meals for the children, Lensley never partook.

Loretty was oblivious of the underlying circumstances why the marriage between Lensley Quane and herself became a reality, but rumor had it that Loretty's father owed Sam Muggerdon a favor, and he requested Dulvert's first daughter as payment. That favor was kept a secret; not even Agnes Dunn had knowledge of it. All this time, C.D. was of the opinion that Muggerdon wanted Loretty for his son Kingsley, so he was never opposed to the agreement, but it turned out otherwise, and he made no effort to object. No one argued with a Muggerdon. If a Muggerdon thought that something or someone was good for you, then it had to be so. When Muggerdon said, "Jump," everyone asked, "How high?" Therefore when Lensley Quane's father, Walton, who was a caretaker on one of Muggerdon's properties in Dartsdam, was approached by his boss and informed him, "I have a wife for your boy, Walton," he had no other option but to accept.

Loretty's friendship with Kingsley Muggerdon drew disparaging responses from his father. Kingsley was appalled that his father's reaction was so unwarranted.

"She is not good enough for you, son. You deserve better than a Dulvert, and one day you will prove me right."

Kingsley did not argue with his father because doing so would make Sam disinherit him, but deep in his heart, he knew he loved Loretty. Sam Muggerdon sent his son to a different part of the country to get away from those he called "the common people." Kingsley went to the University of Thornborough, where he studied business and cinematography. After he graduated, he was hired by Paradise Theater Company (PTC) to manage a number of movie theaters throughout Puca Luca. He also worked part-time as a production manager for a major television station. Not long after that, he became a major shareholder in PTC, and his father, being the astute business-man that he was, organized a major takeover of the company. The elder Muggerdon always got what he wanted, and he wasn't prepared for the fight and resistance put up by Alfred Nollis, the owner of the company. Muggerdon thought of an alternative plan. Because he couldn't get his way, he told his son that the only way the takeover could be accomplished successfully was for him to marry Alfred's daughter, Elfreda.

Arranged marriages were very common in those days, and on most occasions the female was forbidden to complain about her match. The bride's father was always adequately compensated, or in some cases he owed the suitor an obligation. Loretty's fate was sealed. Before long, she would be married to Lensley Quane, a man whom she pretended to like even though she had her heart set on Kingsley Muggerdon. She never let go of her feelings for Kingsley, although they had never become intimate with each other. She always wondered whether the feeling was mutual. He never wrote, or at least that was what she thought. But later in life, she found out that he had written to her, but the letters were intercepted by one of her distant paternal cousins who worked at the post office and was jealous of Loretty. These letters were handed over to Cyril Dulvert, who never bothered to give them to his daughter. For a while, Loretty hated her father for this, but she decided to forgive him. She once read a quotation from the Buddha that said, "Holding on to anger is like grasping a hot coal with the intent of throwing it at someone else; but in the meantime you are the one getting burned."

When her husband began to abuse her and be unfaithful to her, Loretty couldn't resist passing on some of the resentment to her father. She always dreamed of the type of life she would have had with Kingsley Muggerdon.

Lensley Quane's womanizing had the blessing of his mother. In addition to his involvement with Emily Brank, he regularly met at his mother's home with Velma McHerring, who worked as a cashier at the farmers market at Redland Valley. Loretty later discovered that Velma and Emily fought frequently using any objects that they could get their hands on to inflict pain on each other. Clothes were ripped off, wigs were thrown to the ground, and all manner of adjectives were used. Sometimes Lensley stood by and watched, not saying a word. At the least, he appeared pleased that women could degrade themselves over him.

"I am appalled that you would encourage the relationship between Lensley and Velma," Loretty said one day when she came face-to-face with her mother-in-law.

"Velma's mother and I are friends. We work with the same people on top of the hill. It is by sheer coincidence my son happens to be here when the girl and her mother pay me a visit. He needs a place to get away from you. And even if it my son were having an affair with Velma, what could you do about it? At least we know who he is meddling with. Can we say the same thing about you?"

It was no use arguing with Ethel. "I do not want my emotions to take precedence over my self-esteem, so I will try hard to maintain my composure." Other women urged Loretty to confront her adversaries, but she let it go. As an avid churchgoer and a believer, she often said, "I leave it in God's hands. Someday He will remove all the stumbling blocks out of my way."

After a while, Velma came to her senses and realized that it wasn't worth the while to continue seeing Lensley. When she told him she was ending the relationship, he went berserk and threatened violence on her entire family. Her mother, Gladys, went to Ethel and pleaded, "We have known each other for a long time. Please talk to your son— he is out of control. You need to set an example in the community."

Ethel Twipple wagged her finger at her friend and said, "You are more despicable than your daughter. Don't lecture me about my child. Those who live in glass houses should not throw stones. When things were going well, you didn't feel the need to say anything. Let me tell you something, Gladys: my son hates two-timing bitches." That ended the friendship between the two women.

An unusual and unbelievable situation developed. Velma met with Loretty, apologized, and even offered to help her in whatever she needed. But Loretty declined to accept any help from Velma.

Ionnia counted the days until Sunday, which was a special time for her. She would meet her two friends, Ibrau and Tammy. Sunday school classes were a happy event for Ionnia, and she looked forward to making a joyful noise unto the Lord. Her favorite song was "Across the Bridge," first released in 1966 by the late Jim Reeves.

> Across the Bridge, there'll be no sorrow
> Across the bridge, there'll be no pain
> The sun will shine across the river
> And you'll never be unhappy again.

That song was special to her, and with the emotions and enthusiasm with which she sang it, one could really see that it meant something to her. Ionnia thought of all the battered and abused women she had seen or heard of. She wanted a special place for them where they would be safe from harm, and where they could be happy.

Ionnia was the youngest member of the church choir, and Pastor Brathwaite's wife, Kurdelle, constantly complimented her for her melodious voice. "You are like an angel sent from God," she said. This was very comforting to hear, and it made Ionnia feel special.

However, despite all the accolades, Ionnia was not given any angel part in the Christmas plays. If she sounded like one, then surely she could play the part. Instead, she was always playing the part of Rudolph the Red-Nosed Reindeer. The first time this happened, she thought it was a mistake. She remembered her father's words, and it frightened her.

From then on, Ionnia was determined to change the meaning of the word *mistake*, a word her father frequently called her. She elected to be happy regardless of being despised and rejected by her paternal relatives. At a very early age, she loaded up her mind with images of a very successful future, and she was determined not to block her view of this with the experiences of neglect, rejection, and poverty which she suffered. She took courage in the Japanese proverb that said, "The bamboo that bends, is stronger than the oak that resists." And surely she was strong enough to bend and not break despite whatever wind blew her way. She had the character, self-discipline, and tenacity, and her experiences along the way helped shape the course of her life.

Ionnia also saw the need to help other women and children in similar situations, and she was determined to make this a reality. But how would she go about this? She prayed for direction.

Ionnia had recurring dreams of women being rescued and taken across a bridge over the Shafton River toward a newly established community. She saw a large gate that would close when everyone was safely across. She could remember in one of the dreams how some of the women, before they got on the bridge, looked in the direction from whence they came. The story of Lot's wife came to her thoughts. But these women in her dreams were lucky; they didn't suffer the same fate for looking back. Instead, as soon as they started to descend slowly into the river, just before they hit the water, they were rescued by a little girl in the form of an angel who emerged with a huge floating device in the shape of a basket. The angel soared effortlessly upward and placed them safely back on the bridge. They then continued their journey across the bridge to their safe location toward the brightest sunrise she had ever seen.

I could be that little angel, Ionnia said to herself. *And that is why I will always remember the words of Frances Willard, the nineteenth-century American educator who once said*, 'I will not waste my life in friction when it can be turned into momentum.' Now more than ever, her fundamental focus was to create a safe haven in which abused women and children could find refuge as soon as they realized the perils of living at home. Ionnia was aware that every project took money, so she started saving all her money and worked extra jobs. No job was too mundane. She promised herself to not let these jobs get in the way of her interest in her school work and her extracurricular activities, because without an education, she would not be able to be productive and realize her dreams. She ran errands and performed chores for some of the more affluent people in Dartsdam and the adjoining towns. She made dolls from leftover scraps of cloth from her mother's sewing room. She designed and sold dolls' clothing to the girls in the neighborhood. She regularly held doll fashion shows, where she showed off her minor designing talents. She was convinced that this prepared her for bigger challenges. These shows were very impressive and became an annual event. Ionnia was soon making dolls' clothes for most of the girls in Dartsdam, as well as for one small retail outlet. Her dolls' wardrobe won the hearts and minds of almost every little girl in Dartsdam. She was described as one who had potential to grow up and outdo some of the nation's top designers if she continued on this track. She made a pouch from cuttings of cloth and stashed her earnings in it. She was tempted to hide it permanently under a mattress like most of the older folks in the neighborhood, who were fearful of anyone else managing their money. However, Ionnia had learned from past experiences when their father had stolen from them, so she opened a joint account with her mother at the Amstock Savings and Loan Bank in Kerquat. Her brothers followed suit by taking the contents of their piggy bank to ASLB and opening separate accounts. They felt proud of themselves that they had taken the first step toward financial independence.

While the boys and their mother made small kitchen gardens, Ionnia concentrated on a poultry project. She bought a chicken from one of her neighbors and named it Queenie. She took great pride in raising her. When she wasn't playing hopscotch or hide-and-seek with her brothers, she gave Queenie the special attention she deserved, and this bird loved the attention.

Ionnia focused a lot of her attention toward the nurturing of Queenie, and she watched her mature into a beautiful hen who laid an inordinate amount of eggs. She sold some of the eggs and kept some to multiply her brood. Ionnia kept busy with the first batch of four little chicks, three which would grow up to become hens. The other was a proud rooster that responded to the name of Corbie, which was given to him by her brother Kyle.

Ionnia fed her brood with corn she got from some of the small farmers in the area. She would put the grains of corn into a small bag and pound it with a stone so that the little chicks would have no difficulty picking up with their little beaks. Queenie and her chicks found a comfortable spot on a low limb in a guava tree in the backyard, and there they spent most of their nights. As soon as the little ones were able to fly higher, they ascended to the top of the tree. Lensley Quane seemed to be bothered by everything. As soon as Corbie was able to crow in the early mornings, it angered him. He opened the back window of the house and hollered at the innocent rooster, "I swear if you do not stop upsetting my sleep. I am going to teach you a lesson by turning you into a capon or twisting your damned neck off." But Corbie never stopped crowing, and he probably had the bird instinct to know that Lensley didn't like him. As if to spite him, Corbie stretched his neck and crowed louder than ever. Every time he saw Lensley in the yard, he ambushed him and viciously dug his spurs into his flesh. Then Lensley had the nerve to ask Loretty to dress his wounds.

At first, when the villagers saw Lensley's wounds, they thought that Loretty had finally found the fortitude to fight back. When they learned that he was assaulted by a rooster, he was the joke of the community.

"Imagine a man who beats up on women but can't defend himself from a rooster."

"Very soon that cock will be history," Lensley Quane responded, embarrassed.

Ionnia's brothers, with the assistance from other boys in the neighborhood, including Ibrau, erected a small chicken coop for Ionnia, and every night she would ensure that the chicks were secured under their mother's wings. Ionnia felt a sense of belonging when she was among the chickens, and she wrote a lot about them in her diary. "It's amazing," she said as she watched how Corbie protected the other little chicks. "If only my father had as much compassion as a rooster." Ionnia talked to herself and to the chickens, and they seemed to understand when she communicated with them.

She was unaware that she was being watched some days by Myra Biddis, who became concerned and said to Loretty, "This daughter of yours might have to seek psychological help. I just left her back there talking to herself and to the chickens."

Loretty said, "Pretty soon the entire family may have to do just that. I don't know how much more of this we can endure."

"Don't blame the weather, because you chose to stand in the storm," Myra said to her friend. "I can get you some help. My niece, Mystie Brume, is a psychiatrist and psychologist, and she can conduct a few sessions with the entire family whenever you are ready. I'm sure she will charge you what you can afford. If you agree to it, I can make the contact and get back to you whenever you are ready."

"Thanks, I am willing to give it a try if Lensley will go."

"Good luck with that," Myra said.

Eighteen

Hundreds of people from all walks of life and from different religious denominations converged on the community of Dartsdam each year for the Annual Bishops' Conference (ABC), a weekend of learning the ABCs of life. It was a celebration to look forward to, and some people referred to it as the Annual Bishops Carnival. Huge tents were erected on vacant land owned by Basil Oop. The out-of-town bishops would request members who were in need of special prayer to see them after the Holy Ghost–filled service. According to their doctrine, they wanted to be sure that their members were on the right track.

On this particular Sunday, Loretty was the first to meet with Bishop Ryte, the superintendent of the southeastern congregation of the Apostlic Faith, headquartered in Krepston. She had brought her sister Dee Dee with her to make sure she didn't leave out much of the details of her sorrowful life. She poured out all her troubles at the bishop's feet. She held nothing back, and then she said something that stunned the man of God.

"I have to admit that sometimes I question whether it makes sense to continue praying. I once asked God whether He had forgotten about my family, or was He punishing me for something that someone in my family or I had done, or was it just because I was born a woman."

She raised the question of what was her interpretation of the Bible's decree of male supremacy, which has kept women inferior to men for centuries, and she sought clarification about the following passages written by the Apostle Paul.

1. Wives, submit yourselves unto your husbands, as unto the Lord. For the husband is the head of the wife, even as Christ is the head of the Church. Therefore as the Church is subject unto Christ, so let the wives be to their own husbands in everything. (Ephesians 5:22–24)
2. For the man is not of the woman; but the woman of the man. Neither was the man created for the woman; but the woman for the man. (1 Corinthians 11:8–9)

Bishop Ryte pleaded with Loretty, "Please restore your faith in God."

But that did not satisfy Dee Dee, who seemed to take over the discussion. "Bishop, can you please explain what St. Paul meant in the first passage when he called for the submission of women to their husbands? Does that mean that the word *everything* could allow husbands to subject their wives to anything, including all manner of abuse? Are you condoning this behavior? Does God hate women too?"

The bishop evaded the question but instead referred to the section of the wedding vows where the wives pledged to "honor and obey" their husbands. Trying to reinforce his message about man being the head of the home and the church, he continued. "Sister Loretty, why do you think God made man before woman?"

He was surprised with the answer he got from Dee Dee. "Because God needed a rough draft. And then he made us to perfection."

Loretty elbowed her sister, indicating that she should shut up.

"I can't dispute the fact that women play an integral part of our society, but we have to respect God's Word. Furthermore, Sister

Loretty, take comfort in the words of Harriet Beecher Stowe, a famous American author who once said that when you get into a tight space and everything goes against you till it seems as if you could not hold on a minute longer, never give up, because that is just the place and time the tide will turn."

Dee Dee walked out of the room in disgust. "Something has to be done about these brainwashers."

Loretty apologized for her sister's behavior, told him more about her problems, and ended the session in prayer. Later that day, prior to the culmination of evening's activities, Bishop Ryte had a private family meeting with his wife, Berdene, and told her, "The spirit has instructed me to go the extra mile and do something for Loretty. I know that you may want to say something about that, but we should not go against what the Lord has in store for us."

"Exactly what do you have in mind?"

"Adopt her daughter."

Berdene thought for a moment and then said to her husband, "Our two children are grown, and although I kept boarders for a long time, I was really not prepared to raise another child. But who am I to question God and my husband?" She believed in women honoring and obeying their husbands. The bishop held the strong notion that a wife should be submissive, and his wife was no exception to this rule.

"Very well, then. We will eventually meet with Sister Loretty after and discuss this with her."

When this proposal was put to Loretty, she was taken aback. This was not the type of help she was expecting. "I was hoping that the bishop would meet with my husband and convince him to change his attitude toward his family. Can I have some time to think about it? I want to thoroughly discuss it with the boys and other members of the family."

"Take your time, sister," Bishop Ryte said as he consoled her. "We know that this is a huge decision to make at this time, and we would not be upset if you say no. You can give Pastor Brathwaite an answer whenever the time is right. He will also work on getting your husband to attend church. God bless you, sister."

Loretty agonized over the fact that all she was guilty of was being a submissive wife who had given Lensley Quane five children, and now she had to give up one of them, her only daughter. "I'm glad I did not get too confrontational with the bishop when we first met. I want a better life for my daughter."

Word got out about the discourse with Dee Dee and the bishop, and not long afterward, a group of radical, outspoken women (including Dee Dee) launched a campaign against certain passages on the Bible relating to the way to which women were referred and its direct reference to women's submissiveness. They formed a group called the Bold Organization of Non-Denominational Assemblies for Greater Enlightenment (BONDAGE). How ironic, when their mission was to free women from bondage. One of the group's goals was to encourage women to think for themselves and eventually set themselves free from the bondage of submissiveness, which most times led to emotional and physical abuse.

This group was determined to change sections of the existing wedding vows and to enlighten women that much of what St. Paul taught nearly two thousand years ago was irrelevant in today's society. They criticized women who believed literally in certain sections of the Bible as taught by the so-called religious leaders of the community.

They encouraged women to be strong and referenced Matthew 5:5, which warned that the meek would inherit the Earth. They gave their own interpretation of this passage to mean, "If you don't fight for yourself, you will be killed and put six feet under."

Reaction to this group was diverse. New members enlisted monthly, and several people demonstrated. Preachers were furious and enraged. They described the group as blasphemous, likened them to disciples of Satan, and condemned them to eternal damnation. Men went berserk, threatened to destroy the group and accused them for destroying the minds of their spouses. But the more the women were criticized, the more vocal they became.

BONDAGE was the first group that encouraged the staging of divorce parties, which took off at a pace for which not even the organizers were ready. From the monetary contributions they received, they purchased a plot of land on which they established a cemetery. There were no human beings buried there; instead, it contained urns with the ashes of whatever reminded them of their marriage: wedding dresses, photographs, rings, and more.

At the entrance of the cemetery was a sign: "Yonder lie the memories of young loves, cut down in the prime of their lives." This idea took off exponentially, and other cemeteries were established in different locations. One prominent Puca Luca recording artist won the prize for the theme song for this concept.

Loretty had come to realize that it was not worthwhile to be a pleaser. Nothing seemed to be working—not church, psychotherapy, or words of comfort from friends and relatives. She thought of ways to get rid of Lensley but did not share any of this with anyone. Resentment, hatred, hostility, and other emotions toward her husband surfaced in a manner that Loretty could not describe, and these emotion affected her physically and emotionally. *Should I hate myself for harboring these feelings? I know that this is contrary to my Christian belief, so I will have to pray a little harder each time any of these feelings surface. This is the work of the devil. I pray that the situation gets better, especially for the sake of the children. I know that I am not the only woman in the island of Puca Luca who is suffering under the hands of her husband.*

One Sunday evening at the dinner table, Loretty waited till everyone had finished eating, and then she asked them to hold hands while she discusses a very tough situation with them. The suspense mounted, and she looked from Kyle to Tyrone to Ionnia. She inhaled so heavily one would believe she was ready to take a twenty-foot dive in the ocean from the Shafton Bridge.

"What is it, Momma?" Kyle asked.

She finally told them of the bishop's request. First they were stunned, and then they started to ask a lot of questions.

"Momma, are you really going to give away our little sister?" Tyrone asked her in his prepubescent voice. He gazed into Ionnia's eyes to see what effect this was having on her.

Before giving her response to Tyrone, Loretty choked up and replied, "Life consists of a number of hard, difficult choices, and this is one of them." Turning to Ionnia, she asked, "How do you feel about this, sweetheart?"

Ionnia said nothing. She sat with a blank stare and then started cracking her knuckles. At this moment, Ionnia was more confused than ever. She was overcome with emotions, and the tears started streaming down her face, but she hoped to see the rainbow through the tears. She thought that maybe with her out of the way, everyone could be happy again. Ionnia hated the idea that she was regarded as the spoiler in her parents' relationship. A moment of self-hate suddenly emerged. She also wrestled with the idea that maybe her mother really wanted to get rid of her, and maybe her brothers didn't really love her, as they often verbalized. At that time, she felt that she was being given away like a little puppy. She decided to not share her thoughts with them.

She stared at her mother and said, "I just want you and my brothers to be happy, and because the offending adult won't leave, I guess I have no choice."

Her mother drew nearer to her, held her in her arms, and dried her tears. "This is not how I hoped it would go."

"I'm sure you mean well, Momma," Ionnia sobbed, "and I'm sure my father will be more than delighted to be rid of me. But did the thought ever occur to you that you could have discussed this with us first?"

"Are you going to give us all away, Momma?" Kyle asked. "The last shall be the first, and the first last," he grumbled as he shifted uncomfortably in his seat. He could barely control his anger. "Look what this is doing to her."

"Kyle, where is all this anger coming from?"

"Sorry, Momma."

Loretty rose from her seat, straightened her skirt, and gave the children some freshly squeezed orange juice. "Listen. Ionnia will be afforded the type of education that she always dreamed of."

"She is already scheduled to attend Knoxford High, so what's the big deal?" Kyle asked.

As Loretty continued to hug her daughter, she said, "I now have to start working on your transfer from Knoxford High School to Mount Mathuveh Christian Academy, one of the most prestigious high schools in Krepston. Bishop Ryte's sister, Mrs. Gertrude Ott, is the principal. If you continue to show the same amount of interest in your education as you do now, you could attend the University of Krepston or any other tertiary institutions at which you may want to pursue your dreams. I also have a plan B. I plan to ask my former brother-in-law, Ansel McEarth, to investigate other schools, part-time job opportunities, and alternative living situations in Krepston and the surrounding areas just in case it doesn't work out with the Rytes."

"When do you plan to tell Roger and Chad?" Tyrone asked.

"I will write to them tomorrow," their mother promised.

The two boys suggested that their mother request frequent visiting privileges, and if possible an open adoption. Tyrone went on to talk about one of his friends, Merton Phyllop, who was adopted at birth and longed for the opportunity to know who his birth mother was. "He is making plans to find her one day, and I plan to help him."

"Talk to me, baby," Loretty pleaded with her daughter, who listened keenly to everyone and remained quiet throughout most of the discussion.

Finally, Ionnia began to open up. "Anything to make you happy. And honestly, Knoxford, Krepston, or anywhere else—it doesn't matter. I am happy to be out of here, but I feel sad to have to leave behind what little friends I have, and to start making new ones all over again. I'll also have to learn to fit into a new cultural situation, and with what little clothes I have, I wonder whether the new community will make fun of me when I am not in uniform. Most of all, I will miss Queenie and the rest of the fowls, but I know that Corbie will do his best to protect them."

Loretty was shocked to hear her daughter speak like this. "Don't worry too much about your feathered friends," she said. "We can ask Tammy, and Ibrau's little brother Junior, to help me take care of them. Your brothers will take over when they come home for the holidays. Don't worry about the money that I get for the eggs. I will put every penny in your account."

After everyone expressed an opinion, Loretty said, "Let me know when I can inform Pastor Brathwaite to let Bishop Ryte know that we have come to a decision."

"Why the rush, Momma?" Tyrone asked. But he got the silent treatment from everyone.

That night, Ionnia wrote to Chad and Roger asking them to pray for her and to forgive her father for what he has put his family through. "He is sad, misguided, and confused," she wrote.

The following day, Loretty went to see her sister Twyleith and told her about the new developments in her life. They agreed to see their mother on Tuesday. "Mother, what are your thoughts about Ionnia leaving and being a part of someone else's family?" Loretty asked.

Agnes Dunn hugged her daughter and sobbed. "I'm sorry, Loretty," she said through her tears. "I wish there was another way to solve this problem." She placed her hand on her head, pursed her lips, and thought for a moment. "Loretty, why do you stay with that man? Why don't you take all of the children and move to another town? This would make much more sense. You could go someplace where he can't find you. The children don't need to be split up. Don't be a weak person anymore, Loretty. I didn't raise you as one, and I remember how strong you were for your brothers and sisters."

Both sisters exchanged glances, and before Loretty could say anything, all three embraced. Nothing else was said for a few minutes.

"This didn't have to happen," Agnes Dunn continued, and she wiped away the tears from her daughters' eyes. "We all knew that she had to leave for high school, but ..." She stopped short of saying anything that would further upset Loretty. "Do you want some tea?" If she had nothing else in her kitchen cabinet, one could bet she had an ample supply of different herbs with which to make tea. "I think I could come up with some money to help you relocate," Agnes assured Loretty.

"Why now, Mother? And why do you stay with our father, who refused to marry you? Don't you think that that is also a form of abuse?" Loretty fought back.

Agnes was astonished to hear her daughter speak like that. "I never mentioned this to anybody before, but your father always said that he didn't want to be referred to as anyone's second husband."

Twyleith was stunned. "What do you mean, Mother? Were you married before?" she asked.

Loretty said nothing, and her silence led her sister to believe that she had knowledge of her mother's former marriage.

"Yes, I had been married for a short time to someone by the name of Clifton Dunn."

"Then what happened?"

"My best friend, Bobsie Winters, came between us and broke up the marriage."

"Go on, Mother."

"Clifton was thrown off his horse and died before we could be divorced."

"So that is where the name Dunn comes from? We were always of the opinion that this was a family name."

"You are correct in thinking so. Clifton and I are second cousins."

"Do we have a sister or brother out there somewhere?" Loretty asked.

"Ha-ha, I knew you would ask. And the answer is no. Loretty, you are my first child, and I thought I had won the lottery when you were born. Switch up the letters in your name."

The two sisters figured it out and began to laugh.

On their way home, the sisters drove without saying anything until Loretty broke the silence and begged her sister, "Take care of my children if anything should happen to me."

"What do you mean?" Twyleith asked curiously. "Talk to me. If that husband of yours hasn't kill you yet, do you think he will eventually succeed in doing so?"

"No, no, Lethie. I ..."

"Oh, my God, What are you planning?" Twyleith asked.

"I don't know," Loretty sobbed.

"Now you are scaring me. Just don't get yourself into any trouble."

That night, Twyleith appeared very distraught, concerned, and frightened over the previous evening's conversation with her sister. She let out a big sigh, reached over to her husband, and said, "I smell trouble brewing at my sister's. Big trouble."

Harold turned around and asked, "What's new at that household? Lensley is always making trouble, and Loretty refused to press charges to send that disgusting, drunken slob to jail."

"So that means she deserves what she gets? How can you be so cold?"

"You know I didn't mean it that way," Harold said as he rolled over and hugged his wife.

Nineteen

After a sleepless night, Loretty got up early Wednesday morning and walked Kyle, Tyrone, and Ionnia to school, where they would board a bus to the all-island track-and-field championship event in the Corway arena, at the west end of the island. When they left home, Lensley was not there, and she wasn't expecting to see him when she got back. But as she entered the house, the smell of stale liquor and vomit greeted her. Now she was the one who smelled trouble.

Lensley appeared from nowhere and started hollering at her in his usual accusatory tone and derogatory language. "So now you are beginning to sleep out," he intimated. "Did you have a good time with the girl's father?"

She thought she heard a voice saying to her, "This is it." She knew it didn't sound like the voice of God; it rather sounded like the devil. "What are you talking about? So now you are jealous? And will you stop denying your daughter? If you were a good father, you would be the one to take them to school and on the trip. You should see all the other fathers out there."

"Now you are beginning to sound crazy. You damn well know that I, Lensley Quane, could not create a daughter. Look at the four boys that came off my assembly line."

Loretty's gut was on fire, and she turned around to face her accuser. "Remember that you signed the birth certificate." The very mention of that enraged him further because he held on to the misguided fact that he was coerced in doing so by Harold and Pastor Brathwaite. Before Loretty could utter another word, Lensley punched her with his heavy fist two or three times in her mouth, and as he did so, he bellowed, "I thought many times of getting rid of you and your bastard. Now it will be sooner than you think."

Two teeth fell out of her mouth, and Lensley pulled her by her hair into the kitchen and gave her a look that would make the devil cringe. She noticed a clump of hair in his hands, which he had ripped from her scalp, and she saw her life flash before her eyes. *Is this the moment?* she thought. Then the voice said, "It's now or never."

She felt like she was about to explode with all the anger, resentment, and fear that welled up inside of her. Suddenly, an extra burst of strength erupted inside of her that she had never experienced before. Although tears blinded her eyes, she no longer felt defenseless. "Go for it, Loretty," the voice said, "It will be self-defense."

As she groped for a defensive object, she said to herself, *I am going to stand up to this monster for the first time, and hopefully this maybe the last.*

But before Loretty could retaliate, Lensley dropped the hair on the floor, grabbed her again, and slammed her against the kitchen counter. As he did so, he resumed calling her more derogatory names, shouting and cursing as he did so. Loretty felt blood oozing from her scalp, down the back of her neck, and from her mouth where the two teeth had fallen out. She did not beg for her life this time. "Today is judgment day," the voice said. She grabbed a meat cleaver from a nearby drawer and threw her arms wildly. The meat cleaver's first stop was between Lensley Quane's eyes. He made another swing at Loretty, whose actions had caught him by surprise.

He jumped up in the air like an overdone toast popping out of a toaster. "Do you realize what you just did, woman?" he cried. Blood gushed from his face like a broken faucet and blinded his eyes so that he couldn't see where to land his fist.

Loretty swung again as he raised his hands to strike her another time. This time his right arm was the object of her wrath. His groan sounded like a bull in heat, and he spat out some of the blood he was about to swallow. In a moment, he fell to the floor writhing in pain, having slipped in his own blood.

Loretty stood over him and wondered, *Should I chop his head off and end his life instantly?* But the voice said, "Let him suffer in agony a little longer."

She made the sign of the cross and yelled, "Get up, you son of a bitch. I am not afraid of you anymore."

Lensley was losing a lot of blood fast, and at this point, he showed no signs of movement. Loretty reached down and felt for a pulse. The monster was still alive. The disoriented, blood-soaked Loretty stumbled outside, and the first person she saw was Mr. Montaggle riding his donkey on his way to his small farm nearby. He always stuttered when speaking, and this time no matter how hard he tried, he couldn't get a word out. Finally he blurted something out, and if one did not know him well, one would think he had Tourette's syndrome.

"H-h-holy shit, Ms. L-Loretty. What h-h-happened?" Montaggle's donkey began acting up, and he had to pull its reins very tightly to calm it down. Obviously, the old man wasn't the only one who was surprised to see someone looking so frightful.

Her mouth was numb from the punches, but Loretty found her voice and said to Mr. Montaggle, "Please hurry and get to the phone booth by Miss Phoebe's shop. Call the police. Tell Miss Phoebe to call my sister Twyleith, I'm sure she knows her number."

The man and his beast both smelled the urgency, and they took off at full speed as if they were at Quigland Park race course.

The Gobers arrived before the police. Loretty stood in a corner shaking violently and soaked in her and Lensley's blood. She clutched the weapon as tightly as she could.

"Well done," the voice said.

The kitchen looked and smelled like an abattoir. This reminded Twyleith of the time when the family went camping, and Harold had to kill a wild boar to protect them.

"I feel nauseous," Twyleith said, and Harold guided her to a chair in an opposite corner of the room.

Lensley lay on the floor like a half dead pig, his eyes almost cut out of his face and his right hand twisted out of shape. At last he was powerless. Loretty gave one last hateful look at her husband and spat on him. She felt at peace without thinking about the legal repercussions.

Twyleith got up and took the weapon away from her sister. She led her to a less messy area of the house and gave her some peroxide to wash her mouth. She sent Harold out to the car to get some cotton to stuff in her sister's mouth. Loretty was now sobbing uncontrollably on Twyleith's shoulder.

"Holy hell," Harold said as his wife rendered first aid to Loretty.

They waited for the police and the ambulance to arrive, and none of them made any attempt to help Lensley Quane. Twyleith may have felt sorry for her brother-in-law, so she got a pillow case with the intention of wrapping it around the wound to stop the blood from flowing.

"Get the hell away from there," Harold shouted.

By this time, a crowd had gathered outside the Quane residence, and when the police vehicles and ambulance arrived, people were asked to retreat to the nearest cleared plot of land, which Loretty and her boys had prepared to plant vegetables.

"Did he kill her?" Hartley Vichals shouted at Officer Sheila Bluggard, who was about to enter the door Harold was holding open for her.

"Don't know, sir."

"Did she kill him?"

"Don't know, sir," she answered again, sounding like a record.

Hartley Vichals crept quietly behind the house to a window, hoping to get a glimpse of what happened inside. Suddenly someone drew the blinds, and he did not achieve his objective.

Officer Sheila Bluggard and Paramedic Lonnel Watt looked at each other and then directed their attention to Loretty and Twyleith.

"It was self-defense," Twyleith said.

Harold shouted to the women, "Shut up. Zip it. Anything you say or do may come back to haunt you." He looked around at Officer Bluggard and asked, "Am I right, officer?"

"You're correct, sir," came the husky voice of the five-foot-eleven motorcycle cop.

Officer Bluggard asked some preliminary questions, and while the interrogation took place, a few more law enforcement and medical personnel arrived from Farnsworth and the surrounding areas. The scene was so gruesome that one of the attendants puked all over the floor. Lensley was taken away barely clinging to life, and he was pronounced dead on arrival at the clinic.

Loretty was treated for severe headaches and received treatment for the section of her scalp from which her husband had pulled her hair. Her dental problems were also taken care of, and she would later be fitted with partial dentures.

"You and the children will be staying at my house for as long as necessary, and as soon as the police gives us the okay, we will have your house cleaned up," Twyleith said to her.

Later, when the autopsy was being performed on Lensley Quane's body, many curious spectators gathered outside and waited till they were told the cause of death. Very soon they were to learn that the cause of death was listed as a heart attack.

"How can that be?" Ethel Twipple asked with a puzzled look on her face. "That wretch butchered my son and may not have to face the consequences."

When she finished shouting, she stood motionless and looked like a withered plant. Emily Brank came and threw her arms around her. "We will all get justice."

As a matter of procedure, Loretty was detained by the police but wasn't immediately charged for anything. A few days after the medical examiner's report was officially released, the police decided to charge her with assault, and within hours she was released on her own recognizance.

The death of Lensley Quane and the report of Loretty's release generated mixed reactions among all sectors of society. A section of the community was stunned that she wasn't charged with murder, but some thought that Loretty should not be charged for anything whatsoever.

"She has suffered enough, and she had a right to defend herself. Many more women should do exactly this."

Harold Gober's brother-in-law, Boysie Vernetti, a partner at the law firm Vernetti, Tippinger, and O'Hammond, was asked to represent Loretty.

"How will he be paid?" Loretty asked Harold.

"Don't think about that now. If we all have to collect donations, I am sure we will get enough money to pay for your defense. You will not go to jail."

Kingsley Muggerdon heard about the incident, got with Vernetti, and paid Loretty's legal fees. He asked that this be kept confidential. Loretty was unaware of Kingsley's generosity, and each time she asked Harold how the attorneys would be paid, he gave her the same answer: "Don't worry about it."

Meanwhile, the organization BONDAGE, with which Dee Dee was affiliated, pledged their support, and Loretty was left to believe that this was the major source of her defense fund.

Twenty

Never before had the death of any ordinary individual made such news headlines in Puca Luca. These kinds of exposure were reserved for politicians, educators, financiers, religious figures, and other dignitaries. It could almost be said that in death, Lensley Quane had become an overnight celebrity. But when Carolyn Veetely submitted a short and concise report about his death to one of the radio stations, which aired it every hour on the hour with emphasis on the victims of domestic violence, the focus quickly shifted, and the real celebrity status soon belonged to Loretty. The following day, the newspapers carried the story, and most editorials also focused on the perils and consequences of domestic violence and other forms of abuse.

Twyleith went down to the police department and requested permission to return to her sister's dwelling to collect clothes for Loretty and the children. "Mrs. Gober, we don't want you to contaminate the crime scene, so I'm sending two officers with you," Officer Bluggard said to Twyleith.

When she was satisfied that she had enough clothes and other conveniences the family would need, including her sister's sewing machine, she returned home to organize her home for the comfort of her older sister, whom she looked up to. Later, she volunteered to pick up her niece and nephews from school, where they would have been dropped off after returning from the track-and-field meet. She did not want them to walk to their residence and find out what had happened on their own. Neither did she want them to hear the news from other people who may want to hurl insults at them.

The children showed off their trophies, plaques, and medals with such excitement, but they couldn't help but notice that their aunt was not her usual self. The accolades and congratulations were weak, her driving was erratic, and she did not turn the radio on as usual.

They felt cold and neglected. "Are you feeling okay, Auntie?" Tyrone finally asked.

Twyleith sighed and then said, "Your father died today."

"And that is why you look so sad? You should be celebrating with my mom," Kyle said.

"You see, that is the problem. She is not in a celebratory mood. She had to defend herself from one of your father's vicious attacks, and in the process he collapsed. He died on the way to the hospital."

The children's reactions and emotions seemed to come naturally. They shed some tears, but did they miss their father, or were they worried about their mother?

Ionnia inquired, "Aunt Lethie, what is going to happen to Momma? Where is she? Is she hurt? Can we see her?"

"Your mom is at my house, and she will be fine," Twyleith assured her with a smile and a big hug.

"Am I to be blamed for this, Aunt Lethie?"

"No, dear. Don't harbor these thoughts in your head. Nothing that has ever happened at that house is your fault."

But despite her aunt's assurance, Ionnia couldn't help thinking that she was the cause of the situations that led to her father's demise.

Twyleith stopped at a small grocery store to get refreshments for the children. She had left the key in the car's ignition because she didn't plan to stay for any length of time. Sitting in a corner with a beer bottle in hand was Emily Brank. She looked outside and saw Loretty's children in the car. Then she stormed out of the shop as if she had heard someone call her name. She pointed her finger at Ionnia and screamed, "You bastard! He's gone because of you. If you weren't here, Lensley would still be alive. Your wench of a mother is going to pay big time." Obviously she believed the lies Lensley had fed her.

Kyle, who was sitting in the front passenger's seat, slipped over to the driver's seat. In a split second, without hesitation he put the car into gear and inched the vehicle toward Emily. She fell on top of the hood, screaming at the top of her lungs, and tried to hold on to the car with one leg up into the air. Tyrone and Ionnia laughed for the first time since they had heard of their parents' problems.

Twyleith appeared from inside the store. "Kyle!" she hollered, "Stop it, and let that fat thing roll off my car. Enough trouble for one day."

Emily was not hurt but appeared to be extremely embarrassed. Other shoppers emerged from the store and made fun of her. This was the second time she had been attacked by the Quane boys, and she never retaliated to any of the incidents.

"What did you say to my sister's children? Stay away from them," Twyleith said as she looked disdainfully at Emily and shook her fist at her.

"Are you threatening to go to Fist Avenue with me?" Emily asked.

"I wouldn't think of defiling myself with a thing like you."

"Stop that," someone shouted from inside the shop. "Go home, Emily. You have caused enough trouble with this family."

Emily was the only daughter of Wratford and Flossie Brank, who were so embarrassed by their daughter's actions that when she was a teenager, they made several attempts to put her in a convent. Each time they took her to one, she ran away.

Chad was away in medical school and was first told about his father's death by Boysie's daughter Veronica, who also attended a boarding school in the same town. As soon as he heard, he notified his brother Roger. Chad's teachers empathized with his situation and gave him the option of taking off the rest of the school term if he wished to do that. He welcomed the idea because he really wanted to be with his mother. He was given a lot of research assignments to complete and send back by registered mail, and he was requested to do as much volunteer work as possible at nearby hospitals, clinics, and health centers. He then got on a train and came home to be with his family. As the firstborn, he felt that he had an obligation to protect them at this time, especially his one and only sister. "I don't want my sister to grow up thinking that this is the way out of a relationship."

The decision as to where would be the final resting place for Lensley Quane was not an easy one to make. His mother had no money to bury him, and neither did his wife, who didn't care whether the fowls of the air consumed his carcass. To add insult to injury, several people sent notes to Loretty requesting her to pay them back hundreds of dollars that Lensley owed them, much of which he'd spent at the drinking saloons and on his many other relationships.

Lensley could not be buried in any of the church cemeteries, and neither would any minister consent to officiate at the funeral because he was not a member of any of the churches. Despite numerous attempts to get him to attend church in the past, Lensley was defiant and unwilling to attend. He once said to his mother, "Church is for people who are afraid and need something on which to cling. And as for the fashion show that takes place every Sunday, I am not interested."

Ethel Twipple once sought the intervention of her pastor to pray for her son so that he would not become a lost soul, but obviously prayer didn't help.

"Keep reading the Bible, and keep praying until your son realizes that there won't be any drunkards sitting at Jesus's feet," the pastor urged her.

Ethel opted to have her son interred in the small family burial plot situated on the same property that her mother, Vickie, was laid to rest. She asked old Walton to contribute something, but once again he made a promise he couldn't fulfill. Ethel issued a strong warning to him. "You are forbidden to attend your son's funeral." She also sent the same message to Loretty but added that if the boys wanted to attend, she would have no objection.

It was customary in those days, that after twenty-one days, if someone didn't take possession of a body, the medical examiner's office would dispose of it in any way they saw fit. To prevent this from happening, the community collected contributions of cash and material to put their drinking buddy to rest. A few of them made a box from cedar wood, and others prepared the burial site. The night before the burial, a few of people gathered at Ethel's residence to pay their last respects. Lensley Quane was buried on a Thursday afternoon with close to a dozen people in attendance.

Later that night, Loretty managed to sneak to Lensley's grave unnoticed, and she placed a sign on it that read, "RIP (Rise if Possible)."

The death of Lensley Quane and the subsequent arrest of his wife, Loretty, caused more women of Dartsdam and the surrounding areas to begin talking more freely about the abuse meted out to them by their spouses. When asked why they refused to alert authorities about their situations, some replied, "We were too ashamed, and moreover these men convinced us that we made them do it." They stayed for a number of other reasons.

Many women fervently anticipated that their men would change. Some were financially dependent on their husbands, and some said that they stayed in the relationship because of the children. Others refused to acknowledge the nature and extent of the abuse and how this was destroying them physically, psychologically, and emotionally, because they truly thought that that was the norm. Sherlette Traupe was overheard telling someone who rescued her from her battering husband, "He did it because he loves me."

The afternoon segment of psychologist Dr. Mystie Brume's weekly radio show, entitled *How to Cope,* had become the most listened to program in recent years. Women made sure they finished their daily chores by that time, and they would gather in groups at selected places with their old transistor radios. This particular afternoon, Dr. Brume focused heavily on every aspect of abuse and how women could identify the first signs of such. She started out by saying that although physical abuse was easy to identify, researchers had found that emotional abuse created scars that may be far deeper and more lasting than physical ones. With emotional abuse, the insults, insinuations, criticisms, and accusations slowly ate away at the victim's self-esteem until she was incapable of handling the situation and had become so beaten down that she blamed herself for allowing this to happen. An emotionally abused victim could become so convinced that she was worthless and believed that no one else could want her. Her self-esteem got so low that she clung to the abuser, so she stayed in the relationship because she thought she had nowhere to go. Her ultimate fear was being alone while she struggled with the feelings of hurt, fear, anger, and powerlessness. That powerlessness was a psychological condition known as learned helplessness.

Learned helplessness, as described in most dictionaries, is when one has been conditioned to believe that one is so helpless in a situation that whatever one does is futile. As a result, one will stay passive in the face of an unpleasant, harmful, or damaging situation, even when there is an opportunity to change the circumstances of such a situation.

It was ironic that Dr. Brume should speak out against abuse and the women who tolerated it. She was once an abused woman for years who had been married to Dr. Haughton Brume, a dentist from Hampstead. He was a compulsive womanizer who cheated on her with some of his younger patients. She could no longer look the other way and pretend that it wasn't affecting her, so one night she confronted him. "I am not interfering with your life, so stop interfering with mine," he told his wife. He went on to threaten her. "As a matter of fact, I will teach you a lesson." She never nagged her husband again but gave him the silent treatment. He hated to be ignored. He got a chance to "teach Mystie a lesson." One day, she went to him to have some work done on her wisdom teeth, and he did the unthinkable. While she was anesthetized, he pulled out four of her front teeth. He was sent in front of the ethics committee of the Puca Luca Dental Association and was not allowed to practice dentistry for three years. Despite the infidelity and other cruelty, in order to keep up appearances, Mystie stuck with her husband and made no attempt to divorce him.

Other women who were victims of the shame and neglect caused by their husband's infidelity also stuck by their men, and not long after that, a new phrase was coined: Mystie Brume syndrome.

Twenty-One

Although Ethel Twipple had a strained relationship with her daughter Bobeth, she felt compelled to inform her about the death of her brother. She worded the letter as if it were a telegram. It contained no details, just, "Loretty killed Lensley." Maybe she had really intended to send a telegram, but then she learned that Marianne Ernakki's daughter, Jillian, was vacationing in the same location where Bobeth lived, so she asked her to carry the letter for her. She would have liked her daughter to be around, but according to what she heard from sources close to her, Bobeth's marital and financial obligations would not allow her to come home at this time. She had a husband and a daughter to support, and she was the sole breadwinner while her husband pursued his career ambitions.

When Bobeth received the letter and saw the few lines, she couldn't believe that her mother didn't spare the time to say what had actually happened. Perhaps she was relying on the young Ernakki to fill her in. Bobeth's reaction was unemotional at first. "I don't know whether I should feel pity, empathy, or regret, or should say good riddance. I know of my brother's temper and what volcanic wrath he was capable of unleashing, but I cannot imagine that a pious, church-going woman like Loretty could contribute to a man's demise. I bet she snapped. My heart goes out to her. I only wish that I also had the visceral fortitude to dispatch a wife abuser to another world."

Bobeth was no stranger to spousal abuse, and she was one of those suffering from the Mystie Brume syndrome. At a very young age, in order to escape the hardships of upbringing by a single mother, she got married to Ansel McEarth, her first love. She never knew her father, but she heard from her mother that he was struggling to provide the type of good life he wanted her to have. When this young, attractive, ambitious young man came into her life, everyone in the family was elated and encouraged her to do whatever it took to keep him. Bobeth and Ansel dated for six weeks before they got married, which in the long run proved to be a mistake. Before Bobeth had a chance to get used to her new life and all the responsibilities that came with being a wife, they migrated to London, where Ansel was enrolled in a prestigious law school. He would constantly try to convince her, "I am going to be making lots of money as an attorney, and you will be able to enjoy the life you deserve." He did not work while in law school because he was committed to graduating early at the top of his class. Bobeth was the sole provider, and being the devoted wife that she was, she worked more than one job to pay the portion of her husband's tuition that was not paid for by his sponsor. She paid all the household bills and took care of their only child, Polly. She was so committed to her husband's success that when she participated in a drama talent contest and won, she invested all her winnings in him. She anticipated a future that she'd only dreamed of, and that gave her the impetus to devote all her energies and finances to her husband.

Ansel graduated, passed his bar exam, and got his first job. Then he no longer needed Bobeth or her money. His promises of a good life seemed to fade, away and he became financially, emotionally, and physically abusive. She was no longer the beautiful love of his life.

Bobeth desperately needed someone in whom to confide, so she wrote to her former teacher, Cilda Skidhouse, who had remained a mentor to her and with whom she kept in contact all these years. In the letter, she said, "Ansel restricted me from making any contact with most of my friends, and I am not sure how he will react when he realizes that I have maintained contact with you. He belittles me in front of the few friends I have left. If and when he takes me to any social functions, he interrupts me whenever I attempt to speak, therefore making me feel that my thoughts and opinions are not important. He insulted and demeaned me in front of people, and he told me how ugly and unattractive I have become. He ridiculed me for not having a professional nine-to-five job. But how could I become a professional, and how could I find time to go to beauty salons, when I've had to work all the time to support him? All these experiences make me feel like I want to crawl into a shell like a snail and never be seen again."

Her teacher's response was that she should confront her husband and let him know how hurt she was. However, when Bobeth did that, Ansel merely dismissed her and said, "You are overacting and are too sensitive. Get over it. And furthermore, look at all the professional men in my circle of friends: they all have educated women with whom to socialize. How can I take you to any social events? You would be snubbed, and I would be ridiculed."

Ansel decided to return home to Port Knowles without Bobeth, and he wanted to take their daughter, Polly, with him. Bobeth resisted. "She has a little over a month to complete her current grade, and I would not like to let her miss her end-of-term tests." Six weeks after Ansel's departure, Bobeth returned home with almost nothing to show for her years of working as a wife. She was not seen in public for a long time. She was too devastated, humiliated, and ashamed. After a while, she gathered the courage to write or phone some old schoolmates. When they heard what had happened, some were appalled at what her husband had done to her, but some criticized her and said that she'd married too young.

"It's not your fault," most of them wrote back. "It is unconscionable what he did, but you are a good woman, and bad things happen to good people. Hang in there. We know that you are a very ambitious woman, and with time, we know you can make good of yourself. Better late than never."

The most interesting and intriguing piece of information came from Eldorine Brownshoe, who wrote, "It is a tough job being a wife, and what you have to consider when entering into the contract is, How much is a wife worth? Why doesn't a woman get paid for her services? Why does she have to wait till she gets divorced to ask for payment (alimony)? Someone once suggested that as soon as a woman is married, she should begin receiving weekly or monthly payments from her husband."

Eldorine's letter continued. "Men save a lot of money by having a glorified maid and an unpaid whore. Consider what they would have to pay for a housekeeper, cook, daycare worker, shopper, janitor, nutritionist, laundress, facilities manager—the list goes on. Consider yourself a household CEO. But not all wives carry out all the afore-mentioned chores, and with the trophy wives who only perform bedroom duties, even if they receive a salary either in or out of the marriage, they would hate to be referred to as prostitutes. But believe me, it's better to be paid than to receive nothing for your services. So all women should take a look at what she is worth, and demand weekly or monthly payment for her services while she is still married."

This was food for thought, and Bobeth made a commitment to take Eldorine's suggestion into consideration if and when she decided to remarry—but not before she got a profession. She also thought these were wise words to pass on to her daughter, Polly, and her niece Ionnia.

It was no secret that Ansel had found himself a professional woman with whom to socialize. He was dating Christine VonHutton, a bio-chemist who attended the same university as he did. She was made famous for research she did on genetics, placing emphasis on nucle-osides and nucleotides of both RNA and DNA. She presented her research paper at the annual science fair and biochemical convention held in the auditorium at the Trevine Polytechnic Institute, and that year she received the highest award.

At first, Ansel denied the allegations between Christine and him. "I swear unequivocally that the relationship between Christine and me is nothing more than platonic." But the truth became obvious as time went by, and therefore he had no other choice than to admit that they were an item. He finally told Bobeth that he was divorcing her. This further devastated her, and to add salt in the wound, her own mother blamed her for not being able to hold her marriage together.

Christine began working at the coroner's office, and Ansel got a job at the district attorney's office. With his first set of assignments, he was determined to cast an extraordinary impression upon judges and fellow attorneys. Six months after accepting the job, he successfully prosecuted a number of defendants, and several dozen more cases were waiting on his desk.

Having witnessed Ansel's extraordinary talents, the district attorney reassigned him to the position of chief prosecutor, a position he held for two years. During this time, Christine testified as an expert forensic witness for the prosecution. Members of the Bar Association expressed concern and made efforts to replace her.

Bobeth was tired of fighting, so she agreed to the divorce, but not before she demanded sole custody of their daughter, Polly. Ansel was ordered to establish a trust fund for Polly's education and to pay alimony to his wife. The judge also ordered him to set aside monies for Bobeth to return to school, citing the fact that she had put her life on hold while he'd advanced his education.

It took Bobeth a while to really process what happened to her, but when she did, she was determined to move on with her life. "This is like starting all over again." She moved to a different section of the country and did not prohibit Ansel from communicating with his daughter. She enrolled in nursing school, and the pressure of raising a child and attending school at the same time proved difficult at times, but she was determined not to fail in any of these roles. She graduated third in her class and accepted a job at Trevine Memorial Hospital as a midwife.

After working at the district attorney's office for three years, Ansel McEarth made a name for himself as a fearless prosecutor and then left to join the Law Firm of Saddler, Deek, and Fraugh. At this firm, he assumed the coveted position of researcher and consultant. Although the salary was good, he was not satisfied with this position because he loved the limelight. Before long he was a defense attorney, and shortly thereafter he became a junior partner of the firm. The clientele grew enormously in so much that the law firm of Saddler, Deek, McEarth, and Fraugh had to be relocated to a larger building that was adjacent to the courthouse and owned by the Inkst Group of Companies.

Ansel was seen having lunch with his female partner, Fiffie Saddler, on many occasions, and Christine eventually confronted him. "Are you sleeping with your coworker? I know she is a very influential member of the firm, but you should separate your private life from your professional life."

"So now you are jealous and paranoid? If it will satisfy you, Fiffie is a lesbian, and she has been urging me not to let you slip away from me." He put his hands in his pocket, and Christine thought he was looking for his keys to get away from her, but as he slowly withdrew his hand, she became silent. Ansel had a surprise for her. He opened a small box, raised it to her eye level, and said, "This is why Fiffie and I have been hanging out. She has been assisting me with this purchase."

"And this is for whom?" Christine asked as her eyes became dazzled with one of the most enormous, expensive diamond rings she had ever seen.

Ansel laughed. "Who else would it be for except the most beautiful, intelligent woman in the world who happens to be at the right place at the right time?" He watched her reaction, and before she could do or say anything, he popped the question. "Will you marry me?"

"Can I have some time?" Christine responded.

"Don't take too long now."

She accepted his proposal later that evening in the presence of Fiffie and some other friends. They were married in a lavish ceremony shortly thereafter. They had a son, Andrew (Andy for short), whom Bobeth helped to deliver. Ansel made sure that Polly and her brother had a good relationship. The children spent time at each other's homes, and neither Bobeth nor Christine objected to this arrangement. They both loved the children. As for the adults, an atmosphere of civility existed among them. They were seen together whenever there were events and ceremonies involving the children.

Twenty-Two

A little over two weeks after the death of Lensley Quane, his paternal half brother, Harry, an auto mechanic, attempted to forcefully take possession of the house and property. Loretty and her children were still living at the Gobers', so Harry must have taken it for granted that that they had abandoned the premises. But each day before and after school, Ionnia went to take care of her chickens. She would meet up with her two best friends, Tammy Banderson and Ibrau Kraun, who would bring corn for the fowls and play hopscotch and hide-and-seek with Ionnia.

Lensley had died intestate, and Harry told the neighbors, "What belongs to my brother also belongs to me. I'm almost certain that Loretty's father, Cyril Dulvert, cheated our father out of several acres of land, and it isn't fair that she should benefit from anything this family owned, especially given what she did to my brother."

"What about his children?" Earlon Gevannes asked.

Everyone knew Harry as a bully. He was always also a very big person for his age group, but when he reached the age of eighteen, he started spurting up more rapidly and eventually reached a height of seven feet four inches. Some speculated that he had some sort of disease associated with giants because he would sometimes get ill, and doctors were unable to diagnose what ailed him. The prediction was

that he would die at an early age, and because of this he acted as if he
didn't care about anything or anyone.

Earlon Gevannes, a neighbor of Lensley and Loretty Quane, was
one of those who went to school with Harry, and he was one of the
few people who were never bullied by him. Despite Harry's behavior Earlon took a liking to him, and the feeling was mutual. Earlon
thought he could dissuade Harry from bullying other children. Lots
of time Harry promised he would stop, did so for a little while, but
subsequently resorted to the same despicable behavior. Harry would
use his tactics on other children to extort money and food from them,
and also to get them to do his homework. He would display physical
violence when other children didn't comply with his demands. He
displayed arrogance and a superior sense of entitlement toward anyone
who didn't have the strength to go toe-to-toe with him. He loved
it when others showed that they were afraid of him, and he gave a
frightful grin that scared them even more. But all of this did not scare
his friend Earlon.

Harry Quane's past included arrests and jail time for theft, as well
as assault against other defenseless victims, which included women
who were foolish enough to be with him or too scared to say no. He
never committed himself to marry any one of these women. It was no
secret that he hated women, so he remained single. This he attributed
to his mother's neglect and abuse, which caused him to get into a lot
of trouble. At age fourteen, Harry was sent to juvenile reform school,
and it was while he attended this penal institution that he learned the
automobile repair trade. The one good thing people could say about
Harry was that he was a very good auto mechanic, but they knew
that as soon as their vehicles were fixed, they had to pay up or face
the consequences of Harry's wrath.

On one occasion, Eda Lane, a schoolteacher, almost had it coming, but she stood up to him. She brought her car in for minor repairs
one morning, and Harry quoted one price. When she arrived that
afternoon to pick it up, he quoted another.

"Please, Mr. Quane, can we stick to the price you quoted this morning?"

"Are you telling me how to run my business? If so, this is what I will do." As he reached for a chainsaw, he looked at Miss Lane and threatened, "If you do not pay me, I will use this and cut your car to pieces—and maybe you too, if you get in the way."

"You will do no such thing," she snapped back at Harry, and she reached in her purse for her gun. "It certainly is not too soon for another Quane to go six feet under."

He was taken by surprise because most people cowered when confronted by this gigantic bully. "Leave the car, and come up with the money within twenty-four hours."

Eda was at a loss for words. She couldn't believe that Harry had yielded. Did Harry have some tricks up his sleeve? At this point, instead of speculating, she decided to borrow the money from her sister, Glenda Edge, who was married to a detective superintendent of police, Hector Edge, in charge of Whickam County Law Enforcement Authority. Not knowing what Harry would do next, and out of fear of losing her sister, Glenda lent her the money.

Eda left school a few hours early to pick up her car, but when she got to Harry's repair shop, her car was nowhere on the premises.

Her heart started racing, and beads of perspiration streamed down her face. "Oh, my God. What did you do with my car, Mr. Quane? I have your money."

Harry kept on working from underneath a car and shouted back at the teacher, "Someone needed a ride to work, and yours was the only car available. You have a problem with that?" He got up from under the car and stood up in a menacing and intimidating manner, stopping a few inches from Miss Lane's face. "Pay me the money, and come back later when the person returns with your car."

Eda was not in the mood to protest because she'd had a very rough day at school, so she reluctantly paid Harry the money. "I am taking a walk to the post office, and I should be back soon. Make sure my car is here when I get back."

"Or else?"

Ms. Lane didn't give Harry an answer, but as soon as she left, she stopped at a phone booth behind the gas station and called her brother-in-law, Hector, to tell him what had happened.

"I will immediately put a team in motion to search for your car. I hope you remember that your sister has a spare key for your car just in case you gave Harry the only one you had. I will get the other one for you."

"That won't be necessary; I have a spare."

After an exhaustive search by four constables from the Special Constabulary Unit, Miss Lane's car was spotted in a parking lot behind the courthouse.

"Does anyone know who parked this car over here?" Constable Doodsie asked some of the people standing nearby.

"That's the Honorable Judge Daniel Sweet's car. I saw him when he parked there this morning," a young man said politely. They knew what the consequences were for not cooperating with the police.

Eda had had her share of shock and awe for the day, and this information hit her like a ton of bricks. This judge was known to everyone as Judge Dread, and it was he who had ordered Dalvern Deronniapp, the owner of a dry cleaning establishment, to pay for a customer's weight-loss program. This particular customer had left her dress with Deroniapp's establishment, and when she went to get it, she was told that it was misplaced. It took around three months before it was found, and by that time the customer had gained a lot of weight. She sued Deroniapp because she wasn't able to fit in the dress unless she lost the weight.

Special Constable Doodsie called Superintendent Edge and told him who had borrowed his sister-in-law's car. He waited nervously for instructions. Eda didn't wait for any directions. She jumped in the car and sped away. It wasn't her problem how Judge Sweet would be getting home, and Harry had already been paid.

The detestable Harry Quane continued with his loathsome, vile, and iniquitous behavior. This time, he waited until no one was home at his late brother's house, and he committed one of the most horrendous, despicable, and unforgivable acts: setting fire to the premises. He started out with Ionnia's chicken coop by splashing gasoline all over, and he set the birds on fire. The poor little things tried hard to escape but were unable to do so. A strong wind was blowing, the flames spread rapidly, and they were burnt alive. The smell of burned chicken permeated the neighborhood like the annual Independence Day barbecue. At such festivities, almost the entire community was invited, so everyone asked, "Who could be having a barbecue without inviting us? And what is the occasion?" They followed the smell and the smoke, and before long they realized what was really going on.

Earlon Gevannes happened to be on his veranda and looking through his telescope, and he witnessed Harry's every move. It was captured on a recording device which he hooked up to the telescope. He tried calling out to Harry to stop, but he either didn't hear or he didn't care. "Oh, my God. This man has lost his mind. He should not get away with this." Earlon called the police.

Before the authorities arrived, the neighbors who had assembled at different spots used whatever resources available to them to try to save Loretty's house. In the absence of running piped water, they made several trips to neighbors' catchment tanks and to the nearby Shafton spring, where they quickly filled buckets of water to put out the flames. The arsonist did not hang around for the irate neighbors to enact revenge on him. He ran away as fast as he could, and some of the villagers chasing after him with machetes, pickaxes, and four-by-fours. They were unable to catch him because he seemed to be more familiar with the terrain than anyone else, so he managed to elude his captors. He jumped into the lake where the Shafton spring emptied out, and he disappeared on the other side into the community of Bedford Run. It was no use to continue with the pursuit, but the pursuers threatened to enact the most severe form of street justice on

Harry should they catch him before the police did. Others summoned the forces of evil on him.

Melvin Swoon grabbed a few men, and they jumped in his dugout canoe and rowed as fast as they could over the other side to Bedford Run. With the use of his bullhorn, he warned the residents, "If you harbor this very dangerous man Harry Quane, there will be serious consequences. He is a wanted man."

As soon as word of Harry Quane's wretched behavior reached Twyleith, she took her sister aside, gave her a comfortable seat, and said, "Your house caught fire today, but please try to remain calm."

"How did it happen?"

Before Twyleith could answer, Loretty let out a deep sigh and slumped to the ground. When her sister knelt down to revive her, she saw the whites of her eyes, and this terrified her. She had never seen anyone in this condition before, and the first thing that came to her mind was that her sister had suffered a stroke. She started to pull down her eyelids, which only went halfway. Twyleith did the next best thing that came to her mind. She slapped her sister's face a few times, and within a few minutes Loretty was able to speak. She asked for a glass of water, and after gulping this down, she asked, "What did you say happened at my house?"

"Someone set fire to it."

"I knew it, I knew it."

"What do you know?"

"That devil Ethel will stop at nothing."

"Ethel didn't do it."

"Then who did?"

"Harry did."

"I'm not surprised either. I need to go over there right away."

Lensley and Harry Quane were definitely chips off the old block. Their father, Walton, was a violent, out-of-control person who would put the fear of God in the women in his life, as well as the men and women he worked with on Muggerdon's property. Ethel Twipple, Hilda Morraine, and others had stories to tell.

Despite Harry Quane's attempt at evading authorities and the angry villagers of Dartsdam and Bedford Run, he was caught a few days later in the home of one of his girlfriends. He was arrested and charged with a variety of felonies.

Judge Sweet was assigned to preside over the preliminary hearings to determine whether Harry should be granted bail, but under pressure from his colleagues, he recused himself. A trial judge had to come from Trevine to try the case. When Harry appeared in court, he told the judge, "I am innocent. That fire was an accident. I needed a place to store some gasoline and other equipment, but unfortunately the container of gasoline ignited when I lit a cigar."

People were surprised. "We don't know Harry to be a smoker. As far as we know, he hates tobacco products."

"That's right," someone said. "I remembered Harry once threatened to terminate one of his mechanics who was caught smoking."

Harry pleaded not guilty to all charges, but the judge refused bail. "I don't want a dangerous man like you on the street," the judge said. Harry was remanded in custody and remained locked up for four months until his trial. He was unaware that his friend Earlon had evidence that could be used against him and probably put him away for a long time. He had to learn tough love.

Ionnia was devastated. "My best friend Queenie is gone, and this is not the type of departure I had wished for her and her brood. No longer will I be able to gather her eggs and sell to the ladies on top of the hill. But God will make a way."

A few days after the fire, Twyleith and other friends and relatives returned to the house to retrieve anything that they could salvage. Loretty and her children didn't have much to begin with, and with this fire and water damage, it was extremely difficult for them to survive in such a fragile structure. Twyleith and her husband didn't mind having them around, but Loretty wanted her own space. Loretty's pastor offered to let her and the children stay at an unoccupied, furnished, two-bedroom dwelling behind the church that was reserved for visiting guests. In payment for that, the family would take care of the premises, clean the church, and perform any other duties required of them.

Harry represented himself at the trial. Despite the amount of money he made as a qualified mechanic, he claimed that he couldn't afford an attorney, and no one in his family was willing to pay for one to represent him. Ansel McEarth had offered to represent him pro bono, but after thinking seriously about what people would think of him should he represent Harry, Ansel opted not to do so. "I can do without this publicity." His conscience must have stared him in the face when he remembered that Ionnia was his ex-wife's niece. Knowing his strategies and tactics, he would put Loretty's entire family on trial and make Harry Quane out to be an angel.

"You had enough time to think about what you did. How do you plead?" the judge asked the giant.

"Not guilty, Your Honor."

If most people had their way, the only thing they wanted to happen was to see Harry put away for a while because they knew what a menace he was to society. But one thing they knew was that they would surely miss a damn good mechanic.

Harry got the shock of his life when his only friend, Earlon, was called by the prosecution to testify. When the tape was presented as evidence to the court, Harry's eyes popped out of his head, looking like two hard-boiled eggs. He was in disbelief that his friend would do that to him. Other members of the community were called by the prosecution to talk about Harry's bullying and reckless, dangerous, behavior. One by one, they gave accounts of his manipulative tactics and how he drove the fear of God and the devil in others. His school records were summoned, and some of his former teachers testified about his disruptive behaviors in class and how he would threaten them if he were punished. Harry's juvenile incarceration records were also examined. Only at the reformatory did any so-called behavioral change take place because he had no other choice but to conform to the rules. Glovene Hatford and Eda Lane were among those called by the prosecutor, and they held nothing back.

The only other person who said anything positive about Harry was Lizzie Dussle, who was rumored to be his girlfriend, and whose house he was found in at Bedford Run. Her brother Garth, who was Harry's right-hand man, would run the mechanic shop during Harry's absence.

When Harry's mother took the stand, he breathed a deep sigh of relief, hoping she was going to say something good about her only son. Hilda Morraine tilted her head, took off her glasses, and wiped a few tears from her eyes, She glanced at Harry and then addressed the judge. Rather than speaking well of her son, she pleaded, "Your Honor, maybe sending Harry away will teach him a lesson. God knows I want my son to be a good person, and not like his father or his brother."

Harry was stunned. "Why are you doing this, Mother?" he yelled.

"Order!" the presiding judge, the Honorable Martha Finlaw, said as she pounded her gavel. She gave Harry a chance to cross-examine the witness, so he rehashed all his childhood experiences and punishments meted out to him by his mother. "She hated me from the day I was born, Your Honor," Harry told the judge.

Ionnia was called by the prosecution to talk about the many hours she'd spent taking care of Queenie and the rest of her chickens, as well as the amount of money she'd made by selling the eggs and the young chicks. She outlined to the court how she'd saved her money toward the purchase of school books and other educational materials. She told them that Queenie had become her friend and that she dreamed about her every night. She ended by presenting to the court a drawing of how she perceived the innocent birds had perished while fighting for their lives. Her brother Tyrone did a good job with the artwork, which impressed the judge and other people in the court-room; they could be seen drying their eyes from time to time. Then Ionnia turned to the judge and asked her if she could make a state-ment on behalf of women and children who suffered by the hands of men. The judge had no objections. Ionnia continued. "Your Honor and distinguished officers of the court, one thing I would like for you to consider when these bullies and women haters appear before you is not to give them a slap on the wrist, as so many of your male counterparts do, but rather give them the punishment they deserve. It has become apparent that it is the nature of most men to inflict pain on women. No doubt if my mother or I were in that building, we would have been the victims of this arsonist." She pointed to Harry. "Women need to be respected and protected instead of being beaten, tortured, burned, or killed. Please send a message, Your Honor."

The judge asked Ionnia whether she had any questions for her uncle. She turned to Harry and asked, "Why, Uncle Harry? Why did you do it?"

Harry sat motionless, his face devoid of any emotions, and he said nothing. The judge asked him if he had any questions for his niece, and he straightened up and shook his head. "No, Your Honor."

"Then what do you have to say in your defense?"

"It was all an accident."

Harry had begged several of his mechanics to testify on his behalf, but only one, Dalbert Coote, told the court of Harry's excellent auto mechanic skills, and he added, "I think the system could benefit from his expertise. There is always good that emanates from something whom we look at as bad and evil." The judge nodded in agreement. Harry was thankful that Dalbert didn't say bad things about him. The prosecution had no questions for him.

"I am going to set an example here," the judge said. She found Harry guilty on all charges. He was ordered to compensate Loretty and her family in the amount of five thousand dollars for the loss of Ionnia's chickens and for the section of the house that had been damaged. He was also sentenced to two years in prison, and ordered to attend anger management classes and group counseling sessions while he was incarcerated. As if that wasn't enough, Harry was given five years' probation following his release, and would also be fitted with a surveillance tracking device. It didn't stop there. He was also slapped with a restraining order to stay more than one hundred yards away from his brother's family and their property when he got out. Not expecting all this, Harry jumped up from his seat, disrupted the proceedings with an outburst of flatulence followed by expletives, and was charged an additional five hundred dollars and sixty days for contempt of court.

Harry had one request. "Can my friend Earlon Gevannes act as a manger for my business while I'm away? Even though he helped to put me away, I know he meant well. He will be the one responsible to pay Loretty a weekly amount."

The judge turned to Earlon and asked, "Do you have any objections, Mr. Gevannes?"

"No, Your Honor."

"Then I will give you two some time together before the prisoner is taken away."

The first thing that Earlon pointed out to Harry was, "I know how much help you need, and I am positive you will get all the help where you are going. The prison's psychiatrist, Dr. Elsworth Gevannes, is my brother. Feel free to tell him everything about your life so that he can help you."

Harry knew how to manipulate the system so that he could be put in charge of certain activities. How ironic: Harry hated authority figures but liked to be put in a position of power. Harry was put in charge of repairing the fleet of vehicles for the police department, the prisons, and many other government agencies. The experience, responsibility, and total autonomy were probably what Harry needed to turn his life around. At times he thought of tampering with some of the vehicles, but one time when he was about to do so, a car slipped off a jack, and he came within an inch of meeting his maker. Since that time,

Harry seemed to be on the straight and narrow, and he never missed any of his anger management sessions. Whenever he was faced with situations where he could get angry and resentful, he would use the opportunity to go work in the garage, where he would get flashbacks of his near-death experience that had forever changed his life. Harry always expressed his gratitude to his friend Earlon, who never gave up on him and often visited him in prison. He was also grateful to one of his supervisors, George Copelander, for trusting and believing in him.

Harry was the first inmate who benefitted from a new program whereby inmates received compensation for work performed while incarcerated. He was motivated and encouraged to save his money, which he used for restitution to his brother's family. His attitude changed toward women, and at first people were skeptical as to whether his intentions were genuine or whether he was doing this simply to get on them to trust him. But he proved that even the worst among us could change.

Twenty-Three

Boysie Vernetti, who was representing Loretty in her assault case, took on another role: making sure that she and her children would have the proper documents for the Dartsdam property and be able to continue living there in peace. Thus, Boysie needed the expertise of Angelina O'Hammond, an attorney and graduate of the University of Krepston. "I need you to handle the real estate affairs of Loretty Quane and her children. This situation has become a complicated one and needs the expertise of someone like you to straighten it out. Several searches were conducted at the offices of the registrar of titles in Trevine, but no documentation could be found showing Lensley Quane as the registered owner of this property. We sure wouldn't like to see Loretty lose her home and property despite the sad memories that linger there."

"So who has the title, who owns the property, and where does Loretty and her family stand in all of this? Would they be able to live there unprovoked until the situation gets straightened out?" Angelina asked.

"The mystery remains, but left in your capable hands, the family will be able to breathe a sigh of relief that this will be sorted out on their behalf, no matter how long it takes. That's why I want you to keep this as quiet as possible. We wouldn't want her mother-in-law to find out about this, because with the help of Walton Quane, she may suddenly appear with some fictitious documents. Furthermore, maybe either Cyril Dulvert or Sam Muggerdon can provide some answers as to who holds the title to the property. Interview all of them. Do whatever it takes, but just don't let Muggerdon hypnotize you."

Angelina immediately set her machinery into motion and scheduled an emergency hearing in the local magistrate's court before the justice of the peace, Mr. Isaac Finlaw. She wanted some assurance that Loretty and her children would be allowed to stay on the property uninterrupted until the situation was resolved. However, only one bedroom of the house appeared to be livable at this time due to the extensive smoke and water damage from the fire. In the true spirit of a unified community, the neighbors helped the family clean up and make the home more livable once again. Everyone pitched in, but the cleanup took longer than expected due to the amount of broken liquor bottles. The volunteers dug through the ashes and the rubble for any valuables that may have been buried. They found little. Skilled tradesmen of Whickam County contributed their time, money. and materials to the church to help Loretty, and very soon her home was transformed into a beautiful three-bedroom dwelling equipped with modern amenities. Church members, women's groups and other concerned citizens donated clothing, food, money. and furniture. It was such an inspiration in the midst of tragedy.

Loretty's sister Dee Dee offered to move in with her. "You don't need to be alone in times like these."

"So what will you do with your apartment? Have you broken up with your boyfriend?" Loretty asked.

"I don't want to talk about that now, big sis. Let me just say that we need each other at this time. Please do not protest."

Dee Dee did a lot of voluntary work at the schools and the clinic in and around Dartsdam. Nurse Veetley was very impressed with her work, so she offered her a full-time paid position as a medical records technician.

The younger Dulvert, who was always considered a flirt, quickly established a relationship with Edgar Baruke, an ambulance driver who transported patients from the Dartsdam Clinic to Whickam County General and other hospitals. Edgar hailed from San Clewert, was married with six children, and wasn't honest enough to tell Dee Dee, but she happened to get wind of it. When she confronted him, he swore that it was only a matter of time before he divorced his wife and married her. His wife, Maizie, was a teacher at the elementary school in San Clewert, and she didn't follow her husband around or ask questions about him. She was satisfied to see him when he came home once every fortnight. She was an easygoing, submissive human being who always said how much she trusted her husband, adding that he was a good provider to his family. She was one of those women who couldn't believe that her man would lie to her. She was brought up to believe anything a man told her. And moreover, she said that she had enough on her hands caring for their six children and the many others whom she taught. She was a very dedicated teacher, and most of the children regarded her as a second mother.

Dee Dee soon became pregnant and almost went insane. Now more than ever, she really wanted him to fulfill his promise to her, but every time she mentioned marriage, he became very evasive. "I feel tempted to let his wife know of his infidelity," Dee Dee said. "But why burden her with something that is not her fault?"

Dee Dee was not the only woman with whom Edgar had extramarital relations. Sybil Sagoo, a beautician and operator of Boundless Beauty Salon, was one of the other unsuspecting victims. Dee Dee learned about Sybil from her sister Twyleith, who visited the establishment for her hair care and beauty needs. Sybil had been bragging day after day to her customers about her newfound love. Twyleith was incensed when Edgar showed up one day when she was there. She never said a word to Sybil that her sister had fallen head over heels with the same man and was pregnant by him. She was torn as how to handle the situation. Should she tell Sybil about Dee Dee, or should she tell her sister about Sybil? She never wanted another sister of hers to be mistreated, so she informed Dee Dee about Sybil's relationship with Edgar, warning her to not create any confrontation with her. "She may not even know about you or his wife, so go easy on the girl. As a matter of fact, let me go with you and talk to her. We all may be able to teach him a lesson."

At around closing time one afternoon, the Dulvert sisters paid a visit to Sybil's beauty shop. All the customers and staff had left, and Sybil was alone. When they pushed the intercom button, Sybil shouted from the storage room, "We're closed."

"We are not here for services, we are not here to sell you anything, and we are not cops. Please let us in. We have something urgent to talk to you about. We are here because of Edgar Baruke."

"What about him? Is he in some sort of trouble? Did he have an accident?" Sybil rushed downstairs and opened the door. She was trembling, and her face had an inquiring frown. She recognized Twyleith, so she beckoned the pair to enter, took them upstairs, and then offered them seats. She sat opposite them on a stool without a back. "Well?" she inquired as she looked from one woman to another.

Twyleith introduced her sister and there was a long pause.

Dee Dee was the first to speak. "I don't know how to say this to you without breaking your heart," she said calmly.

"Will you please stop keeping me in suspense and tell me why you are here?" The tears ran down Sybil's cheeks in torrents, and one could hear her heartbeat. Obviously she cared about this man, and she thought he cared about her too. She reached for a small washcloth, and Twyleith gently took it from her and dried her tears. Sybil got a hold of her emotions and stared at the two women.

"Did you know that Edgar is married?" Dee Dee asked Sybil.

She was speechless. She sat motionless, frightened, and absorbed in thought. "This is absurd. We plan on getting married," she said with strong convictions. "Where did you hear that? Are you the wife?" Before Dee Dee could answer, Sybil stared at them threateningly and said, "If you two don't get out of here, I swear I will throw you over the balcony!"

This doesn't look good, Twyleith thought to herself. Then she turned to the grieving lover, held her hand, and said, "Calm down and listen to me."

Dee Dee chipped in and said to Sybil, "Don't believe what he says. He has a wife and six children, and one other woman that I know of. And just in case you are doubting my last statement, this is the proof." She pointed her finger at herself. "I'm one of those whom he also promised to marry, and I am pregnant."

"Why are you telling me this? What do you hope to gain? Do you expect me to just leave him at this point in our relationship? I waited a long time before I found true love, and I am not going to give it up just because you two want me to do so."

As Sybil began to sound more hostile, Dee Dee assured her, "I hold no animosity toward you. I am fully aware of the fact that you did not know about my relationship with this man before you got involved. Now is your chance to come to your senses and do the right thing before it's too late."

"Too late for what?" Sybil asked.

Twyleith began to feel sorry for Sybil and asked her, "Pardon me if I sound presumptuous, but are you also pregnant?"

The poor girl, who by now looked a complete wreck, said, "I'm not sure." Suddenly she began to regurgitate. She grabbed one of the salon towels, covered her mouth, and ran to the bathroom.

"Oh, my God!" Twyleith exclaimed in a sympathetic manner.

On her return, Sybil turned to Dee Dee and said, "If I am pregnant, I am definitely not going to have his child. Are you going to keep yours?" Before the young lady could answer, the beautician added, "Another thing I can tell you that I am absolutely sure of: if you will agree to it, we can teach that testosterone-laden SOB a lesson."

"How would we carry this out? What do you have in mind?" Dee Dee asked.

"Give me some time to process all of this information," Sybil

Sagoo said to her. "I will get back to you as soon as possible so that we can put a plan together. I also promise that I will not confront Edgar before that plan is put in place, and I hope you won't confront him either."

"We have a deal," Dee Dee said.

"Thank you. You seem to be a very understanding person."

Both women crossed their hearts to seal the pledge, and then the sisters helped Sybil lock up the salon.

Twenty-Four

Ionnia's legal adoption was taking longer than everyone anticipated. In the meantime, Ionnia was anxious to drop the name Quane, so she put in a special request to her mother. "Can I drop the name Quane and use the name Dunn in honor of my grandmother?"

"Sure, anything you wish. I will have this taken care of right away."

"Would you consider doing the same?" the young girl asked her mother.

The mother thought for a moment and then replied, "I'll think about it."

Loretty asked her sister-in-law's husband, Ansel, to take care of the name drop for Ionnia before the actual adoption by the Rytes became a reality. Ansel knew the right strings to pull and got this done as quickly as possible. He was very supportive to the family, as if they were directly related to him, and he knew how much his ex-wife cared about them. Loretty had one last assignment for Ansel: notifying Knoxford High that Ionnia wouldn't be attending as scheduled. He would then ask that all documentations be sent to Mt. Mathuveh Academy. He personally visited the school and had this done in the blink of an eye.

The Rytes were anxious for the new addition to their family and wrote to Loretty, asking her if it would be all right if her daughter could come as soon as possible. Their son-in-law Charley Gress, an attorney, was responsible for monitoring the procedure. He was familiar with Ansel McEarth's ability to get things done, and so he solicited some assistance from him.

It was summer holidays, school was not in session, and all four of Ionnia's brothers were home. They had completed their summer jobs and were looking forward to returning to high school and college in a few weeks.

The day arrived for Ionnia to leave to her new home with her new family. Mrs. Gertrude Ott, lovingly called Aunt Gert from then on, had made arrangements to pick her up on Friday, August 23, a week after Ionnia's eleventh birthday. Ionnia woke up early that morning and continued her packing, carefully selecting suitable things to wear. She had lost most of her belongings in the fire, but thanks to the church community and family members, she had enough to last her a while. Loretty had made Ionnia four sets of uniforms (avocado green skirt and yellow blouse) from materials given to her by Harold's brother-in-law, who owned a department store in Eppon Harbor. Loretty assisted her daughter by packing her school documents, vaccination records, baptismal certificate, medical and dental records, financial documents, and most important her diary.

"This is much more difficult than I thought it would be," Ionnia said.

"Make sure you understand that you are not the only one making an adjustment. I'll also have to adjust my life without you here," Loretty told her daughter. "But your adoption will be an open one, the family will be allowed to visit you in Krepston, and you will visit us whenever you can."

The excitement and enthusiasm had waned, and then Ionnia opened a letter she had received from Mrs. Finlaw the day before congratulating her on passing the entrance exam to Knoxford High. Her words of encouragement remotivated Ionnia. Mrs. Finlaw gave her the name of one of the retired instructors who could be a mentor to her, and she also enclosed a small amount of money, which Ionnia could really use.

"As soon as you settle down, you will have to let Mrs. Finlaw know that you are not at Knoxford High," Loretty reminded her daughter. "She will be just as pleased to know that you are at Mount Mathuveh and that more than anything else, you will be around family."

The goodbyes were long and tearful for the family, and each of Ionnia's brothers gave her something to remind her of him.

Chad was exceptionally kind and encouraging to his sister. As the eldest sibling, he assumed the role of father and gave Ionnia the necessary guidance he thought was important. He told his sister that it was okay to look back at life's journeys, but if one forgot to continue looking forward, one would run off the road.

Roger had the following words for her: "I know much you want to escape your tormentors and forget the past, but please do not forget your humble beginnings."

Kyle and Tyrone also had their say, but Tyrone was the one who asked, "What is all the fuss about? Let's treat Ionnia's departure as if she were going off to high school. No one made all this fuss when we were leaving."

"This is a different scenario," Chad reminded him.

Ionnia hugged her mother tightly and said, "I am scared to leave you, but I promise to pray for you, write to you, and visit you as often as possible."

"Listen, baby. I want you to save whatever money you have, as well as any that you may be making while in Krepston. I will be fine. You don't have to travel unnecessarily. And don't forget to write and thank Mrs. Finlaw."

"I am going to miss my friends, and I don't know how soon I will be able to make new ones, or how will I be accepted in a new community."

By the time Aunt Gert got there, everyone's eyes were red and swollen. When she saw how devastated the family was in bidding goodbye to Ionnia, she said, "I can understand how everyone feels. Take all the time you need." Turning to Loretty, she added, "If you change your mind, I also understand." Aunt Gert held Ionnia's hands, looked at everyone, and said in a very humbling tone, "Look on the bright side. This time in your life may seem like one of the darkest hours, but don't forget that the sun that sets today will rise again."

Aunt Gert turned to the rest of the family. "Boys, I wish you well in your pursuit for a higher education." She gave them some pointers about goal setting, self-awareness, resilience, assertiveness, and self-esteem. "You are a wonderful family," she told them, "and nothing but the best will come of it. Just believe. And lest I forget, I am really sorry to learn about the family tragedy. We will be praying for you. Loretty, we are so sorry that we didn't intervene as soon as we learned about your woes. What happened could have been avoided, and I understand that the bishop has been making changes to ensure that the people of the community are well ministered to. Can we talk elsewhere for a moment while the children have some time together?" They went into the bedroom and resumed the conversation. Then Loretty walked Gert to the car. When they came back inside, Ionnia indicated that she was ready to go.

Ionnia kept silent for the first part of the 150-mile journey to Krepston. Aunt Gert was determined not to let this be an exhaustive journey, so she reached for a cassette tape and inserted it in the deck. Suddenly Ionnia heard the voices of the members of the Mount Mathuveh choir singing her favorite song, "Across the Bridge." The two looked at each other and smiled. "I know that that's your favorite," Gert said, "so I had it recorded." Soon Ionnia opened up to Aunt Gert, and the immediate bond they formed was unbreakable.

Gert slowed the car, reached in the glove compartment, and handed Ionnia a small box. "I want you to have what's inside."

At first the young girl was hesitant. "Open it," her aunt pleaded. So as not to disappoint her aunt, she did as she was told. When she opened the box, she didn't know what to say. Inside was a beautiful gold wristwatch with a stretchable band and Roman numerals.

"It belonged to a grand-aunt of mine," Gert said. "It was given to her by her husband, and when they divorced, he demanded it back. She hid it safely where he couldn't find it."

Ionnia was about to ask her why she didn't give it to her daughter, but Gert must have read her thoughts, and at that point she interrupted. "I don't have a daughter, and I was waiting to give it to my first son's first daughter, but he ended up with all boys."

"Thank you. It's beautiful. Can I put it on now?"

"You deserve it. I have heard of all your achievements, and how little you have been rewarded and appreciated for your efforts and ambitions by some people close to you. I am not trying to make up for all the neglect. I know you will always remember the past, and that's a good thing; it makes one stronger and more resilient. Also, if you do not know from whence you came, you will not be sure where you want to go."

Mrs. Ott drove slowly in order to afford Ionnia the opportunity to appreciate the different sceneries. This section of the island had acres and acres of citrus trees, coconut trees, and sugar cane. From a distance, one could see some old sugar cane factories, some of which were currently in use. When Ionnia saw the smoke rising from the huge chimneys, her mind suddenly went to Hollers Valley.

Halfway through the journey, in the vicinity of Bregmar Creek, they ran into heavy rain and dense fog that impacted visibility, making it extremely difficult for them to continue. Aunt Gert was familiar with the reckless behaviors of the drivers of these areas of Puca Luca who would overtake on the narrow roads in section where they weren't supposed to overtake, even around hairpin corners. There was evidence all over the side of the road of burned-out vehicles of all shapes and sizes, and from time to time, people in need of spare parts for their vehicles could be observed retrieving these parts, posing as extra hazards to vehicular traffic. Gert was being cautious with her precious cargo, and she tried to avoid having an accident on the road. They had just managed to reach the foothills of the Shafton Mountain, so this very cautious driver thought it would be best to stop at the Marberg Inn and spend the night. This was around a quarter of a mile from Deliverance Park, where a religious crusade and revival was scheduled to start under a huge tent. The park was so named because it was the chosen venue for most religious events that were not held inside any church, and where many people claimed that they had received divine deliverance from their burdens and healing of their bodies and spirits. The event attracted numerous people, both locally and from out of town. This was the same venue where many politicians held mass meetings and promised their constituents deliverance from poverty and all other ills that stood in their way of prosperity. It was at this very spot where Basil Oop talked about income inequality and predicted that the ordinary person would one day experience freedom from oppression of the rich folks. He promised them equitable distribution of property and reminded them that all people were created equal.

All the rooms at the hotel were sold out, but Gert stared the receptionist in the face and said, "I'm sure you must have an extra room in case of emergency. I will pay you extra if I have to."

At that moment, a tall gentleman with salt-and-pepper hair and a black pin-striped suit appeared and heard the exchange. He identified himself as Horatio Blevick, the manager. He smiled and, in a voice as refined as the suit he wore, turned to the receptionist and said, "Let me take care of this." He and Gert spoke for a moment or two, and then he informed her that he could let her occupy one of the suites reserved for visiting executives. Gert was about to protest when Mr. Blevick said, "A lady of your caliber should not refuse a generous offer in a time such as this, unless you two want to go out and hurt yourselves. Bear in mind the nearest hotel is twelve miles away from here. And if this will calm your spirit, the suite will not cost you anything extra." Mr. Blevick beckoned to one of the bellhops. "Zey, take these folks to suite number 534."

"Yes, sir," he said as he straightened his uniform. He looked around wide-eyed at the other employees, who had a suspicious, questioning look that Gertrude Ott was one of the hotel's executives, and at that moment every employee who was standing idly by scrambled to find something to do.

"This way, ma'am," the young man said in an unusually polite tone, and he walked toward the elevator. Gert thanked the manager, and then she and Ionnia followed the bellhop to the suite reserved for the executive director.

"Did you know him, Aunt Gert?" Ionnia asked.

"No, but he did look like someone I knew while I was studying at university."

"Then what did you say to him to convince him?"

"Nothing much, but as time goes by, you will learn the art of negotiation." This was not the only thing that captivated Ionnia's attention. This was her first ride in an elevator, and she remained silent until they reached the fifth floor.

The start of the revival was delayed two hours due to inclement weather. Gert and Ionnia savored the hotel suite before heading for the tent. They enjoyed the scenery from the balcony of their suite and then snooped around for any evidence of the identity of the executive director of the Marberg Inn. "Oh, no," Gert said. Ionnia looked at her questioningly, but neither one said anything else.

The rain ceased, the fog disappeared, and the radiant evening sun shone through the trees. The huge gathering at Deliverance Park was a reminder to Ionnia of the day she was rescued out of the Four Eyes Cave. A very diverse group of people was seated and waiting patiently for the start of the event; some walked around aimlessly throughout the park. Ionnia recognized Carolyn Veetley, who was the recipient of many awards for her human interest stories. She was ready to report on the many miracles supposedly performed by the pastor, Reverend Frederick Kremp from Ridgewood.

Kremp was a man in his mid-forties and was tall and muscular.

Although he was always immaculately dressed and would change suits
during intermissions, his face had a peculiar expression that seemed to
cause a degree of awe and fear from the gathering. When he preached
of hellfire, one could almost immediately feel the heat. Many people
left his meetings satisfied that they were healed physically and that
the demons blocking their efforts at achieving success in life were
removed. They could be heard shouting at the top of their lungs,
"Deliverance!"

Those who attended Reverend Kremp's revival meetings were
always generous with their donations, which were collected in
twenty-gallon paint buckets passed around the park by other faithful
followers. But there was always the odd person in the midst. One
man was caught trying to put a handful of the money in his pocket,
and when Reverend Kremp was notified about this, he publicly humiliated him but offered him a chance to return the money in front
of the huge gathering and ask them for forgiveness.

When he was finished, Reverend Kremp addressed the crowd.
"Not one of you must attempt to lay your hands on this man. He has
confessed his shortcomings before God and this gathering, and we
have forgiven him. The devil is always at work, ready to test us, but
we must not yield to temptation."

Mrs. Ott recognized many familiar faces. One in particular was
Iris Snipp, now Iris Depping, a schoolmate and cousin of her first
husband, Bernard Snipp. They talked for a while, and Ionnia was
introduced as Gert's new niece. *Oh, my God, did the bishop cheat on his
wife?* Iris said to herself. They never got into the details of how this
came about, although Iris had that "tell me more" look on her face.

Iris beckoned to her granddaughter, Lorna, who was standing
nearby. "Come and meet my friend's niece." Iris thought that by doing so, Lorna might learn the whole truth. "Her name is Ionnia, and
I have a feeling that this is the friend you always wanted to have." She
was right because as soon as both girls were introduced, there seemed
to be instant chemistry between them.

While the adults conversed, the teenagers, who seemed to have a lot in common, talked as if they'd known each other for a long time. They talked about school, their friends, their hobbies, and their goals. They leaned against one of the oversized speaker boxes that were placed strategically at various locations of the park, and they were scared out of their wits when suddenly there erupted a loud boom from the piece of equipment. The girls must have thought the whole place was going to blow up. The box started to vibrate, and a strong voice said, "Testing, testing, one, two, three." This was a signal that action was imminent. The crusade was about to commence.

The girls got over the fright, composed themselves, and moved to a different location, but they stayed in clear view of their guardians. Lorna and Ionnia shared similar interests. They had ambitious goals and wanted to be successful. Both had mothers who had been abused by their spouses, and both were fatherless.

Twenty-Five

Lorna had a devastating story to tell, and she begged Ionnia not to tell any of her friends about it. Ionnia placed her hand over her heart and made a solemn vow not to reveal Lorna's secret. Some of what she was about to tell her was what she'd heard from others, or what she had read from newspaper clippings in her grandmother's scrapbook hidden away from her and her sister, but they managed to locate it without anyone finding out. Some of the information was what she actually remembered after having repressed it for a little while.

Lorna's mother, Brenda, was savagely beaten and humiliated for years by her husband, Norman Tottenberry. She became a regular patient at the hospital, and at times she would be treated and sent home, but at other times she was kept for days due to the severity of the assault. Despite all this, Brenda refused to press charges or leave her abuser. She did not want to return home to her mother or to other relatives or friends. She was scared that Norman would find her and kill her. This was how Nicole Linzi, an insurance sales agent, came to rest permanently at Dove Lawn cemetery. Nicole had escaped from her husband and was staying with a friend, but the husband had found her, killed her, and threatened to pour acid on the friend. Furthermore, when Brenda was confronted by anyone and asked why she didn't leave her husband, she would always reply, "I love him."

This response got many people giving her the strangest look ever, but she didn't care. After a while, if Brenda should start to relate her story to anyone, they would walk away and say, "You fool." Like so many battered women, Brenda would always return to the batterer and looked forward to the day when she hoped he would become a changed man. She would blame herself for being clumsy, and she'd make up excuses, telling the hospital staff that she'd fallen or that she'd stumbled into a piece of furniture with a sharp edge.

Ionnia's thoughts were on her mother, and she briefly told Lorna about her own situation.

"I'm so sorry," Lorna said. "It must be very hard for you."

Brenda's situation worsened rather than improved, and her mother, Iris, was never fully involved in her life because she had warned her against marrying Norman. One Christmas eve when the children were very young, Norman came home and started a verbal fight with his wife. She ignored him, and that was the worst thing that she could do to him. He kicked and beat her so severely that she passed out. He didn't call for help but left her to die, and he stormed out of the house. She was discovered by her sister-in-law, Cislyn, who had come over with presents for the girls. Norman was not there, and no one knew where he had gone and what time he would return.

Cislyn, called Cissy, grabbed some clothes for Brenda, and the children and hurriedly took Brenda to the hospital. Then Cissy went to her home with the children. One week later, Brenda was released into her sister-in-law's custody per her request to the hospital authorities.

"I am determined to not let my sadistic brother torture his family anymore."

When Norman realized that his wife and children were at Cislyn's house, he decided to show up unannounced. "Please send my family back to me, I promise to be a changed man, and I will never hurt Brenda again," he pleaded with his sister.

"Go away, Norman. You ought to be ashamed of yourself. Our

parents did not raise us this way. I ought to have you arrested." He left but returned later with gifts for his family and tears in his eyes as he declared his love for them. At this point, he showed some signs of remorse.

"Norman, you need to seek professional help before I release Brenda and the girls into your custody."

"Okay, then tell me where to go and whom to see. I will do anything to have my family back. Life is not the same without them."

Cissy gave him a name and address and said, "Make sure you schedule this appointment soon. I will be checking to see that you do."

Norman did see a psychotherapist and was scheduled for anger management treatment. This convinced Brenda that he was on the right path and that he would not abuse her anymore, so she told Cissy that she wanted to return home. However, pressure was brought to bear on her from family and friends for the couple to attend marriage and family therapy sessions. "Norman has a problem that needs to be addressed," her mother, Iris, stressed. "And you have a self-esteem problem, or else you wouldn't put up with such crap. You need to leave Norman. Once a batterer, always a batterer. You need a lot of help, and no one is able to help you until you are ready to accept that what is happening is not normal and needs to stop."

Norman really had a problem: that of having to disclose private family matters to a stranger. "I am very uncomfortable with this," he said, so he discontinued the sessions. But the few sessions they had completed seemed to have an effect on them, and calmness prevailed in the Tottenberry household until Valentine's Day.

The couple had an argument because Brenda didn't pick up his dirty socks out of the living room the day before, and his friends saw them when they came over. Later, on their way to his mother's house, Norman pulled the car to the side of the road, pounded Brenda in her face and head, threw her out of his car, and almost ran her over as he hurriedly tried to escape from the scene with their screaming children in the back seat of the car. Luck was on Brenda's side. She was picked up by a passing motorist who happened to be Captain Reuben

Brumely of the Puca Luca military. He took her to the nearest health center, but her injuries were so severe that he summoned his headquarters to dispatch the air ambulance to the area. Brenda was airlifted to the main teaching hospital in Trevine, and the stranger gave his name as her next of kin. He gave special instructions not to allow her husband near her, and when Norman showed up with flowers and a love letter, he got the shock of his life. He couldn't see his wife. The lengthy love letter described how much he loved and missed her and couldn't wait for her to come home. But otherwise, he was having a lot of fun taking care of the girls.

Brenda was worried about her children, but she seemed to be satisfied that they were being taken care of by their father, so after her release from the hospital, she never returned home. Due to the frequent beatings in her head and face, Brenda developed a condition called Bell's palsy. This was a paralysis of the facial nerve, which resulted in twitching, tingling, facial spasms, and inability to control facial muscles. Other symptoms included headaches and neck pains, dizziness, clumsiness, and balance problems. The last two symptoms were probably the reason why Brenda kept falling into furniture. She sought treatment from an acupuncturist, and most of the symptoms disappeared so that she was able to live a normal life. Then she disappeared from radar. No one saw or heard from her for a while.

Lorna and her sister Olive were left with their father, who appeared to be a loving and caring dad at first, so there was no urgency for Cissy or the rest of the family to take them away. Cissy still saw the need to supervise them or to have them over on weekends. But Norman Tottenberry had a dirty secret. He started molesting the girls, and when they rejected his sexual advances, he choked them until they passed out. He laughed at them and then committed his sinful act. He would frequently tell his daughters, "I'm the one who supports you, so no one else is going to get what belongs to me. And don't ever think of telling anyone, because you won't be believed."

They felt trapped and helpless, but when they decided to speak out, people did believe them, including law enforcement personnel. Time had caught up with Norman. He was arrested and charged with incest and child rape. He was also charged with the assault and the attempted murder of his wife who had resurfaced, testified in court, and disappeared again. At his trial, the jury, which was made up of mostly young mothers, wasted no time in returning a guilty verdict on all charges. Norman was sent to prison for fifteen years on each count of rape to run consecutively, ten years on each count of incest to run concurrently, and twenty years for the assault and attempted murder of his wife. He was also to receive eight lashes with the cat-o-nine-tails. The children were taken away and raised by different relatives. Lorna lived with her maternal grandmother, Iris Depping, and Olive lived with her paternal grandmother, Essie Tottenberry.

Iris Depping never stopped looking for her daughter, and she agonized over the fact that if she had gone on and rescued her daughter, she would be okay today. Seven long years passed before she finally found her. This time she was living with Kethune Brumely, sister of the captain who had rescued her. Iris persuaded her daughter to start divorce proceedings against her husband, but before this was finalized, Norman was savagely attacked by prison inmates and killed. They had planned this from the first day he was brought in, because they had heard of his charges; even the worst criminals who were incarcerated had no sympathy for child molesters. Norman had been taken out of the general population and placed in solitary confinement, but he was wrestled out of the hands of the warden by five hardened prisoners, who stabbed Norman over two hundred times with various improvised weapons they had made in their cells.

Although Brenda had no further need for a divorce, she was anxious to get rid of the name she'd acquired from being married to Norman Tottenberry. She returned to her maiden name, Depping, and planned later to change her daughters' names. Brenda and Cissy continued to establish an unbroken bond.

Cissy was an advocate against domestic abuse, but she let her guard down when she met Evan Curley, a warehouse supervisor at Verley Nollis's lumberyard. She couldn't believe that she had endured physical and emotional abuse at the hands of her husband, but she thanked her lucky stars that she was fortunate enough to not have any children with him. Her marriage to Evan lasted for nine years, and despite his cruelty, she felt she couldn't live without him. She could not believe that she had ceased to be herself. She had become Evan Curley's property. She lived and breathed for this despot. Now it was Brenda's time to remind Cissy of what she had been enforcing. Of the nine years she was married to Evan, only two of them could be described as good. She finally summoned her courage and split up with him. She cried herself to sleep every night and tried numerous times at reconciliation, but Evan had already started a new relationship with Nicole Linzi's cousin, Kaithlyn, from Falcon's Bend. She had three children for him over a period of three years.

"How could he not miss me? Has he thought of those times when he couldn't resist me?" Cislyn cried. During the period when they were separated, Cislyn made unwelcome contact with Kaithlyn until she became tired of her.

"I am fed up with your wife interfering in our lives," Kaithlyn told Evan. "You are free to reunite with her—she's all yours. I'm taking my children and going as far away from you as I can get."

During the time Evan and Cissy were separated, she had gone back to school and become a licensed realtor, and she was making lots of money selling real estate to the rich and famous.

Around six weeks after Evan and Kaithlyn broke up, he lost his job at the lumberyard and went pleading to his wife to forgive him and to take him back. He knew that she would come running in his arms, but she never realized that he was simply using her. Obviously, she was in love.

Evan convinced Cislyn to lend him a few thousand dollars to make a down payment on a car so he could find a job in an adjoining town. Cislyn looked at him suspiciously but reminded herself that they had made a promise before God and their friends to love each other as long as they both shall live. But this was not what she had been encouraging other women to do. It was a case of "Do as I say, not as I do."

After much pleading and convincing from her husband, Cislyn was convinced that he wanted to make things right. She believed his stories and loaned him the money. She was surprised to learn later on that he'd used that money as a retainer for a divorce lawyer. When she realized what was happening and confronted him, all he had to say was, "Give it up peacefully."

Cislyn almost lost her mind. Those words cut through her like a saw cutting lumber down at the mill. She felt sick and played the events over and over in her mind. "What will the other women think of me? How could I let this happen? How could I not have control over myself?" Cislyn cried. "That bastard!"

When Cislyn finally got it together, she confronted Evan and demanded to know why he'd treated her that way. He laughed at her and said, "Do you really think I was serious about wanting you back?" She asked Evan for her money, but he cursed her out and refused to pay her back. His response was, "Shut up. You damn well know that you paid me to screw you."

Shortly after the divorce was final, he reunited with Kaithlyn and married her for the sake of the children. But Kaithlyn was smart. She had Evan sign a document committing himself to a five-year marriage, after which she may consider renewing the vows.

After Cislyn recovered from the shock, she was more resolute and determined to put the past behind her, regain her independence, and forget about men. She made herself a promise not to let worry devour her life, and she reflected on the words of Dorothy Galyean, who once said, "Worry is like a rocking chair, it gives you something to do but it gets you nowhere."

Cislyn and Brenda maintained their close relationship, and Brenda was introduced to a women's support group Rescuing Abused Women (RAW), headed by Clover Fishley of Mumfries Harbor. They also teamed up with the BONDAGE group from south Whickam County. With the establishment of these groups that declared war on abusive men, the government was forced to take a serious look at domestic violence. A national survey was done to ascertain the number of victims, and the results were frightening. Another follow-up survey was done to identify the monetary burden on the healthcare system brought about by domestic violence, which had reached an alarming proportion. Women were treated for physical and mental health injuries such as head and brain injuries, broken bones, and miscarriages.

As more and more women became fed up with the intolerable physical and emotional abuses, they expressed a desire to learn to use guns and engage in other self-defense methods. They saw the need for women to arm and protect themselves against their aggressors, so Brenda and Cissy decided to open a shop that specialized in various types of self-defense.

Sheila Bluggard, who had since resigned from law enforcement, joined RAW, opened a gun range, and taught women the proper techniques of using guns of different calibers. Women were obsessed with the idea of defending themselves, and Sheila also taught martial arts to everyone who wanted to learn such techniques. She knew what these women were going through because she had responded to too many domestic violence situations when she was a cop, and she felt empathy for them. The various police departments were overwhelmed with applications from women for gun licenses, and there was a sudden upsurge in gun sales, but in the meantime, the men complained that they were denied the opportunity to obtain the same firearm licenses.

There were several chapters of RAW established throughout Puca Luca and the surrounding islands. Those who preferred to remain single were encouraged to make the most of singlehood, enjoy their independence, eat out, and socialize without having to worry about a spouse. These individuals soon became the envy of many wives and girlfriends at parties and other social events because they could dance with and talk to whomever they wished without the possibility of jealous men's repercussions. This was such an unimaginable, priceless freedom. One could not help feeling sorry for those women who were still suffering in unhappy relationships but were too afraid to leave. But despite the savagery and ugliness of the men's behavior, marriage remained popular.

Twenty-Six

Even though Lorna may have felt some embarrassment talking about her ordeal to a total stranger, she never showed it. Once she started opening up to Ionnia, she said that it felt therapeutic. As for Ionnia, she continued to think about how all these situations would influence her future—and the future of women who needed help. Lorna and Olive were no strangers to therapy. For a long time, they received weekly psychotherapy at Kotchette Cove from Dr. Mystie Brume. They benefitted tremendously from these sessions, Olive more so than Lorna. Lorna's sessions were reduced to once per year or as needed, but Olive was transferred to another psychologist for once per month sessions because she had begun to develop other psychological and psychiatric issues and needed additional medications. She also battled self-esteem and a weight problem; at one time children started calling her a rotten berry, and that was when she became suicidal. She was hospitalized for a while and then transferred to another school, and she was able to continue her education, although she had to repeat grades. Brenda reunited with her daughter, and after a while, Olive's condition significantly improved. Kethune "Kettie" Brumely was involved in her life as a life coach and mentor.

One of Lorna's biggest concerns was growing up and not getting a husband. In those regions, marriage was the cultural norm. "I'm damaged goods, Ionnia. He will find out that I'm not a virgin, and then what will he do? He may turn on me and start abusing me. I could not endure conditions to which my mother and my aunt were subjected."

Ionnia pleaded with her. "Lorna, stop. Please don't think about that now. No one knows what the future holds. There is plenty of time to think about this, and you may want to discuss that topic a little more with your therapist." Ionnia encouraged Lorna. "There will come a time when abuse against women will be a thing of the past. Furthermore, there should not be a need in any woman's life for a husband."

The two discussed their situations so maturely that if one had heard them and not seen them in person, they would assume these were adults talking. "You are very optimistic," Lorna remarked. "So, how about you? How are you going to cope with your situation?"

"The best way I can. Think positively and focus on the future. Have a goal in mind and reach for the stars. I will be starting high school in a few weeks. As a matter of fact, I am on my way to Krepston. I will be attending Mount Mathevuh High."

Ionnia was thrilled to have met Lorna, and she promised to maintain a long-term relationship. She felt a sisterly connection for which she had always longed. When the girls rejoined Gert and Iris, the women were discussing the many charm schools that Iris had established all over Puca Luca and the surrounding islands. At these schools, young girls were taught etiquette, poise, and more. The schools also catered to young women and girls whose ambition it was to enter beauty contests. Iris also focused on refining and enhancing the skills of those who wanted to be successful businesswomen. Much of her time was taken up with some of the 4-H groups from many of the government schools in Whickam County. Iris was very involved in assisting and organizing shows and other competitive events in home economics, speech, drama, modeling, and beauty pageants. She had a very capable group of people who worked for her, some of whom were past students, and she knew she could depend on them to promote the business and to provide quality service. That gave Iris time to spend with her two granddaughters, whose futures were now the top priority in her life. Iris mentioned the names of several successful models and prominent businesswomen with whom she had the pleasure of working, and one of them was Vivette Reglon.

Gert remembered the name. "Whatever happened to her?" she asked Iris.

"She is married to Dr. Hal Beuhling, one of the best plastic surgeons in the country."

"Any word about Nereen DesLandis?" Gert asked. "She was such a natural beauty."

"Nereen was one of the top runway models for Zeme's at one time," Iris said with pride, knowing that she was in some way responsible for her success. "The fashion industry could not exist without me, if you know what I mean."

"Oh, yes, I think I remember seeing her on the cover of magazines. The last time I heard anything about her, she had her own modeling agency and was in charge of the annual Miss Puca Luca teen beauty pageant."

As Ionnia listened to the conversation between Gert and Iris, she visualized herself attending a few of these classes after her ordinary school day was over. She needed some of those qualities that Iris Depping had utilized in the past to shape the lives of many women. She knew she could cope. She was an A student with a high IQ. She could also attend on weekends or whenever possible. This was a chance to get together with Lorna, who was now her new best friend. Ionnia put in her first request to her new aunt, and Gert had no objections.

"I'm glad you are interested. As soon as you settle down, I'll talk about this to your new parents."

The pair stayed at the convention for quite some time before starting on their way back to the hotel. "Let's get out of the way before the convention comes to an end, and we won't be able to get away from this crowd for at least another three hours. Moreover, we won't be missing much."

They bade goodbye to Iris and her granddaughter, who would be staying the night at a friend's place by the beach. As they squeezed their way through the crowd, someone tapped Ionnia in the shoulder. When she looked around, she recognized a familiar figure. There was Samanthley Whitelace dressed in her flowing white robes and cheap jewelry. Ionnia was overcome with the overpowering scents of musk and incense, and she began to cough.

"Hello, Miss Whitelace," Ionnia said politely, never once forgetting that this woman had led a team that had saved her life.

Samanthley smiled and slipped a small amulet in Ionnia's hand. "That's for good luck," she whispered. "Keep it with you at all times."

Ionnia quickly slipped the object in her pocket before Aunt Gert had the chance to notice, because she knew Gert wouldn't approve of her taking this item from Samanthley. Her thoughts went to one of the Ten Commandments, which made reference to idol worship, and she reminded herself of the passage from Deuteronomy 31:6, which said, "Be strong and of a good courage, fear not, nor be afraid; for the Lord thy God will go with you. He will not leave you nor forsake you."

Psalm 23 also came to her, and she wondered whether taking the amulet from Samanthley meant choosing between God and the devil.

"Who is this, dear?" Aunt Gert inquired of Ionnia. Judging by the frown lines on her forehead, there was a sign of disapproval.

"Someone who was there when I needed help," Ionnia said politely.

Ionnia introduced the two women and then gave Aunt Gert a brief summary of the cave incident, stating that Samanthley was the one who had rescued her. As she said that, she smiled at Samanthley as if still thanking her. Then the tears welled up in her eyes.

Gert listened intently and then shrugged and said, "Bless her heart." She turned to Samanthley and said, "Thank you. You will always be in our prayers."

Samanthley studied Gert's facial expression and tone of voice, and as if to taunt her, she asked, "Would you like me to give you a reading and tell you what your future holds?"

Now Gert was impatient, and she looked at Samanthley despicably and said, "In the name of the living God, I rebuke you."

Samanthley backed away, and while doing so, she shouted at Gert with both arms raised, "Okay, okay, but keep this child away from your brother."

Ionnia pretended not to hear, but she was always mindful of her surroundings whenever any males were present. She had begun to fear them and was building a wall brick by brick, the dimensions of which she was not sure about at this time. Despite the fact that she had built a fence around her, she had plans to soar to higher heights so that she wouldn't continue to see it but was always conscious of its existence. She needed a protective armor that would keep her from hurt but wouldn't stop her from growing.

Gert and Ionnia were back at the hotel in the two-bedroom suite. The bedroom that they were allowed to occupy was furnished with a king-size bed and a pullout sofa that could be used as a queen bed. Ionnia hesitated as if waiting on her aunt to make a decision about who would sleep where. "Take the bed, dear. I will use the sofa." This was the first time that Ionnia had a bed this size all by herself. Before they fell asleep, Aunt Gert further discussed the idea of Ionnia attending charm school, reiterating that she would use her influence on her brother and his wife to allow her to go on weekends. Gert knew of the benefits and had seen the results.

Gert used the phone to call the Rytes and let them know not to expect her and their adopted daughter till the following day. She assured them that everything was all right; it was just a case of bad weather. They breathed a sigh of relief and engaged Gert in conversation for a little while.

Ionnia struggled to fall asleep as several things went through her head, including Samanthley's last words. She was looking forward to having a father figure in her life for the first time—someone she could look up to. She was not prepared to suffer anymore at the hands of any man. Not even a man of God.

The more she thought about Samanthley's words, the more frightened she became. Was it too late to change her mind? Ionnia glanced at the sleeping, snoring, Gert and wondered, *If I should run away, will she find out before tomorrow?* But where would she run to? Ionnia was not familiar with the area, and she knew no one. She thought of an escape route but decided against it. It was too risky a move, so she drew the covers over her head, curled up in the fetal position, and tried to sleep.

Twenty-Seven

Early Saturday morning, just as the sunshine was beginning to filter through the trees and slowly burn off the mist visible in the cool morning air, Gert and Ionnia prepared for the final leg of the journey to Krepston. They traveled through several small towns and a few large cities, and very often Gert reduced her speed or stopped so Ionnia could get some local history and geography lessons. She pointed out some historical landmarks, including the sugar factories and the old rum distilleries. Gert had stories to tell about some of the old sots who used to be employed at this and other distilleries in Puca Luca. At some point, the wharves from where sugar and rum were exported were visible from a vantage point.

"If it is not too much to ask, could we stop at the Burning Wheels Mall? Ionnia asked. "I've heard so much about it."

"Sure. That will give us a chance to have breakfast and take a peek in an art gallery owned by a past student of mine. I'm sure you will like what you see there."

Ionnia was fascinated with the various displays of fine clothes, furniture, and jewelry in the mall. She had only read about these products and merchandise in various magazines; she had never seen them up close except for the short time when she worked at the Ernakki residence. She had dreams of becoming a designer one day. The pair never bought anything. Ionnia held on to whatever little money she had with her. She was very thrifty, and moreover, she did not want to depend too much on her new family for pocket money. They had a hearty breakfast of fish fritters, cornbread, and hot peppermint tea at the ancient, rustic restaurant where an old sugar mill once stood. The manager gave them a complimentary bottle of sugar cane juice and a jar of molasses. He offered Gert a twenty-year-old bottle of rum, but she politely refused.

The gallery's sign, "Varthea's," was visible from a distance. No one could miss it. It was named after the owner, Varthea Bellaqua. The place was filled to capacity with high-priced displays by famous artists and sculptors from all around the world, and which attracted customers from a diverse culture. Today was no different. The gallery was astir with affluence and the chattering of the richly dressed crowd of socialites and wannabes.

Gert was familiar with artwork and the artists, whose names were visibly placed on their pieces. She and Ionnia browsed the displays and walked around the gallery with an air of sophistication reserved for the rich and famous, even though they weren't wearing the expensive clothes like most of the patrons. But as the saying went, "Clothes never make a man," although this was a highly controversial and disputed topic.

Gert and Ionnia could feel the stares coming from the snobs as they gave them the "What are you doing here?" look.

"Like that one?" a voice said to Gert as she admired a painting by Varthea's husband, Barrique Bellaqua, who was Barry by his wife, relatives, and close friends.

Gert recognized the voice and spun around. "Look at you. You have not changed a bit," she said to Varthea.

"Though I walk through the valley and the shadow of cash, I'm still me," Varthea said with a laugh, and she looked at Ionnia when Gert introduced her as her niece.

Both women were delighted to see each other, and Varthea offered Gert the painting she was admiring.

Gert spun the price tag round and round, looked into her past student's eyes, and said, "I couldn't accept this, Varthea."

"What are you talking about? You were my favorite teacher and the predominant motivating force behind my success. Please don't deny me the opportunity to show my gratitude. I remember back in the day when all was lost, and I thought that I couldn't succeed. Everyone had told me that I was not good enough and wouldn't amount to anything. You used the baseball analogy on me. You sat me down, looked me straight in the eye, and asked me if I was prepared for my home run. Then you told me to keep swinging my bat and do it with all my effort, because someone may one day pitch my way."

"And I can see you have hit that home run."

"Yes, finally. I had swung and hit once before with Fitzgerald Larnes, but I only got to first base."

"You mean the Fitzie Larnes who was the director of the Puca Luca Bureau of Standards?" Gert asked. "What happened?"

"He cheated on me."

"And you found out how?"

"He frequented an establishment owned and operated by his cousin Arlette."

"That doesn't amount to cheating."

Varthea placed her finger over her mouth and whispered in Gert's ears, "This was an escort service. Arlette was a madam. And he owned up to it that he used the services of nearly a dozen of the girls. He said that those girls gave him all that he wanted, that I was too sophisticated to try new things in the bedroom, and that I was always too tired when he came home."

"So you were working outside of the home?"

"Yes. I was a loan officer and counselor at the Farmers' Loan Bank. Going through those loan applications was no easy feat, and believe me, I was exhausted when I got home."

"Good for you to know when to break off a relationship."

Varthea beckoned to one of the attendants. "Please package this piece for my favorite teacher." She turned to Gert and said assuringly "You won't see this anywhere else. This is a one-of-a-kind piece."

"I don't know how to thank you."

"Yes, you can. I will be staging the next exhibition of amateur artists the first week in October, and I would like you both to attend."

"How can I say no? This is a small price to pay for this invaluable gift."

Ionnia was fascinated with some of those pieces in the section reserved for amateur artists, in particular those by the person who signed his name as Simm Yun. She said, "Maybe I could get to meet him one day."

"He is a very nice young man, and he is destined to go places."

As Gert and Ionnia walked out with the piece of artwork given to them by Varthea, the same set of people who'd snubbed their noses at them earlier began engaging them in conversation. Gert smiled broadly and said politely, "Have a nice day."

"Never judge a book by its cover," one woman uttered under her breath, but it was loud enough for Gert to hear.

The next stop for the two was at a service station to fill up and wash off the hundreds of small bugs that had splattered on the car. While the car wash attendant took care of the vehicle, Gert and Ionnia walked across the street to a souvenir and curio shop. There was Samanthley Whitelace at the checkout counter, this time wearing a less flamboyant outfit and getting ready to pay for her purchases. She looked so different, almost distinguished, and could possibly pass as one of Puca Luca socialites except for her candles, incense and other items that would be regarded as bizarre by most folks who called themselves normal.

Standing next in line and towering over Samanthley's tiny five foot frame was this well-dressed, family-type hunk showing off his well-fed appearance. As Samanthley started to walk away, her gaze met his, and he said to her, "I've been admiring you from the moment you walked in the store. Can I ask you to have dinner with me sometimes?"

Samanthley stared at him and blurted out for everyone to hear, "And then you would kill me like you did your first wife?"

Without thinking, the stranger exchanged his smooth lyrics for a more defensive tone. "That was an accident. The brakes on the car gave way, and it rolled down the embankment." He paused for a moment in wonderment. Had he given too much information to a stranger?

Before he could say anything else, Samanthley said to him, "Don't continue. This was big-time news, but did the media get it right? Remember now, you have the right to remain silent. Look around at all the people who would bear witness to your confession, which could be used against you in a new trial. Don't incriminate yourself."

Suddenly the sweat started pouring from his face like a waterfall, and the lines that had formed on his forehead looked like a train line. "Who are you? Are you a cop?" he asked.

"What does it matter at his time? You are so busted. Confess, turn yourself in, and get a damn good lawyer. It's not too late. This will be adequate closure for your wife's family and to all the other battered women who happen to have a disgusting specimen of a human being like you for a husband."

The man looked at the shock and surprise on all the customers' faces and blurted out, "What are you looking at? I'm the Elliston Cliphorn from Orange Blossom who was accused of pushing my wife's car down a precipice at Brackette Hill, but I swear as the sun shines today that it was an accident. I was never charged, and if another trial was to happen, no jury would convict me." Cliphorn was fully convinced that most everyone believed in his innocence and no one was going to stop him from enjoying all of life's pleasures.

Gert and Ionnia exchanged glances with raised eyebrows, and then Gert looked at the man and said, "I remember that incident. Sadie was a teacher, a great one, and I'm sorry for your loss.

"Yes, but she just wouldn't stop taking advice from those so-called friends of hers who were probably jealous of our relationship."

"A relationship? Imagine. Other people would describe what existed between you and your wife as death in slow motion," Samanthley added before making a hasty exit.

There was laughter throughout the establishment. Ionnia had believed in Samanthley before, and this time was no different.

Elliston Cliphorn's wife, Sadie, met her untimely death allegedly by his hands one Ash Wednesday, but it was finally ruled accidental. They and their six year-old twin boys, Derrick and Merrick, went to visit Sadie's parents. Joe Medley was a prominent banker, and his wife, Margaret, was a teacher. They lived in a mountainous area of Puca Luca called Brackette Hill. No one believed his version of the way his wife died, but there was not enough evidence to even indict him on charges of murder, manslaughter, or reckless endangerment. Did the police in Brackette Hill not do their job properly, was Elliston Cliphorn one of the untouchables, or was he in fact really innocent? The only person who could answer those questions was Sadie, and she couldn't do so unless she spoke through a medium, such as Samanthley. Was this what was happening?

Elliston was a self-employed truck driver who loaded up in Trevine with various items from construction material one week, foodstuff another week, and furniture the next. He would then make deliveries to different areas of Puca Luca, and he was quite familiar with the terrain of the island.

Sadie was a high school teacher just like her mother, but unlike her parents, she and her husband fought constantly, both physically and verbally. If anyone should question why she put up with the abuse, she would tell them, "I'm not ready yet. I believe in staying married, especially for the sake of our twin boys, even if it kills me." And it really did.

Twenty-Eight

While Sadie was at Brackette Hill that fateful Ash Wednesday, she reunited with three of her high school friends: Merlene Bishop, a flight attendant; Doris Keenley, who owned a travel agency; and Jannis Crustanzie, a former nurse. There was a lot to talk about as they reminisced on the past, drank red wine, and played Scrabble, dominoes, cards, and Monopoly.

When Sadie finished telling them about her miserable life, which she chose to tolerate, she waited for the girls to give her the juicy details of what was going on in their lives. Jannis choked up with emotion and told the group of the time she'd been arrested for allegedly stealing a baby from the hospital where she worked as a senior delivery nurse and midwife. She was childless, couldn't have children, and wanted to please her husband, who always wanted children. "I always obsessed with the idea of being a mother, and when I looked at young mothers with their children, I felt like an empty, useless person—or as some people would put it, a mule."

Sadie and the others remembered the incident as the media reported it, and this was the first time they had heard all the details from Jannis—those details to which no one else was privy. At one time, Jannis faked a pregnancy; as a matter of fact, she'd imagined it, and for nine months, she'd felt all the symptoms.

"They have a medical term for this false pregnancy condition, but I can't remember it just now," Doris said.

"This condition is known as pseudocyesis," Jannis said.

Sadie then reached for one of her mother's encyclopedias and summarized the definition of the condition. "Pseodocyesis can cause many of the symptoms of pregnancy, and it mimics the condition in every way except one: there is no baby. In some instances, some women report the sensation of fetal movements. Abdominal distension is the most common symptom of pseudocyesis, and one noticeable physical sign is menstrual irregularity. The woman also experiences morning sickness, tender breasts, and weight gain."

The girls were curious to know what happened next, so Jannis went on to tell them that in the ninth month of her phantom pregnancy, a fourteen-year-old pregnant young lady, Dorcie Hollis, was admitted to the hospital with labor pains. This was Jannis's opportunity. She reassigned the other nurses to other wards, saying, "I think I can manage alone." They were very much aware of her competence, so they departed. Jannis heavily sedated the young mother, delivered a perfectly healthy baby boy, and secretly had her accomplice, Jean Beacon, take it away to an undisclosed location. When Dorcie awoke, Jannis gave her a sad story that her baby was stillborn. Jannis went on vacation, and her symptoms went away. Her body went back to normal, and she claimed Dorcie's baby boy as her own.

"But how did your husband not know that you weren't really pregnant?" Sadie queried.

"Did he not want sex when he came home?" Doris asked.

"I found excuses. I simply told him that I had a difficult pregnancy and it was too risky to have sex. I also said that it was against my religion to have sex while I was pregnant. He didn't object. He was very supportive and too excited that he was going to have a son to carry on the Crustanzie name, and he didn't want anything to happen where he'd miss out on the opportunity to make that a reality."

Doris kept piling on the questions. "Didn't you worry that he may be getting satisfied elsewhere?"

"I didn't have time to worry about that. I was too busy putting a plan together."

"So what happened to the baby?"

"I had to give him back to his biological mother. This was the hardest part, because I had already bonded with the little boy, whom I named Ronny."

"Why? What happened?"

The questions came in quick succession, and Jannis never had the chance to answer them all.

"Did you ever find out the reason why you can't have children?' asked Merlene.

Jannis put her head in her cupped hands and let out a heavy sigh.

"You don't have to talk about it if you don't want to," Sadie and Doris assured Jannis as they wrapped their arms around her.

"Promise me you won't judge me. I know I am a horrible person, but I already asked God to forgive me. I've been to my Gethsemane and back."

The girls looked at each other, not knowing how to interpret that statement. Jannis never bothered to explain or elaborate. But they knew of Jesus's story: just before He was crucified, He went to the garden of Gethsemene and prayed all day in the sun till He had a nosebleed.

Jannis told her friends how she'd gotten pregnant at age fifteen, and when she broke the news to her then nineteen-year-old boyfriend, Elton Sagoo, he never wanted to have anything to do with her. "He said that he was not ready to be a father because he wanted to focus on his career as a medical doctor. I had ambitions and goals too: I wanted to go to college and become a registered nurse. I knew of his ambitions, and we would talk about him setting up his own medical practice, and I would be his nurse. This plan was never going to materialize. But if he had decided to take responsibility, I would have been content to be a mother and raise the child on my own." Jannis agonized over the responsibility of raising a child alone without fulfilling her dreams while Elton pursued his career. "It just isn't fair for us women to put our lives on hold while the men continue with theirs."

"So what did you do?"

"Jean Beacon, the same one who'd kept the baby for me, took me to someone who specialized in herbs and other alternative methods of administering health care. The doctor performed an abortion in the most horrific and unconventional manner."

"Did you parents know about the procedure?"

"No, and at that time, I became so badly scarred that I am not able to carry a child to full term. All subsequent pregnancies have ended in miscarriages."

"Have you regretted this?"

"Oh, yes. I wish I had kept my baby."

"How did Elton react when he realized that there was no baby?"

"He accused me of lying about the pregnancy, and I left it at that."

The group was awestruck. They empathized with Jannis and promised to support her in whatever way they could. Doris began singing "Lean on Me," and they all joined in.

"Have you ever thought of adopting?" Merlene inquired.

"No, because every time I look at a child, I am reminded of the other two."

"So what eventually happened to the baby-stealing case?"

"At the trial, my husband, Martin, an army lieutenant, begged the court for leniency. The judge was an old schoolmate of his, and he pleaded with him not to impose the maximum sentence on me because, according to him, I was a very sick person. Dorcie's grandfather, who also had some influence, interceded on my behalf. I was given two years' probation and was ordered to receive psychological treatment until I got better. My husband divorced me shortly after the trial and married Dorcie's aunt, who has since borne him three children. He also bonded with Dorcie's baby boy, Ronnie, which was the name I gave him."

"How does that make you feel?"

"This made me depressed most of the time, but I am determined at this time to move on with my life. I continue psychotherapy with Dr. Bruce Thelweld. Martin pays for it as part of the divorce settlement. I also have a job now. I own a clinic that specializes in counseling and therapy for infertile women."

The four women brainstormed in between the games and red wine, and they came up with other alternatives. One thing Jannis was sure of was that she wanted to get married again. She never gave up hope of finding someone, and she craved for that day. She told her friends how lonely she felt being single.

"Do you know that loneliness is a choice?" Merlene asked. "Don't be too anxious to get hooked."

Jannis investigated the possibility of signing up with several matchmaking agencies, one of which was called Lunch Meet and was operated by Allison Boswick of Port Downs. This agency had a 90 percent success rate and was structured around working-class professionals who were able to visit only during their lunch hour. The services did not come cheaply, and after checking this out, Jannis decided that she could not accommodate this expense at this time.

"Perhaps you need to start looking in other directions," Sadie suggested.

"Explain," Jannis pleaded.

"There are a few good men working in the factories and in the agricultural sector," Merlene suggested. "You don't have to marry a professional person."

Merlene tilted her wine glass, drained it, and examined the empty bottle on the well-polished coffee table. She asked Sadie, "Any more wine?"

Sadie realized that Merlene had consumed most of the wine, so

Sadie did not think it was a wise idea to open another bottle. "No more. That was the last bottle. Have some water this time."

As Merlene twisted the glass of water nervously in her hand, she remarked, "Where is Jesus when you need him?"

Twenty-Nine

Elliston Cliphorn, who was a very bossy, manipulating, and controlling individual, was resentful of Sadie's friends and made no effort to conceal his feelings. His tone sometimes suggested that she got what she deserved. Elliston complained that Sadie had been neglecting him and spending too much time with her friends, especially one of her coworkers and best friends, Georgette Melvys. Sadie's husband accused her friends of filling her head with falsehoods and innuendoes, so on this particular afternoon when Doris, Merlene, and Jannis left, all hell broke loose.

Elliston Cliphorn made such a fuss with his wife that his father-in-law intervened and gave a few words of advice. "Take a ride, you two, and get some time to cool off. The mountain air will do you good. Leave the children with us. Their grandma will put them to bed."

Elliston and Sadie welcomed the suggestion and acted accordingly. On this night, the moon peered intermittently through the cloudy sky that at other times was overcrowded with stars but now was barely visible. Everyone was concerned about the condition of the roads in case it started to rain. Elliston was the one doing most of the talking, and it made him very angry when Sadie didn't respond. He stopped the car at a section that most people would compare to Croakers Mountain, and here was where she met her fate.

Around ten o'clock, after the boys had gone to bed, Elliston returned to the house on foot, slightly bruised and out of breath. He pounded on the door so hard that his in-laws were afraid the boys were going to wake up. Joe Medley looked through the window and saw that Elliston was alone—no car, no wife. He rushed to the door and opened it, and before he could ask what had happened, Elliston began to ramble.

"Slow down, for God's sake," Joe Medley said to his son-in-law. "I cannot understand you." Joe sat down in a chair on the porch and beckoned his son-in-law to sit opposite him. Looking at him like a pit bull, he shouted, "Where is my daughter?"

Forcing a tear, Elliston said, "The brakes on the car gave way, got out of control, and rolled down the steepest precipice around a mile from here. Then the car burst into flames. Sadie was driving, and she went down with the car. My door flew open, and I rolled out." He stretched out his hands and said, "See? Look at my wounds."

At that moment, Margaret Medley emerged from the house, still buttoning her silk robe. Joe hugged his wife, who was shaking uncontrollably.

"I am sorry I didn't do enough to save Sadie," the allegedly grieving husband said.

"Tell us again what happened. Do you think she could have fallen out the same way you did? Did you call the police, or did you tell any of the neighbors?"

Joe gently led his wife back inside, placed her on the sofa, gave her a glass of water, and said, "Stay here. I am going down to the police station. I am willing to put up the funds for additional manpower, and I will pay for any overtime the additional cops are be asked to do. Sadie is my only child, and we will do anything to find her." When he returned to the porch where Elliston was sitting nervously and constantly looking at his watch, Joe said sternly, "You are coming with me, and your statement had better be accurate."

Joe could see that Margaret was not prepared for this, and he realized that she should not be alone at this time, so he assured her,

"I will stop by Jannis's house and ask her to come over and be with you right away."

Elliston got in the car with Joe, and they didn't exchange a single word till they arrived at Jannis's house. When Joe told her what had happened, she almost fell to the ground in shock. Elliston looked at her as if to say, "You are responsible for this." The men did not tarry but hurried to the police station. Meanwhile, Janis contacted the other girlfriends who had been with Sadie earlier that evening, as well as some other friends and coworkers. When they arrived at the Medleys' home, Margaret had just finished preparing a pot of coffee, and they sat around the oval mahogany table in the dining room and drank coffee from Margaret's fine china. No one said anything till they had finished the coffee, and it was no surprise that not one of them believed Elliston Cliphorn's version of his wife's accident. Jannis contacted her ex-husband to ask his commanding officer to provide a helicopter to assist in the search for Sadie. Martin obliged without hesitation. Sadie's badly burned body was found the following day, a few yards from the charred remains of the car.

An extensive investigation was carried out into the death of Sadie Cliphorn, and although there were many inconsistencies in the husband's statements, there was no conclusive evidence to prove that he was responsible for his wife's death. When it was eventually ruled an accident, the case was closed. However, the husband was judged as a murderer in the court of public opinion. He was suspected all along for having pushed the car down the precipice with Sadie inside, and people believed that the bruises he'd sustained were self-inflicted.

Sadie's death was a devastating blow to the entire family. Margaret Medley could not be convinced that her daughter was not murdered, but she had to restrain herself from showing any signs of her suspicion in the presence of the children. She objected to her son-in-law raising her grandchildren, and she petitioned the court for custody, but the final ruling was made in the father's favor. Nevertheless, the judge granted the grandparents unrestricted visitation rights. Among the many tributes paid to Sadie Cliphorn was one from the Orange Blossom PTA, which erected a bronze statue at the school in her memory. Another was a scholarship in her name, established by the Puca Luca Bankers' Association, of which Joe Medley was a board member; his colleagues were more than happy to do this.

Back in Orange Blossom, Elliston Cliphorn tried to raise his twin boys by himself, but he soon found out that this was not an easy task due to his work schedule. When Sadie was alive, she had made these responsibilities look effortless as all women do. The boys took their mother's death very hard, and for thirty-one days, both refused to speak to anyone except each other and their mother's friend and coworker Georgette Melvys.

Elliston's friendship with Miss Melvys was now closer than ever, and she had no problem assuming the extra responsibilities of taking the children home in the evenings and acting as a surrogate mother for them. She missed Sadie and wanted to do everything possible to help the family deal with their loss, so three months after Sadie's death, she moved in at the Cliphorn residence and took over from where Sadie had left off, both with her children and with her husband. It was unimaginable to most people who knew Miss Melvys that she and Elliston could be romantically involved because everyone knew the polarity of their personalities, but this only went to prove that opposites attract. The two denied the relationship at first and insisted that they were merely acting in the best interest of the children. Elliston Cliphorn collected two hundred thousand dollars from an insurance policy he had taken out on Sadie's life. His father-in-law made sure that he was not going to benefit from his daughter's death, so he demanded that he put away the bulk of the money in a trust fund for the twin boys' education. Elliston also had his car replaced by another insurance company. This he gave to Georgette, but he kept the registration and title in his name. She somehow managed to obtain change-of-owner forms, and without Elliston's knowledge, she had everything changed over in her name.

Elliston never gave up his job in the trucking business, and as always he was away most of the time. Georgette appeared to be comfortable with this arrangement, and she never questioned his whereabouts because she knew beforehand what she was getting into. She looked forward to the day when she would be Mrs. Georgette Cliphorn, and she would always take comfort in the hope that she was special and that whatever he was doing meant nothing as long as she didn't see it. But would her dreams be realized? Could she handle this abusive individual, or would he be a changed person?

While Elliston was away on his trips, he would phone home every evening, and at one time Georgette had to tell him, "Do not spend all your money in telephone calls. We are okay with you calling every other day."

"This isn't costing me much. My cousin Courtney Shackleworth works at the telephone exchange, and most of the calls are for free."

Georgette assumed that Courtney was a guy because she knew several male students with that name, but she was soon to find out otherwise. Not only was Courtney a girl, but this was one of the many female lovers that Elliston Cliphorn kept while on his trucking route, and it seemed that she held a special place in his heart. She obviously knew of his wife's death, and she knew that he had not remarried. Georgette found a photograph and love letters in a secret compartment in Elliston's truck, and their relationship deteriorated from there. As soon as Derrick and Merrick were away in boarding school, Elliston's true colors reemerged.

Things came to an end one Thursday afternoon when Georgette returned from a workshop in Vannadoo County. She was not supposed to come back until the following day, but neither was Elliston supposed to be home, so she was surprised to see his truck outside. Georgette opened the front door and was about to call out to Elliston, but she decided against it. "I'm sure he is tired and is taking a well-deserved rest. I will put my luggage in the boys' room." As she walked toward the boys' bedroom, she heard sounds coming from

Elliston's room: moans, groans, and other lovemaking sounds. Her knees buckled, and she fell to the floor in a convulsive state that lasted a minute or two. When the dizzy spell that had engulfed her receded, she garnered her strength, tiptoed to the bedroom door, and opened it with her key. Elliston and Courtney were too busy getting it on, so they did not see or hear Georgette enter. Their eyes were closed.

She sighed deeply and made an unexpected gasping sound before saying, "Good job."

The sex act ended abruptly, and the two lovers grabbed the lavender satin sheet that Georgette had left on the bed, covering their sweaty bodies with it.

"Don't stop because of me."

"Who is she?" Courtney asked Elliston.

"She is my tenant."

As Georgette walked aimlessly toward the closet and grabbed whatever clothes she had there, she stopped briefly and asked Courtney, "And what would his tenant's clothes be doing in his closet?"

Elliston raised his voice. "Those are my dead wife's clothes."

She held up a pair of her size sixteen jeans and asked, "Such as this one? Sadie was a size eight."

"Don't try my patience, or else ..."

"Or else I'll meet the same fate as Sadie? I'm not afraid of you." Georgette reached for the shotgun that Elliston had in the closet, pointed it at him, and said, "I have a mind to shove this up your ass, pull the trigger, and blow out your guts."

Courtney couldn't listen to the exchange any longer, so she ran to the bathroom and locked herself in.

"I can't believe that someone who had once proclaimed his love for me could treat me the way you treat me," Georgette said. She was disappointed and ashamed. But she reminded herself of an African proverb: "When one goes in search of honey, one must expect to be stung by bees." She left the house and immediately went to Orange Blossom Elementary School to hand in her resignation, which the principal reluctantly accepted.

A few days after this encounter, Elliston made an attempt to take back the car he'd given to Georgette. "I only allowed you to drive it because you had to take the boys back and forth from school and athletic and soccer practices."

She showed him a copy of the registration and title and said mockingly, "This is for services rendered, you sadistic pig." Georgette relocated to Bunkers Ridge and accepted a position in a high school as an English teacher. Elliston lost both Sadie and Georgette. Now he was back on the market, hoping that another fool would fall for him.

Thirty

Saturday, shortly after midday, Gert and her new niece arrived at the rectory, where a select group of fifteen people were waiting to welcome Ionnia into the Ryte family and into the broader Mount Mathuveh community. The setting was informal, and people were dressed in everyday clothes. As the two female made their entrance into the hall, the laughing, babbling, and chattering abruptly ceased, replaced with loud clapping and cheering. This was like a surprise birthday party, which Ionnia had only read about.

The men, women, and children turned curiously to look at the young lady whom they had all been longing to meet ever since Bishop Ryte had announced to the congregation that there was going to be an addition to his family. Ionnia's new parents greeted and embraced her and then made the introductions.

Louise Klute, the church organist, turned to Deacon Eustace Ryte and whispered, "She is so thin. Looks like she could use a lot of nourishment."

The bishop must have heard Louise's comments and gave her a disapproving look that could scare a maggot off a meat wagon. He withheld his rebuke and instead put her on the spot by making the following request. "Sister Louise, will you please offer a prayer thanking God for the safe arrival of my sister and my daughter?"

Louise, who was wearing a striped sleeveless dress, came to the front of the room. She raised her arms overhead and asked everyone to close their eyes and bow their heads. Everyone's eyes were supposed to be closed, but Ionnia, just like any other mischievous preteen, used this opportunity to sneak a look at the gathering. Just before Louise lowered her arms, Ionnia could see that the woman had enough hair under the armpits that could easily be tied in a ponytail. In those days, some women from certain areas of Puca Luca did not believe in shaving their armpits because they held the belief that by doing so, they would be deprived of certain wisdom and strength. It was obvious that Louise was one of those who believed in the story of Samson and Delilah in the Bible, where Samson lost his strength when Delilah shaved his head.

Louise prayed for around three minutes, which seemed like an eternity, and she specifically asked God to keep the child safe.

Ionnia remembered Samanthley's words, and as soon as everyone's eyes were opened, she looked at them questioningly but did not detect any unexplainable expression on anyone's face. While she remained unemotional, she hurt inside, not knowing what to expect. *I hope that there will be an explanation or revelation soon. In the meantime, I must keep reminding myself to be extra cautious while being around any males,* she said to herself. There were four people in her life with whom she felt like sharing what Samanthley had warned: her mom, her grandmother, her aunt Twyleith, and her former teacher Lillian Finlaw. This weighed heavily on her. However, she decided to wait a while before sharing this warning with anyone. She would observe and analyze. The welcome ceremony was very overwhelming for Ionnia. She felt as if she was wide awake in a dream.

A buffet style meal was served. There was an abundance of different foods, including spaghetti and meatballs, chicken, rack of lamb, vegetables, and various types of seafood. Refreshments were in abundance: fruit punch, grape juice, and lemonade, to name a few. Ionnia ate very little. She was not used to seeing so much food in any one place at any one time, much less eating a lot of it.

"Eat up, dear. Don't be shy," Mary Blades said to her.

It was strange that Mary should encourage someone to eat because she looked like she could use a good meal herself. But looking at the pile of food on her plate, one could not determine whether this was the issue. Mary was very thin with bulging eyes and sunken jaws, and she appeared to weigh no more than 105 pounds. Maybe she had some intestinal bacteria that prevented the manifestation of good nutritional habits. The hair on her head, which was fixed in a bun, resembled a bird's nest just like Miss Areneldie's. The only difference was that there were no birds to perch in it. There was a look of woe about Mary that seemed to indicate the magnitude of a less than healthy and productive life.

Mary was currently married to Abraham Blades, the bell ringer at the church. Her first marriage to Bertel Yutz, a dipsomaniac, was a total disaster when he was alive, and no matter how hard she'd tried, she couldn't get him to go to church with her. She was the butt of jokes among the community as her drunken husband got wasted and stripped naked in saloons. Sometimes the other patrons hid his clothes and then called Mary to bring some over. She got so tired of this behavior that after a while, she stopped responding to the calls. One particularly cold night, it was suspected that someone had put cornmeal in Bertel's drink, which made him disoriented and sick. He was disrobed by the patrons and pushed out of the bar at closing time. He attempted to walk home but fell among the tall grass and shrubs a short distance from the establishment, and he was not found till two days afterward. He died of pneumonia within a week.

What a way to start a new life, Ionnia said to herself as she socialized the best way she knew how. She definitely had charm school on her mind. She didn't speak much but rather observed every little detail of the new environment of which she would be a part for a very long time if nothing happened to short-circuit her. Ionnia did not want to appear as a shy country bumpkin, which she was not, so she respectfully smiled at each person as the introductions were made.

She avoided eye contact as much as possible because she wasn't sure whether doing so was a polite thing to do in this part of the country. The group applauded her, especially when they heard of her academic and athletic achievements, as well as the many awards she'd received for these and other activities, including spelling bees, her school's debating club, and her singing and athletic abilities.

The bishop's granddaughter, Nickie Gress, who was about a year older than Ionnia, took an immediate liking to her. "So you are my new aunt? I wish I could be like you. I wish I had all these achievements."

"Are you saying that something or someone prevented you?"

Ionnia learned that Nickie's mother, Bernadene, was married to an attorney, Charlie Gress. She loved to entertain, so when Charlie brought home a young lady and introduced her as his cousin, she believed him and had her stay over for the weekend to assist her with one of Nickie's pageants. The so-called cousin, Natalie Spout, did not attend the pageant, and it was a shock to Bernadene when she returned home and caught Charlie kissing her. Charlie confessed that he and Natalie had a long-term relationship, but he asked that his wife not embarrass anyone in front of her guests, who were there to celebrate one of Nickie's performances. Without hesitation, Charlie left with Natalie and quickly returned. He had taken her to a nearby hotel and probably made arrangements to hook up with her later.

There were significant differences in the way each parent chose to raise his or her daughter. Charley was a strict authoritative parent, whereas Bernadene was the soft-hearted one who would always give Nickie whatever she asked for. For these actions, Charley would always refer to Bernadene as spineless.

There was a contrast in appearance between Ionnia and Nickie. The latter was plump and precocious, and Ionnia was thin and naïve. Nickie was a spoilt little girl, whereas Ionnia was already molded into an independent human being. At three years old, Nickie had possessed almost an entire room full of toys. Ionnia had owned only toys that she and her mother could make from scraps of cloth leftover in Loretty's sewing area. At six years of age, Nickie was dressing like a princess, participating in beauty pageants, and placing less emphasis on school, and her mother did not tell her that an education was equally important. The opposite could be said about Ionnia. When Charlie objected and demanded that his daughter focus on academics in order for her to go to college, her mother said that Nickie was too pretty to go to college.

Nickie was always a runner-up in the various beauty pageants, and as time went by, she and her parents were faced with the reality that unless she had an education, beauty alone would not be the determining factor in winning these contests. She would always be an also-ran because she was unable to answer questions relating to academics or anything that required her to think.

Nickie developed an eating disorder that went from one extreme to the other, from anorexia to bulimia to obesity. Her parents spent enormous sums of money in treatment programs for her, and by the time the parents were divorced, Bernadene realized that it was time for her to dedicate more time to her daughter's education. She hired private tutors for her, and before long, Nickie showed signs of academic improvement. She also had to participate in eating disorder programs and have a good nutritionist to get her weight under control.

"Get acquainted with your aunt," Berdene said to Nickie. "Show her to her room and give her a brief tour of the rectory." Each girl grabbed a suitcase and left the adults to converse with each other and consume the rest of the food. Nickie headed toward the elevator, and this time Ionnia got to push the buttons. Nickie was impressed. Little did she know that this was Ionnia's second time using an elevator.

Ionnia was in awe at the opulence of Bishop Ryte's dwelling, although the building and most of the contents were the property of the church. The upper floor of the three-story mansion was reserved for visiting church dignitaries and was out of reach to the regular members.

Ionnia was shown to her room on the second floor. She had her own bathroom and a huge walk-in closet. Her bedroom was between the Rytes' bedroom and the library, where Bishop Ryte spent a lot of time reading the Bible and preparing his sermons. This arrangement made it hard to escape in case she ever thought of it. Suddenly, she remembered what Samanthley had said, and she shuddered.

"Are you all right?" Nickie asked.

"I'm just tired."

Nickie appeared skeptical when she saw the expression on Ionnia's face. "Is this room too small for you?"

Ionnia did not reply. She glanced over at the bed on which her small suitcases were placed, and as she mentally counted the pieces of clothing inside, she wondered where she would get clothes to fill all that closet space.

"Excuse me, please," she said politely to Nickie, "I need to use the bathroom." She was overcome with emotions. She broke down and shed a few tears as she thought of ways to fit into this new environment. Ionnia also thought of her mother and brothers, but she quickly regained her composure, washed her face, and rejoined Nickie. She knew she would gave a few more of these episodes until she settled in. She thought of how this would have been compared to boarding school environment at Knoxford High. Material things were important, but the emotional love of a family should take precedence. She remembered the days when there was nothing to eat, but the love was present, and that had made the situation easy to cope with. She had no doubt about the Rytes' love for her. She was sure that she would not be the victim of any indoctrination regarding female submission to the male. If they tried, she would resist, and maybe they would not want to keep her any longer.

The walls of the library were covered with paintings and photographs of distinguished bishops and other church dignitaries from near and far, dead and alive. But the one that stood out most admirably was that of the late Bishop Josiah Mathuveh, who was responsible for the establishment of the church and the high school that started as a small preschool for orphaned children. Amid the photographs and portraits was a humongous painting of the Last Supper signed by Simm Yun, a name that Ionnia remembered from Varthea's Gallery.

An old eighteenth-century grandfather clock stood in one corner of the library and signaled the top of the hour with sounds equivalent to what suspicious people in some areas of Puca Luca called the Rolling Calf.

"This is going to take some time for me to get used to."

The entire south wall of the library was transformed into a massive bookshelf that contained encyclopedias and other books depicting all world religions, from Christianity and its various denominations to Buddhism. There were also history books, medical and psychological self-help books, and a large scrapbook containing all sorts of events dating back to 1835. In one corner of the library was a purple hammock in which the bishop spent most of his leisure time. This was given to him by a bishop from an East African country who promised that a few minutes of relaxation per day in this hammock would produce unbelievable cognitive transformations. Anyone who tried it believed it.

Very interesting place, she thought to herself. This was the largest and most well-equipped library to which she had been exposed.

The ceiling, which was illuminated by the stained-glass windows and crystal chandeliers, was painted sky blue and adorned with angels and stars of different sizes. It was certainly an outstanding depiction of the heavens, and if this were on the top floor when the sunlight streaked through, it would truly be a sight to behold.

Ionnia and Nickie talked about family and future goals. It was evident that Ionnia was the one who had clearly defined goals; Nickie was undecided as to what path to take. "Perhaps you can give me some guidance in that direction," Nickie said to Ionnia.

"That will be no problem," Ionnia responded.

When the girls rejoined the group, Ionnia was bombarded with questions about her biological family. She plainly refused to answer some questions. Her new parents made sure that each person did not overstep his or her bounds when questioning Ionnia. They were such an inquisitive group of people.

"I'm sure she is tired and would like to lie down," Berdene Ryte hinted.

The group got the message and stopped questioning Ionnia. One by one, they bade goodbye, leaving Berdene, Gert, and the bishop with Ionnia. Berdene spent time with her new daughter till close to nine o'clock, not under the pale light of a kerosene lamp but this time with bright electric lights. She familiarized Ionnia with their Sunday routine and promised her that later that week, Berdene would let Ionnia know what her duties and chores would be.

It must have been hours before Ionnia fell asleep, and she got just around three hours sleep. This new experience was a bittersweet one. She woke up very early and drew the curtains from the French windows to let in the sunlight which was just coming over the horizon. She pushed open the window a little bit and drew a deep breath as she smelled the sweet smell of jasmine, roses, and orchids coming from the garden. She admired the dandelions, the sunflower, and the gladiolas by the fountain. Farther afield was a vast layout of agricultural crops.

Ionnia watched the scarecrows swaying in the breeze, and that reminded her of her early years in Dartsdam, when these had to be placed in gardens to scare away predial larcenists and small rodents.

As she stood by the window and listened to the sounds of church bells ringing, she was reminded that it was Sunday morning. "I need to select an outfit for church. But what shall I wear?" She sat on the bed lost in concentration, and she did not hear the first knock on her door. The second, louder knock caused her to jump up, and she made a few long, athletic strides toward the door. It was her new mother, Berdene, who had come to find out about her first night.

"Good morning, dear. Did you have a good night?"

"It got better toward the latter part of the night, ma'am," Ionnia told her.

Berdene handed Ionnia a garment bag, kissed her, and said, "See you at breakfast, and later in church."

"Thank you, ma'am. I'll be there."

Berdene smiled, hugged her, and said lovingly, "Try getting used to calling me Mother, but I will understand if that makes you a little uncomfortable at this time. It may take a while."

When Ionnia unzipped the garment bag, she could hardly believe her eyes. Inside was one of the most beautiful dresses she has ever set her eyes on: light pink with white polka dots. She stood with her mouth agape for three minutes. She hurried to the bathroom, showered, and then tried on the dress. It fitted perfectly. She looked in the mirror and spun around so many times that she almost became dizzy. She later found out that her mother had made it and secretly given it to Gert. Ionnia took the dress off, hung it in her closet, made her bed, and got ready for breakfast. "Mom was right: it will take a long time getting used to this type of treatment. This is the opposite to which I'm accustomed, and it is truly overwhelming."

When breakfast was almost over, Ionnia made an attempt to remove the dishes from the table.

"Remember, now, you don't have to do that, dear," her father said to her. "Your primary responsibility here is to your books. I'm sure that everyone who cares for you wants you to succeed. Just in case you are thinking of how these household chores are going to get done, don't worry. We have a housekeeper and cook, Clementine St. Hugh. We call her Clemmie. She has been with us for a very long time. She hails from the seaside Village of Sandy River and specializes in the preparation of the most sumptuous seafood anyone has ever tasted."

"Now I know who was behind the elaborate buffet served yesterday."

"And when you look at the beautiful garden, Clemmie's husband,

Marty, and the Lord are responsible for that. He supervises a group of farmers who work very hard to grow most of the food and vegetables that are consumed at the church and the school."

"I'd like to help somehow. I like tending to flowers, and I like to sew and decorate. Please let me help whenever possible."

"If you really want to help, we won't object," Berdene said. "I'm sure you can, and you will learn a lot from Clemmie. She is an artist in her own way, and it runs in the family."

When Ionnia returned to her room later that day, there was another surprise. Her mother had filled her closet with new clothes, and shoes, and in her bureau drawers were underwear and nightgowns in her favorite colors: lavender, baby blue, yellow, and white. It was no surprise that there weren't additional school uniforms. That was because the Rytes knew how much effort Loretty and Ionnia had put in by making whatever she came with. Berdene planned to send the material to Loretty whenever new uniforms were needed.

Thirty-One

We want you to be familiar with the Mount Mathuveh property as much as possible, so Nickie and I will take you on a tour tomorrow," Berdene told her daughter after an exhausting day. She packed a picnic basket laden with various goodies: sandwiches, bread pudding, cookies, and drinks, all prepared by Clemmie. As the sun came over the mountaintops and the dew on the grass began to disappear, the trio started out on the journey in the refreshing morning air. They secured the picnic basket onto a folding cart with wheels, which they took turns pulling and pushing. They chose a path lined in some areas by oleander bush, royal poinciana trees in other sections, and pine trees in another. Ionnia was used to walking far distances, but it was obvious that Nickie and her grandmother were not used to doing this activity on a regular basis and therefore found it a little strenuous. After walking for about an hour, they spotted a location suitable for rest under one of the huge lignum vitae trees that was strategically planted on the compound. They sat down in close proximity to a small stream where several ducks were swimming. Ionnia spotted a white duck, which reminded her of Queenie, and suddenly her countenance changed. Lucky for her, no one noticed, and if they did, they did not comment.

Berdene pointed to an area with four huge buildings. "Those are our halls of residence. They are named after certain flowering plants or shrubs found on the grounds or in the gardens of Mount Mathuveh: Dandelion and Sage for the males, and over there are Sunflower and Gladiola Halls for the females. If you would prefer to be among the other girls, you can speak up before you get too comfortable. We wouldn't have a problem. You are still our daughter no matter where you put your head at nights."

"Sounds challenging," Ionnia said.

"We've gotten enough rest. Let's move on," Nickie said. She seemed jealous that Ionnia was getting all the attention.

After resuming the walk for five minutes, they were joined by Myrna Myerston, who was out on one of her regular morning jogs. Myrna was the house manager and nutritionist for Sunflower Hall, one of the largest on the property. She was a freckled-face woman in her late forties who was a very strict disciplinarian, and she upheld the moral values of Mount Mathuveh. She had survived years of abuse by her ex-boyfriend and would sometimes say that she'd lived in hell and managed to escape the heat. Although she socialized with people of the opposite sex, she trusted none of them with her love and emotions, and after a while, she vowed to be single for the rest of her life, saying, "If you are not satisfied loving yourself, then don't expect someone to do it for you." She would always remind people who would question her singlehood that this was a gift. In addition, she would also quote an old German proverb: "He who has once burned his mouth always blows his soup."

Myrna could give women and young girls quite a few lessons about the dos and don'ts of relationships. Her strong opinion was that if the teenage girls were exposed to the realization that most males entered a relationship simply to be adventurous and show their friends how many girls they could have sex with, then society would not have to deal with the massive number of physically and emotionally abused women.

"Hi, Sister Berdene," Myrna said as she slowed down and wiped the perspiration that drenched her face. "It's so good to see you."

The two women hugged each other so tightly that when they released themselves from the embrace, they were almost breathless. They had known each other since elementary school, gone their separate ways, and ended up in different areas and with different situations until Myrna reappeared five years ago and was appointed house manager for Sunflower Hall.

Ionnia was introduced to Myrna, who expressed disappointment at not having her in her hall of residence. But then she added, "I'm delighted that you are living at the rectory with Sister Berdene and the bishop." Myrna assumed that Ionnia was a boarder at the Rytes, and Berdene did not make her any wiser.

Before she had a chance to ask any questions, Berdene said, "Myrna, we never really got a chance to catch up about our past."

"Do you want to go first?" Myrna asked.

"No, you go."

Myrna told Berdene that when she was nineteen years old, she left her parents' home and cohabited with Noel Darrighan, an older man who worked as a biochemist at a fertilizer plant in Dillisberg. He never married her, and each time they discussed marriage, Noel made promises which he never kept. Only once did he appear to be serious about getting married. He asked Myrna one day to meet him at a jewelry store so that they could select the rings, and after the overjoyed Myrna made her selection, she waited for hours for Noel to come and pay for the rings, but he never showed up. She took pictures of the rings and kept these throughout the relationship.

"What do you think happened?"

"I justified his actions by saying that he must have had urgent business to do for his company and therefore could not get away." Myrna didn't see Noel for a week after that, and on his subsequent visit, he started with his sorry excuses. She bought his story hook, line, and sinker and became known as Sister Faithful.

She was one of those submissive women whom many described back then as a spineless person who never stood up for her rights and who was always being pushed around. Her submission bordered on insanity. One of her aunts who saw how submissive she was had this to say about her: "If you spit in her mouth, she will swallow it."

With four children at the age of twenty-five, Myrna had little hope of being successful in life like her other sisters, and she was constantly told that she would not amount to anything. After much encouragement, support, and challenges from the progressive members of the family, she took the children to her uncle's house, left them there, and then disappeared. Noel looked everywhere for her, and when he got frustrated, he said, "I will surely clean the bottom of my shoes on her face if I find her."

But he was no match for her uncle Gabriel Myerston, who never traveled without some of his many shotguns and revolvers. Gabriel caught a glimpse of Noel hiding in a bamboo clump near his house one afternoon, and he scared him into oblivion as he emptied every round of a shotgun in that direction. Mr. Myerston raised his grandnieces and grandnephews, sent them to good schools, and was able to boast of their achievements before he died.

How different everything looked now that Myrna's eyes were opened. She was now a member of several women's groups, among them RAW and BONDAGE, and she began advocating for the safety of abused women. She went back to school, got an education, and received a degree in hospitality management.

When Myrna had finished talking to Berdene, she had a few words of advice for Ionnia and Nickie. "Girls, focus on getting an education before you think about dating."

Nickie gave a little snicker on hearing this. The women pretended not to notice, but Ionnia stepped slightly on Nickie's toes, and she immediately wiped the smile from her face. She was a good actress and was accustomed to smiling or not smiling on cue.

"You are not too young to know that if and when you decide to date, you should thoroughly investigate the individual before making a commitment," Myrna added. After looking at her watch, she realized that time had slipped by very fast. "We will play catch-up another time," she told Berdene, who was glad that the conversation had come to an end because she didn't want Myrna to know how submissive she was to her husband.

If only I was old enough to join some of the organizations that help these women, Ionnia said to herself, and she shivered at the thought of how abuse had become an acceptable form of social behavior. She was very mature for her age and was able to comprehend, process, reason, and analyze situations better than most adults. She mentally meandered into the future, and what she saw was an image that could one day become a reality. Just as in the recurring dream, she saw a place linked by a bridge where women would be safe from the emotional and physical wrath of their male companions, and where young women would learn the art of letting go and finding themselves. The word of her favorite song, "Across the Bridge," came to mind. "I'm on my way," she whispered, and the others looked at her.

"Whom were you talking to?" Nickie asked.

Ionnia caught herself and said, "Myself."

"Do you always do that?" Nickie asked.

Ionnia did not elaborate. By now she had slipped out of her daydreaming trance. Myrna continued her morning jog, and Ionnia, Nickie, and Berdene walked for another half mile along the edge of the creek that ran through the property. Then they decided once again to sit down, this time to munch on some of the goodies in the picnic basket. When they had had enough and were about to close the basket, they spotted a woman with a little boy who looked like they could use the rest of what was inside. With curious fascination, Ionnia watched the woman and her son as they approached them. The woman was slightly overweight and walked in a henlike manner, again reminding her of Queenie. The lady had long black hair that was marinated in what smelled like the castor oil Ionnia's grandmother used to make. Ionnia noticed an expression of kindness in her eyes as she slowly removed the sunglasses she wore. She also noticed that at times there was a strange grimace on the woman's face that made it appear as though she wanted to sneeze or was in pain, but Ionnia detected an air of sophistication in her voice. The little boy wore a broad-brimmed hat that almost concealed a strange, frightened look about him—a look that could be mistaken for some beings that belonged to another world.

"Hi," Ionnia greeted the pair, and she started a conversation about the weather. The woman, whose name was Erma Leven, was careful at first not to say too much. She introduced her ten-year-old son as Ezra, and as she talked, it became obvious that she was an intelligent woman. But why was life so unkind to them? Ionnia was not one to judge books by their covers. "Today's ugly caterpillar is tomorrow's beautiful butterfly," she concluded.

Erma had been a very successful sales representative for one of the most reputable insurance companies in Puca Luca, but her life took a downward turn some eight years ago when her husband, Bradley, conned her out of her home and property, which had been an inheritance from her late father. She had a mental breakdown and had to send her son, who was two at the time, to live with her great-aunt, Dulcie. When Ezra was six years old, he witnessed the death of Dulcie's husband, and that traumatized him. Recovery for the both of them had been slow but steady. Every time Erma talked about her domestic incident to anyone, she would say, "I can't believe it happened to me. But I guess that's how love makes you blind. I'm optimistic that I can rewrite my life's script with a happy ending."

Berdene asked everyone to hold hands while she prayed for the lady and her son. When they finished praying, Berdene said, "Time is a great healer."

"If you don't mind, let me show you another side of Krepston," Erma told the trio.

They took the back road over a hilly, stony path lined by oleander shrubs, and then they came to a broken turnstile that led them on a narrow footbridge over a huge pond.

At first, Berdene and Nickie were scared. "Is there another way of getting there?" Nickie asked as she focused on the brackish water below. Ionnia wasn't scared, and she lit up like a candle when she saw the bridge.

"Yes, but I prefer not to take the easy way out. The harder the struggles, the sweeter the reward," Erma remarked. "Just hold your heads high, look straight ahead, and do not look down."

They held on to the handrails of the footbridge, which was made of ropes from the indigenous sisal hemp plant. Then they entered a small village with about a hundred homes and some huge willow trees. Some of the buildings were made of mud and grass with tin roofs, and some were sturdy concrete structures. It was a very unique place and reminded Ionnia of her birthplace of Dartsdam: one section for the haves, and another for the have-nots. The houses were numbered from one to one hundred in no special order.

"This development is called Chowden," Erma told them. "The property is owned by Roscoe Rackman and managed by Vercus Menningly, who makes sure all the tenants pay their rent on time."

"Sounds like he is related to the late Peter Rachman of Britain, that unscrupulous landlord who threatened, exploited, and intimidated his tenants, and from whom the term Rachmanism was coined," Berdene noted.

"No, Miss Berdene. Their names are spelled differently. The Brit spelled his name with the fourth letter as *k*, whereas our man spells his name with an *h*. But despite that, Roscoe exhibits similar traits. What's in a name?" As Erma reached her destination, number twenty-two, she said, "I think I will leave you with the story behind how we were assigned this particular dwelling."

They listened with rapt attention as Erma explained that on the rental agreement, when they put the initials, E. Leven and E. Leven, Vercus's response was, "Because two elevens make twenty-two, it would be most fitting for you to occupy number twenty-two."

Everyone had a hearty laugh except Ezra, who went inside to put away the contents of the basket.

"Thanks for everything, Erma," Berdene told the lady. "Please take Ezra to Sunday school sometimes."

"I am the one who must thank you, because this is the first intelligent conversation I've had in a long while with people who would listen. Everyone seems to be afraid of us, so we keep away from them."

"Once they get to know you, they will find out that you are two of the nicest people around." Berdene said to Erma. "And if you need to talk, please come over to the rectory and sit with me."

For the first time since they met on the compound, Erma forced a smile. Turning to Nickie, she said, "Now you can go the other way; it is less treacherous."

Berdene and the girls began their reentry into Krepston from a different direction. It was a breathtaking and picturesque view. This was the type of scene that appealed to artists. Nickie breathed a sigh of relief. Overall, the place looked more beautiful from this vantage point, and they recognized a mini trading post, a shoe-repair establishment, a small community center, a huge playground, and other amenities that made up a community. Ionnia was shown more of the Mount Mathuveh property. "Over that side is where we call the bread basket of the community," Berdene said as she pointed to many acres of a farm. "Not only is there a section for the rearing of livestock of all variety, but a vast expanse of the land is subdivided for the growth of various agricultural produce. Another section is earmarked for aquaculture from which we get our freshwater fish, lobsters, and shrimps. The entire place is overseen by Dr. Jacob Packston, a graduate of Brackette Hill Agricultural College, and his competent assistant, the aquaculturist Clarice Blevick. And don't forget Marty; his contribution to the farm is invaluable."

Thirty-Two

The environment at Mount Mathuveh Academy was very different from the one at Diamond Globe, but both institutions had one thing in common: very strict rules against any form of unsupervised interactions between the male and female populations outside of the classroom. The dorms at MMA were situated at opposite sides of the school, and students could socialize only in a specially reserved area close to each of the vice principal's residence. The house managers for the different dorms were very strict when it came to visitors from the opposite sex, and an adult would always be present at visiting time, which would be over by 8:00 p.m. sharp.

The first Monday in September marked the beginning of the new school year, and Ionnia was registered in school as Ionnia Dunn. She was placed in third form because she had completed first- and second-form curricula at Diamond Globe. Her first day at school started out very hectic but somewhat pleasant, and then something happened. A sixth-form student, Nancy Creshawn, was assigned to be her mentor, and it was Nancy's duty and obligation to properly orient Ionnia and make her familiar with the various classrooms, science labs, and other areas of the school. This student may not have been a physical bully, but she spoke to Ionnia in such a condescending manner that Ionnia had flashbacks as she recalled what a different

Nancy, Nancy Reglon, and her friends had done to her at Dartsdam Elementary. She held her head high and didn't appear to let it bother her. She had her goal, and no one was going to prevent her from achieving it.

Most of the students in Ionnia's form were much older than her. Some of them could barely maintain a C or D average. The teachers showed extraordinary interest in her when she successfully completed her work before many of the others, so she was asked to tutor other students in first form. After a while, she was tutoring nearly everyone from first to third form. It frustrated Ionnia when she observed the lack of interest that the students displayed in getting an education. She knew how important it was, and it had always been drilled in her by her family and other mentors. She was disappointed with these privileged people's behavior. They were raucous and rowdy when no one was monitoring them, they weren't focused, and they didn't have goals. Tuition wasn't cheap, but these students were from very affluent families and could afford every penny. When asked why they were there, some would say, "My parents forced me to come."

There were some students who resented the idea that Ionnia was assisting them with their lessons. They felt that they were being imposed on by this young girl. They snubbed her at first and called her Miss Know-It-All or a teacher's pet. At times they would ask, "Should we refer to her as Miss Dunn?" Then the reality hit them: if they wanted to pass their term exams and move on to a new form the next school year, they had no choice but to accept the extra help. They hated being kept back and made fun of by others. Before long, some students who were getting low grades and had repeated forms began to improve one or two grade levels in the subjects with which Ionnia assisted them, and they were finally able to advance.

"How did you do it?" some of the parents asked Ionnia. "In the history of the school, this has never happened. Normally, it would be senior students doing the tutoring." To show how much they appreciated Ionnia's help, they offered her money and other tangible gifts.

Ionnia could do well with the money and valuable gifts, but prior to accepting anything, she discussed these offers with her parents. At the end-of-year recognition function, Ionnia was highly recognized for her work with the students and the convalescent home.

Ionnia developed a friendship with Ordrette Booke, a good friend of Nickie Gress, both of whom were in the first form. Ordrette's mother, Dorothy, was head of the school's music department, and she taught students at her home who needed extra piano lessons. She promised to teach Ionnia for free as a token of her appreciation for helping Ordrette with some of the subjects in which she had not been doing well. Ionnia was elated, but again she had to discuss this offer with her new parents, who were hesitant to give their consent for her to be tutored at Dorothy's home.

"We have nothing against Dorothy, but we are concerned that you will have to take these lessons late in the evenings, and we fear for your safety. We will not always be there to walk you home."

Samanthley came to mind. Her parents did not elaborate, but Ionnia was soon to find out that Dorothy's seventeen-year-old son, Jeremy, an aspiring recording artist, was known to be a very wild young man. There was no telling what he would do, although up to this point, no one had lodged any formal complaints against him.

This youth reminds me of Cordell, Ionnia said to herself.

Although the Rytes seemed overprotective of Ionnia, they didn't want to appear judgmental of anyone, so Berdene Ryte suggested to Ionnia, "I am confident that you will learn enough in Dorothy's music class at the Academy, but I will also teach you to play the church organ so that your visits to Dorothy's home will be minimal."

"Will I be able to continue studying with Ordrette?"

"Yes. You can study here or at the library at school."

When Dorothy was told that she would not be giving piano lessons to Ionnia at her home, she felt hurt. "I think Berdene is jealous. However, we can work around that. I am sure we can find some extra time to do this at school during the days."

Ionnia was a quick learner, and in no time she was playing the piano and the organ perfectly. Apart from athletics, music was her life. Some Sundays when the full-time organist, Louise Klute, was not in church, Ionnia was asked to play, and she loved this. She outperformed Louise by playing extra notes to some of the songs to give them more rhythm.

"This young lady surely could be Louise's successor," Valriss Packman said. She thought she was whispering, but she spoke loudly enough for others to hear.

Ionnia and other students from Mount Mathuveh Academy participated in music and singing competitions and contests, both locally and nationally. It would be difficult for the coaches and teachers to supervise the students and concentrate on the competition, so the school provided a chaperone to accompany them to the different venues. This was a priority for the parents and teachers, so they decided on Thea Tweeler, the assistant librarian, to be the chaperone.

Thea was a successful, independent single woman in her mid-thirties, and she was well respected by everyone. She was the assistant choir director at the church and also found time to volunteer at the Krepston convalescent home. She was a role model to most of the school's female population.

Thea was a fierce defendant of women's rights. She encouraged them to protect themselves from anyone who chose to attack them. She maintained that no woman should be taken advantage of and that they should never believe when men blame them for doing things to provoke an attack. Her brother Barry, who was a personal trainer, body builder, and martial arts instructor, owned a gym in Krepston, and Thea was one of his more advanced students. When he was not there, she would teach the classes, and on several occasions she would be asked to assist the academy's gym teacher whenever he was not available.

Once, while carrying out her duties as a chaperone, Thea had to subdue a young man who made unwanted physical advances on one of the female students in her group. The young man, Herbert Rusk, was caught off guard, and his companions made fun of him for having been overpowered by a woman.

Ionnia was enthralled by Thea's ability in self-defense techniques, and at a later date Ionnia would use some of the money she saved to take some classes at Barry's Gym. She was determined that no man would treat her the way her father had treated her mother, let alone what she had witnessed and heard about with other women. But one thing she was sure of: help was on the way. It may take a long time, but as the older folks would say, "Slowly but surely."

Thirty-Three

Ionnia battled the homesick bug while trying her best to blend in with the new community. This new environment was inhabited by families from various cultures who continuously engaged in dialogue of their areas of origin, and sometimes she couldn't tell whether they were talking about her or not. At first Ionnia felt strange, and the memories of rejection came back to haunt her. Because of this, she quickly learned different languages and dialects and was able to communicate with everyone at different levels.

On occasions when Ionnia was not tutoring her friends and schoolmates, she sometimes went to the servants' quarters that Clemmie shared with her husband Marty. Clemmie, who reminded Ionnia a lot of her grandmother, was a much-needed source of comfort for Ionnia. Clemmie used her spare time well by immersing herself in her favorite pastimes, knitting, crocheting, and embroidery. Ionnia also had a passion for these types of needlecraft and felt that she could learn a lot more from Clemmie, and vice versa. Clemmie had an excellent memory, and Ionnia loved hearing stories from her about everything from the war to ghost stories and other folktales. Clemmie had no sad stories of her relationship to divulge, especially to a teenager. She and Marty were model citizens. Marty had been her first boyfriend, and they maintained a tremendous amount of respect for each other.

Clemmie and Marty kept souvenirs from the ocean, and on a three-shelf cabinet in the small living room were evidence of these. Among them were dozens of conch shells of various sizes, shapes, and colors.

As Ionnia looked on, Clemmie stepped closer to her and handed her one large conch shell. "Would you like to hear the sounds of the ocean?"

Ionnia held the conch shell close to her ears and was fascinated by the calming sounds of the ocean's waves. Clemmie watched the expression on the young girl's face as she enjoyed the new relaxing experience. "You can keep that shell, if you'd like. It will bring calmness and serenity after a hectic day at school. I can always get more." Clemmie talked about her grandchildren and the expression on their faces when they first held one of these conch shells to their ears.

"Where do your grandchildren live?"

"They are from Brackette Hill but go to college in Trevine.

"How old are they?"

"Simeon is nineteen years old, and Simone is seventeen," she said, as she reached for a shoebox underneath the coffee table in the living room that contained about two dozen black-and-white photographs of different members of her family. Pointing to Simone and Simeon, she said, "These two belong to my younger daughter, Nervalee. Here she is with her husband. This was on their wedding day."

"What a beautiful couple, as are their children."

She reached in a medium-sized envelope and produced a picture of a beautiful young lady. "Here is my older daughter, Raylene. She is married but has no children."

"Where is her husband?"

"You are looking at him."

Ionnia took the photograph and eyed it meticulously. "I think I have very good eyesight, but I don't see a male in this picture."

Before she could say anything else, Clemmie said, "She is married to herself, and I think she says there is a special name for that." She reached in the envelope and added, "I had her write it down for me." She handed Ionnia a piece of paper that had the word *sologamy* written on it.

They both laughed so hard, and Clemmie started to cough. Ionnia was scared, and her bout of hilarity came to an abrupt end. She became concerned about Clemmie and feared the worst. She had once read about a woman who was attending an opera performance in 1782. The woman had burst out laughing so loudly and uncontrollably that she had to be expelled from the theater. That woman had laughed continuously all night long and the day after, and she'd died early in the morning, the following day. There was another man, Pietro Aretino an Italian author, playwright, poet, and satirist, who in 1556 was said to have died of suffocation from laughing too much.

"Are you going to be okay, Miss Clemmie?"

"I'm fine, my dear." When Clemmie stopped laughing, she continued the conversation. "Raylene swears she does not want to be married to anyone. She dated someone in the past, but she said that her fiancé got married to another woman, and she didn't find out till six months afterward."

Clemmie flipped through the remaining pictures from the box, briefly mentioned names, and then closed the box and replaced it under the table and continued, "I come from a large family, twelve children in all. I am the oldest girl and dropped out of school in the second grade to assist our mother with the household chores. I was denied an education, and you cannot imagine the animosity I carry toward my parents and my siblings."

"Yes, ma'am, I think I understand how you feel. My mother also had to drop out of school to take care of her brothers and sisters. The only difference is that my mother dropped out at a later stage."

"I don't think she tried to kill her parents, like I did?" Then she made the sign of the cross. Ionnia was a good listener and decided not to ask Clemmie about the details of her attempt on her parent's lives. When she saw the inquisitive look in Ionnia's eyes, Clemmie continued. "That did not work out as planned, so I ran away with my first love, Marty. As part of our arrangement, I told him that I was determined to not have more than two children, and I warned him what I would do to him if I got pregnant a third time."

"Do you have any contact with your brothers and sisters?"

"My sisters Margaret and Veta are the only ones who showed some gratitude for what I did for them."

Ionnia was sure she had recognized Veta McDode in the pictures that Clemmie showed her, but she said nothing. It was obvious that Clemmie and Ionnia had taken a liking to each other. Ionnia always enjoyed the company of older people because she learned a lot from them. After several visits, Clemmie seemed to trust her new friend, and the feeling was mutual.

One day Clemmie said, "I have a favor to ask of you."

"I hope I can help you, Miss Clemmie. I know how to clean, cook, sew, and do a lot of other things."

"No, no. I am not asking you to help with chores." Clemmie beckoned Ionnia to sit down on the sofa, and as she sat beside her and held her hands in hers, she let out a little girl giggle and said, "Can you help me from time to time write letters to my two grandchildren?" Before Ionnia could answer, Miss Clemmie went on. "Sister Berdene always helped me in the past, but I don't want to impose too much. And moreover, you will know how to write so that young people understand.

"Yes, ma'am. I'd be happy to oblige. I could also teach you to read and write, and then you could take some evening classes at the academy if you are interested. Miss Margaret and Miss Veta will be prouder than ever." Ionnia felt that this would be her way of thanking Miss Veta for rescuing her.

Clemmie shrugged and softly asked, "Does that mean you are not going to help me with the letters?"

Ionnia detected the tone of disappointment in Miss Clemmie and replied, "I didn't mean it that way, ma'am. But you know the Chinese proverb about teaching a man to fish?"

"Oh, yes. It goes something like this: 'Give a man a fish, and he will eat for a day. Teach him how to fish, and he will eat for a lifetime.'"

"Miss Clemmie, it's never too late. I knew a lady who became a teacher at the age of fifty-five. She used to be a stay-at-home farmer's wife who became severely depressed due to her husband's treatment toward her. She escaped and went to live with one of her nieces who tutored her, and then she took two subjects at a time at the community college until she was accepted into the teacher education program."

"Sounds interesting. So when do we start? I won't promise you that I will be a teacher. I am sure my sister Margaret will be happy to know that I finally decided to do something to improve my life. She has been encouraging me for a long time and even offered to help, but I thought her generosity was out of guilt." Clemmie picked up another photograph. "This is my husband, Marty. He has a way with plants and animals, not to mention his fascination and amazing knowledge of the ocean. His friends used to wonder why the fishes gravitated toward him, and they would speculate about his special skills in catching so many. When other fishermen would go home with a meager catch, Marty had enough grouper, red snapper, mackerel, and king fish to sell to the entire village and have enough leftover for his family."

"So what was his secret?"

"Just hook on the second bite, whatever that means. And guess what? He taught others how to fish, and soon they were able make a living out of it." Laughter erupted again but subsided quickly, and Clemmie remarked, "I have not laughed so much since ..."

"Since what, Miss Clemmie? Or since when?" Ionnia asked inquisitively. But before the lady had time to relate a story and laugh herself to death, Ionnia said to her, "Please hold that for another time. We will certainly be able to engage in another laughing session. It is good for us; it is healthy. Would you like me to bring you some books with knitting and crochet patterns? In that way, you can expand your abilities to create new designs."

"Certainly. That would be awesome. I may not be able to read, but I am pretty good at looking at a pattern and figuring it out. If I miss out, you can read for me and have me do it the right way."

Thirty-Four

Mount Mathuveh Academy was known for many things, and one of them was a strict sex education program that espoused its values on abstinence. Regardless, some of the students' behaviors did not demonstrate this, and they would end up getting suspended or in some cases expelled. It was as though they were making a mockery of this reputable and renowned institution. Word got around the high school that Ionnia was still a virgin, and as a result she was constantly teased, mocked, and ridiculed by some who thought that it was a crime to be of a certain age and remain a virgin. But Ionnia thought differently, was proud of herself, and pledged that she would remain a virgin as long as possible.

This was put to the test one afternoon in the school's science lab, and she had to physically defend herself against three male students who had requested tutoring. The three boys, Wilfred "Willie" Brownshoe, Malcolm Banderson, and Derval Bruce, asked Ionnia to help them with a project, but when she arrived at the lab, she immediately sensed that they weren't there for tutoring. The boys were seated around a table with no books and no equipment, and when Ionnia looked around, there was no adult in the room. A red flag went up, and her suspicion heightened. "What are these boys up to? Are they there for some erotic aerobics?" If so, she was prepared to show them that that wasn't going to happen. She had the option of making up a story that she had forgotten a book and then leaving hurriedly, but she wanted to give them something to remember. As a student of Barry Tweeler's gym, Ionnia was confident that she could surprise them.

Malcolm Banderson was the first one who grabbed Ionnia and covered her mouth with a dirty handkerchief. Willie and Derval attempted to hoist her on top of one of the tables, and they looked at each other and laughed. In a split second, as Willie attempted to rip off her top, she was resolute in defending herself so as not to be dehymenized by these thugs. Her kicks and punches caught them by surprise. She poked one of the boys in the eye and then grabbed the nearest object available to her, a lab stool. She swung it wildly, and at least two of the boys got struck. They lay on the floor of the science lab trying to regain their composure and process what had just happened. They had underestimated her.

How ironic, Ionnia said to herself. *I always thought it unladylike to fight, but now I have to fight to continue being a lady.* Other women's situations flashed in front of her, and she decided that she wasn't going to be a statistic. She was familiar with the location of the on/off switch for the gas, so without hesitation, she went to that location and flipped it on. She summoned her athletic ability, buttoned her blouse, and dashed from the lab screaming while the boys lay on the floor inhaling the fumes.

Ionnia was furious. What unlucky star had she been born under? She had had her share of struggles and calamities affecting her life. "Enough is enough," she kept saying to herself. "Is it worth staying alive? Perhaps I should go back in and die with the bullies."

While making her escape, she ran into Dr. Egbert Digginboss, head of the chemistry department and one of the vice principals of Mount Mathuveh Academy. The name Digginboss was synonymous with frankness and discipline, and he had a voice that would rattle window panes. He had a strong personality and was a devout Christian. Digginboss was an impartial and conscientious individual who was sometimes described as brutally honest. He inherited many of these traits from one of his many foster parents, police inspector

Vinnie Digginboss. One could love him or hate him; it didn't matter to him. He wasn't one to beat around the bush.

Dr. Digginboss was not always a Christian. In the past, he hadn't cared much about religion or spirituality despite his early teachings from his adopted mother, Imogene Kopper. His conversion to Christianity came about when he reportedly had a close encounter with death following a boating accident. He loved the ocean, and he loved his whisky. His permanent job back then was a lifeguard.

Before his conversion to Christianity, Egbert was described as a fun drunk instead of a violent drunk. He was accustomed to using a lot of profanities, and he was never afraid to voice his opinion about any matter, even if he wasn't asked. Back in his worldly, carefree days, Egbert had many enemies, one of whom was Ezekiel Drysdale, who was suspected of tampering with his boat. Zeke, as he was known by most people, had a long-lasting beef with Egbert, which neither of them publicly discussed or disclosed. However, he never hid it from anyone that he wanted to get even with Egbert no matter how long it took. Once Zeke hardened his heart against someone, that individual had better exercise extreme caution or get out of his way.

One afternoon, Egbert decided to go fishing as usual in his thirty-two-foot boat, which he named *Lady Digsie*. His only companion was his bottle. Not far from shore, the boat began to sink, and in the blink of an eye, water was knee-deep in the vessel. Egbert had time to grab his life jacket and jump overboard, and he wasn't found until fourteen days later. Everyone thought he was dead, and as the community mourned his demise, some said, "Egbert, the expert diver who always saved people from drowning, couldn't save himself this time."

Arrangements were made for a memorial service before word got out that he was found alive. Ivan Montaggle, a fisherman, found him one Sunday morning. Egbert was disoriented, amnesic, dehydrated, and exhausted, and he was unable to provide Montaggle with his identity. Most everyone who heard the story said, "It was the mercy of God that kept him alive."

Ivan wrapped Egbert with whatever he could find on the boat and took him home, where his wife wrapped him in more blankets and gave him some hot tea. "It's best if we take him immediately to the hospital," she said.

Egbert remained in the hospital for several days, and as soon as he began to improve, he spent many hours in the hospital chapel thanking God for his survival, but all the while he wanted to get even with Zeke.

"Why not attend regular Sunday services at the Moravian church half a mile away?" the chaplain, Ephraim Morette, asked Egbert. Egbert accepted the invitation, got baptized, and turned his life over to the Lord.

With a lot of therapeutic interventions, Egbert got his memory back, returned to his home in Flaming Acres, and began to pursue his ambition to become a marine biologist. He acquired a second degree in chemistry. Dr. Digginboss also acted as an advisor to Dr. Clarice Blevick, the aquaculturist at the academy.

There was no corroborative evidence that Zeke was responsible for Egbert's close encounter with death, but if anyone messed with him, he would ask them, "Remember what happened to Egbert Digginboss?"

Egbert loved singing his favorite song, "Amazing Grace." He always gave testimony of the many times he had been lost and then found. "I am grateful that I was given another chance in life." He sold his home and moved to Krepston, where he got the position as a science professor and dean of the department, and he made it to vice principal status. He was very active in the church and would often comment, "I have seen the works of the Lord and His wonders in the deep."

The moment Ionnia saw Dr. Digginboss, she shouted, "Hurry! They tried to rape me, and one of them turned on the gas to kill me, but I knocked them out and escaped."

The vice principal hastened his steps as he listened to Ionnia's story. Then he donned his mask and hurried to where the boys lay unconscious. He stopped briefly to shut off the main source of the gas leading to the science lab and pull the fire alarm alerting the authorities of the imminent emergency. As soon as he opened the door, he was almost overcome by the smell of gas, which started to permeate the afternoon air.

"This is serious," he said.

Ionnia wanted so badly to be with her parents, but immediately the emergency siren sounded, and a voice was heard on the public address system. "This is a total lockdown. All students are asked to remain inside until the fire department gets here and has the situation under control." She found refuge in the arms of the music director, Dorothy Booke, and she felt safe.

The boys were transported to the hospital. All three suffered brain damage, underwent extensive rehabilitation, and were never the same. They were expelled from Mount Mathuveh Academy after internal investigations were completed. Charges for attempted rape were never filed because the authorities concluded that the perpetrators had suffered enough. Ionnia was satisfied with this decision, and she never disclosed to anyone that she was the one who had turned on the gas.

Since that incident, different arrangements were made with regard to tutoring. It was mandatory for an adult to be present at all times whenever students received tutoring from their peers. Even then, a number of students refused to engage in this activity. The academy sent letters to the parents of those students whose academic achievements were a little behind, and it gave them the following options: get tutoring outside of campus, or contribute toward the cost of hiring security guards to keep watch during tutoring sessions. The parents fought back, and their outrage was brutal. Despite the many accolades Ionnia received, some called her the evil one. Meanwhile, Mount Mathevuh struggled to regain its prestige and prominence among the country's top education institutions.

Thirty-Five

Ionnia's adoption was finalized six months after she arrived at the Rytes' home in Krepston. A party was organized at which she would be presented with her change-of-name certificate, which listed her last name as Dunn-Ryte. This celebration was her first semblance of a birthday party, and when it was first discussed with her, she told her parents that she would rather not have a party. She had lived without birthday parties this long and had not grown up to be dysfunctional, so she could continue without one. This time her parents insisted that she have on because it was a tradition in their family. Her close relatives from Dartsdam and surrounding areas were the top invites, along with her grandmother and Claudia Bundle from Redwood Vale. Her brothers couldn't attend, so they sent recorded messages and other gifts. She was also allowed to invite some of her new friends from Krepston, and she didn't forget Lorna Tottenbery, whom she had kept as a pen pal ever since the day she'd met her at the revival on her way to Krepston. Their relationship became closer, so much so that they began to refer to each other as sisters. Lorna came with her grandmother Iris, and they both stayed with Gertude Ott for a few weeks before returning to Castorvale. Nickie Gress and Ordrette Booke were also among the list of invitees. From then on, the four girls formed an unbreakable bond.

"I'm overwhelmed," Ionnia told her parents. "I am thankful that you agreed to share my life with my biological family. I am fully aware that in many adoption cases, one would have to sever all relationships with one's family, and I am overjoyed that this didn't happen in my case."

"We saw the love you have for your family, and vice versa, so we couldn't let anything come between you. We love you too much to deny you your family's love and affection."

Ionnia posed for pictures with her adopted and biological families as a group, and then with each family separately. She also took individual pictures. Everyone was happy for her. They soon realized how unnecessary were their apprehension about her being adopted versus being away at a boarding school. Upon her return to school, Ionnia was introduced to her class with her new name: Ionnia Dunn-Ryte. Everyone was curious to know why she'd been adopted. Many of them had assumed she had been boarding with the Rytes like many of the past students who'd attended Mount Mathuveh Academy and other schools in the area. Ever since all the new residential complexes of the academy were completed, the Rytes had discontinued the practice of accepting boarders. Some students found it difficult at this time to conceal their resentment toward Ionnia when they learned of her background. Some referred to her as the "slaughter's daughter." The male students kept away from her, assuming that if they got close to her, she would kill them too.

"It's in her blood. No wonder she tried to kill those boys in the science lab," someone pointed out. Others were more empathetic and supportive, especially Vanice Boot, who was adopted by her half sister's maternal aunt, Adelaide. Vanice's mother, Ivene, could no longer care for her due to physical abuse by her husband, Reuben Veller, so she was delighted when Adelaide intervened and decided to adopt Vanice.

Ionnia became withdrawn, and both Aunt Gert and Berdene couldn't help but notice the changes. They attributed this to the drastic changes in environment and socioeconomic status that had been suddenly thrust upon her. "But she should have gotten over this by now," Berdene said. "Anyhow, this too shall pass. I am aware that each individual handles situations differently."

But as time went by and Ionnia struggled with the different situations that faced her, she could no longer keep things bottled up inside her. She attended a few counseling sessions with the school psychologist, Dr. Childie Wee, after which there was significant improvements. She wrote to her mother and her brothers, who sent her all types of motivational books and magazines. She also reread some of the magazines given to her by Ms. Arineldie. Kyle sent his sister some poetry he had written, and her grandmother Agnes, accompanied by Claudia Bundle, came to see her every three months.

Ionnia continued to attend Iris Depping's charm school on weekends. Her friend Ordrette also attended, and Ordette's mother, Dorothy, was available to chaperone them. Ionnia continued to see Miss Clemmie and brought over the books she'd promised her. Clemmie was making progress with the three Rs, and both she and Ionnia were proud of the improvements. Clemmie was a quick learner. Ionnia had her read some of the instructions from the books and made sure Clemmie understood what she read.

"There is no turning back now. I really didn't know what I was missing. I can imagine how a blind or deaf person feels whenever it becomes possible that he or she is able to see or hear for the first time. Marty is very proud of me and asks every day what he can do to repay you."

"I'm sure he will have an opportunity to show his gratitude some time. Trust fate."

"My grandchildren are coming to visit for the Easter holidays, and I want you to meet them."

"Then you can show off your skills."

"Yes, like I have been doing all along." Clemmie beamed.

"You mean they don't know?"

"Not in the least, and it is going to remain that way."

"You have my word, ma'am."

Simeon was a multitalented individual. He was a very good artist, a creative barber, and a poet, but his ultimate goal was to be a geologist. He was the top student in biology, chemistry, and physics classes at his high school. He was very concerned at impressing his grandmother, and he showed off his artistic ability by sketching a portrait of Ionnia. He signed it using his pseudonym, Simm Yun. Ionnia was tongue-tied, and when she was able to get the words out, she said, "I have seen pieces of your work before, and I truly admire them. I never imagined that I would have the opportunity to meet the artist so soon. It is really a pleasure."

He was as cool as cucumber. "What would you like to do with it?" he asked Ionnia as he looked at the portrait and then back at her. Not waiting for an answer, he went on to say, "You have three options: give it to Grandma, keep it, or let me display it in a gallery."

Ionnia opted for the latter when she thought of all the exposure she would be getting. "Thank you," she said as she extended her hand to Simeon.

While they shook hands, Simone appeared from the kitchen, where she'd been helping her grandmother with refreshments. "Are you flirting with my brother?" she asked somewhat jokingly.

"Not all young girls are like you," Simeon said to her. "Instead of aiming to fulfill your aspirations, you'd rather put it on hold and obsess about marrying and starting a family with that evil Gladstone Bibb."

Ionnia was taken by surprise at the sound of that name, but she managed to keep her cool and asked, "Do your parents or grandparents know about her plans?"

"No. They think she has teaching on her mind, like Aunt Sadie. God help her that she doesn't meet the same fate as her."

All at once, sad movies started to play in Ionnia's head, and for a moment she looked away and said nothing. "Is this the same Gladstone Bibb from Redwood Vale?"

"Do you know him?" Simone asked with a big grin on her face.

"I knew him when I attended Redwood Vale Elementary School."

"Then you know that he is not an evil person," Simone said.

"Then why would your brother say so?"

"What Simeon is referring to is one isolated incident that occurred a few years ago, when Gladstone was in the company of two of his friends, and a girl was attacked with stinging nettle and hit on the arm with a baseball bat. They said that it was to prevent her from participating in the school's essay competition. Aunt Veta told me that it was miraculous how the young girl survived, and everyone hoped that she was not left permanently disfigured. Gladdie swore to me that he didn't hurt the girl."

"If he wasn't the one who hit the girl, he was an accessory. He was there," Simeon said. "I hope you meet that person one day so that she can tell you the whole story. And if I were you, I would still be afraid of him. This time he may break every bone in your body."

Ionnia showed no emotions, although it was hard not to cry as she relived that fateful moment. She was not ready to give them any clue that she was the victim of that vicious attack. The only thing she said to Simone was, "I'm sure you believed him and will continue to do so."

"Of course. He would never lie to me."

"Have faith in the one you love," her brother chimed in mockingly.

"Well, did anyone think of reporting the boys to the police?" Ionnia asked her.

"Do you know what their parents would do to anyone who turned their sons in? They are powerful people."

The silence that followed showed how much Ionnia pondered whether she should say anything about which only the victim or perpetrator would know. That would be a dead giveaway. If she didn't restrain herself, she feared Simone would piece together the puzzle, and she was not ready to give her a shock seeing how much she believed in Gladstone. She bade goodbye. Simeon walked her to the back gate and then sauntered off in the direction, where his grandfather was tending to some vegetables. As soon as Ionnia got back to her room, she reached for her journal and documented what had just transpired. She wished she had it on tape so that later on, when she was ready to confront Gladstone Bibb, he would not be able to dispute it. She actually felt sorry for Simone.

Thirty-Six

A few weeks following Loretty's return to Dartsdam, she became severely depressed and had to be hospitalized. The anxiety of the impending trial and the absence of her children had taken an emotional toll on her. Because of her fragile mental situation, her attorney submitted a motion to the court rendering her incompetent to stand trial for the assault that had led to her husband's death. Loretty was also diagnosed with PTSD and admitted to Blovingworth Mental Hospital, twenty-seven miles from Dartsdam. Once again she left Dee Dee at her home. She worried about her children and expressed to her doctor and family members that she sometimes felt guilty for having contributed to their father's death. Her children had never really told her how they felt or what they thought about it, and she never asked them. Maybe she was afraid of the answers she would get.

Loretty had never been in a hospital for any length of time before, and she was scared. "I hope my diagnosis does not escalate into any serious condition, like many of the inmates in Ward R. I also don't want to get hooked on medications." She had many visitors, one of whom was Nurse Veetley, who proved to be an invaluable source of moral support; she was also a member of the hospital board.

Ward R, labeled the Rejected Ward, had been built more than

two centuries ago and stood on the site of the first sugar factory and rum distillery in Puca Luca. It was ironic that some of the people who worked at the distillery ended up with problems that landed them in the same spot where they'd worked. Ward R was one of the most rejected and neglected buildings on the hospital grounds, both inside and outside, and patients with the most severe mental illnesses were housed there. Those patients were the ones whose families and friends had given up hope. Advocates for people with mental illnesses continued to make representations to the Health Ministry to demolish the building and do something about the occupants and the conditions there, but all they got were promises. The patients received minimal treatment, and reports were that once a week, the patients were herded to an empty warehouse nearby, where they would receive electroconvulsive therapy. Some Ward R patients showed signs of progress, but others chose to curl up in a corner, mutter incoherently for hours, and toss feces and other body fluids on the walls. As time went by, some patients whose conditions were assessed were determined to be ready for transition to the regular population. One such patient was Fitzroy O'Rigby, who was nicknamed Barley and Brains; her earned the latter nickname because of the birthmark on his right shoulder in the shape of a brain. Gradually, two more were integrated and would receive the much-needed care that they'd been denied over the years, including enrollment in an experimental drug treatment program. Unfortunately, a lot of the occupants of Ward R died before they were ready to be moved. Finally, the media disgraced Blovingworth Mental Hospital and the Health Ministry for the existence of Ward R. Immediately the ministry allocated funds for additional staff and for the demolishment of the building. The old warehouse was remodeled and refurbished, and the remaining patients were transferred over there. A modern, three-story structure was erected on the site where Ward R once stood. The second and third floors served as living quarters for members of staff, and on the first floor was a convention center where various organizations chose to hold their annual meetings. The very first organization that held its meeting at that location was the Puca Luca Association of Research Scientists (PLARS), whose members were employees of schools and colleges, the police department, the medical examiner's department, and pharmacies, as well as private individuals.

As soon as Loretty showed significant signs of improvement, she was assigned various tasks at the hospital. Her first assignment was in the laundry room, and she would do all the mending and repairs that needed to be done. When the director, Steven Sagoo, discovered that she was good at dressmaking, he met with the members of the hospital board, and they came up with a plan to capitalize more on these skills. Loretty was transferred to a separate wing of the hospital, given some equipment, and put in charge of making the hospital gowns for the patients and the medical staff. She was paid handsomely for her work. The hospital saved thousands of dollars that it would normally have had to continue paying the company contracted to make the gowns. Three evenings per week, Loretty taught dressmaking to other patients, and two days she taught nonpatients who came from nearby communities.

Loretty and a select group of patients were chosen to attend classes at Blovingworth Adult Technical School (BATS) to advance their education and enhance their potentials. This was the opportunity Loretty had been waiting for, and she obtained a diploma in higher education six months after she enrolled. This was one level higher than high school and one level below college. She was encouraged to go to college, but instead she concentrated on her dressmaking and designing skills. She spent additional time at BATS learning how to use the modern, industrial-type sewing machines and other equipment. Some patients began to resent Loretty because they thought that she was getting preferential treatment from the director. She would address the criticism by saying, "Whatever you are assigned to do, do it well. Stand out, and you will be recognized."

The hospital was awarded a contract from a renowned and lucrative garment company in Trevine, (MUJALI Group of Companies, owned by Muggerdon, Javeng, and Lifurdy. This company exported finished garments to different countries and also had a contract to make uniforms for the prisons in the area. Thousands of cut pieces of garments were received at the hospital each month. The ladies would put these together, and the finished products were collected the last Friday of each month. Loretty and her crew worked tirelessly to complete the assignments on time, and the company was featured in MUJALI's monthly magazine. Soon thereafter, MUJALI was contracted to make uniforms for a number of schools, hotels, and airlines.

Kingsley Muggerdon, who was one of the board members of MUJALI, visited the institution so he could have firsthand knowledge of the operation and be more familiar with the dedicated group of people who made them wealthy. Loretty had not the slightest idea that this was the same Muggerdon whom she'd had a teenage crush. Kingsley Muggerdon's surprise visit caught Loretty off guard, and they stared at each other for a while. This was the first time she had seen him since his father had sent him away many years ago.

"I am pleased that you are a part of this successful venture," he said politely.

She was unsure how to express her feelings without making a fool of herself, but the politeness was reciprocated. Kingsley knew much more about Loretty that he wanted to reveal.

They talked for almost about an hour about business and personal issues. He talked about his marriage, and said that for the first few years, whenever he held his wife, it felt like he should have been holding Loretty instead. He added, "Look what our fathers took away from us. Look what Lensley Quane took away from me."

Kingsley couldn't resist holding Loretty in his arms, and he kissed her. She felt like she was in the middle of a dream.

"I wanted to do this for the longest while. I hope you enjoyed it as much as I did," Kingsley said.

Loretty did not respond. She was frightened by what she was feeling. Was she in love with this man? Had she been all along? If so, why had she suppressed this for such a long time?

"Say something, Loretty, or I may assume that you are mad with me for kissing you."

Her response was interrupted by a knock on the door. It was the director, Steven Sagoo. "Mr. Muggerdon, I would like to speak to you before you leave."

"Certainly. Give me a few more minutes."

"Oh, my God, I'm in trouble. Do you think he saw what happened?" Loretty asked.

"If he did, I can handle it." He hugged Loretty and with the strongest of convictions said, "Don't think I am going to forget you this time."

The gods had finally smiled on her. "What about your wife?" Loretty asked.

"She is very sick."

They said nothing about themselves or Kingsley's wife, instead focusing on the business. Then he bade goodbye and went to meet with the director.

Blovingworth Mental Hospital now had an independent living facility for those patients who had nowhere to go immediately after being discharged. This facility accommodated fifteen people and had a separate wing for a supervisor. Guess who was assigned as a supervisor? Loretty Quane. She stood out among the rest and was highly respected and trusted. To her surprise, the facility was named the Kinglore Center, a name suggested by Kingsley Muggerdon, for Kingsley and Loretty. Her self-esteem shot up like a rocket going into space.

Thirty-Seven

Loretty visited her house in Dartsdam infrequently, and when she did, she said that there were too many sad memories, so she only went twice per year. Her sister Dee Dee, who was still employed at the health center in Dartsdam, was allowed to stay at the premises. Loretty spent a lot of money fixing up the house, and Dee Dee was very aggressive with the workmen. She made sure her sister wasn't ripped off. Dee Dee took very good care of the property, made good use of the land, and planted all different types of catch crops for herself and the canteen at the health center. Ethel Twipple was jealous that Dee Dee was able to work the land and produce a quality of foodstuff that surpassed expectations. It was quite noticeable that as soon as the crops were ready to be reaped, someone had helped themselves to some of the vegetables. Almost everyone suspected Edith Twipple, but no one saw her doing it.

There was no date set for Loretty's trial, and she was beginning to worry. She was anxious to have this over and done with and resume normal life with her family. Her four sons, who were in boarding schools in different sections of Puca Luca, had most of their tuition and books paid for from Basil Oop's scholarship funds, and their lodgings were paid for by contributions from several women's organizations that were sympathetic to the cause of battered women and their children. Loretty sent money and care packages to them, but they had to work part-time jobs for pocket money, especially to pay fare to visit their mother in Blovingworth and travel home. They felt a sense of pride and independence in doing so. If they came home during the holidays, they stayed with Twyleith or at the family home with Dee Dee and her son, Herbie. With the children away and attending different schools, Loretty often said to her sisters, "I feel empty and lonely at times. I miss my kids, but each time I remember the meeting with Kingsley Muggerdon, my spirits are lifted."

"Don't tell me that you are substituting those memories in place of the love for your children?" Dee Dee asked.

"Oh, heavens, no," she declared emphatically.

"So do you know if he feels the same way about you?"

"I don't know. But it certainly seems likely."

"Well, even if he does, he is not going to leave his wife."

"I know, but …"

"But what? Are you planning to have an affair? This is a game, Loretty. He knows that you are vulnerable."

"If that's the way it should be, then I don't think we should defy fate," she said. "His wife is very sick."

When the boys wrote to their mother, they expressed how much they missed her.

"Leaving home and living at a boarding school is the hardest decision that I have had to make," Tyrone wrote. "There is also this unexplainable feeling of the splitting up of the family, and the first few months away made me very scared. I miss my friends and family. I was slow in making new friends when I got here, and I don't trust my roommate. I was afraid of my dorm master at first, but after a while, I was reassured that there was nothing to fear. I have adjusted pretty well, and I have participated in a number of athletic events, particularly swimming." He sent a photograph of all the trophies he'd won and included newspaper articles of his championships.

Kyle didn't write often, but when he did, he was always asking for money because he only worked when he felt like doing so.

Ionnia didn't depend too much on her mother for pocket money. She performed various part-time jobs, one of which was at the post office in Krepston, where she worked evenings and weekends. The post office was always giving students the opportunity to work at least ten hours per week, and Ionnia had an advantage over many of the other students because she was used to the operations of the postal service when she'd lived in Redwood Vale. She also continued her crocheting, knitting, and embroidery. She made stuffed toys and designed dolls' clothes, which she sold to her schoolmates for their younger sisters. She sent some of the stuffed toys to her mother to give to the patients at the hospital, and she gave some to Clemmie to distribute at the orphanage at Christmastime.

When Ionnia visited her mother in Blovingworth, she traveled by rail. She avoided flying because she was aerophobic and aviophobic, so one summer she headed that way on one of the trains owned and operated by Metropolitan Express (MET-EX). She made herself comfortable in a window seat so that she could enjoy as much of nature as possible. When she got on, every car was packed to capacity, but as soon as they pulled in at the Pinewood station, most people got off to attend the annual Whickam County fair, so she was able to occupy a twin seat all by herself.

Farther down the road at the Fairstone station, there was a delay for almost an hour, and everyone became concerned as to what was causing this. Some people became panicky and said that the delay would cause them to be late to work. They were concerned about losing their jobs.

"Your attention, please," one of the train's attendant said on the public address system. "A little girl around five years of age was found sleeping on the train all by herself. Will the parent or guardian please report to the reception area? Thank you."

When no one came forward, the employee said, "The person with whom this little girl was traveling probably got off at Pinewood and either forgot that she was still on board, or deliberately left her there. We will transmit an urgent message to Fairstone and wait here to see if someone will call or catch a cab to this station to get the child."

How could anyone forget a child? Ionnia's first reaction was that the little girl was traveling with her father because it was hard to conceive that a mother would abandon a child.

Another fifteen minutes passed. No message was received, and no one claimed the little girl. The police were called. An attendant on the MET-EX hugged the little girl, who was crying her little eyes out and using her pretty little frilly pink dress to wipe her nose and her eyes.

"What's your name?" the attendant asked the scared little girl.

With the tears streaming down her face, she hiccupped and said, "Bubbles."

"Where did you get that name? What does it mean?"

"It is because I like to blow bubbles."

"And your real name? Do you know what it is?"

"Daisy," she said.

"A pretty name for a pretty girl," the attendant remarked, trying to make her feel relaxed.

"Where's my mommy? I want Mommy," Daisy said between sobs.

At that time, they speculated that Daisy, or Bubbles as she preferred to be called, was traveling with her mother. But where was that mother now?

"What's your mommy's name?"

"Her name is Cassie. Can you get her for me?"

"Was she with you today?"

"No. I was with my aunt Naomi, and she told me that she was taking me to see my mommy."

"We are going to find you mother and your aunt, I promise."

The attendant looked around, and standing there were three ladies: Officer Athlene Bluggard from the police department, accompanied by two others from Children's Services. Bubbles had stopped crying and began sucking her thumb.

The MET-EX employee bent over, took Bubbles by the hand, and asked, "Will you go with these ladies? You will be safe with them till we find your mommy and your aunt."

Daisy forced a smile and nodded twice. Someone had come over with a bottle for Daisy to blow bubbles. She seemed to forget everything about her mother and started blowing bubbles in some of the most beautiful patterns.

Ionnia asked her if she wanted a stuffed toy, and she gave her a grey teddy bear with a lavender ribbon tied around its neck. "You can give her a pretty name. Hold her close to you and take very good care of her," Ionnia told Bubbles.

"Thanks. I'll call her Dimples."

Another MET-EX employee was busy searching the records for ticket information, and eventually he found a stub for a ticket which was purchased in another town around twenty miles away from Fairstone for an adult and a child. They were purchased in the names of Naomi and Daisy Felder. Officer Bluggard and the people from Children's Services thanked the MET-EX employees for their cooperation, and they left with Bubbles to find Cassie or the woman known as Naomi Felder.

Did this mean that Cassie had used an alias, or had she really asked Naomi Felder to travel with Bubbles?

This situation was very disturbing, frightening, and confusing to Ionnia. She found herself comparing her life to Daisy's. Did the two of them have something in common? Was giving a child up for adoption the same as walking away and leaving a child on a train full of strangers? She asked herself a lot of questions. What reason would a woman have for abandoning a child? She quickly dismissed any negative thoughts from her mind and instead replaced them with positive ones. She was not abandoned. She still had a relationship with her family. She had two sets of people who loved her. But would poor Daisy ever find her mother? Had Naomi kidnapped her and, when she thought the authorities were closing in on her, abandoned her?

Ionnia's thoughts were interrupted when a young woman boarded the train at Fairstone and was directed to the empty seat beside her.

Ionnia was happy for the company because she needed someone to talk to, especially about what had just happened. It didn't take long for them to engage in conversation, and this took a lot off Ionnia's mind so she was able to relax a little bit, but it didn't last long. The woman, Sherna McKraugh, was carrying a small bag, and inside was a dog named Navette. The dog peered at Ionnia with a pitiful look, and as Ionnia attempted to play with it, it leaped out of the bag, jumped on Ionnia, and savagely tore into her flesh. It bit her numerous times on her face and other parts of her body.

As she screamed on top of her lungs, Sherna could be heard saying to the dog, "Navette, Navette, calm down. Where did you learn this?"

Sherna made no effort to help Ionnia but instead hurried to get her dog, which had taken off running down the passageway with blood all over its face.

Ionnia bled profusely and cried uncontrollably. Her face was almost unrecognizable from the lacerations, the blood, and the tears. *Is this the kind of pain my mother and other women felt when their spouses assaulted them?* she thought. *Or is this the kind of pain Lorna's mother felt when her husband pounded her face?*

Many people looked on in shock, and they hesitated to help or call for help. This lack of involvement was what social psychologists referred to as the bystander effect. However, a young man sitting across the aisle ripped off his shirt without hesitation, ran over to Ionnia, and covered her wounds as the train's attendants came to her rescue. The medical staff who'd heard her screams also came to her rescue, and they took her to the medical facility on the train, where emergency treatment was rendered.

The train pulled into the New Mahoe station around fifteen minutes later, and Ionnia was rushed to the emergency department of the small hospital. She writhed in pain. Immediately she was given rabies and tetanus shots, and she was hooked up to an IV line with painkillers and sedatives.

"This dangerous beast that did this to this young lady should be put to sleep immediately, its body buried in the county's trash dump," someone declared angrily. "We understand that this was an unprovoked attack, and people should be protected from such a savage creature. I'm sure it was a male dog." Someone had already contacted animal control and told them to meet the train at the New Mahoe station, where the dog would be taken from its owner and disposed of as seen fit.

Sherna McKraugh was thunder-truck. She could not believe that such a situation was happening to her beloved dog as it was snatched from out of her arms. "How am I supposed to live without Navette? She was a birthday present given from my grandmother. This is my baby!" she cried. "Please don't dispose of her in the garbage. Can they cremate my baby and give me the ashes? I have a plastic bag here." Sherna laid all the blame on Ionnia. "If the girl had not been sitting there, he would not have scratched her. We should have been by ourselves."

"Are you out of your mind?" an older lady shouted. "This was no scratch. Look at the young lady's condition! She is suffering, and that is all you have to say?" The lady pointed her cane at Sherna and said to her, "You should be the one in that bag, you stupid, heartless, inconsiderate little bitch." The dog was disposed of in the hospital's incinerator, and Sherna got nothing to hold on to.

At the hospital, Ionnia had a surprise visitor: the young man who'd covered her wounds with his shirt. He brought her two flowers that appeared to have been taken from the vase at the nurses' station and appeared to be a couple days old.

"How are you? I'm Stuart Dent, but you can call me Stu. I tried to give blood in case you needed it, but we are not a match. You are type AB negative and I'm type O positive." He pointed to a short lady in a straw hat and remarked, "She gave blood, and also another man who was on the train who identified himself as Randolph Montaggle, the deputy superintendent of public works in Whickam County."

"Neither of us knows you but we are sympathetic to the situation," Mr. Montaggle said. "I have children."

Ionnia was heavily sedated, but she forced a painful smile. "Thanks to everyone," she muttered weakly. She then closed her eyes and drifted off to sleep.

When she awoke, Stu was still there. The pain had subsided, and she managed to scribble a request on a piece of paper asking Stu to call her aunt Twyleith to let her know what had happened. Twyleith would then call the rest of the family, including the adopted parents and guardians.

Stu made the phone call, and on his return to her bedside, he said to her "You forgot to give me another number."

"What do you mean?" she asked. "The number I gave you didn't work?"

"What about your boyfriend? Shouldn't he know what happened to you?"

"I don't have a boyfriend," Ionnia muttered.

Stu looked up in the ceiling and smiled, as if to thank God for having just stumbled upon a jackpot. "You don't have one now, or you've never had one?" Stu asked in a suggestive manner that all teenage girls should have a boyfriend.

"Never had one, and I don't need one."

"I didn't mean to get you all worked up. I'm sorry." He kissed her on her forehead. "Get some more sleep."

Ionnia's brother Roger was the first family member to arrive at the hospital. He was doing an internship as a financial analyst ten miles from New Mahoe, and he had purchased a five-year-old car from one of his classmate's father who owned a used car lot. "How are you, sis?" he asked as they hugged each other. Roger looked inquiringly at Stu and then back at his sister and asked, "Who is this young man? You left out this major detail in your last letter." He assumed that Stu was her boyfriend. Stu filled him in, and they shook hands. "Thank you for being attentive to my little sister," Roger said.

Stu handed Roger a piece of paper. "I did a little investigation on my own. This is the name and address of the girl who owned the dog. I need to give you two some time alone," he said politely, and then he exited.

Roger held his sister's hand until she fell asleep again. Then he sat in a chair and read from the company's policy manual he had brought along with him.

When she awoke, Ionnia mustered enough strength to ask Roger about the rest of the family.

"This may not be the right time to tell you this, but I guess you will find out eventually. Grandma is very ill," Roger said. "She has pancreatic cancer, which is terminal. I'm sorry to have to give you the bad news at this time, but I know you can handle it."

Ionnia's body ached all over, and her soul ached for her grand-mother. She felt like getting up and running to her. "Where is she?" Ionnia asked.

"She is at the hospital in San Clewert"

"Why San Clewert?"

"She went to visit her uncle, Zaccheus Mann. When he saw how sick our grandmother was, he made the call to Chad. He told him that at times Grandma could hardly breathe because of how much pain she was in. He her rushed to the hospital, and that's how the story goes. Chad can explain it better when you see him."

"Can you take me to see her as soon as I get out of here? I would really like to be able to see her before she passes away." She would al-ways regard her grandmother as her tower of strength. "Please, God," she whispered. "Keep her alive until I am able to get to her." With that, she drifted off to sleep. As she did so, the only words she could remember were *terminal* and *dying*. She was scared. Ionnia processed the events of the past few days very well. She was a very strong person for her age and had learned a lot of survival skills.

While she slept, more visitors arrived, including her mother, her adoptive parents, and a number of other family members.

Chad called. "I have exams, and I promise to be there as soon as I can get away." He was not able to visit, but he called at least twice per day and consulted with Dr. Leroy Boot, the doctor in charge of Ionnia's care.

"The prognosis is good," Dr. Boot assured the family, "But she will need to have plastic surgery in the future."

The family held hands while Bishop Ryte prayed.

Stu Dent reappeared and then bade goodbye as suddenly as he'd arrived. He respected the family's need to have time with Ionnia. "I promise I'll come back tomorrow." Looking at his watch, he turned around and said, "I have errands to run, so I will hurry back to the train station and catch the next train to my destination."

Berdene sat by her daughter's bedside and comforted her. Ionnia asked for a mirror and was terrified when she saw the bandages on her face. The only areas not covered were her eyes, her nose, and her mouth. She tried to let out a gasp but restrained herself.

"My face is going to look like a pineapple," she said, and she couldn't stand the thought of it. She started shaking. Was she going to be teased at school? Was she going to be rejected? Were her new parents still going to keep her? All these emotional wounds started bleeding, and she mentally searched for bandages to cover them.

"Shh," her mother said. "You will be okay. We will see to it."

The staff nurse entered the room, and one couldn't help but notice how her demeanor stood out above the rest of the hospital staff. She didn't appear to be more than nineteen years of age, and Roger, who was standing in the hallway, was mesmerized with her. On her way in, he glanced quickly at her name tag and made mental note of her name: Tourmaline.

"Can everyone please relax in the waiting room for a few minutes while I attend to the patient?" Tourmaline asked. In less than fifteen minutes, she was finished in Ionnia's room, but to Roger her stay seemed like an eternity. He waited anxiously to start a conversation with this petite, red-headed caregiver.

Tourmaline smiled at the group and said, "You can go in now, but don't stay too long. The patient needs to rest."

Roger, who had already positioned himself in the doorway away from the group, was impressed with the professionalism that Tourmaline exuded, and he couldn't wait any longer to strike up a conversation with the nurse. He smiled at her and said, "Excuse me, can I have a word with you?"

She hadn't noticed him earlier, and even if she had seen him, he could have been any other visitor. "I cannot discuss a patient with you. Are you a relative?" she asked.

"Yes, I'm Ionnia's brother. And although I'm anxious to know of my sister's condition, that's not the reason I want to talk to you," Roger whispered softly while gazing in her eyes. "The others will fill me in. All that I want to discuss at this time is standing right here in front of me."

Tourmaline blushed, and smiled uncomfortably. "You have a beautiful name. Is there a special meaning to it?"

Tourmaline explained to him the meaning of her name; it related to gemstones.

"Very impressive. I'm sure you are real a gem to the people in your life. Can I call you Gem? May I also invite you to have lunch with me on your day off? I won't take no for an answer. I will be hanging around for a few days." He didn't bother to ask whether she was already spoken for, and he didn't care. This was love at first sight.

Before Tourmaline could give Roger answers to all these questions, he gave her information where he could be reached, and then he rejoined the group. The name Gem stuck with her from then on, but she didn't mind at all.

Thirty-Eight

Ionnia spent a week in the hospital, and she was overwhelmed by the outpouring of cards, flowers, gifts, and well-wishes from people who didn't even know her. During her confinement, her brothers Kyle and Tyrone had also come to see her but didn't stay long. Aunt Gert, who couldn't be there, contacted Dr. Sarah String, a close friend of the family, to stop by and assist Dr. Leroy Boot with Ionnia's treatment. They trusted her competence.

Dr. String had once had a relationship with Gert's son, Robbie, but he broke it off when she refused to make a commitment to marry him. She kept in touch with the family and held Gert dear to her heart. She would always refer to her as the greatest mentor she'd ever known.

At the end of the week, some of Ionnia's stitches were removed, and it was time for her to be discharged. She contemplated whether to go to her maternal family or to her adoptive family. She settled on the latter, and Dr. String volunteered to accompany her to Krepston.

Ionnia placed a call to Chad. "Can you get away? I'm being discharged today, and it would be nice if you could be here."

He didn't send back a reply but decided to show up unannounced and surprise her. She admitted that she felt much better when she saw him.

Tourmaline, now known as Gem, was not on duty when Roger, Chad, and Dr. String picked up Ionnia to go to lunch. Roger had already put her on notice, so he had requested time off, which was granted. She was immediately summoned to join the group. Stu was elated when he was asked to join them as well, and all six of them headed to the Universal Yacht Club, a few miles from the hospital and near Roger's internship site.

Before they departed, Dr. Boot gave Ionnia a list of names of competent plastic surgeons. The list included some doctors who had performed various cosmetic procedures on models and beauty contestants. Stu made a few suggestions too. He recommended Dr. Hal Beuhling in Trevine, who was a close friend of his sister's husband, and promised to have him make contact with the renowned doctor.

Stu turned to Ionnia, squeezed her hand, looked into her eyes, and said, "When it's all over, you will be more beautiful than before. I am looking forward to spending plenty of time with you. I hope you won't mind."

"Thank you." She did not know what to think of her new friend, but she was curious to know whether he paid this much attention to all the strangers he met. She enjoyed all the attention that Stu was giving her, but in the meantime, she was suspicious of him and very cautious about his intentions. Who was he? There was something strange and weird about Stu Dent. Ionnia did not want a boyfriend, and she informed Stu that she would rather pay attention to her education at this point. She loathed what she observed happening to other girls in her high school who had steady relationships—and the emotional pain they endured as a result. She used her own mother's experience as a deterrent to get involved with guys, as well as some of the stories she'd heard about other women. She wanted to be a successful fashion designer, an entrepreneur, and an advocate for abused women and children, so she had no time to waste on relationships. As far as she was concerned, being involved in a relationship would be a retrograde step and block her path. She had a mission to accomplish, and nothing was going to get in her way.

"Let's leave the girls alone while we get to know this kind young man. Go ahead and order some appetizers. We will be back in a few minutes." Roger led the way, with Stu and Chad following behind. They were outside for approximately fifteen minutes. Perhaps they were trying to figure out Stu's weirdness or what his relationship was with Ionnia. Or maybe they were thanking him again for being there for their sister, and they were attempting to compensate him in some way.

The females ordered crab balls and salmon fritters with peanut sauce. They chatted about everything from medicine to relationships to politics. Tourmaline whispered to Ionnia, "I like your brother."

"Which one? Chad is already spoken for."

"No, I am referring to Roger. Don't misunderstand me, Chad is a great person, but who needs to be talking hospital stuff when we meet?"

Tourmaline bombarded Ionnia with a lot of questions about Roger, hoping to get as many answers as possible before the men returned. *This is good,* Ionnia said to herself. *I hope if there is a relationship between these two, it will mature into marriage. I am looking forward to having her as a sister-in-law. From what I have seen, she seems to be a nice person, an intelligent person, and a good role model.*

When the males rejoined them, they began ordering lunch from a menu that had a variety of seafood dishes. Ionnia ordered grilled grouper on a bed of curried eggplant and coconut rice with a side of green peas. This was her first nourishing meal outside of the hospital, and she did not want anything or anyone to retard her appetite. She needed a lot of TLC and assured herself that when she got home, she could rely on her new parents and Clemmie for this. She had already suffered much from ill health, and she was determined to press forward in the pursuit of her dreams. She was giving herself that emotional push, and she forced a smile.

Ionnia had never asked Stu what he did for a living, but maybe her brothers had already asked. She had learned from her past not to measure a person's status through one's vocation. Women had come to resent men as soon as they met for inquiring where they worked, because in most cases this was used as a yardstick to determine social acceptance.

It was Tourmaline who asked Stu where he worked. "I work with my mother, who owns a funeral home and crematorium. She is a professional embalmer and cremator. I also work part-time at the medical examiner's office as an autopsy assistant, and one of my assignments is to collect John Does and Jane Does." Stu's mother, Velma, was president of the Whickam Organization of Registered Undertakers (WHO-RU). These undertakers were contracted to properly dispose of all the unclaimed bodies from the county's morgue, and it was their responsibility to dispose of them in any way they saw fit. So as to retain scarce prime land for agriculture and housing purposes, most of the bodies were cremated. He further divulged how his mother enjoyed her work, especially when she had to cremate a man who was a spouse abuser. Stu spoke in graphic details how the funeral establishment specialized in making dead girls prettier than when they were alive. He opened his wallet and showed the group before and after pictures of some of these women. He seemed rather obsessed with this technique.

"Who is responsible for this work of art?" Dr. String inquired.

"Dent's Mortuary and Crematorium has on staff one of Puca Luca's top aestheticians, Nickolas Enderone."

"Nick works for your mother's establishment?" Dr. String asked.

"You know him?" Stu and Chad asked in unison.

"Yes. I remember him when he had a company called Endless. He used to do facials for beauty contestants and models."

Memories of Ionnia's father's abuse and his death resurfaced, and Stu's obsession with the dead made her feel nauseated. Ionnia excused herself to go to the ladies' room.

"I didn't mean to spoil anyone's appetite," Stu apologized. Just then, his pager made that familiar beep that signaled that he was needed for probably another assignment. He glanced at the number and did not seem to recognize it, but he decided to make contact anyway. There was a happy and sad expression on his face as he excused himself to make the phone call. He was enjoying the company of his new friends and he did not want this to end.

No one commented on Stu's behavior, but his fascination with death was deeply etched in Ionnia's mind. That was just one side of Stu. She also never forgot how he'd helped her when she'd been in trouble. On the other hand, did he think she was going to die? Was she another one he wanted to make pretty? She freaked out.

On her way to the ladies' room, Ionnia almost bumped into a pregnant female who was carrying a mop and bucket and wasn't paying much attention to where she was headed. Ionnia looked at her name tag and recognized the name: Jaylene Bullock.

The girl looked at Ionnia but seemed not to recognize her. Or if she did, she did not show it. Maybe she was not expecting her to be in this side of town, or perhaps it was the condition of Ionnia's face, or maybe Jaylene was too ashamed to face her, knowing what she and her friends had done to Ionnia in elementary school.

Jaylene was working as a bathroom attendant, and Ionnia thought it best not to extend any greetings or hold any conversation. Ionnia stretched her imagination in all directions, wondering about the fate of the other members of the clique. Most of all, she was curious to know who had knocked up Jaylene. There was no wedding ring on her finger. It was more than likely Jaylene didn't know, if she'd continued to be as promiscuous as she used to be.

When Stu returned from making the telephone call, his expression had changed. This time he was more than excited. He wore a broad grin on his face almost exposing all of his teeth.

"Well?" the group said as they gazed at Stu.

"You wouldn't guess with whom I just spoke."

"Nick?" Dr. String asked.

"No."

"Well, don't keep us in suspense," Roger said.

Before anyone could say anything else, Stu said, "The chairman of the board of MET-EX. He wants to give me an award for helping Ionnia."

"Oh, that is great. Not all citizens are rewarded for their heroic efforts," Tourmaline said. "You deserve it."

"There will be a special ceremony at the Fairstone station tomorrow afternoon at three, and you are all invited to attend."

"I wish I could be there, but I can't," Roger said. "I have to be back today." He shook Stu's hand and said, "Best of luck. I am sure you are happy that you were able to help in the way you did. On behalf of all of us, thank you very much."

Turning to Stu, Dr. String said, "I'm sure between Tourmaline and me, we can make overnight arrangements for you, Chad, and Ionnia so that you will receive the moral support that you deserve."

There were no objections, and the group focused on finishing their scrumptious meal. They looked forward to the next day's event. During lunch, Roger learned a lot about Tourmaline. She talked of her struggles while growing up and what had happened to her and her two older siblings. Her mother, Bessie "Bibbie" Brandstalk, also a battered and abused woman, died while giving birth to Tourmaline. Her father, Armand Brandstalk, was left to raise the children all by himself, and after a while, he decided not to do so anymore. She was told that her father had left her on the steps of a church when she was five months old, and he'd left her siblings, Opal (age three) and brother Jade (age five), at the local farmers market in Dolby with a woman named Murdell Kiffin. The cleaning lady at the church, Either Wee, found Tourmaline and took her. She was in no financial or physical position to take care of a baby, so she notified the pastor's wife, who began making inquiries as to the identity of this child. When no one stepped forward, she was ready to place the baby in the orphanage run by the church. That was when Tourmaline's maternal aunt, Priscilla, heard the news and went to get her. Murdell would have been more than happy to have another addition to her family if Armand Brandstalk had informed her that there was a third child.

Tourmaline grew up with her aunt Priscilla Dutte, her mother's half sister, while Opal and Jade were raised by Murdell and her husband, who had five children of their own: Carol, Laura, Chester, Glenda, and Fern. Murdell and her husband made no distinctions between their children and Bibbie's children. They taught everyone the same moral values and did their best to give them the best education. Tourmaline and Murdell's children grew up like brothers and sisters, but her cousins, Jessica and Arlene, were resentful of her. They and their mother would treat Tourmaline like an outcast and a maid. She had to do most of the chores, was the last to be fed at mealtimes, and was forbidden to have friends over. When word got to Murdell about the mistreatment, she allowed Tourmaline to spend most of her time at their home, and Priscilla and the girls never seemed to mind.

Jonas Kiffin, a butcher known as Butch to his friends, and his wife, Murdell, a basket maker, were a happy couple and role models in their community. Their relationship was based on love and respect, and they encouraged a strong family relationship. They may not have been rich financially, but they didn't consider themselves poor. They were the envy of most of their acquaintances. Whenever people made reference to a perfect marriage, they would always mention the Kiffins. Some even went as far as to say that if one should look in the dictionary for the words *compatible* and *perfect*, one would find the Kiffins' picture. People always asked them what was the secret of their success in marriage, and their response was, "Respect each other, and the love will follow." Others were constantly urged to take a leaf out of the Kiffins' book.

Aunt Priscilla did very little to help her niece become self-sufficient, but she assisted her two children in getting the best holiday jobs available. Priscilla's husband, who held a prestigious position with the Puca Luca Public Service Company (PULUPSCO), offered Tourmaline a job, but it wouldn't come without a price. He wanted to sleep with

her, and when she told her aunt about it, she was beaten with a piece
of PVC pipe and accused of wanting to break up her marriage.

Despite the hardships, Gem persevered. She was determined to make
something of her life. She did odd jobs from time to time while in
school. She helped Jonas in the butcher shop and saved her money
to help her while in nursing school. She got good grades in school
was promised a scholarship from the Basil Oop Foundation. After a
while, her grades plummeted, and she lost the opportunity for the
scholarship. Financial issues stared Tourmaline in the face, and the
Kiffins helped as much as they could. She remembered getting word
of where her father was living, and she wondered whether he would
help her at this time. Armand Brandstalk was now married to a cousin
of Tourmaline's former teacher, Doreen Packston, with whom he'd
fathered two children. Tourmaline decided to write to him, asking
for help of some sort, and she waited with much anticipation, hoping that he would be proud of her and would therefore try to assist
in whatever way he could. She remembered how excited she was
when she received a letter postmarked from her father. Tourmaline
could barely control herself as she ripped the envelope open, and although there was no money enclosed, she was happy at first to know
that her father had responded to her letter. But that happiness was
short-circuited. She was in for a big surprise: half the contents of the
letter sent to Tourmaline was from Armand's wife, Doreen, requesting that Tourmaline not continue to write to her husband and upset
the family. To rub salt in the wound, the second half of the letter was
from her father, who stated strongly in colorful language that he did
not know her and did not wish to have anything to do with her, and
that she should leave him and his family alone. The tears welled up
in her eyes as she relived that moment.

"I'm sorry," she said as she held back the emotions and wiped away
the tears. "I'm not looking for any sympathy here."

Roger reached across the table, took up a napkin, and tenderly
dried Tourmaline's tears. He moved closer to her, hugged her, and

then reminded her of the Chinese Proverb that said, "The gem cannot be polished without friction, nor man perfected without trials."

It was at that moment Ionnia returned from the ladies' room, and she could see that Tourmaline had been crying. She didn't ask what was wrong and wondered if Roger had said or done anything to upset her. As she glanced in his direction, he held up his hands and said, "I didn't do anything to hurt her. She was just reminiscing on her past."

At first Ionnia was scared that Roger had begun to turn into someone like his father, because there were studies that showed that children who experienced or witnessed abuse often grew up to be abusers themselves.

Thirty-Nine

Dr. String and Ionnia arrived in Krepston safely, and the first order of business was to contact the medical staff at the health center, which had already received her chart and was aware that she needed biweekly follow-up visits. After she got this out of the way, she spent a few days with Gert, who was thrilled to see her. Not once did they bring up the relationship between Robbie and Dr. String, but when Gert mentioned that her son would be visiting over the weekend, Dr. String found an excuse to make a hasty departure.

Ionnia was scared to look in the mirror, and each time she looked, she panicked. "Will I ever be normal again?" she wondered. "But what does being normal mean? Are we to go by society's standards?" She was terrified by thinking that she would be teased and bullied, and the thought almost immobilized her.

Ionnia's wounds were healed, but the terrible scars remained. She didn't look the same, and she had begun to experience regular panic attacks. When she returned to school, she knew that she would be stared at, but she was ill prepared for the reactions she got from the students and some of the teachers. She was definitely not emotionally prepared for the intolerance, indiscretion, and verbal comments from her peers. They treated Ionnia as if she was afflicted with some kind of plague, or as if she were some animal in a zoo. Her friend Olivine

Deroniapp ignored her and no longer wanted to sit beside her and socialize with her. "She is so ugly," she told Lyrette Sykone, the girl who had become her new best friend while Ionnia was away.

"This doesn't matter much to me. It only means I no longer have to help her with her assignments. She has done me a great favor," Ionnia told herself.

Olivine and Lyrette were vocal with their verbal abuse, and it got so bad that they were summoned to one of the vice principal's offices and reprimanded. "The school has a zero-tolerance policy toward certain behavior, and if you do not cease and desist, you will be suspended for five days." The girls apologized to the vice principal, who reminded them that they should also apologize to Ionnia. They were reluctant at first, but when they were told that the suspension would come with a request for their parents to administer corporal punishment, they sent Ionnia a written apology and gave a copy to the vice principal to keep in their file.

Ionnia couldn't help but wonder, "Is there an end in sight?" Once again, fear and panic gripped her, and she wondered whether this had now become a reality. However, she preferred to reflect on the people who loved her, so she quickly dismissed whatever negative thoughts that crept into her head, replacing them with positive ones. "I am determined to learn something positive from this experience. How can I help others when I don't have the strength to cope?"

Another comment that haunted her was the one that abusers always used: "See what you made me do?" Those words reverberated in her head, and she thought of the times when her father had beaten her mother and then looked at her apologetically while uttering those words. One night as she took a shower, the hot water beat down her back, and the tears streamed down her face as she relived the moments on the train and asked herself, "Did I do anything wrong to cause that beast to attack me?" She had no simple answer for everything that happened in her life, but one thing she was sure of: if she could avoid it, she wouldn't get near a dog as long as she lived. She couldn't bear the sight of a dog even in pictures, and she freaked out whenever she heard one barking.

Despite the adversities that confronted her, Ionnia found courage beyond her own expectations to exhibit resilience and courage, continue forging a path to success, and fulfill the purpose for which she was destined. She remembered a wise saying: "If shadows remain in your life, maybe you are standing in your own sunshine."

Due to her facial disfigurement, Ionnia chose to exclude herself from most of the school's extracurricular activities that required students to compete out of town. She no longer participated in the singing competition, athletics, the drama club, and the 4-H club. She theorized that audience members would focus on her face and not her accomplishments, and she wasn't used to anything other than first place.

"I will use these extra hours to concentrate on my academics. I will not let anything mar my efforts for achieving my goals. The sky's the limit," she told herself. She reflected on some words she once read from Thomas Huxley, a nineteenth-century biologist and writer. "The rung of a ladder was never meant to rest upon, but only to hold a man's foot long enough to enable him to put the other somewhat higher."

With that, Ionnia became more determined than ever to excel and show everyone that she could be whatever she wanted to be despite what others thought of her, especially because of her outward appearance. At times she examined the amulet given to her by Samanthley, and she convinced herself that this added a little bit of luck. However, she never forgot her spiritual faith, and she remembered what the Bible warned about idol worship.

Charley Gress, who was waiting for a break to take on a major insurance company, volunteered to represent Ionnia in the case against Sherna McKraugh and her insurance company. One of his counterparts, Vince Huggins, presented the case against MET-EX. After months of postponement and the inability to find an impartial jury, Gress and Huggins argued for an out-of-court settlement.

At first the management of MET-EX refused to accept culpability and to settle out of court. "Let the jury decide," they said.

The insurance company, however, settled out of court. "We do not need all this publicity," the CEO said. "This would be bad for business."

The plaintiff's team applied an aggressive approach in presenting its case. All parties who were witness to the attack were called to testify. The jury returned a verdict in Ionnia's favor and awarded her a substantial sum of money. This was enough to pay for her plastic surgery and other expenses associated with the injuries.

The court ordered MET-EX to put new restrictions on the way animals were transported on their trains. Half-page ads were taken out in the country's major newspapers, and fliers were posted in all the trains and at their stations. Fliers were also stapled to light poles and on walls of businesses. These notifications informed passengers who traveled with small pets that they would be riding in a separate car away from most people.

"This is a good idea," some commented. "Let them turn on each other while in isolation."

These new rules did not sit well with animal rights activists, so they took to the airwaves and picketed the MET-EX headquarters. Some people went so far as to tamper with the tracks to cause derailments. One afternoon, a group of people led by the president of the Animal Lovers Association, Enos Hatford, was seen disconnecting brackets from the railroad tracks. All of them were arrested and charged with malicious destruction of property, with the possibility of bringing about mass fatalities. They were found guilty, but the punishment was not as severe as the citizens wished. The guilty defendants were ordered to work with the Department of Public Works to replace the brackets, and Enos was ordered to assist the director of transportation in lecturing civic groups and organizations on various aspects of railroad safety.

"They should be charged for attempted murder," said Gladys Pickerns, who rode the train every day to work.

This incident brought about the introduction of optional passenger travel (OPT) insurance on all modes of transportation, and suddenly there was an upsurge in the writing of insurance policies.

Forty

No one liked to receive a telegram because it usually signified bad news, and Ionnia knew this firsthand by working part-time at the post office. About 75 percent of telegrams sent and received brought bad news, so when Ionnia got one from Aunt Twyleith, she hesitated in opening it. Different scenarios crossed her mind, including what may have happened to her mother or grandmother. When she composed herself, she decided that it would be best to be with her parents when she read it, so she handed it to her mother. Berdene Ryte carefully tore the edges of the folds in the envelope, opened it, and read it to herself. Everyone waited with bated breath as she did this slowly. There was no expression on Ionnia's face because she didn't want to experience the shock reaction to which she was accustomed.

Then Berdene looked at everyone and said in her usual calm voice, "This is top priority."

"Will you please tell us what it says, dear?" the bishop pleaded with his wife.

Finally she looked at Ionnia, drew her close to her, and said, "Your grandma was readmitted to a hospital in San Clewert, and she wants to see you one more time before she passes."

Ionnia cried on her mother's shoulders.

"So sorry," her father said as he helped comfort her. "This takes precedence over everything else. We are aware how much you love your grandmother, so we will not stand in your way. Start packing, and take enough so that you can stay as long as you want. We will be offering our prayers."

Ionnia put everything else on hold and made preparations for the trip to see her beloved grandmother. She was nervous as she made a decision to travel by air even though she was afraid of flying. Taking the mail boat would take too long, and she would have to walk from the pier to the hospital. Among the items she packed were schoolwork to complete, photographs of her family, a Bible, and other books to read. She tried to assure herself that she would be okay. Pastor Ryte's nephew, Gert's son, Robert "Robbie" Snipp, taught history at the academy. Robbie offered to take his cousin to the airport. On their way, Ionnia talked about Dr. String and Nurse Tourmaline and how attentive they had been to her while she was in the hospital. She leaned sideways and said to Robbie, "The nurse is already spoken for by my brother Roger, but maybe if you meet Dr. String, I'm sure you would like her. She's a lovely person."

Ionnia was unaware that these two had already met, dated, and broken up.

"She may be a great doctor, but certainly not."

"Not what?"

"Forget it."

"You know her?"

"Yes, and this is not a conversation I should be having with my little cousin."

"Why not?"

Robbie told Ionnia a little bit about his relationship with Dr. String. He painted the picture as if the breakup was her fault. "She puts her profession as the number one priority."

"And you have a problem with that?"

"So, when would she get time to raise our children if and when we got married?"

"Are you saying that she should give up her job and commit her life solely to you? That's very selfish of you, Robbie Snipp. There are a lot of women out there without a profession who would be happy to fill that role, and then you can control them. You are too egotistic. Professional women want to maintain their independence. However, there are three sides to a story: my side, your side, and the truth."

"If you should spend some time with her outside of the hospital, you would agree that she is the selfish one," Robbie said.

"Oh, no, that's where you are wrong. I have spent time with her. She did the most unselfish thing and volunteered to take me home after my stay in the hospital."

"Don't tell me she was in Krepston."

"Yes. Your mother didn't tell you? And if there were pleasant memories of the relationship between the both of you, she would have looked you up."

Robbie was silent for a while, as if he were reflecting on the relationship with Dr. String. He sighed. "I guess I misjudged your maturity." He said nothing else, so to indicate that the conversation was over, he turned on the radio. Ionnia listened and sang along, especially when her favorite songs were played, "Across the Bridge" and "Something Inside so Strong."

"Nothing lifts the spirit more than music."

Traffic was in their favor, and the journey took considerably less time than anticipated. As they neared the airport, Ionnia read the signs along the road, and the first one that caught her eyes was the word *Terminal*. Her brain somehow misinterpreted this word and associated it with the act of dying. She thought about her mortality, and fear gripped her. She started to perspire, her heart raced, her mouth became dry, and after sipping on the bottle of water she had with her, she turned to Robbie and told him she wanted to change her mind about the trip.

"But your grandma needs to see you. How would you feel if she passed, and you didn't get the chance to say goodbye? What suddenly happened?"

"I can see myself falling to my death," she said. "Memories of plane crashes still haunt me. I can clearly remember when I was around seven years old, and I witnessed a small plane plummet from the sky into a cornfield, killing all six occupants on board. I can also recall reading in the papers of a large commercial plane carrying a group of athletes and exchange students that crashed while on its way to Australia after a flock of birds came in contact with the plane. Of the eighty-five passengers on board, only two survived."

"I can definitely see why you have a fear of flying." They talked about her phobia, and Robbie comforted her. "Many people have overcome different phobias through the utilization of various thera- peutic interventions and techniques. I can remember reading that the odds of being involved in a fatal air crash are one in nine million," Robbie said. "Various empirical data show that people die more fre- quently in car crashes than in plane crashes. Calm down. There is nothing to worry about. I have flown many times, and here I am; I am not a ghost. Or is this what a ghost looks like?" Suddenly he made a violent swerve to avoid hitting a car that had cut in front of him. He let out a loud laugh, which infuriated Ionnia.

"That's not funny. If you were to listen to some people who have survived airplane crashes, you would feel just like I do."

"Did you purchase that travel insurance?"

"Yes, and I put you down as my beneficiary," she said sarcastically.

"Lighten up, cousin. I mean well."

The closer they got to the airport, the word *Terminal* could be seen more often, and Ionnia shared her thoughts and fears with her cousin. He drew her attention to the numbers beside the word and explained about the different areas of embarkation and disembarkation.

"Of course. I should have known better." She became less tense, and she and Robbie talked about more pleasant subjects.

During the check-in process, Robbie spoke to one of the ticket agents, a very pleasant young lady whose name tag bore the name Marie. She looked to be around twenty-two years old. Ionnia thought he was flirting with her, but then she learned that he was informing her of Ionnia's phobia.

"We will try to make her as comfortable as possible," the young lady assured Robbie.

He was about to leave, so he kissed Ionnia on the forehead and said, "You will be all right. Marie is going to make sure of that. I have to get back to work. I hope everything goes well with your grandma. God has a way of working miracles."

"Thanks."

"And don't forget that He needs angels in heaven," Robbie said.

Ionnia's flight was delayed, and during those waking moments, she was taken to a private room, where she received counseling from an airline psychologist who happened to be at the right place at the right time. She introduced Ionnia to some activities to calm her down, gave her books to read, and provided a list of titles to purchase in the future. She was also taken on a virtual tour of a flight. Ionnia felt better after the session, and she was escorted to the aircraft by another crisis counselor prior to the scheduled embarkation of all the other passengers. On the way to the gate, she studied the faces of different people in an effort to detect any signs of fear or nervousness in them, or probably to spot a hijacker, although she was no expert at any of these. Everyone seemed at ease. The counselor took Ionnia to an area where she could watch the planes take off and land. She exhibited a lot of patience and compassion before showing Ionnia to seat 7A. "This will be your seat. Make yourself comfortable."

"Have you encountered a lot of passengers like me?"

"Yes, every day."

Before the counselor exited the aircraft, she spoke to Charlette, one of the flight attendants, but Ionnia couldn't hear what they were saying. They both went into the cockpit to talk to the pilot and co-pilot. Ionnia was focusing on her exercises when the flight attendant returned and said, "Today is your lucky day. Captain Clifford has consented to show you what goes on in the cockpit."

"Do you always treat all your passengers this way?"

"No, you are a very special passenger."

"Is it because I'm disfigured, and you feel sorry for me?"

Before she could answer, Ionnia recognized the captain, Mr. Lynval Clifford, who was the father of one of Chad's friends, Ronnie. He explained the plane's mechanisms to her.

"How is Chad, and what is he up to these days?" the captain asked.

"He is studying to be a doctor."

"I should have guessed."

"How is Ronnie?"

"He is pursuing a course in civil engineering at the University of Trevine, and he does summer jobs with Puca Luca's Ministry of Public Works. He recently supervised an assignment where a group of people were court-ordered to work on the railroad tracks after they had vandalized it."

Ionnia told Captain Clifford that she was familiar with the situation, and she gave him a brief summary that led up to it. "Thanks for everything, Captain."

Ionnia walked back confidently to her seat. By this time, the rest of the passengers had begun to take their seats. They seemed so relaxed. She read her Bible and immersed herself in the other printed materials given to her earlier. She closed her eyes and relived the simulation. She said a silent prayer not just for the safety of herself but for everyone else, being the unselfish person that she was.

Just as Ionnia opened her eyes, she saw a tall, overconfident man putting his carry-on luggage overhead. He looked at his boarding pass and said softly, "Seat 7B." Then he rested his travel documents in the seat while he continued to shove his luggage in the compartment. The document revealed his name, Carlton Drysdale. When he was ready to sit down, he stared at Ionnia's face and turned away disdainfully.

He beckoned to the flight attendant and said, "I do not want to sit beside this person with the mask. What time of year she thinks this is, Halloween?"

Lots of thoughts flooded her mind. *I am not a violent person, but this is one time I would have eviscerated someone if I had a knife handy.* Then she thought of her mother and decided to remain calm in her seat.

The passenger went on a tirade about his beautiful wife and then said, "It would be nauseating for me to sit the entire flight beside someone with a face only a mother could love. If I'm going to do this, I will need a double scotch on the rocks," he bellowed to the flight attendant.

The other passengers looked on with disgust and expressed how uncomfortable they were at being on the same flight with him.

The senior flight attendant, Merlene Bishop, approached him and said, "You are aware that you can be thrown off the plane and charged with disruption of a flight? I suggest you sit down and behave yourself."

Ionnia had not yet scheduled her appointment for plastic surgery but wished she had. She planned to do that as soon as she got back and completed her final exams. She ignored Carlton the best she could, although she was fearful of him because of his size.

Charlette Buttons, who had taken Ionnia to the cockpit, approached the area. Without looking at anyone in particular, she said rather politely, "I have a seat in business class."

Assuming that Charlette was addressing him, Carlton immediately attempted to remove his overhead belongings so that he would sit in business class section. As he did so, Charlette ignored him, extended her hand to Ionnia, and said, "Come with me."

Carlton's eyes nearly popped out of his head as he stood with his outstretched arm, still trying to get his things.

The passengers laughed uncontrollably, and they clapped and booed Carlton.

"Crawl up in the overhead compartment for the duration of the flight, 'cause we never want to hear from you anymore, you rotten, good-for-nothing you-know-what," shouted one outraged passenger. "I have a son with a physical disability due to a rare skin condition, and I would hate to know he is treated this way by anyone."

Merlene asked everyone to calm down because they wanted to get going as soon as possible, adding that the pilot was not going to leave in the midst of the commotion. Charlette assisted Ionnia with her luggage from the overhead compartment and placed it in an enclosure near the cockpit usually reserved for the crew. Captain Clifford was informed of the situation and offered Ionnia more comfort. He approached Drysdale and repeated what Merlene had told him earlier. The man became subdued and appeared remorseful, and he plopped down in the seat all by himself.

Ionnia was seated comfortably in the business class section of the plane and looked around to see whether anyone there was going to make fun of her. No one did; these were sophisticated businesspeople who didn't have time to discriminate. She was amazed to see the difference between coach and business sections—the comfortable seats and the one-on-one attention. She loved this. Her demeanor, intelligence, and conservative grooming said a lot about her and reminded her where she really belonged. She fought hard to forget what her face looked like now, and she visualized herself on the covers of various women's business magazines after her plastic surgery. She opened one of the books she'd received earlier during her counseling sessions, and she began reading.

Shortly after liftoff, a stocky gentleman who appeared to be in his late twenties or early thirties and a lady of the same age introduced themselves to Ionnia. "We heard what happened back there," he said. He gave Ionnia his business card with the name Victor Zeme printed on it.

The name Zeme rang a bell. Ionnia was familiar with the names of some of Zeme's companies at home and abroad. *Is this the closest I will ever come to someone with that name?* she thought.

Victor was the nephew of the famous fashion designer Ryland Zeme. He described himself as an actuary with a major investment firm that controlled some of Puca Luca's prosperous banks and some insurance companies. Victor once taught accounts and economics at the Trevine Polytechnic Institute. He told Ionnia that his father, Kevin Zeme, maintained little or no contact with his half brother Ryland, but he kept track of his success.

Victor's wife, Mavis Zeme, née Muggerdon, talked with Ionnia about her ambitions, her goals, and her education. She was fascinated with Ionnia's interest in Zeme Industries and referred her to various magazines. Ionnia asked a lot of questions about the famous fashion designer, and the couple was impressed. "Here, I just happened to have these," Mavis said. She gave her some magazines.

Ionnia felt good. She loved to associate with dreamers. She had high hopes of turning adversity into something positive.

"Tell me, why are you traveling alone? And where are you headed?"

Ionnia told them about her grandmother and showed Mavis Zeme pictures of her family. Mavis's countenance changed as she probably recalled some of the injustices meted out to poor people by her family, and for the first time it appeared that she felt remorse and guilt. "You said you have relatives by the name of Dulvert?" asked Mavis. "Where are they from?"

When Ionnia told her, Mavis told her about her cousin Kingsley and how he constantly talked about a young girl from Redwood Vale by the name of Loretty Dulvert. "It seemed as if he was in love with her."

Ionnia became silent. Many thoughts raced through her head. "I never heard my mother mention that name to anyone. On the other hand, that's a discussion for adults, not children. But imagine how different life would have been if I were a Muggerdon instead of a Quane. Anyhow, it's no use crying over spilled milk."

Ionnia listened intently as Mavis told her about her family's achievements. She told Ionnia that Kingsley Muggerdon was the manager and owner of a chain of movie theaters throughout Puca Luca, and he was also a board member and partner of the MUJALI group of companies. She had heard her mother talk about that company but didn't know that Kingsley Muggerdon was affiliated with it.

Ionnia planned to ask her mother if she remembered the name and what would happen if she should see Kingsley Muggerdon again. What Ionnia didn't know was that Loretty had indeed met with him recently.

Ionnia was very relaxed and had almost forgotten about her phobia when Charlette's voice was heard over the intercom asking everyone to fasten their seatbelts. The aircraft made a jolt and a rapid descent because of turbulence. Charlette saw how scared Ionnia was and gave her literature that explained everything one needed to know about turbulence. Ionnia composed herself when she looked around and realized that the other passengers had exhibited no unusual signs of fear at this time. They were frequent fliers and were obviously used to these situations.

Carlton Drysdale had a lot to drink during the thirty-minute flight. He probably downed an entire bottle of whiskey. He periodically took out his wife's picture, held it up, and said, "People, now look at a beautiful woman."

No one looked his way, no one commented, and no one was interested.

Charlette approached him and said in a stern voice, "Please be quiet, Mr. Drysdale. If you keep this up, when we land, I will have you escorted off the plane by the police."

Forty-One

The day's excitement was truly eye-opening, and Ionnia looked forward to an uneventful evening. The aircraft touched down in San Clewert without any incident, and passengers in business class were the first to disembark. Ionnia retrieved her luggage and proceeded to the main entrance of the building, where she would wait to be picked up by her aunt Twyleith, who had arrived a few days earlier. She didn't have to wait long. Her aunt pulled up at the curb before she could put her luggage on the sidewalk. "Perfect timing, I don't have to wait here and be humiliated by anyone else."

They were putting the luggage in the car when Carlton Drysdale stumbled past them in a drunken stupor and headed toward the car rental area. "Freak!" he shouted in a very distasteful manner.

Twyleith spun around and asked, "What was that all about? I hope he wasn't referring to either of us."

Ionnia related the incident on the plane.

"Good God!" Twyleith said in amazement, her mouth agape. She grabbed a lug tool and looked in the direction where Drysdale was headed, and she just missed him as he hopped into a golf cart that was taking passengers to the rental area. She slammed the trunk of her car so hard that one could hear it from miles away.

"How did that monster's comments make you feel? I know you

were taught not to have confrontations with adults, but this time you would be excused for telling him what you thought of him."

Ionnia smiled at her aunt and said, "Auntie, a thoroughbred does not bark at a mongrel."

"Lethie Dulvert!" someone shouted from behind.

Twyleith turned around and recognized an old school friend, Priscilla Lennox, who had been married to Winston Dutte, otherwise known as Mr. Handsome.

"Imagine meeting you here," Twyleith said. "What brings you to this part of the world?"

"I could ask you the same question. But let me answer you." She smiled and said, "I am on a sleuthing mission."

"Are you with the media, or are you with law enforcement?" Twyleith asked.

"Neither."

Twyleith listened intently as her friend talked of the abuse meted out to her at the hands of her former husband, and how he'd left her for a younger woman. Priscilla had two children to raise on her own. She refused to divorce him. She monitored and traced his financial assets and transactions, making sure that his new girlfriend got nothing.

A leather-faced guard approached the trio and said, "Keep moving. You've been here for over fifteen minutes."

Priscilla looked at him questioningly and was about to tell him that they had been there less than five minutes, but he stood there pulling his beard and held his baton high in the air. They got the message.

"Look, Lethie. I had intended to rent a car, but can you give me a ride to Copper's Run so that we can continue talking about the good old days?"

"No problem. Hop in, and give me the address and directions."

The two women covered a lot in a short period of time. One could say that in these brief moments, Twyleith knew of more negative things in Priscilla's life than what she knew twenty years ago. "So tell me about of the good things that have occurred in your life," Twyleith said to her pal.

"My two children turned out well. Both graduated from the Trevine Polytechnic Institute and are now working for the government. I also had to raise one of my sister's children. Remember Bibbi? She died in childbirth. That girl of hers, Tourmaline, turned out to be a real ungrateful wench."

Ionnia sat in the back seat reading one of Zeme's magazines, and it almost fell out of her hands when Priscilla made the comment about Tourmaline. She couldn't help saying, "Wow."

"Is everything all right, dear?" Ionnia's aunt asked.

"Yes, Auntie. I was just looking at how awesome these designs are," she lied.

Priscilla switched the conversation from herself to Twyleith and said, "I have talked enough. You tell me what's going on with you these days, Lethie. Did you ever get married to Reginald Blevick?"

"Our friendship never matured into any meaningful relationship. Reggie completed high school and went on to the University of Trevine, where he studied political science. I heard he got married to Pauline Wrenlock. I'm happily married to Harold Gober. Remember him?"

"How could I forget Harold? He was the skinny boy who was the first to raise his hands in class. Mr. Know-It-All."

Before dropping Priscilla off in Copper's Run, the women exchanged addresses and phone numbers. "Please keep in touch," Twyleith said to her old schoolmate. "You certainly could use a shoulder now and then."

Twyleith and Ionnia headed down the highway toward the hospital. It began to rain. She veered to avoid the puddles of water in the huge potholes and nearly hit a young man who had attempted to hop onto the back of a pickup truck and lost his balance. When she merged on to the highway, she was held up for close to an hour due to an accident. Emergency, fire, ambulance, and police vehicles blocked both lanes, with the news helicopters hovering above. One rescue helicopter sat on the median, waiting to take the injured to the hospital.

While they waited, they talked about numerous topics from family to politics and the many rejections Ionnia had faced as a result of her disability. She talked about Ryland Zeme and Zemes Industries. She was almost obsessed with Zeme's success.

"Aunt Lethie, I know this is none of my business, but I'm curious to know about someone by the name of Kingsley Muggerdon. I heard he had a crush on Momma when they were much younger. How much do you know about that?"

"I know about my sister's and Kingsley's crush on each other; we talked about it once. There was nothing to it. You stay in touch with the Zemes, and if possible the Muggerdons. It is always good to hang out with dreamers. By the way, how and when did you learn about your mother and Mr. Muggerdon?"

Ionnia told her aunt what Mavis Zeme had told her on the plane.

Finally, the traffic started to move again. Ionnia changed the channels on the car radio. They heard the news of the traffic accident and how the rescue team had to use the Jaws of Life to get a drunk driver out of his car that had gotten stuck under an eighteen-wheel tractor trailer. Oh, what a tangled mess—literally. As a result of the impact, the cab of the eighteen-wheeler had smashed into two other vehicles. Several people in those other cars sustained injuries, but none as extensive as those sustained by the man who had caused the accident. He had to be air-rescued to the same hospital where Ionnia and her aunt were headed. The other injured people were taken to the hospital by ambulance.

As Twyleith and her niece arrived at the hospital, a doctor was heard shouting to a nurse, "Get me a few pints of AB negative blood, stat!"

"That's my blood type, Auntie," Ionnia said.

"Mine too, but you are not old enough to give blood. You have to be at least eighteen years old."

They noticed a voluptuous blonde in the waiting room crying uncontrollably. Ionnia recognized her from the picture Carlton flashed around in the plane. This was his wife. She was beautiful, all right, but she had a pair of breasts that would sink a cruise ship. The woman could hardly see her shoes. She ran clumsily back and forth from the elevator to the hallway and the waiting room, obviously confused.

"Please don't let my husband die," she screamed.

"Oh, no," Ionnia and Twyleith said simultaneously. "Could he be the one involved in the highway crash?"

Carlton should never have been behind the wheel of a car after the way he'd drunk on the plane. In many instances, blame could be placed on the airline crew for serving a passenger too much alcohol, but not in this case. It was reported that after Carlton disembarked, he'd stopped at one of the duty-free shops in the airport, purchased additional bottles of whiskey, and gotten himself wasted after he got into the car. A half-empty bottle was found in the car when it was towed to the police parking compound.

"Do you think the doctor wanted the AB negative blood for him, Aunt Lethie?"

"Maybe, but let someone else worry about that. You wouldn't be thinking of asking me to donate? Not even if he were going to pay me a million dollars, which I doubt he has."

They walked toward the elevator to get to the third floor, where Agnes Dunn lay dying.

"Hi there," came a voice from the other side of the hall. Ionnia swore she had heard that voice before. She looked around, and her eyes met with those of Stu Dent's.

"Stu, what are you doing here? You are like a spirit. You seem to show up at the right place and at the right time." Facing her aunt, she asked Stu, "Remember my aunt?"

"Sure. Hi, Miss T," he said as he offered his hand to Twyleith.

He stared at Ionnia for a long while and then said, "I'm running an errand for my mother."

Is he here to pick up a dead body, or bodies? she wondered. *Whatever the case, please don't let him start talking about it.*

Stu sensed that his friend and her aunt were curious about his presence at the hospital, so he said, "I'm here to look around for a bigger space to expand the small funeral home that we have not far from here." He directed his next comments toward Ionnia. "I hear that your blood type is in short supply."

The confused, weeping, top-heavy woman heard the conversation and turned around to face the trio. "Is that so? You have it? Then please help my husband."

Twyleith looked at her scornfully and said, "Freak."

"He is a good man," she sobbed. Pointing to her breasts, she said, "How will I finish paying for these if Carl dies? This can't be happening."

All three laughed so hard that they couldn't control themselves. Their laughter turned to tears. Twyleith bent over hysterical, her face almost touching the floor. When she caught hold of herself, she thought, *Maybe I should be feeling sorry for this woman after all, and also her pathetic husband.*

Ionnia told Stu what had taken place on the plane, so he got off the elevator and told Mrs. Drysdale the whole story. "Woman," he said, "would you really want any member of this young lady's family to save a man like this?"

"Carl will pay her whatever she charges, please," she pleaded. "Can you forgive him? I have never known him to be like that. Someone must have provoked him."

"Here we go again. Put the blame on someone, even the devil," Ionnia said.

"Good luck," Stu said scornfully to the weeping woman. "Bye, ladies," he said to Ionnia and her aunt. Then he continued on his errand, which was in the direction of the hospital morgue.

"Come on, Nevlyn. Let's go," Mrs. Drysdale's friend, Brenda, said as she hugged her and walked her back to the emergency room. "Someone will turn up with the right blood type and be willing to donate."

Carlton Drysdale remained in the hospital for a lengthy period, during which time he was slapped with many charges. There was also much controversy about whose insurance should pay the hospital bills: his, or his employer's.

When Twyleith heard the name Nevlyn, she spun around before the two disappeared. She pulled Brenda aside and whispered, "Tell me, is your friend from Brownsbridge?"

"Sure is," she responded. "Will this make a difference?"

"No. I just didn't recognize her. No wonder she behaves this way. The poor girl was hit in the head so many times."

In defense of her friend, Brenda said, "She may be behaving nutty now, but she sure is a very influential and persuasive person, both in her job and the organization with which she is affiliated."

"Do the place of employment and the volunteer organization have a name?"

"Nevlyn is the front desk person at the Listert Hotel, and she's a member of RAW. I'm sure that woman from Dartsdam who killed her husband could have benefited from my friend's seminars."

"Hold it right there, Brenda. That woman from Dartsdam is my sister, and she did not kill her husband. She has been charged with assault, and I can assure you that she will be acquitted because it was an act of self-defense."

So much for an anticipated uneventful day.

Forty-Two

Oh, how times changed people and events, and how events and time changed people. If anyone knew about abuse more than Loretty, it was Nevlyn Drysdale, née Vassale. She suffered physically and emotionally under the hands of her first husband, police corporal Clifford Ashvern. Her situation made the news headlines week after week, but with the help of caring relatives, she overcame. She grew up in an area where so-called pretty girls were not encouraged to get an education but rather were pressured by their parents, relatives, and friends to find someone, marry early, and have children. Nevlyn took their advice and married at the age of seventeen to someone much older than her, hoping that he would take care of her. Everyone thought that Cliffie was a nice gentleman who was paid to uphold the law and keep the peace, but he turned out to be cruel, jealous, and possessive toward this naïve country girl. Soon after the marriage, he started behaving as if he owned her. He treated her like property.

Nevlyn's parents owned a hospitality establishment; a restaurant, a bar, and a lounge downstairs, as well as a five-bedroom, five-bathroom lodging upstairs. Nevlyn helped out in multiple capacities, from housekeeping to being a waitress and hostess. Everyone was surprised that her husband allowed her to continue working at the establishment, but he found time while on patrol to visit her place of employment and pick fights with male patrons who held any type of conversation with his wife. He often threatened and intimidated people, continuously reminding them that he was in a position to arrest and slap charges on them that they would not be able to fight.

One such patron, Axley Washbuckle, experienced Clifford Ashvern's wrath in an incident that he would never forget. He had complimented Nevlyn for the string of pearls she was wearing, and Clifford decided to teach this man a lesson for flirting with his wife. Clifford had overheard him in the bar borrowing money from a friend to pay the insurance on his car, so the corporal set up a road-block, seized the man's car, and arrested him for driving an uninsured vehicle.

Clifford constantly sent his subordinates to spy on his wife, and if he ever received a report of her socializing with anyone, then when Nevlyn got home, he would beat her senseless. If and when she went to the emergency room at Whickam County General Hospital, she would tell the medical staff strange stories about how she got her concussions, fractures, lacerations, and bruises. None of the stories added up, but if the woman didn't want to press charges, the medical staff couldn't pursue the arrest of the abuser. Clifford Ashvern got away with assault on his wife time after time. His abuse and neglect continued until Nevlyn decided that she would report this to her husband's supervising officers, but they looked the other way and did little to help her. They dismissed the allegations, claiming that they did not believe her—and even if they did, they would ask her what she did to provoke her husband. He would report some made-up stories by telling them that his wife was an epileptic, and when she fell, she hurt herself. However, when an appointment was made to admit her for an evaluation, he refused to have her undergo the procedure.

Nevlyn became pregnant soon after the marriage, but that ended in a miscarriage due to her husband's beatings, and so did the second pregnancy a few months later. Her husband blamed the miscarriages on the stress of her having to work, so he talked to her parents and convinced them that he could take care of his wife, and there was no need for her to continue helping out at the establishment. By keeping her at home, he avoided having to explain her wounds to her parents or anyone else. He isolated her from her parents, who could visit only after making an appointment with him.

Nevlyn stayed home, cooked, cleaned, and performed her wifely duties whenever her husband demanded it. She reluctantly performed the bedroom duties, which she came to resent and viewed as a chore rather than something to be enjoyed. Most of the time, she faked it, and her husband told her that he was experienced enough to recognize what she was doing. He was also experienced enough to know that he could do something to get her in the mood, so one night he forced a kiss on her after coming home after midnight without any explanations. The kiss nauseated Nevlyn so much that instead of reciprocating or even pretending enjoyment, she vomited in his mouth. If Clifford should come home and the domestic chores weren't done, he would threaten her with his service revolver. He would drop his socks and other pieces of clothes all over the house and then shout at her to pick them up and put them away. He never fired a shot at her, but he hit her on her head with it on different occasions.

Nevlyn never saw her husband's paychecks. He did all the shopping. He even bought her clothes, saying that he did not want her to dress like a slut. If she were lucky, he might give her a small allowance. She no longer could keep her longtime friends because Clifford was afraid they would influence his wife, but his friends and coworkers would be allowed to visit the home. Nevlyn did her best to entertain them when they came over, but because she wasn't very educated, she was not allowed to participate in their conversations. If she attempted to do so, he would shout at her and tell her to shut up. He would later tell her not to embarrass him in front of his friends.

A frequent guest at the Ashvern residence was Inspector Marion Klute, one of Clifford's girlfriends. Nevlyn was so naïve that she never suspected anything was going on between them, despite hints from some of his own friends. Moreover, what could she say or do about it that would cause the relationship to end?

Clifford never ran out of made-up stories about his wife's mental state, and he claimed that many of her wounds were self-inflicted. He told people who would listen that he suspected his wife of suffering from a factitious disorder called Munchausen syndrome. This was a psychiatric disorder in which someone feigned or exaggerated an illness in order to draw attention or sympathy to themselves. He once tried to get Nevlyn committed to the psychiatric ward at Whickam County General Hospital, but the doctors found no reason to commit her despite the fact that they said she was suffering from postpartum depression after having her second miscarriage. Instead, she was kept under observation for eight hours and then sent home.

Nevlyn thought of using her husband's service revolver to kill him when he was asleep, and she convinced herself that her actions would be justified because he had already labeled her as insane. However, she didn't want to sacrifice her freedom for someone the likes of Clifford Ashvern. "There's got to be a different way out," she said, She finally revealed to her parents the magnitude of the abuse. They could no longer sit idly by and watch what was happening to their daughter, so one time when Clifford was out of the area on a special weapons training course for a week, Mr. Vassale went to his daughter's matrimonial home, packed her belongings, chartered a ferry, and sent her away to Mumfries Harbor to stay with one of his sisters, Clover Fishley. He was afraid to use the public ferry system in case people realized what was happening and alerted Clifford. Clifford would likely alert the coast guard to intercept the ferry and retrieve his wife.

When Clifford returned home from training, he was stunned to discover Nevlyn gone. He contacted her parents and some friends he knew she'd had before they were married, but he could not get any information as to the whereabouts of his wife. The parents pretended to grieve, kept mum throughout, and promised, "We will let you know should she make contact with us."

Clifford had no idea that they were involved in rescuing their daughter from a life of tyranny. "I swear I am going to teach her a lesson when I find her."

"Don't you dare think of doing anything that you would regret. You think you are untouchable, but I would have a big surprise for you," Mrs. Vassale warned.

Corporal Ashvern was taken aback to hear his mother-in-law express herself this way, but instead of humbling himself, he shot back, "Well, then, you should have taught her how to be a faithful wife."

"So now you are blaming me for your inability to be a civilized human being?"

Mr. Vassale interrupted the heated exchange between his wife and his soon to be former son-in-law. "Get off my premises, you sadistic son of a itch. We are not afraid of you, and you are not the only one who knows how to use a gun."

Nevlyn settled down in Mumfries Harbor under the assumed name of Totlyn Borgarn. Her aunt Clover encouraged her to join Rescuing Abused Women (RAW), of which Clover was president. Clover distributed Clifford Ashvern's pictures among the group with instructions to report any sightings of him. This was the first time in three years that Nevlyn displayed any semblance of happiness.

But after six months passed, one afternoon Nevlyn said to her aunt, "I was thinking about Clifford, and I feel it's time for me to go back home to him."

"Are you for real?"

"I love my husband, and I miss him a lot. I keep wondering who is cooking his food and doing his laundry."

Clover was appalled. "And I'm sure you are also wondering who is screwing him. You may have physically left him, but you seem to be still psychologically connected. Your wounds may have appeared to be healed, but apparently you have not learned your lesson. How do you plan to go through life being stupid?"

That really got to Nevlyn, so she took Aunt Clover up on her earlier offer to help her file for divorce. She retained the services of one of RAW's attorneys, Sarihey Bell-Dourhey. Clifford Ashvern contested this and tried to mediate reconciliation, which didn't work out. He was ordered to stay away from Nevlyn and to direct all communications through her attorney. Nevlyn received an adequate amount of money, and Clifford was obligated to pay her alimony until she remarried. She would also receive half of his pension when he retired whether or not she remarried. Needless to say, he was more than livid about this decision. Nevlyn was now a free woman. She went back to school and got a diploma in hotel management.

While working at the Listert Hotel, she participated in a radio call-in contest and won a weekend cruise on the maiden voyage of the *Rigvonette*, a prestigious ocean liner owned by the MUJALI Group of Companies. This was her first time going on a cruise, and she was very excited. She would be meeting people of consequence and would be able to hold intelligent conversations with them.

Many of the company's employees were privileged to get specially reduced rates to go on this cruise. After sailing for three hours, the ship entered rough waters. Huge waves slapped the *Rigvonette,* and she rocked back and forth. The passengers were taken off guard.

This incident conjured up memories of the *Titanic.* The ship leaned to the port side, mainly from being top-heavy, and the majority of passengers were hurled in that direction. Some passengers held steadfastly to whatever and whomever they could get their hands on. Some fell on top of other people, and others puked all over each other. These were scary, frightful moments.

Nevlyn fell on top of Carlton Drysdale, a sales associate for MUJALI. When the ship straightened, they looked into each other's eyes. Nevlyn became very nauseous and regurgitated all over Carlton's face. He took her to a comfortable area of the ship, grabbed a bottle of beer that had rolled to his feet, and used that to wash his face. Then he accompanied her to her cabin. She was suffering from the worst case of motion sickness, and the ship's medical team distributed medication to Nevlyn and all others who were affected.

Carlton befriended Nevlyn for the duration of the cruise, and he was kind, loving, caring, and compassionate to her. She concluded that this was a blessing in disguise. She was happy that someone showed her so much attention. He kept in touch with her after she returned to Mumfries Harbor, and their friendship blossomed into a romantic one. Carlton impressed Nevlyn as the perfect person. She was swept off her feet with flowers, generous gifts, and frequent trips to various locations. They had fallen in love with each other, but she approached with caution. "Once bitten, twice shy," she often repeated.

Four months after the memorable *Rigvonette* trip, on Nevlyn's birthday, Carlton held her in his arms and said, "I love you too much to wait any longer for you to be my wife." Not waiting for her to say anything, he kissed her passionately and popped the question. "Will you ...?"

Before he could finish the sentence, she said, "Yes," but not with much enthusiasm. There was no engagement ring, but Nevlyn never seemed to mind. She loved Carlton and believed him when he told her that the following week, they would buy the rings.

She told her aunt about the proposal. "I am happy for you," her aunt said, "but never let another man put his hands on you. If he ever makes an attempt, you know what to do."

Weeks went by, and all this time Nevlyn was unaware that Carlton was making secret plans to get married as soon as possible. He managed to get hold of Nevlyn's private information and subsequently obtained a marriage license. He had spoken to two of his friends,; Judge Edgar Rusk and Desty Nation, a coworker, and invited them to his wedding. On their way from the jewelry store, he said to Nevlyn, "Call your cousin Erica and another friend, and ask them to meet us downtown at the restaurant in the Dalfries Hotel for lunch, I want it to be a very special occasion."

Nevlyn made the call to her cousin Erica Vassale and her friend Pam Tweedley, who both worked with the Public Works Department in Mumfries Harbor. "What's the occasion?" Erica asked.

"I just want you to get to know my fiancé."

After a sumptuous meal was served and several bottles of liquor were consumed, Carlton took out the rings and showed them to the group. Each person took a turn holding them, and the gasps could be heard across the restaurant. Patrons seated at other tables stretched their necks to see what the commotion was about. Some even came over and offered their congratulations to the couple. Nevlyn and her friends were still clueless that this was her wedding day. When it was Judge Edgar Rusk's turn to hold the rings, he looked at everyone and asked, "Well, does anyone have any just cause why these two should not be joined today in holy matrimony?"

The girls were taken by surprise. Nevlyn sat motionless as a rock. The others had barely got over Carlton Drysdale's extravagance and were just now processing the judge's question. No one was dressed for a wedding in the traditional ways, but Carlton didn't care.

"Is this a joke, an inebriated prank?" Pam asked. Soon they realized the seriousness of the judge's question, and Carlton had arranged for this day to make Nevlyn his wife.

"How could you do this to me, Carlton?" Nevlyn asked.

"I just want to make you happy," he said as he pulled her closer to him, grinning like a teenager.

Nevlyn said, "I was hoping that if and when I decided to get married again, I would have the opportunity to invite my parents and Aunt Clover to my wedding."

"We can have a church wedding later and invite all your friends and relatives. Then we can have a huge party afterward," Carlton promised.

"We need pictures," Desty interrupted. He looked around for someone carrying a camera. "Bingo!" he exclaimed as if he had won the lottery. Over at one of the tables in the far corner of the restaurant, he saw a young lady with a camera with her handbag.

"That's Sally Kastrineckiss," Judge Rusk said. "She is our crime scene photographer and always carries different types of cameras with her.

Desty went over and whispered something to her. She smiled obligingly, got a bigger camera out of her bag, and accompanied Desty to the table, where his group was sitting. She recognized Judge Rusk, who introduced her to everyone. "She is single too," he added, looking in Desty's direction.

"Let's get this show on the road," Carlton said.

Carlton took Nevlyn's hand gently and beckoned to Judge Rusk. The ceremony was over in less than five minutes. Sally took the pictures and gave the negatives to Carlton, who compensated her handsomely for her efforts. She made quite an impression on the group and one person in particular, the irresistible Desty Nation.

Nevlyn's friends and family were shocked at the news of the wedding, but they wished her well and hoped that this marriage would be a happier one than the first.

Not long after the wedding, Carlton began making snide remarks about the size of Nevlyn's breasts, comparing her to other women he knew. He made her feel uncomfortable as a 34B, and he constantly referred to her as his flat-chested wife. Her self-esteem was shattered. She began obsessing about a 38DD or 40D, so finally Carlton decided to let her have breast augmentations. Neither one could get an insurance company to pay for it.

Forty-Three

When Ionnia and her aunt arrived at her grandma's room, Agnes Dunn was in good spirits considering what she was going through. She looked beautiful, her complexion was clear, and whenever she opened her eyes, they shone like new coins. She was getting morphine intravenously and didn't appear to be suffering. She seemed to have taken comfort that the end was near, and she wasn't afraid.

"This is the calm before the storm," Twyleith said as she held her niece tightly and gave a big sigh.

Nurse Baruke entered the room and paused the flow of morphine and sedation fluids so that the relatives could have a conversation. Ionnia hugged her grandma and cried. She filled in the blanks about her life. Grandma said very little, but when she did, she urged Ionnia to continue excelling in school.

Agnes had a very pleasant and humorous roommate, Mrs. Geraldine Penny, who told Ionnia folk stories and real stories of her own family. She went on to tell Ionnia that she should see herself as a special person who was born to fulfill a special purpose in life, and she should never get discouraged.

Ionnia thanked her and gave her a big hug, and then she went back to Grandma's side.

"One last thing before my sun sets: do not let your mother's experience deter you from getting married. Promise me," Agnes pleaded with her granddaughter.

Ionnia felt badly that she would probably not be able to grant her grandma's dying wish, so as she moistened the woman's lips with pieces of ice that lay in a small cup on the night stand, she said, "I'll think about it, Grandma, but I really didn't have that on my agenda. Momma has four sons. She really doesn't need a son-in-law. And remember, my name has already been changed, I don't have to go through life using the name Quane."

The nurse reappeared and noticed that Agnes may be in pain, so she resumed the flow of morphine and sedation fluid, which soon took effect on Agnes. As the two continued their conversation, Agnes drifted off into a deep sleep. Ionnia pulled the sheets up to her grandma's shoulders and went with Aunt Twyleith to the gift shop on the second floor of the building.

"Can I get you anything, Miss G?" Ionnia asked her grandma's roommate.

"Just run along and promise you will take care of yourself. My boyfriend will be here soon. I don't know what's taking him so long."

As soon as Ionnia and Aunt Twyleith walked into the gift shop, the attendant approached them and politely asked, "Can I help you?" Twyleith's eyes met the woman's, and they stared at each other. It was Cassandra Lawfries. That was the second high school friend Twyleith had run into that day.

"Imagine meeting you here after so many years," Twyleith said as the both women embraced each other. Aunt Lethie beckoned to Ionnia. "Select the flowers and other gift items for Grandma while Cass and I reminisce on the good old days."

Before they began to talk about personal issues, Twyleith told Cass about her mother, and Cass promised to visit her as often as possible for the few days she had left on this side of heaven.

Just as Priscilla had done, Cassandra had nothing good to say about her husband, Elwin Dutte, brother of Priscilla's husband, Winston Dutte. The most shocking part was that he'd left her for her own mother.

"Most merciful God, how could a mother do that to her own daughter?" Twyleith asked. "You could never be the same again. You poor soul. This may be a little harsh, what I am going to say, but remember it. Your family is your misfortune, but your husband is your fault. You just happened to pick the wrong man. How did you meet him?"

"During the redevelopment of Dartsdam, men from various areas of Puca Luca were brought in for the installation of the area's infrastructure. The Dutte brothers were members of the team employed by Puca Luca Public Service Company to run telephone lines and erect electric lights in Dartsdam and the surrounding areas. Many of the men stayed in a guesthouse in Farnsworth run by my mother, Zelda. Obviously, she was not only serving food to these men, and no one knows how many others she slept with."

"How long were you married to this jerk?"

"It lasted 17,640 hours."

"Come on, Cass. Give it to me simpler than this. Math is not my strongest subject," Twyleith said as she leaned slightly on one of the display cabinets and waited for an answer.

"Two years and five days," Cassandra said.

"Any children?"

"One little girl, Daisy. We call her Bubbles."

On hearing these names, Ionnia spun around. She couldn't believe what she was hearing. First, it was Priscilla talking about Tourmaline. Now, Cass was talking about Bubbles. Ionnia hit the rewind button and went back to the events at the train station. *Have I just stumbled on the woman who abandoned her child on the train?* she asked herself. *Should I confront Cass?* She restrained herself, and opted to tell her aunt later on. *Let the adults handle it.*

"Thank goodness your mother didn't have any children with him," Twyleith said to Cassandra.

Cass let out a little moaning sound and gazed blankly at Twyleith. "She has a little girl by the name of Jasmine. That is Bubbles' sister and aunt, and my sister, all in one. How do I explain this complicated situation to Bubbles? Will she understand this confusion?"

"So where is Bubbles now?" Twyleith queried. "You will have to tell her someday, or she will find out from other people. What if her father wants custody?"

Cassandra walked away and started attending to another customer without answering the questions. It was then that Twyleith realized how fragile Cass was. When Cass returned to where her friend was standing, she was a little shaken, and then she opened up about her past mental breakdown. She told Twyleith that not long ago, she had been a patient at a hospital after her attempted suicide. That was when she again mentioned Bubbles and said that the girl was living with a friend in another town. "I can't take care of her now. I'm sure when I'm stable enough to raise my daughter, Naomi will not be selfish and will give her back to me. At least, that's what we had agreed on. My little Daisy deserves her mother, but right now she needs a very loving and stable family. Elwin Dutte will never know where she is."

Oh, my God. If she only knew what was happening to her child, Ionnia said to herself. *It was good that I didn't say anything.*

Cass told Twyleith that close to her release from the hospital, the social worker assisted her in getting the job in the gift shop, as well as an apartment at an affordable rate. This allowed her to reestablish her independence and gain easy access to the hospital for treatment because she didn't drive. She lived in a two-bedroom apartment across the street, and she invited Twyleith and Ionnia to have supper at her place and stay over if it became necessary.

"Thanks, but we are staying with a relative down by the ocean."

"Who?" Cass asked.

"Zaccheus Mann."

"You mean the retired commander of the Puca Luca coast guard who now owns a fleet of mail boats?"

"That's the one."

Cassandra spoke to Twyleith about her therapy sessions with her psychiatrist, Dr. Elsworth Gevannes, adding that she felt very safe with him. The way she spoke about Dr. Gevannes was almost suggestive that something in the form of a relationship was going on between them, but Twyleith knew that Dr. Gevannes upheld the ethical principles of his profession and would not be intimately involved with any of his patients. Dr. Gevannes was on the mental health team that treated and evaluated Loretty at Blovingworth Mental.

Before Twyleith could poke her nose further in her friend's business, Ionnia rejoined the group. Cass rang up the items, and they headed toward the elevator to return to Agnes's room. Once again they bumped into Nevlyn Drysdale. This time the drama subsided because the doctors had assured her that her husband was in surgery and that would be okay. He had gotten the blood he needed from Desty's new girlfriend, Sally Kastrineckiss. Carlton's condition was critical but stable at this time, and the battle waged on as to who would be responsible for paying his hospital expenses. Would MUJALI accept the claim knowing that the accident was caused by Carlton due to his inebriation?

Ionnia wanted so much to tell her aunt about Bubbles and what had happened on the train, but she again decided against it. *Cass couldn't know about this. She would have another breakdown.* She posed other questions instead. "Auntie, what do you think happened to this little girl? Do you think she is safe? Do you think Cass really knows where her daughter is?"

"Maybe she is telling the truth, and maybe the child is better off where she is. Remember that Cass was hospitalized and in outpatient treatment for a while. She did not have the capacity to raise a child during that period." Twyleith said. "And even if Bubbles is found, do we hand her over to Cass? How do you think the new parents would fccl about giving her up at this time?"

"Auntie, I know where to find Bubbles."

"Say what?"

Ionnia finally gave her aunt the details of what had happened on the train.

Forty-Four

Agnes Dunn's final exit came at 9:30 that night. Her treating physicians reported that she didn't suffer in her final moments on Earth. Ionnia placed a call to Velma Dent's Mortuary and Crematorium regarding the embalmment of Agnes Dunn's body. Luckily, Stu was still in San Clewert, and his mother immediately made contact with him. When they met this time, Stu offered some much-welcomed comfort to Ionnia during this period of bereavement. This was the first time that they both hugged each other like they wanted to, not as though they had to.

"I will be there for you. I will attend the funeral not just in my official capacity but also as your friend."

"Thanks, and I hope you understand how much I appreciate your friendship."

"It's mutual."

Twyleith contacted the rest of the family to give them the bad news. When she told Cyril Dulvert that Agnes had died, his response was, "Thank God."

She tried to figure out what he meant but preferred to wait until she met with him the following day to make arrangement for the funeral and interment. Dee Dee was with her when she confronted him about this. "I was only expressing my feelings that Agnes's suffering had come to an end. I just couldn't bear to see her suffer for a long time like Lucille Butts," he said.

"Let me remind you," Twyleith said, "my mother was nothing like that woman. You have to remember that Lucille was a very hateful person who had nothing good to say about any human being. She showed her preference to dogs and cats."

Dee Dee had to say her piece. "Don't forget that the old, dried prune never told her stepdaughter, Lyneithe Butts, that her father had died. It was on Father's Day when Lyneithe called to wish her father a happy Father's Day, and the woman told her he had died three months prior and she shouldn't call her house anymore."

"So what was the reason why this girl did not keep in touch with her father?" Ionnia asked.

"The woman was so jealous, controlling, and obnoxious, she wouldn't allow her husband to answer the phone. If she found out that he made contact with his daughter, she would threaten to throw him out. She forbade him to leave anything in his will to his daughter."

"What did she do with his money and property?"

"She left everything to the animal hospital in Wellane."

Agnes Dunn's funeral was scheduled to take place a week after her death, in her hometown of Redwood Vale. Ionnia had made contact with the extended family in Krepston. "I won't be back till after the funeral," she told her mother.

"Our sincere condolences," Berdene Ryte said. "This family and the church members are here for you. Is there anything you need? We definitely plan to be there."

"Could you please bring my black-and-white polka dot dress for me? This is my favorite dress."

Arrangements were made to bring along the Mount Mathuveh Youth Choir, of which Ionnia was a member. A request was made to the minister at the Redwood Vale Church to have Bishop Ryte assist with the ceremony. Ionnia's three friends, Lorna, Ordrette, and Nickie, would also attend to give her support.

An hour before the start of the service, the casket was opened, and friends and relatives got their last opportunity to view Agnes Dunn's body. As she lay in the casket, light from the stained-glass window fell on her face and gave her a pleasing look that was suggestive of peace and comfort. Her face also wore an expression as if she was dreaming of something extremely pleasant and unforgettable. The Dents did a god job covering up the dents in Agnes's old body. She deserved this and was a good woman.

The chief officiating minister at the funeral, Pastor Duke Blaggin of Redwood Vale, had this to say of Agnes Dunn. "She was a woman who lived and touched many lives with her kindheartedness and humility. She was one who helped others and never boasted about it. She was faithful to her family, her friends, and her God. In life, she was very forgiving, and she was willing to intervene and fix things. She never did anyone any harm."

He challenged the congregation to follow Agnes Dunn's example, and should they choose to do so, they too would receive the crown of life from their heavenly Father. He referenced her life as one filled with precious memories, and immediately the Redwood Vale choir erupted with the hymn "Precious Memories." They were joined by the Mount Mathuveh choir.

The visitors from Krepston were well received. Their performance received standing ovations from the congregation, who asked for an encore. This was like a concert rather than a funeral, and it was the biggest event Redwood Vale had ever seen since the memorial service held for a Muggerdon some years ago.

Ionnia eulogized her grandmother and sang her favorite song, "Across the Bridge." She did not wander through events that were less memorable in Agnes Dunn's life; rather, she spoke of the values for which the woman stood. She came down from the rostrum, kissed her fingertips, and slowly pressed them to her grandma's forehead. An eerie sensation overcame her, followed by a calm that indicated to her that letting go would be easy.

Cyril Dulvert spoke and forced a tear. Everyone knew him as a heartless person and wondered whether these tears were real. Maybe these were tears of guilt. Cyril spoke of his love for Agnes and stated that she was his only true love, and he would certainly miss her. Someone at the back of the church let out a deep sigh and said, "Liar."

Inside the church, Cyril sat beside Claudia Bundle, Agnes's close friend and neighbor. Rumor had it that one of her children was fathered by Cyril Dulvert, but because Claudia was married at the time, no one made any extra trouble by trying to prove whether this was true. Mr. Bundle was one of those men who believed that when a man was married to a woman, he took responsibility for her children whether or not he was the biological father. Darrell and his brother Leroy had distinct characteristics that came from their father, Nathaniel Bundle, so as time went by, the matter was laid to rest.

Other prominent people remembered Agnes as a caring, loving person who would go out of her way to help anyone in need. Darrell Bundle, now a county commissioner who was close friends with Agnes Dunn's first son, Curtis, said, "Miss Agnes was my second mother. I can recall those difficult days when my father was very ill and my mother had no food. Miss Agnes shared whatever she had with us. We could always depend on her. I can also remember how Miss Agnes would collect pieces of board, old nails, and other waste construction material, giving them to her sons and me to make go-carts. Because of her, we won many prizes in the annual Redwood Vale Go-Cart Derby."

There was laughter among the congregation. "Thank you," Darrell continued. "We are here to celebrate this wonderful woman's life, not to mourn her passing. So cheer up, and as she was famous of saying, 'In the midst of adversity we should find comfort.'"

Outside the church, Darrell Bundle spoke with Loretty and consoled her. He let her know that he was familiar with the charges she'd faced as a result of the death of her husband. "If there's anything I can do to help, please let me know. I will keep my promise to you to ensure that your children get part-time summer jobs to help offset the cost of their education."

Stu introduced Ionnia to his mother, who already knew a lot about her. Mrs. Dent patted her on the shoulder and said, "I am truly sorry about all the things you have been through. Stu told me. How are you holding up?"

"Better than expected," Ionnia replied politely. "Thanks for asking, Mrs. Dent."

Ionnia then quoted Garrison Kellior, a twentieth-century author. "'It's a shallow life that does not give a person a few scars.'"

"I'm impressed," Velma Dent remarked.

Ionnia also remembered the analogy of the pencil told to her by Mrs. Penny, and she said, "I think my life has purpose, and whatever it was that I was born to accomplish, I am determined to fulfill this accomplishment, which was strongly encouraged by my grandmother. All the struggles I've been through have prepared me for what lies ahead."

"I would like to talk with you some more. Can I invite you to my home?" Mrs. Dent said. At no time did she mention Stu's interest in Ionnia. How much did she know? What had he told her? "My younger daughter, Sharlette, is around your age. The two of you should get together sometimes. She could learn a lot from you. You are certainly an inspiration."

Stu never discussed his siblings, and she never asked him, so Ionnia asked Mrs. Dent, "Is Sharlette an only girl, just like me?"

"No, I have another daughter, Petronia. She is ten years older than Stu."

"Does she live with you too?"

"After she finished college, she got married to Basil Oop's youngest son, Sylvester. They lived in a mansion at Pointer's Bluff."

Pointer's Bluff, a community for the very rich and famous, was a well-designed community established ten years ago by wealthy real estate developer Armond Bevitt. He took great pride in ensuring that the quality and security of the community were maintained. The homes were built around a small airport, with each resident owning his or her own airplane. Everyone also owned a medium-sized boat anchored in the Pointer's Bluff Marina.

Despite Petronia being a Pointer's Bluff socialite, people always turned their heads whenever she signed her name, "P. Oop."

Petronia's husband, Sylvester, had acquired most of his fortune and his generosity from his grandfather, who was popularly known as Mr. Philanthropy. He continued to support his grandfather's charitable organizations after his death. Sylvester's pet project was education, and each year a number of children received scholarships to different secondary and tertiary institutions in Puca Luca and the surrounding islands.

Ionnia met some elementary school friends and family acquaintances at the funeral. For the first time, she met all of her mother's brothers and sisters, and for the first time since Leonard Dulvert had dropped her off his bus in the middle of nowhere, Ionnia got the chance to confront him about it. Lennie pretended that he didn't remember anything about the incident, but his son Max overheard the conversation and intervened. His father tried to shut him up, but Max insisted, "It's time you apologize to your niece."

"It's okay, Uncle Lennie. Be a man. Go ahead and apologize. I have learned to forgive," Ionnia assured him.

"Okay, I apologize," Lennie said reluctantly, and he appeared embarrassed as he did so. It was so insincere that she couldn't help being reminded of the saying "All wood and no ply make Jack a dull board."

Max added his apologies too. "I'm sorry, cousin, and I wish that I'd known who you were before I told my father about the fare. Can you forgive me too?"

Ionnia hugged Max and told him that she forgave him. But she reminded him that that was no way to treat a child no matter who that child was. They also talked about what could have happened to her while she waited by the side of the road.

"Would you and your father have felt guilty if I had been attacked, kidnapped, raped, or killed?"

Max hung his head. "Guess what? I am not going to wait any longer to ask God to forgive me." With that said, he headed back into the church and kneeled at the altar. He must have been there for a good five minutes, and when he came back, he was teary-eyed.

His mother, Maxine, who had overheard the conversation, followed her son into the church and threatened to drive the fear of God into him if he didn't repent. This was the first time Maxine was hearing the story. She took her son and her husband aside and told them, "I am appalled at the both of you for treating Ionnia the way you did. I am surprised that Agnes did not tell me about it."

At the cemetery, Loretty's youngest sister, Arthel, walked past her and muttered, "Murderer."

Loretty was not going to let her get away with this. She followed her and said, "If I were a killer, I would have killed all of you and disposed of your frail little bodies when my mother deprived me of an education to take care of you. Your lives were in my hands, remember? But at this time, I am proud of my success and the educational achievements of my five children. Tell me something, Arthel. Can you say the same about your family—the ones who were fortunate to survive? The nerve of you to call me a murderer. How dare you! How many abortions have you had? How ironic that we should find a cemetery within a cemetery."

With that said, Arthel took off so fast that she stubbed her toe on the root of a tree and almost fell flat on her face.

Loretty's father, Cyril Dulvert, avoided Loretty and her family as much as possible. He barely spoke to her, even when she made attempts to speak to him. As for Ionnia, she said little to her grandfather beyond "Hi, Grandpa," and she didn't even wait for a response. She resented him in a way that when she introduced the members of her extended family to her biological family, she did not include him. However, Bishop Ryte went over to him and offered his condolences.

Claudia Bundle gave Ionnia a big hug. "I am so proud of you for having turned into the focused young lady you have had grown up to be. I had no doubt in my mind that you would be anything less than successful."

Ionnia and Claudia talked briefly about Cordell, who was popularly known among racing enthusiasts as the Whip because of the thinness of his frame, his riding talent, and his expert mastery of the riding crop. Ionnia had read in the newspapers, heard on the radio, and seen on the television the great jockey Cordell had become. He had taken Quigland Park by storm, winning sixty-eight races in one year. He was the top jockey in Puca Luca and was sought after by owners of different stables. His latest accomplishment was winning the Atlantic Derby aboard the famous racehorse Rice Pudding, from the stables of Melton Locksley. Cordell was also named Jockey of the Year.

What Claudia conveniently forgot to tell Ionnia was one incident that occurred at the track in which Cordell had almost lost his life. He fell during a race and was trampled by several other horses. It was his father, Darrell Bundle, who filled in Ionnia. Cordell sustained many broken bones and internal injuries, and he had to be out of commission for a long while. At first his prognosis was good, but then things took a turn for the worse. But luck was on his side. He was treated by one of the best doctors that Melton Locksley's money could pay for. Cordell recovered satisfactorily, and his father and grandmother discouraged him from returning to Quigland Park. However, racing was in his blood. He loved what he did and was soon back in the saddle as an exercise rider for a few months. Then he regained his place as the number one jockey.

The first thing that went through Ionnia's mind was that time when she had been trampled by Cordell's mule. *So now he knows how it feels to be trampled by animals that size.* She was so absorbed in her thoughts that she didn't notice her two older brothers standing beside her.

"Hey, sis, are you okay?"

Ionnia spun around and held their hands. "I'm fine. I just miss my grandmother so much."

They complimented her for her performance earlier. "We might just start calling you Star," Chad remarked proudly.

"And this star owes her life to you. I have heard the whole story over and over from different relatives and friends," she said to her big brother.

Nine days after Agnes Dunn was buried, Cyril Dulvert was hell-bent on burning her clothes, but Claudia Bundle heard about this and put a stop to it.

"How dare you dishonor Agnes's memory in this fashion!" she hollered at him.

After the scolding from Claudia, Cyril hung his head like a wounded dog. Was this a sign that he regretted his actions? Claudia almost felt sorry for him. She gathered Agnes's belongings and stored them in one of the empty rooms at her house. "She is not coming back to do you any harm, although God knows she certainly should."

Some of Agnes's daughters were told about their father's actions and how Claudia had stopped him. They took offence to their father's behavior, and Felicity, Arthel, and Dee Dee threatened to stay away from him.

Forty-Five

This phase of the celebration of Agnes Dunn's life was over, and now it was time for the members of the church group from Krepston to return home. Bishop Ryte, Berdene, and Nickie stayed at a small hotel in nearby Brownsbridge that owned and operated by Cassandra Dutte's mother, Zelda. They wanted to be with Ionnia until she felt comfortable to leave her biological family.

The driver and owner of the chartered bus was accountable for all her passengers, so she did a head count and discovered that Minta Turnston, one of the female members of the choir, was nowhere to be found. Although everyone was concerned about her, they could only hope that she would find her way back home safely.

"She is an adult," the driver said, revving up the engine. "I'm sure she can take care of herself. We've got to get going."

It was observed that earlier in the day, while everyone was celebrating Agnes Dunn's life in the church, Minta was thinking of something that she knew best: having sex with a stranger. While she sang on the choir, she surveyed the congregation, and her roving eyes met those of Ashton Denton. He worked at a meat-packaging plant in Gravadee County, where his cousin Grant Dulvert was a supervisor. He seemed to be unable to compose himself and control his emotions over the death of his favorite aunt. Unlike most of the other members of the family who attended the funeral with their wives, Ashton was unaccompanied and was still a single man. As soon as the choir ended the last note, Minta headed toward the young man, offered him words of comfort, took his handkerchief, and wiped his eyes. He held her hands throughout the rest of the service, and she cherished every moment of the attention. Minta was seen leaving with him, and no one thought anything at the time because everyone was headed to the cemetery where Agnes's body would be interred. Everyone made it to the cemetery except Ashton and his newfound comforter. They were later seen around thirty miles from Redwood Vale in the LeCoserve Motel, Restaurant, and Bar.

"We knew she was up to something," Lavern Wrecketts, the bus driver, said.

Minta had a very interesting past. She was always in the habit of picking up men wherever she could find them, and her parents feared that one day she would be killed by one of those strangers.

After finishing high school, Minta was sent away to a Catholic university to pursue a course in social work, but as the saying went, "A leopard never changes its spots." Minta's out-of-control libido resulted in her expulsion from the university after having completed only one term. When men talked about Minta, they would refer to her as Breezy or Nightmare.

When men used her and disposed of her, they would remark, "No one wants a serious relationship with this easy person. We only want a piece of the action."

Minta's first serious relationship started when she began working as a classification clerk at one of the jails in Blackburne County. The convicted prisoners were placed at this facility while they waited to be transferred to different prisons or jails based on the crimes they'd committed and the length of the sentences that had been handed down. It was Ms. Turnston's duty to prepare the list for the transfers.

One of the wardens, Ivanhoe Banderson, couldn't get enough of Minta, so he persuaded her to marry him. But if he wanted a monogamous relationship, this was the biggest mistake he could have made. Minta couldn't resist sleeping around with family members of some of the prisoners in exchange for them being sent to a facility nearer home, or to declassify them from a medium-security facility to a minimum-security facility. When her husband found out, he went to her parents and said, "Prepare yourself for a funeral, because I swear to God I am going to kill your daughter."

The Turnstons brought their daughter home and offered to help her free herself from the grips of marriage. "Instead of a divorce, you can get an annulment," her father suggested.

"What's the difference?" she asked.

"If you do some research, you will find out that an annulment is the legal invalidity of marriage. Your marriage will be declared null and void."

"Void from its inception, as if it never happened," her mother added. "This is better than a divorce."

"Really?"

"Yes. Divorce is not retroactive."

After leaving Dragon Bay in Blackburne County, Minta got a job as a clerical assistant and sales associate with a major chain of furniture store in Krepston. She was a very productive employee who devoted a lot of time to her job. The company profited from her expertise and gave her several awards. Minta started to change her life around, displayed ladylike behavior, and joined the Mount Mathuveh Church. After she decided to get baptized, her promiscuity seemed to be under control. She claimed that she was getting treatment from an unknown source to decrease her libido.

After two days at the LeCoserve Motel, Minta called in at work and told her manager, "I met an old school friend who took me out to dinner, and while on our way back to the motel where I was staying, we had an accident."

"Are you okay?"

"I'm not seriously injured, just a few bumps and bruises, but the doctors want to keep me for a few days under observation. I should be back soon."

"You can take your two weeks' vacation at this time," the manager told her.

Minta was happy to be away from work and in the company of Ashton Denton, who treated her well for the first four days. He convinced her that she was the only one in his life, that she was his soul mate, and that she was the one he'd been waiting for all these years. But while she waited to see him that weekend, he didn't show up, and he didn't leave any forwarding address or telephone number. After checking her purse, she realized that he had taken most of her money, leaving her just enough to pay for the hotel. She paid for the room, checked out, and started asking if anyone knew where she could find Ashton. Finally, she heard about a night club that Ashton frequented, so she decided to go there and claim her man. On her arrival, she was horrified to see him sitting at the bar with another woman on his lap. She took a seat in an inconspicuous spot and observed as much as she could take; they didn't see her because the place was dimly lit. When she couldn't endure it any longer, she made her move. She approached the pair from behind, grabbed both their heads, and slammed them together. She didn't wait for anyone of them to retaliate and made a hasty exit. By the time Ashton and his female companion stopped seeing stars and realized what had happened, Minta had disappeared. Now, that was a weekend they would never forget.

Forty-Six

I want to thank you again for your support. You are a very wonderful friend," Ionnia told Stu in a phone call when she got back home.

"I also feel privileged to have a friend like you," he said. "When are you planning to fix your face?"

"Stu, you sound so mean. If I didn't know you like I do, I would think that you are just like other people who hate me for the way I look. Do you think you could continue being my friend if I do not have the surgery?"

"I'm sorry, that's not the way I intended it to come across. You know I couldn't be that mean to you."

"I accept your apology."

"Do you still have Dr. Buehling's number?"

"I think I do, and as soon as I hang up, I am going to make the appointment."

Ionnia made her appointment to have her cosmetic surgery, and her aunt Kervis and cousin Thalia accompanied her to the capital, Trevine. Aunt Kervis left within a week after the procedure, but Thalia remained with Ionnia for the remainder of the time.

Ionnia spent four nights at the clinic and then another five weeks at the Maravella Hotel and Spa by the beach, which was easily accessible to the clinic. She saw the doctor every other day as part of the follow-up care. The Maravella was quite a contrast from the hotel Aunt Gertude and Ionnia had stopped in on their way to Krepston a few years ago. This one stood twelve stories tall with more than five hundred rooms and suites. This all-inclusive hotel was like a paradise and a haven for society's elite. The guests on the northern side of the hotel enjoyed the spectacular scenery of the waterfall that let out millions of gallons of water each day into the ocean. Ionnia was mesmerized with this hotel, and she paid attention to every little detail. "Could I own something like this one day?" she asked herself. She answered her own question. "Oh, yes, I will. Nothing is impossible. Visualize it, and it will happen. Reach for the stars."

While walking the grounds of the clinic on one of her follow-up visits, Ionnia saw an old acquaintance, Jillian Ernakki, the older sister of her friend Penelope. Jillian was also there for plastic surgery.

Upon seeing Ionnia's face, Jillian's first assumption was that the disfigurement was caused by a member of the opposite sex. "I hope you put him away for a long time," she said.

"Already dead and cremated," she told Jillian.

"Good."

But what Ionnia did not reveal immediately was that the perpetrator to which she was referring was four-legged. Ionnia told Jillian the story and assured her that she was telling the truth.

Jillian had a hearty laugh and then remarked bitingly, "I thought you had followed in your mother's footsteps." Ionnia's color changed, and when Jillian saw her nonverbal response, she said, "Oh, God, I'm awfully sorry. I didn't mean to hurt you, and I wouldn't hold it against you if you continue to hate me."

"Do you want to explain the reason for my hatred toward you? Would you like to get it off your chest?"

In the early years, when Ionnia had done menial jobs for the family, Jillian had treated her disrespectfully. Ionnia sighed deeply as she recalled some of the unpleasant encounters with Jillian, but she tried to remain calm and poised. However, at times she clenched her fists to hold back the anger and rage. She wasn't sure whether Jillian noticed, but if she did, she didn't comment. Ionnia had vivid memories of an incident where Jillian's mother had given her some of Penelope's clothes, and Jillian had accused her of stealing them. Jillian had grabbed them from her, ripped them apart, and then stepped on them. "You will never wear any of my sister's clothes," she'd said angrily. "These are expensive."

Ionnia never went back to work for the Ernakkis after that embarrassing incident, however she remained friends with Penelope, who apologized for her sister's behavior. Her mother also apologized.

Jillian looked her straight in the eye and begged for forgiveness. Jillian knew firsthand about physical, mental, and emotional abuse. She had been married to Byron Inkst, a chemist from Danbury Heights who worked in his uncle, Bertram Inkst, in the racehorse industry. He was a very jealous person and would constantly accuse Jillian of having affairs. She was one of those people who kept in touch with her exes despite the fact that her mother told her that there was no need to talk to someone with whom she had severed the relationship.

During one of Byron's tirades, he splashed a chemical substance all over his wife, causing her disfigurement. She almost lost her sight and had to undergo extensive treatments. To date, she had had seven surgeries. Jillian had many months of psychotherapy and mental health counseling due to the trauma caused by the chemical assault.

Jillian told Ionnia that prior to this latest incident, her husband would beat her and call her names. A few days after each verbal and physical assault, Byron would come home with flowers and other gifts, telling her how sorry he was and how much he loved her. He'd say that it was a mistake that would never happen again, and he begged for her forgiveness. He continually drilled into her head, "You made me do it." Each time, she believed that she was really at fault, and she forgave him.

Ionnia listened. *Another stupid battered woman,* she said to herself. *Can't someone knock some sense into these women's heads?*

Ionnia saw the pain Jillian was reliving, and she asked the usual question. "Why did you stay in such an abusive relationship?" Ionnia had seen the determination with her own mother, who had stayed because of her children. But Jillian had no kids.

"I liked the spotlight, the trips, the fine dining, and the elite circle of friends. Most of all, I loved him," she said. "At least, I thought that was love. Now that I've had the chance to look back at the situation, I can call it insanity."

It was very interesting how Jillian opened up to Ionnia, but as the saying went, "If you hide your painful truths, you will get nowhere."

She could see how empty and lonely Jillian was. If loneliness were an ocean, Jillian looked and sounded like she would drown in it. But one should remember that loneliness was a choice. One decided how lonely one was, and one could choose to be alone but not be lonely. Although loneliness could not be quantified, it could be looked at as a yardstick to show how much one was at peace with oneself.

Ionnia thought for a moment and then said, "I would hate for any man to tell me that he loves me. I have seen too often the result of love."

Unlike her sister Penelope, Jillian had chosen not to attend college. Here was another young woman who had opted to n to pursue a career but rather believed that marrying a man was the most popular, rewarding, and productive thing to do. She snubbed her nose disdainfully at professional single women and referred to them as weirdoes. She convinced herself that these women were unable to get a husband and that something was wrong with them. Jillian was married and divorced twice before her twenty-first birthday; one of her marriages lasted only four months.

Jillian was stuck in her third relationship, with Byron, but she had endured all sorts of physical and emotional abuse of some kind or another. Her mother warned her that if she didn't come to her senses and cease marrying these types of men, one day her family would find her dead. She divorced Byron, returned home to live with her parents, and had started making plans about where to find her next husband after her final cosmetic procedure.

Byron hired a very good attorney and plea-bargained his way out of prison, insisting all along that what had happened to his wife was an accident. He received five years' probation and was mandated to pay for Jillian's treatment. He relocated to another section of Puca Luca but found it difficult to blend in because the news media had done a good job of describing him as Chemical Byron, warning all females to stay away from him.

During her stay in Trevine, Ionnia was frequently visited by members of her family. When Loretty got some time off, she did not always go alone. She brought along Claudia and her sisters Twyleith and Dee Dee. Aunt Gert and the Rytes came every weekend. Ionnia knew that all these people loved her and cared about her. She also got a chance to spend some time with Penelope whenever she visited her sister.

When Gert visited, she had the privilege of reuniting with an old friend, Vivette Reglon, who was now married to the famous plastic surgeon Dr. Hal Buehling. Gert and Vivette had lunch together, and Gert asked her to give Ionnia special attention. The two women talked of past experiences and some of the events in their love lives.

Gert asked Vivette about Berris Nation, a prominent attorney who specialized in real estate and to whom she had once been engaged for almost two years.

"He is one lowlife."

"Explain."

"Do you remember my first house I bought? Well, after I decided to relocate, I rented the house to a family friend. After a while, she stopped paying rent, and my mother asked Berris to intervene. He had an eviction notice served on my tenant and was able to force her to pay my mother some of the rent she owed. Two months after that, I got a letter from Berris informing me that his girlfriend, Mathilda

Karr, with whom he cheated on me, was attending the University of Trevine and needed pocket money. Therefore I should send her eight hundred dollars—the amount he claimed I owed him for taking care of my rent situation. I could hardly believe it."

"And did you send it?"

"Heavens, no. After all the things I'd done for him, and believing all his lies that he was not going to be unfaithful to me?"

"So did Mathilda complete her studies?"

"She did, and he never mentioned anything about the money again."

"What happened to the relationship between them?"

"They eventually got married. Have you heard of the Hotelier Mathilda Karr-Nation? She operates a franchise of the Island Cove chain of hotels, and they have a little girl named April who thinks she is a princess."

As the days wore on and Ionnia's self-esteem grew, she made more friends, many of whom were older than her, but she liked being in their company. One such person was Thelma Wreckitts, the senior accountant at the hotel. Ionnia found out through their many conversations that Thelma was Cordell Bundle's mother. She was a beautiful woman, and Ionnia found it hard to comprehend why Commissioner Bundle had let her slip out of his hands.

I'm never going to mention anything to Thelma about what Cordell did to me years ago. She seems so very proud of her son's achievements as Puca Luca's top jockey, and I wouldn't want to be the one to upset the apple cart. However, she did reveal that she knew Cordell.

Thelma kept pictures of Cordell in her office, as well as a scrapbook of all the newspaper reports about him and the races he'd won. Many sportswriters described him as "a young man with immeasurable potential who infused fresh vigor in the sport and brought immense financial returns to owners and breeders."

Forty-Seven

Within six weeks of returning home, Ionnia returned to Trevine for a follow-up examination. Her cousin Thalia accompanied her once again. On the second night that they arrived, Thelma sent a message to Ionnia that she urgently wanted to see her.

"Oh, my God. Did Cordell tell her what happened? Did he place the blame on me?" Again the famous lines by perpetrators came back to haunt her: *See what you made me do.*

She prepared herself for the worst but got a pleasant surprise when Thelma said, "I am inviting you and Thalia to an awards luncheon at the nearby Vistran Hotel, to be held in honor of outstanding jockeys and other prominent persons in the racing industry in Puca Luca. It will be attended by the who's who of the industry. I'm sure Cordell would want you there."

"I can't accept the invitation."

"Why?"

"Because I don't have anything appropriate to wear."

"I wouldn't worry about that, if I were you."

Thelma discussed it with her son and asked him to contribute some funds so that she could rent two outfits for Ionnia and her cousin. He didn't protest. That was the least he could do for Ionnia, considering what he had done to her.

Ionnia told Thalia about Thelma's invitation, and her response was same as Ionnia's. "Imagine how the snobs would look down on us plain Janes if we were to show up wearing casual clothes."

Around 9:00 p.m. that night, Thelma went to Ionnia's room and presented her and Thalia with the tickets to the event.

"Oh, Ms. Wrecketts, I told you that we ..."

She stopped Ionnia in the middle of her speech and presented her and Thalia with two of the most gorgeous dresses bearing the Zeme label, which she had rented from the hotel's boutique.

"We can't accept these."

"Just make sure they are returned within forty-eight hours," Thelma told them as she made a hurried exit.

The two young ladies spent half an hour trying on the dresses, spinning around like a top in front of the mirror, and giggling like a couple of ten-year-olds. They didn't hear another knock on the door. The knock became louder, and when Thalia looked through the peephole, she saw that Thelma had returned. They quickly undressed and put the dresses in the closet.

"Oh, my God, she has changed her mind." Thalia's countenance changed as she slowly opened the door.

When Thelma saw that the girls' enthusiasm had faded, she asked, "Didn't like the dresses?" Before anyone could respond verbally, Thelma handed them an envelope. Inside were gift cards from the jewelry store across the street for accessories to go along with their outfits. "Buy whatever you want—and those are for keeps."

"I am so excited, I don't think I will be sleeping," Thalia said after Thelma left.

"Do you think the high society guests will wonder how we are able to afford this extravagance?" Ionnia asked. "Now is the time to implement all that I learned in charm school and to not behave like a misfit. I always dreamed of being with rich, famous, intellectual people and engaging in meaningful conversation with them."

At the awards ceremony, Cordell was named the Sportsman of the Year and was the recipient of the top award, the coveted Breeders' Cup, which was presented by Dan Gelner, the chairman of Puca Luca Racing Commission. Other cups and trophies were presented to other jockeys, stewards, track announcers, trainers, breeders, and owners. Special awards went to the senior veterinarian, Dr. Alexander VonHutton; the first female jockey, Susan Faugh; one of the track's photographers, Verron Ungers; and other prominent names synonymous with the sport. The guest speaker for the occasion was Quigland Park's public relations manager, Timothy Inkst.

Cordell's father and grandmother attended the luncheon and were seated at the table reserved for the famous Locksley family along with Ionnia, Thalia, and Thelma. Ionnia felt like a celebrity, and Fenton Locksley couldn't take his eyes off Thalia. It seemed to be love at first sight, and when Ionnia glanced at her cousin, she appeared to be blushing.

Thalia had never been married, although she'd dated before. She told Ionnia that she had dated a minister of a small church, who'd proposed to her after three months. Thalia had been the center of his life, and she'd been happy. Her parents had started planning for a wedding, but the rules of the game had changed as soon as he'd realized that she wouldn't have premarital sex with him, and he'd broken off the engagement. His reason had been that the Lord had told him that she was not the right woman for him. He'd also said that he'd had a dream and heard a voice saying, "Never buy a cow without first tasting the milk."

"Where was this woman all along?" Fenton asked Cordell. "I can't see myself going on without her in my life."

"Well, do what you have to do," Cordell encouraged him.

Fenton was a well-sought-after bachelor who had dated many young women, but he'd had no serious relationships with them. He was described as a philandering Casanova. Was he willing to give up this lifestyle, or was he planning to use Thalia and forget her as he did the rest of them?

Thalia was cautious. "I will not commit myself to anyone until I fully investigate the individual and am satisfied that all my concerns are addressed."

She played hard to get at first and didn't want Fenton to think that she wanted to be with him because of his money, although that was important.

Ionnia felt happy for Cordell's achievement, but at the same time, she couldn't forget what he had done to her, so she felt a little bit uneasy. Others must have felt the tension too.

Claudia took Ionnia aside and said to her, "I know the sight of my grandson has brought back sad memories, but this is a time for celebration. For my sake, please try to remain calm and composed."

"It was a spontaneous reaction. I'm sorry. I'll do my best."

Was Claudia expecting Ionnia to not have any emotions about the incident? Was she suggesting that it was time she put this behind her and move on?

Cordell joined his grandmother and Ionnia just as she put her arms around her in a comforting and understanding manner.

"Well, do you have something to say to Ionnia?'

"You look ravishing in that dress."

"Cordell, for God's sake, I can see that up till now, you have no remorse for what you did."

"I didn't mean it that way, Grandma."

Ionnia appeared as if she wanted to cry, but she held back the tears and forced a smile.

"I am so, so sorry for my actions. I was young and foolish, and I regret it to this day. Please, can you forgive me? Tell me what I can do to make it up to you." Cordell seemed honest and sincere in his apologies, and he offered a handshake. As Ionnia reciprocated, Cordell's countenance changed, as if a big weight had been lifted off his shoulders. "This means more to me than all the trophies and awards I received today."

The function was proceeding according to schedule, but shortly before lunch was served, there was to be a musical interlude, and the vocalist and pianist were nowhere to be found. The organizer of the event, Eda Lane, was frantic to find someone at this late stage to fill in. She knew that her reputation would be in jeopardy if this was a flop. She approached the public relations manager of the hotel, Orville Singleberry, and said, "I need to save face. Can you provide me with a substitute? There has to be someone around here who is musically inclined."

Cordell overheard the conversation and said to Ms. Lane, "Don't worry. I know just the perfect person to fill the position, and I can assure you she is better than the people you booked."

"I hope you are right."

"The Sportsman of the Year can never be wrong," he replied cockily, and he gave her Ionnia's name. Cordell felt obligated to allow Ionnia the chance of a lifetime to show off her talents. Eda took the microphone and announced, "Ladies and gentlemen, the moment we have all been waiting for. Please put your hands together and welcome one of Puca Luca's most talented pianists and vocalists, a member of our audience: Miss Ionnia Dunn-Ryte."

It took Ionnia by surprise, and she was overwhelmed. She couldn't fail this distinguished group of people. As she was escorted to the stage by Miss Lane, she saw the surprised look on the faces of some members of the audience and imagined they were saying, "This must be a mistake."

She would prove to them that she wasn't a mistake one. She asked Miss Lane for the list of songs she wanted her to sing.

"The stage is yours. Sing whatever you think is appropriate. I trust you."

Ionnia performed extraordinarily, and she closed with two songs near and dear to her heart, "Across the Bridge" and "Something Inside so Strong."

She was given a standing ovation. As she bowed to the crowd in recognition of its appreciation, the public relations manager, Timothy Inkst, appeared on stage and handed her an envelope and a bouquet of flowers. Almost everyone wanted to take pictures with her.

"If you are interested in recording your voice, I have a close friend who owns a recording company and who could make you famous," Timothy promised.

"Thanks. I will give it some thought."

Miss Lane met with Ionnia and thanked her personally, and at that point she discovered that this was Harry Quane's niece.

"Would it matter if you had known prior to me performing?"

"Not at all. I wouldn't blame Harry's relatives for what he did to me."

Ionnia and Thalia had planned to return to Krepston by MET-EX, but Fenton Locksley intervened and said, "You will do no such thing. It would be my pleasure to take you lovely ladies home to Krepston."

"We already have tickets."

"I'll reimburse you, if that's what you are worried about."

Fenton was so persistent that Thalia and Ionnia could not reject his offer.

The result of Ionnia's treatment pleased everyone. Her face was more beautiful than ever, just as Stu had predicted. She returned to Krepston feeling like a new and normal person. "Now I won't be the subject of ridicule, scorn, and rejection. Maybe I can even enter a beauty pageant."

Although it was obvious that Ionnia was away for plastic surgery, it had been rumored that she was pregnant and had gone away to have an abortion. Berdene was not about to have the family name dragged through the mud. She was determined to get to the bottom of this and to put an end to the rumor. It didn't take long. She met in the faculty lounge with Noreen Heavely, who was the Sunday school teacher and assistant youth director at the church and a library assistant at the academy, to assign her to conduct an investigation. Noreen was regarded as a role model to many of the young girls in the academy and around Krepston in general. Whenever Thea Tweeler couldn't travel, Noreen was the one who would be sent as a chaperone with the young students who participated in competitive literary events out of town, and she could always be relied on to keep them safe.

"What do you think should happen to the person who is responsible for this?" Noreen asked.

"Haven't thought of that as yet, but I am sure the punishment will be severe. Do you have any suggestions? We were all taught to observe the Ten Commandments, and someone has broken this one that says, 'Thou shalt not bear false witness against thy neighbor.'"

"Our code of moral conduct would be meaningless if there were no consequences or punishment for those who violate it."

Noreen's heart started to pound. She sweated profusely and slumped across the table in front of Berdene Ryte. A bottle of smelling salts was at the right place at the right time, and this was used to revive the young woman.

"Are you all right? What freaked you out like that?"

"I don't know where to start, but I'll tell you of a discussion that Kelly Bashington and I had. It seemed as though certain aspects of it were taken out of context."

"Go on; I'm listening. No, hold on a moment. There are three sides to a story: your side, his side, and the truth." Berdene reached for the intercom and summoned Kelly to the lounge.

While they waited, Noreen explained that they were discussing a newspaper article about girls who got pregnant and were sent away to have abortions or give it up for adoption and then return home. Kelly refuted Noreen's version of the conversation, and she was forced to recant her story. She cried, confessed to having started the rumor, and was forced to apologize to Ionnia and the rest of the family in front of the entire congregation one Sunday. Every one of her responsibilities was taken away from her, and many people lost respect for her.

"How could someone with such an honorable reputation behave in such a dishonorable manner?" everyone asked.

The embarrassment was too much for Noreen to handle, and a few weeks after that, she relocated to a different section of Puca Luca where she changed her name, opened a preschool, and began writing children's books.

Forty-Eight

Ionnia was anxious to let Stu know the results of her cosmetic procedure and thank him for the referral, so she made a call to Velma Dent's business place to ask for him and give him an update.

Velma's secretary, Betty, answered and said, "Stu is not around, but it would be best if you hear the details from his mother." She then abruptly hung up the phone.

Her actions were more than strange because Betty was someone with whom Ionnia always had lengthy conversations. *Whatever the problem is, it sounds pretty bad.* A million scenarios went through her head, but none made any sense to her. The suspense was killing her. When she ran out of speculative options, she made contact. She had given the Dents ample time to deal with whatever the problem was.

When Ionnia finally got through to Velma Dent and asked her what had happened, her response was, "Are you sure you want to hear these ridiculous allegations that have been leveled against my son?"

"Please, Mrs. Dent. Stu is my friend, and I'm sure he needs me. This is the least I can do. Stu was there when I needed him, and now it is my time to return the favor."

"I may as well tell you now before you read it in the newspapers. I'm so mortified and embarrassed. The charge is necrophilia, but I can assure you he is innocent. I know my son."

This can't be so, Ionnia said to herself, and she dismissed the thought about the grotesque accusations and allegations. She was aware of his nerdy actions and his obsessions with dead girls, but never once had she harbored any thoughts that he would be accused of screwing one of them.

Ionnia was silent for a while as she tried to process what Stu's mother had just told her. "So where is he now?" she asked with a trembling voice.

"He was placed in the notorious Kotchette Hill Prison, where he was refused bail. I fear for his safety. Already there have been rumors that he is suicidal," Velma Dent told Ionnia.

"I would really like to come out there, and soon."

"If it will help, I will send someone to come and get you."

As soon as the conversation ended, Ionnia started planning her journey to Kotchette Hill Prison to visit Stu and provide him with moral support. Her parents had no problem with that. Prior to her arrival, Stu had been removed from the original location in which he was placed and admitted to the infirmary for psychiatric evaluation. Afterward, he was returned to his cell, which was a ten-feet by six-feet enclosure with a small opening around nine inches in diameter for a window. A concrete slab was his bed, and he had a straw mattress. An aluminum bucket was placed in one corner of the cell to be used as a toilet. Built in the wall was a small concrete table, and on it was placed a washcloth, a piece of soap, and a banged-up enamel basin with a little water. There were guards at his door twenty-four hours per day. There was no peace and quiet at the prison. There was the constant clanging of locks and bolts on the heavy institution doors, as well as the almost musical noise of bunches of keys carried by the wardens. Stu was unhappy to the nth degree. He was frightened, and most of all he maintained his innocence. No wonder he contemplated suicide.

On one of the walls were names engraved of notorious prisoners who had once inhabited that cell. One such name was Jarew Zep. Stu sweated profusely as he recalled that a person who had committed one of the most heinous crimes in Puca Luca had died in prison, and here Stu was in the same cell. Jarew Zep had decapitated his wife and disposed of her head in a well that supplied the community with drinking water, thus contaminating the entire supply.

Stu shuddered, and he began to scream. "Someone get me out of here!"

Two guards immediately opened the door and found Stu on the floor foaming from the mouth. What they didn't know was that before he'd screamed, he had placed a piece of soap in his mouth, which resulted in the foaming. One would think that the guards would be familiar with most of the tactics of the inmates, but obviously this one was new to them. Stu was removed and again sent to the infirmary, this time for medical observation, but not before the psychiatrist restrained and sedated him.

"Dent, you have visitor—a live one this time," one of the guards shouted at him.

Stu was happy to see Ionnia, although he wished that his attorney was there too. "Have you seen anyone around here looking like an attorney?"

"No, not yet. But your mother is doing everything to get you out of here. Tell me what happened."

Stu hung his head, wrung his hands, and told his story. "There was this dead girl who was identified as Vonnie Alvers."

"Wait minute—I knew her."

A teardrop clung to his eyelash like the early morning dew on a blade of grass. "At the time, Vonnie had been having problems with her boyfriend, Justin Kayse, who was addicted to some unknown substance and would beat her every chance he got. This day in question, he allegedly forced Vonnie to engage in the drug activities with him. She appeared to have overdosed, and then he made an anonymous call to authorities about an unconscious female. He disappeared, and the authorities had difficulty locating who made the call, knowing only that it was made from a phone booth. When the medical team arrived on the scene, they pronounced the girl dead and called Dent's

Mortuary and Crematorium to pick the body up and take it to the medical examiner's office for an autopsy."

"So what happened? Why were you accused?"

"I was dispatched and carried out my mission as I always do. I swear to God I didn't do anything wrong. That boyfriend or someone else screwed her before I got there and told the cops that he saw me do it."

"Good God, what an awful thing to do to someone. Stu, I want you to know that I believe you, and I know you will be exonerated."

After a short pause, he looked at Ionnia's face, smiled, and said, "By the way, you look beautiful."

"Thanks, Stu. Dr. Beuhling and his team did a good job." She couldn't help but feel sorry for the person in front of her. He was had a smiling face and a kind heart. If hearts had windows, Ionnia would see at this time how much Stu's was aching. He didn't deserve this.

As Stu explained the incident to Ionnia, he tried to suppress the spasmodic sobs that almost choked him at times. Clearly he was suffering, and he intended to prove his innocence by all means possible.

What an interesting and embarrassing trial this might turn out to be. This story was an extraordinary amount of fodder for the news media, especially when dealing with someone with the last name Dent, which many people linked with the race horse mogul Morgan Dent. The Dents were no strangers to the public's wrath and resentment. A generation of people had contempt for Stu's great-grandfather Horace Dent, the loan shark who lent money and other consumer goods to people; when they were unable to repay, they would experience the harshest punishment ever meted out to human beings. No wonder they transferred this resentment to the third and fourth generation of Dents.

As Stu buried his head in his hands, he lamented in a weak and sorrowful tone. "No woman will want to marry me after this scandal. They didn't want me before, and imagine now."

Ionnia comforted Stu and then turned around to leave just in time to see Velma Dent arrive. "Is there anything else I can do to help, Mrs. Dent?"

"Not unless you can come up with another exceptional lawyer to join my team, which I already have in place. Money is no problem. Thanks for caring, Stu really needs a friend in these times, and most of his so-called friends have turned their backs on him."

"I will get you the best," Ionnia promised.

When Ionnia returned to Krepston, she contacted Charley Gress, Nickie's father, who was listed with the Puca Luca Bar Association as one of the best defense attorneys in the country. He agreed to meet with Velma Dent, who readily retained him to serve on a dream team with five other lawyers to defend her son. Stu was granted bail at the first hearing and returned to his mother's home. The judge ordered that he should not be allowed to participate in any activity pertaining to the business. He was also put on paid leave at the medical examiner's office, where he worked as an autopsy assistant.

Velma's business was also named a party in this whole mess due to the fact that Stu was sent by Dent's Mortuary and Crematorium to pick up the body. The company was represented as a separate defendant with a separate team of lawyers.

Velma Dent summoned all her energies to keep up appearances. Her son was in trouble, her business was in jeopardy, and her social image was at stake. Reporters hounded her on a regular basis and questioned whether she harbored any resentment toward her son for this alleged action.

"My son has not been found guilty of anything, and moreover, maternal love conquers everything."

Whether one wanted to call this fate or coincidence, the prosecution's only so-called eyewitness to Stu's alleged necrophilia was Gladstone Brownbelt, a homeless peasant who had a history of mental illness. He was a victim of Horace Dent's unethical and unscrupulous business operations and had lost his property and family while trying to make life better for them. He'd carried this resentment for years. After that, he'd tried to commit suicide by hanging from a tree, but the rope was too long and the tree branch was too weak, so he was unsuccessful in his attempt. However, he suffered oxygen deprivation in the process and was never of sound mind since.

Gladstone did see Stu that day, and also someone else who bore a striking resemblance to Stu: a homeless drug addict and convicted rapist named Phillip Auguston, who was recently out of prison and apparently took up temporary residence in abandoned buildings. Was it a case of mistaken identity, or did Gladstone Brownbelt know what he was doing and wanted to enact revenge on a member of the Dent family?

Charley Gress and his team presented expert witnesses to refute the prosecution's allegation against Stu. Justin Kayse, who testified for the prosecution, told of the two men he had seen in the building that day. The physical description was almost identical except for identifying marks on Phillip Auguston's body. He was picked up and roughed up by law enforcement personnel. When he was called to testify, he actually confessed to the crime. He said that when he'd approached the girl, she was still alive, and she'd pleaded with him to have sex with her.

"So you are actually admitting that you screwed her to death?" Charley Gress asked him in cross-examination. "Do you realize that you are admitting to murder with a deadly weapon, and that carries a penalty of death?"

The people in the gallery, the six-man jury, and the news personnel were amused at Charley's line of questioning and his approach in general. Another lawyer on the Gress team added, "Young man, contrary to your testimony, the evidence showed that the subject was already dead when she was sexually assaulted. You are a vile and despicable human being and should not be breathing the same oxygen as the rest of us."

Stu was acquitted of the charges, and his mother's business was also cleared of any wrongdoing. However, the stigma remained, and her bank account drained. Stu was reinstated at the medical examiner's office but restricted to desk duties. He was so ashamed and embarrassed that he resigned.

Gladstone Brownbelt was charged for submitting a false police report. His credibility as an eyewitness was brought into question, and since then the law enforcement community had no confidence in eyewitness reports.

Forty-Nine

The bishop, his wife, and other dignitaries from Mount Mathuveh took regular trips to churches in different locations of Puca Luca and the surrounding islands. One Easter, they left for a week to Gravadee County and would be attending the annual Bishops' Conference. Deacon Eustace Ryte was left in charge during their absence. The bishop's last charge to the congregation was that they give the deacon the same respect that had been shown to him over the years. To his brother, he gave permission to continue using the library to prepare his sermons. This was the first time since Ionnia's arrival in Krepston that her mother would be away from her for such a long time. Berdene promised to call as often as possible and informed Ionnia that Aunt Gert and Clemmie would take good care of her.

The Friday afternoon before the delegation was scheduled to return to Krepston, Ionnia came home from school, dropped her books on her bed, and stripped off her clothes to go take a shower. Then she got the scare of her life. There was Deacon Ryte coming aimlessly out of her bathroom and staring blankly at her. She quickly grabbed the blanket off her bed and covered herself.

"What are you doing in my room, sir?" she asked in a scared but stern voice. She never bothered to pick up her books, which were scattered all over the room.

Deacon Ryte wore a slight grin on his face and said nothing. Ionnia inched her way backward to the window and hollered out to Marty, who was attending to the orchids and roses just below her window. "Help me, Mr. Marty!" Ionnia cried in a trembling, stammering voice that sounded like she was having hiccups. "I am having an emergency problem, and I need your help right away."

The deacon held out his hands toward Ionnia and said, "You don't have to be afraid. I was just looking for a hymnbook that Sister Berdene told me you had borrowed. I'm sorry I startled you."

Marty did not even blink. He saw this opportunity to help as payback for everything that Ionnia had done for his wife. He dropped what he was doing and bolted toward the nearest doorway to the building, which led to the kitchen. As soon as he got to where his wife was preparing afternoon snacks, he beckoned to her to follow him. Marty observed Ionnia wrapped in the blanket and Deacon Ryte still standing there, frozen like a statue. He turned to the scared teenager, "Tell me he didn't." When Ionnia didn't answer, Marty turned to the other male presence in the room and said, "Good God, what have you done to the poor girl, Deacon?"

Clemmie ran in, out of breath and not expecting anything of this nature. She grabbed the trembling and frightened Ionnia, picked up her clothes, and shepherded her to the guest room downstairs so she could get dressed. Then she gave her some tea. The compassionate tears welled up in Clemmie's eyes, and Ionnia saw the pain she was going through. "Sorry," she said as she pulled a white embroidered handkerchief from her apron pocket and dried her eyes.

"Was this incident a reminder of something in the past?" Ionnia asked herself. Had Deacon Eustace Ryte done this or any other heinous unholy act to any other girl before? Was there something else she needed to know? Ionnia remembered the words of Samanthley Whitelace and was overcome with grief and anger. Was Samanthley a very good clairvoyant? Ionnia wished that her grandmother was around. As she tried to make sense of what happened, she couldn't help thinking whether it was the power of Samanthley's amulet or the protective hands of God that kept her safe from the deacon. Just then, she remembered Deuteronomy 31:6, which said, "Be strong and of good courage, do not fear nor be afraid; for the Lord your God, He is the One who goes with you. He will never leave you nor forsake you."

Marty and Deacon Ryte went into the library to talk about what had just transpired.

"You ought to be ashamed of yourself, calling yourself a man of God and trying to rape your niece."

Deacon Ryte sat motionless with a strange expression on his face. "It wasn't like that at all, Marty. I can't explain it, but I swear I didn't touch her."

"Whatever it is, it is truly an unforgivable indiscretion. And you know that the bishop has to hear about this? You'd better have an explanation then."

"Pray with me, Marty," Deacon Ryte pleaded with a scared child's look on his face and a voice that evoked empathy.

The request sounded so sincere that it reminded Marty of the time when his son Simeon was around six years old and saw a spider in his room, which made him so afraid that he pleaded with his father to let it leave. When it didn't leave quickly enough, he asked his daddy, "If I say my prayers, will it leave?"

Was the deacon of sound mind? Was he thinking like a little child? Would the problem go away if he prayed? Did he have some kind of mental illness that no one knew about?

Downstairs, Clemmie and Ionnia chatted, and Ionnia told her the truth about what had taken place in her room. Trying to make sense of this, she turned to Clemmie and asked, "Do you think the deacon took a nap in his brother's favorite hammock and started to sleepwalk? I hear that the hammock affects people in extraordinary ways."

"Don't try to rationalize his behavior, my child. A man of God doesn't sleepwalk. Such a thing only happens to people with deep psychological problems, or people possessed by the devil."

"Well then, Miss Clemmie, do you believe that he was really looking for a hymnbook? I don't remember borrowing one from anybody. I have my own."

"What deacon doesn't own a hymn book? Moreover, if you were to take a look in the library now, I'm sure you would see several copies. The bishop always has enough copies available to lend copies to those members of the congregation who don't have any. However, one thing I am certain of: if Marty believed 100 percent that the deacon touched you, he wouldn't be breathing now."

"Well then, do you think he just wanted to use the bathroom?"

"There are two bathrooms in the library." Clemmie wasn't ready to believe the deacon's explanations. Neither was she quick to forgive him, whatever his true intensions were. "When I was a little girl, a preacher was accused of inappropriate behavior with a four year-old child whom his wife babysat on weekdays. His excuse was that his wife spent more time with the little children than with him, and he had become lonely and neglected. He instead sought comfort with a child. Can you believe that?"

"Is he still preaching?"

"No, dear. One weekend when his wife went to visit her sick mother in another town, the villagers set his house on fire when they knew he was alone. He was burned alive."

"Was anyone arrested for arson or for the preacher's death?"

"No, child. Do you think the police would have space in the jail to keep the entire village of Sandy River?"

"There must be someone who organized this."

"Can we not talk about this anymore?"

When the deacon told his wife, Cedelle, what had happened, her first response was, "I can't believe it. If Marty hadn't seen you in the girl's room, I would swear she was making it up. If word gets out, we are doomed. How are we going to explain this to the children? We have to swear those three to secrecy. No one else except Berdene and the bishop can hear about this, and it sure isn't going to sit well with them."

On the bishop's return, upon hearing what had transpired in his absence, he made this a matter of high priority. He met with each party separately and got their statements and reactions.

When he summoned his brother to the library, he paced the room with his eyes set steadfastly upon the picture of Jesus. He got hold of a Bible, placed his hands on it, and said, "I swear before God and before you, my dear brother, that I was looking for a hymnbook, which I thought I heard Berdene say she had lent to Ionnia. I agree that I had no business snooping around Ionnia's room looking for anything, but the door was unlocked."

"That does not give you the right to enter her room, even if the door was wide open," the bishop said. "This behavior is inexcusable. You will have to get seriously involved in some prayer and fasting."

No one else in the congregation knew about the incident, and the bishop asked everyone involved to let it remain that way. "We have to protect the integrity of the church, the family, and the Mount Mathuveh community on a whole." But there was one thing he never forgot to do: he frequently preached about God's wrath upon those who lusted after the flesh.

Berdene Ryte was deeply saddened that Ionnia had to have this experience in what should be one of the safest places in Krepston.

The deacon's conscience must have bothered him immensely because he elected to lock himself in their guest room for one month of fasting and praying. After fourteen days, no matter how much his wife and others begged him to end this activity, he ignored their pleadings. Late one Saturday afternoon, a group of church members led by Cedelle decided to make a joyful noise unto the Lord with their singing and clanking of cymbals, hoping that this would lure the deacon out of his room. When this didn't happen, Cedelle pleaded to whoever would listen, "This is a waste of time. Someone please do something. I need my husband."

Marty finally broke the door down and found Eustace Ryte unresponsive. "Help! The deacon needs a doctor."

When his wife went in and tested for a pulse, she looked up with sad eyes and said to everyone who was standing there, "He's probably in a coma."

They all stared in horror at his emaciated body. He lay on his back with his eyes wide open. Marty knelt down by the bedside and tried closing them. "He is as cold as ice," he remarked, and he asked someone to get a blanket to cover the deacon. "Sister Cedelle, he's gone. He starved himself to death," Marty said as he rose to his feet.

When she looked up at Marty, one could almost hear her saying, "How dare you suggest such a thing." But instead she choked back the tears and said, "I would leave that declaration for the doctor. Someone please run along and notify the bishop so that he can get the doctor over here as quickly as possible. In the meantime, no one is to touch anything. We will wait for the bishop and the doctor to arrive."

As Marty looked awkwardly at the deacon's wife, he seemed compelled to utter additional remarks, but he caught himself and said, "I'm sorry for your loss." He could see that she was at a breaking point, so he gently seated her in a sofa and beckoned to Delise Gevannes to bring her a box of tissues.

News of the deacon's death spread fast, and more mourners, including his sister, Gert, arrived. Gert lit four candles, placed them at the four corners of the room, fell to her knees, and prayed. Then she asked everyone to join her in the singing of the hymn "There's Rest for the Weary."

Soon, the bishop and the doctor arrived. Dr. Ashvern pronounced Deacon Eustace Ryte dead, and at that time Cedelle put her hands on her head and started screaming. The doctor didn't ask too many questions because he didn't want to compound the family's sufferings, but he assured them that the cause of death would be made known as soon as an autopsy was performed. He added, "This being a sudden death, you are aware that the police have to be notified. And don't forget there will have to be an inquest in the death of this beloved brother."

Cedelle wanted to blame her husband's death on the bishop because he was the one who'd recommended that Eustace engage in fasting and prayer, but she withheld her comments because there would be too many questions as to why he'd found it necessary to make that recommendation. "It is going to take some time for this tragedy to sink in, and I don't know how I am going to take care of the bills," Cedelle sobbed.

With her hands around her friend's shoulder, Delise said to her, "I'm sure you will be able to do so if there is any life insurance money to collect."

While they waited for the medical examiner and the police to arrive, the bishop took Cedelle aside and spoke to her. Whatever he said must have lifted her spirits because amid the grief, shock, and disbelief, she returned to the sofa. One could see that she was no longer in a lot of pain, but how long would this last?

Silently, Ionnia was aching. She felt partially responsible for the deacon's death. "My room had been unoccupied for a long while, and if I hadn't been here, this would not have occurred," she said to her mom.

"Don't blame yourself for this—and don't think that anyone is blaming you," her mother said.

That night, Samanthley came to Ionnia in a dream. The woman said nothing but began digging up dirt in the front of the premises. When Ionnia woke up, she was sweating profusely. "I guess that means there is dirt to be dug up about this family, and I should be the one doing the digging." She also remembered Samanthley's words when they'd met at Deliverance Park. Ionnia knew that the Ryte family hailed from Hampstead, and she remembered Miss Arineldie, whom she had met on the bus, also came from that area. She still had the magazine with her and decided to write to Enid and tell her about the adoption and of her academic progress. She didn't mention the deacon's death or the incident leading up to it.

A response came within two weeks. Enid wrote in her letter that Eustace Ryte had been married to her sister, Velvet, who'd died of cancer a few years back. His only desire was to be with her, and because of the loss, he lapsed into deep depression. When his brother realized how distraught he was, he decided to relocate him to Krepston, where he met his second wife, Cedelle.

Ionnia wrote back and asked, "Do I have any cousins? I would surely like to know them, as well as get the chance to meet with you again. You were truly an inspiration to me."

Another letter came, and Ionnia learned the names of four of her cousins: Rick, Churchill, Georgette, and Dawlene. "There may be others," Enid wrote. "Rumor has it that while he was operating his secondhand furniture store, he used to stay over late and entertain a woman by the name of Ruth, who was the wife of one of his church brothers. The union produced three children, but Ruth's husband agreed to raise them as his own. However, the children found out that their "father" was not their father, and they coped the best they could with their other three siblings. My sister also dealt with this the best she could."

After the funeral, it appeared that there were going to be some problems with the insurance policy. Georgette was an executive at an insurance company owned by the MUJALI group, and before he remarried, when she saw how fragile her father was, she personally conducted the business of underwriting the life insurance policy. What surprised everyone was that Georgette had included Ruth's two children as beneficiaries on the policy. There was nothing for Cedelle. To add salt to her wounds, the home in Hampstead belonged to Eustace's first wife. Although Cedelle felt somewhat connected to the Mount Mathuveh community, she left Krepston to be closer to her family in Bethany.

Fifty

Ionnia graduated from high school a few months shy of her four-teenth birthday, and she had already been enrolled at the University of Krepston, to which she was awarded a full academic scholarship. She was the school's valedictorian and graduated with a variety of honors. She was a remarkable student who, despite the numerous setbacks and absences from school, had managed to complete the program in less time than the average student. Her ambition was to pursue courses in business, communication, and fashion design. She wished she could have lived on campus, but there was no space available in the dorms for the local students because these dorm rooms were reserved for as many out-of-towners as they could accommodate. Ionnia had to continue living at home. Her parents made the daily commute, but there came a time when she felt that she shouldn't be putting so much pressure on them. Six months after enrolling, she asked them per-mission to get an apartment somewhere closer to the institution. She understood the risks of living on her own as a minor, but she promised to choose the safest boarding house that had a vacancy at the time.

So as not to leave any stone unturned, Ionnia sent a request to her biological mother. "Please get in touch with Aunt Bobeth and let her know that I need her help in finding a suitable place for me to stay." Bobeth had connections, and it didn't take long before she and her daughter Polly paid a visit to Ionnia. Bobeth took her to a boarding house in Woodwind known as Skidlet. It was owned by two sisters in their early seventies who hailed from Sassawhackia. One of them was widowed, the other was divorced, and both ladies chose to be called by their maiden names, Skidhouse.

Ceta, the younger one, had married a wealthy haberdasher, Alphonso Millory, who'd divorced her for a younger woman who had been managing one of his stores, Anita De Piper. Ceta's husband never allowed her to work in any of the stores because he proved to her that he could support her and she didn't have to work. They'd had no children together, but Anita had two for him, Kurline and Suzanne.

Ceta lived a lavish lifestyle while she was married. She had a six-bedroom house with a living room almost the size of the school's auditorium. She had a butler, three housekeepers, gardeners, and people to take care of her horses. She entertained once per month, and those who were invited always looked forward to the event, especially the food that was prepared by Ceta and her butler and served on her best silver trays and fine china. No one could surpass her with the excellence of her dinner parties. Her guests craved the hors d'oeuvres, their favorite ones being fried oysters, grapes soaked in vodka, and duck's wings flambéed in olive oil and brandy. The expensive wines, champagnes and other alcoholic beverages were the talk of the party.

Ceta was one of those hostesses who took the time to acquire some background information about her guests. But no matter how deep she delved into their past, sometimes she missed the juicy stories about the skeleton in someone's closet.

Cilda, a retired teacher, had taught Bobeth in elementary school, and Bobeth never forgot the impression she had made on the young minds then. Cilda had married Emilio Blashkent, and the union produced one son, Thomas. Emilio worked at the Arriango Printery, where most of Puca Luca's schoolbooks were printed. It had a contract with the Ministry of Education to prepare test papers for the different levels of examinations given each year, from elementary schools to universities. Emilio was fired in disgrace when it was revealed that he was selling test papers to certain teachers who would prepare their students accordingly. The mystery had been solved. No one knew why some schools continued to have 100 percent passing grades. A number of teachers got fired because of this, except for Cilda, who swore she had no knowledge of what her husband was doing. He corroborated her story.

Emilio then got a job as a production manager at a silica mining plant but resigned after two years, claiming that he was allergic to the raw materials. He started selling carvings and sculptures that he and his three-man workforce produced from mahogany and cedar wood.

After five years of marriage and one son, Emilio disappeared. He left with a carload of his craft to sell in the tourist area of Villard Bay in the southeastern section of the island, but he later took up residence in one of the smaller islands called Rockson Ridge. He established a relationship with Lydia Hardensfield, and that union produced a daughter named Rayla. He never contributed anything to his son's development and education in his formative years. Cilda never filed for divorce.

Fourteen years later, Emilio showed up at Cilda's doorstep with a lot of problems. He'd developed diabetes following a motor vehicle accident, and his left leg had had to be amputated. He'd been fitted with prosthetics but complained of discomfort and bruising due to an improper fit.

Cilda took him in, and when she was asked her reason for doing so, she said, "I'm doing it for my son, Thomas."

Furthermore, Emilio told her, "I will be receiving a monetary settlement from the accident, and you and our son will benefit. You will be set for life."

Cilda believed him and took the best care of him, but unexpected complications set in, and at the age of fifty-five, she was left a widow.

The El Prizzone Mortuary and Funeral Home was in charge of the final arrangements for Emilio Blashkent, and based on the verbal promise made regarding payment from proceeds of an insurance settlement, he was laid to rest. But the worst was yet to come. Cilda contacted the insurance company but got the surprise of her life: there was no settlement to be had. Emilio had already gotten the money and had bought a house for his girlfriend, who'd thrown him out when his medical situation became too severe. She didn't want to have to spend the rest of the money on him. She told everyone who would listen that she was not prepared to deal with it and die penniless.

When word reached the El Prizzone that the bill was not going to be paid, the body was exhumed, and its whereabouts were unknown. Cilda made no extra effort to have her husband rest in peace.

Cilda retired early and used her retirement income to start the boarding house with her sister, who had come into a large sum of money following her divorce.

Ionnia was first shown a lovely neat room on the first floor, but her cousin Polly and aunt Bobeth requested one on the second floor instead. Polly had lived in a boarding home in the past and had witnessed undesirables attempting to enter through first-floor windows to molest the female boarders. However, there had never been any such incident at this particular residence. Bobeth negotiated the price for Ionnia while she and Polly chose the room, making sure that it was the best one available. She was shown a twelve feet by fifteen feet furnished room on the second floor that contained a twin bed, a small bookcase, a round table twenty-four inches in diameter, two chairs, a dressing table, and a small leather sofa. The room also had a small closet and its own bathroom. She was told that she could have visitors, but they would have to be first approved by the Skidhouse sisters.

The sisters assured the trio that this was a safe place to be. And God knew Ionnia wanted to be safe. Her room was adjoining Sharonique Vorgeston's room, and that family would never have placed their daughter in an unsafe environment. Sharonique was a second-year student at the University of Krepston majoring in sociology.

In assuring the young lady's safety, Ceta took the trio around the perimeters of the building and showed her the piles of broken glass bottles at the bottom of the windows covered by rotting vegetation. She showed her the sturdy locks on the doors and pointed to the huge light bulbs that illuminated the entire grounds at night.

"I'm impressed," Bobeth said.

The trio was introduced to the chief handyman for the premises, Amos Noah, who was also the person in charge of security. Amos was a broad, tall man whose presence cast fear upon anyone who first met him, but he was a very sweet and humble person.

The Skidhouse sisters first met Amos ten years prior at church one Sunday. While the pastor conducted the service, there came through the rear of the building a stranger looking like a huge, overfed bull. He had teeth that looked like piano keys, and he laughed continually. His thunderous laughter, which reverberated throughout the church, terrified the congregation, especially the little children. He did not speak much, and when he did, it was incoherent. The deacon took him to an outer building and was soon joined by a doctor who was a member of the congregation. Amos was taken to the clinic but couldn't remember anything about himself. As soon as he began to get better and his memory returned, he gave his correct name and where he was from, adding that he needed work and a place to stay. The sisters took the chance on him and had had no regrets. Amos didn't bother to keep in contact with his relatives, who had disowned him because of the physical and psychological problems he'd sustained as a soldier during a period of political upheaval in Puca Luca. Cilda helped Amos through his adjustment period by making the necessary contacts with the commanding officer of the army, and Amos received the well-deserved physical and mental health care he needed. He also received some overlooked retroactive payments.

The Rytes were very pleased with the selection of Ionnia's living arrangements in the town of Woodwind, and the rent was affordable. Berdene and Aunt Gert made regular visits and enjoyed the company of the Skidhouse sisters.

The community of Woodwind was a quiet one with less than two hundred people, and many people yearned to call home. Apart from the well-kept homes and the prestigious Skidlet Boarding House, Woodwind had a small elementary school, two telephone booths, a grocery store, a savings and loan bank, a furniture store, a farmers market, a bicycle repair shop and petrol station, a nondenominational place of worship, a night club, and a bookstore specializing in afford-able secondhand books, some of which looked more like tenth-hand. In the center of the community sat an old, eighteenth-century build-ing that housed the library, the clinic, the post office, and a police station manned by three people who took eight-hour shifts.

Ionnia could have obtained part-time jobs with department stores on the other side of town and earned considerably more money, but she instead opted to work at the library. She felt that by doing so, she was making a more valuable contribution. She assisted with the adult literacy program and helped the children prepare for their annual reading competition. Ionnia was very instrumental in organizing fundraising efforts for the purchase of new books and furniture for the library. She arranged a book collection drive, and before the community knew it, the library had more books than it could hold and there was an urgent need for its expansion.

Ionnia made many friends while at Woodwind, one of them being Carolyn Mulnavis, the daughter of Roslyn and Percival Mulnavis, owners of One-Stop Furniture. Both girls had similar interests. They were both athletes, they were both the last child and only girl in their respective families, and they were both motivated to be the best in whatever careers they chose to pursue.

But one day the friendship between Ionnia and Carolyn came to an abrupt end, marred by one single incident that could have proved fatal for Ionnia. It wasn't clear whether or not Carolyn was aware that Ionnia was scared of dogs, so one afternoon when they were on their way to the library, Carolyn started teasing a neighbor's dogs. In a split second, before Ionnia could finish telling her that she was scared of these animals, two huge dogs jumped the fence and charged after the girls. This time, Ionnia had the opportunity to run, and as adrenaline pumped into her body, she summoned all her strength and energy. *I am not going to have any part of my body disfigured again by another dog—or worse yet, I wouldn't like my tombstone to say that I was killed by a dog.* She was sickened at these thoughts and the physical and emotional trauma that accompanied this.

Of the two, Ionnia was the faster runner, and she didn't care whether Carolyn was the one savagely torn to bits. Ionnia screamed at the top of her lungs while she outran the savage beasts, and she was able to seek refuge in a fig tree. She was young and tomboyish and was used to climbing trees and sharing spaces with lizards and other creatures.

Meanwhile, Carolyn ran into Irving Gatsworthy's yard. Everyone knew Irving as Mr. Briggs because he was a retired brigadier lieutenant in the army. He came out with his shotgun, fired a few shots in the air, and scared away the dogs.

Ionnia felt sick to her stomach. Fear replaced reality, and one could almost hear the beating of her heart like the reverberation of a drum. She heard rapid gunfire and didn't want to be hurt, so she shouted, "Stop shooting!" She froze and held on to the tree limb tighter than before despite the coaxing from the small group of people who had gathered. Ionnia tried to speak again, but her mouth was so dry that she could hardly move her tongue. Her lips quivered while beads of perspiration covered her face. One woman, Darcey Brank, sent her little seven-year-old son, Ibrau, up in the tree with a pint of cold fruit punch for Ionnia to drink. She was glad to see him, especially when she heard his name. She remembered her days in primary school where one of her best friends, Ibrau, always come to her rescue. *What a coincidence.*

"Relax and take it easy. The dogs pose no immediate danger to you at this time," Miss Darcey encouraged Ionnia. "They are gone thanks to Mr. Briggs."

Carolyn had now emerged from Irving's yard, and she told Irving's wife and the other people that Ionnia had been the one who teasing the dogs.

"You should be ashamed of yourself, young lady, for having engaged in such childish behavior. Don't you know that it's wrong to tease dogs?" someone shouted at Ionnia, and she turned her back to walk away.

The young girl was horrified to hear this. She found her voice and shouted back, "I swear I was not the one who teased the animals." She related the train incident and how much she'd suffered as a result. "I would never, never tease a dog."

They looked at each other and then at Carolyn, who hung her head in shame. "Carolyn, you sounded so convincing. Speak the truth now" said her mother.

She came clean. "I'm sorry for teasing the dogs." She turned to Ionnia and said, "I am so sorry for accusing you. Can you forgive me?"

"Maybe, but this is it. Our friendship is over. Put yourself in my shoes."

The lone policeman on duty, Corporal Freddie Gonthers, whom everyone referred to as Corpie, arrived on the scene to find out what the commotion was all about and who was firing a gun. He was a man who looked like he had made a career on the battlefield as he ambled like a shrapnel-wounded vet. Irving explained what had happened but didn't tell him that he was the one who'd fired the shots.

Gonthers looked everyone in the eye and said, "The Woodwind police takes care that this community remains as incident free as much as possible, so I pledge to take action in seeing that the person or persons who caused this unnecessary problem be punished."

When Carolyn heard this, she got scared. She knew that he meant every word, because he told the gathering that while he was in elementary school in Balderton, his fifth-grade teachers took them on a field trip to a butterfly farm, and they had to pass a home where attack dogs were being bred. Four of the dogs, a mastiff and three pit bulls, escaped from the backyard and mauled some of the children. He said that the mastiff knocked the children to the ground, and one of the pit bulls tore violently into one little girl. The teachers, although scared, tried to rid the children of the dogs. The little girl suffered a punctured lung, broken ribs, and bites all over her body, and she was on a ventilator for a long time. Some children were treated for leg, face, and arm injuries, and one boy needed nearly 150 stitches to close the wounds all over his body.

"Did any of those children live?"

"I don't know about the rest, but you are looking at one of them," he said.

There were loud gasps. Carolyn tearfully and shamefully confessed to Corpie, who instructed her to report to the station that afternoon.

"What happened to the dogs?" someone asked.

"A policeman who happened to be driving by shot all four of them."

"Is this what you are going to do to these?"

"Well, they are a menace to society and need to be put down. There is no need for anybody to have animals like these around. Who is the owner?"

Everyone looked around at each other, refusing to rat out the owner. "Speak up." Gonthers stomped his feet in anger. "Or else I'll charge all of you with something, and you will not like it, especially when you have to appear before Judge Dread."

They knew he was a man of his word, and after surveying the crowd to see whether the dogs' owner had left, someone shouted, "They belong to Miss O'Faddich. They are her guard dogs. She says she needs them for protection."

"Well, she can say goodbye to them as of today," Gonthers said as he cocked his gun and stormed off angrily. "Animals. Some are pets, some are food, but these are pests," he grumbled. "And Miss O'Faddich can always get a two-legged guard. There are lots of them around, even though some of them behave like the four-legged ones."

Someone else shouted back at him, "Corpie, you could be a rich man if you were to bottle your anger and sell it."

Carolyn's mother, Roslyn, offered Ionnia a ride in her car back to Skidlet. Turning to her daughter, she said, "And as for you, I will deal with you on our way to the station. The nerve of you to do something like this! Be prepared for some community service. You are too old for this sort of behavior. Leave this to little kids who don't know better."

Carolyn's eyes welled up with tears. "Will I get to choose? I don't want to be placed in environmental services, where I will be required to pick up dog poop off the streets and down by the market."

"Wrongdoers don't get to choose how they serve their punishment. Just be happy that the situation wasn't any worse. You could have been looking at spending a few years in reform school or jail."

Fifty-One

Dorm rooms were eventually made available on the university campus, but there were so many students on the waiting list that the school had to come up with a procedure where the selection would not only appear to be impartial but would actually be impartial. The lottery process was implemented. Ionnia and some of her friends were lucky enough to win the lottery and get assigned to some of these rooms. Ionnia was placed in a dorm at the north end of the campus with students who were in their final years of college. She was welcomed with open arms, and although she was tall and did not appear her age, she was referred to as the baby of the dorm. When the seniors graduated and left, twenty new students were placed in that dorm, and among them were Ionnia's three friends Lorna, Ordertte, and Nickie, who had just enrolled as freshmen. Whatever the reason, they were all placed in the large corner apartment near the vice principal's suite. These four longtime friends referred to themselves as *the Lions* (**L**orna, **I**onnia, **O**rdrette, **N**ickie) and their room was known as *the Lions' den.'*

Ionnia's longtime roommate Olivine, who was also admitted to the same institution, was placed in an adjoining building and got the opportunity to frequently visit the girls. She was a very different person compared to Ionnia and her roommates. Olivine came from a privileged family, had expensive tastes in her clothing and jewelry, and annoyed everyone with her extravagance. She mocked Ionnia for spending most of her time in the library rather than socializing. Olivine's attitude toward Ionnia had taken a complete 180, yet Ionnia kept expecting that things would be okay for old times' sake.

"I don't like her," Ordrette protested. "How do we tell her politely that she is not welcome here?" Her protest stemmed mainly from the fact that Olivine spent an awful lot of time in the company of the male students and partied heavily rather than focus on her education. When time caught up with her, and she desperately needed help with her research and assignments, she begged Ionnia for help. Without this kind of help, Olivine would receive failing grades. She remembered the good old days and displayed what one would refer to as niceness of convenience. She even offered to pay Ionnia to do her assignments for her. She was a very charming and charismatic person and would rely on these qualities to persuade the professors to allow her to prepare and submit makeup assignments.

"I don't need your money," Ionnia told her on one occasion. "You need to be more focused and should concentrate on your studies. Do you think you can always buy your way to the top or sleep around with the professors and anyone who wears trousers? How will you cope when you get a job?" she asked.

"Who needs to work when one has a face and a body like this?" Olivine asked as she spun around twice. This attitude was a blatant reminder of incidents that had occurred at Dartsdam Elementary.

Olivine was a sex fiend, or perhaps she could be described as a nymphomaniac. One wouldn't be surprised if she were related to Minta. She constantly made reference to her money and her beauty, and she described people who didn't look like her as ugly. She had to be reminded by her guidance counselor, "Outside beauty will fade with the passage of time, but inner beauty never fades."

There finally came a time when Ionnia no longer helped Olivine with her assignments because of her own volume of work and extracurricular activities, and pressure from her roommates. This infuriated

Olivine, and now she was out for blood. What the girls weren't aware of was that one key fitted all the doors to all the buildings, and when no one was around, someone quietly slipped into the Lions' den and hid Ionnia's design displays so that she was unable to make a presentation the following day at the school's annual design exhibition and art festival.

No one had ever seen Ionnia that upset, and she didn't know on whom to place the blame. She wanted to show off her work to the visiting public, especially to those from high-end department stores that offered contracts to students whose work was outstanding. It could have been any one of the friends who visited Lorna, Ordrette, or Nickie. Rather than create a scene, Ionnia reported the matter to her fashion design professor, Dr. Hal Buyer. He understood the situation and empathized with her. He was aware of Ionnia's dedication to her work and so had no reason to doubt her. When one heard "Your attention, please" on the public address system, one knew that an announcement of some importance was about to be made.

What Professor Buyer had to say stunned everyone. "The displays and presentations scheduled for tomorrow have been cancelled indefinitely. One of the judges cannot make it due to circumstances beyond his control." The professor had been on the phone all morning with the judges, the purchasers, and the models who would be showing off the students' work. They all agreed to reschedule.

The students from the design class who had begun to arrange their displays expressed disappointment, but many were happy for the extra time to perfect their skills. As for Ionnia, her immediate response was, "Where will I get the money to purchase all the material I need? And will I complete the project by the time another presentation is scheduled?" She told her mother Berdene about this.

"Let me have a list of everything that you will need," Berdene he said. "I will make sure nothing is left out."

It came as a surprise to the perpetrator that Ionnia was given a second chance, and it must have been overly disappointed that Olivine's plans had not brought about the result that she had hoped for. Surprisingly, Ionnia's displays showed up a few days later, some of which were badly damaged by what appeared to be a caustic sub stance, but she was able to use some of the other pieces. Ionnia was speechless, and a volcanic wrath burned inside her. But rather than concentrate on revenge, she worked diligently day and night on the rest of the project and was able to replace the damaged ones. From that day onward, whenever she completed assignments and got them graded by Professor Buyer, Ionnia placed them in a locked safe in the vice principal's office, or she asked Berdene to put them away. Ionnia's roommates carried out their own investigations, and they were mor- tified when they found out that Olivine was the culprit and how she gained access to the room. Other students feared for their safety when they learned about the one-size-fits-all keys. Immediately, all the locks were changed, and students were given individual keys to each room. This was a huge economic burden on the university, and Olivine's parents were asked to contribute 75 percent of the expenses to replace the locks.

At first, Olivine thought that the whole incident was funny, but when she realized that she would be suspended for ten days, she decided to come clean. She approached Ionnia in a rather lighthearted manner. "I am so sorry for what I have done. Can you see it in your heart to forgive me? Remember how happy we were when we were at Redwood Vale?"

Ionnia asked Olivine, "What are you really apologizing for? Is it because you get caught, or because you didn't mean to do what you are accused of doing? Do you know the seriousness of what you did? You could be charged with breaking and entering, burglary, theft, and malicious destruction of property."

Olivine could not reply. Instead, she handed Ionnia an envelope with a large sum of money.

"Here we go again—buying your way out of trouble." Ionnia grabbed the envelope out of Olivine's hands and told her, "I am going to donate all of it to the Woodwind library, and I will make sure it goes to the children's art projects."

"Maybe you should also consider reimbursing the school for the inconvenience of having to cancel the displays," Ordrette shouted.

"That's a good idea," Nickie said.

The university imposed its own brand of discipline on Olivine, and as a result, she dropped out of college and began working as a personal assistant to Raphael Dexter, the assistant commissioner of police at the Krepston police headquarters. Commissioner Dexter was as obsessed with this young woman as she was with him. His attitude and treatment toward his wife had started to change dramatically, and when Mrs. Dexter protested about her husband's treatment toward her, he interpreted her actions as a threat to Olivine. He told his wife in no uncertain terms, "If anything should happen to this girl, you will be held responsible. I will not hesitate to personally slap on the cuffs on you."

Raphael divorced his wife of twenty-five years and married Olivine, but the marriage didn't last long. Olivine was unfaithful to him, and he made several attempts on her life. He then went to his first wife, begging her to take him back, but she had already moved on.

Would any of these experiences force Olivine to change her ways? According to a nineteenth-century American-born pianist, Caroline Schroeder, "Some people change their ways when they see the light, others when they feel the heat." When would Olivine begin to feel the heat?

Toward the end of Ionnia's second year at the University of Krepston, she was presented with an opportunity to assume a position of responsibility. The student's council president-elect had been transferred to another institution, leaving that position vacant. Several final-year students in their twenties were vying for the position. Ionnia was just a teenager but toyed with the idea of getting in the running. She was young but competent and experienced, although not everyone readily accepted it. These were some of the questions asked by the seniors: "Who does she think she is? Who would vote for her? What will her message be?"

It was bad enough that the students protested Ionnia's involvement, but some faculty members discouraged her too. She was summoned to the office of the professor in charge of student affairs, Dr. Abbie Mann, and was also told in no uncertain terms that she was too young for all the responsibilities that came with the position of student council president. Dr. Mann asked Ionnia to reconsider.

Ionnia looked her straight in the eye without being disrespectful and quoted 1 Timothy 4:12, which said, "Let no man despise your youth, but be thou an example to the believers, in word, in conversation, in charity, in spirit, in faith and in purity."

"So does that mean you won't reconsider? You have time. Perhaps you could try again next year."

Ionnia stood her ground and remarked, "One should never procrastinate. Do what you can when you have the opportunity, because tomorrow may be too late."

"I must say that some people may describe you as ambitious and resilient," Dr. Mann said. "But I would say you are obstinate and hard-headed."

Ionnia politely said to Dr. Mann, "Have you heard of Henry Ward Beecher?"

"Who is he, and what's your point?"

"He is a nineteenth-century US congressional clergyman and social reformer who once wrote that the difference between perseverance and obstinacy is that one comes from a strong will, and one comes from a strong won't."

Among the contenders for the position of student council president was a final-year male student, Denville Linzi, whose parents owned several businesses throughout Puca Luca, had powerful connections, and had contributed a lot of money to the university. They would stop at nothing to get what they wanted, even if it meant going to the extremes. They were ruthless and influential and knew how to pull the right strings. Denville behaved as though he was entitled to the position. The more the students and faculty members discouraged Ionnia, the more determined she was. It was a bitter campaign.

The debating of tough issues was not the only battle that Ionnia had to fight. As a matter of fact, that was the easiest—the older candidates were no match for her. After the first three debates, almost everyone said how impressed they were with her. But Ionnia had to deal with the smear campaigns and vicious, unwarranted rumors that were posted on notice boards and printed in flyers that were distributed all over the campus and in the local community. Various groups on and off campus could be seen gossiping, and as soon as Ionnia got closer, there was a hushed silence broken by whispers. She could sense that they were plotting against her, but what was it they were planning to do? Those thoughts frightened her. Her roommates could not always watch her back, but this time they spent their waking moments finding out what her enemies had in store for her. The plot was worse than anyone could imagine. She found out the hard way that physical harm was a part of the plot. She relived the pain inflicted on her by Bibb, Morette, and Dutte, as well as the rape attempt by the other three in the science lab. For the first time in the campaign, Ionnia feared for her life, but she was not going to back off. A part of her upbringing was to hold on tight to what she believed in. Her motivation was based on her perseverance and persistence. She remembered reading a quote from Publius Ovidius Naso, a Roman poet also known as Ovid: "Dripping water hollows out stones, not through force, but through persistence." She also remembered one from Socrates that stated, "He is a man of courage who does not run away, but remains at his post and fights against the enemy."

Weeks went by, and nothing happened, so Ionnia almost dismissed the thoughts. But her enemies had not forgotten and were watching her every move. One Friday afternoon, Ionnia went to a small copy room adjoining the library to get her flyers ready for the next day's distribution. Someone must have seen her go in but didn't see her depart. She was always mindful of what older folks used to say: "Always choose an alternative route. Always have a plan B." She left through a side door with the art professor's secretary, Natasha Hitty-Houm. Just as they were leaving, they met another student, Marjorie Baruke, coming through that side door. Not many people knew of this door. Ionnia's opponents assumed that she was the only one in the copy room and would be coming out the way she'd entered, so they placed a piece of oiled plastic at the door and then pulled the fire alarm lever, setting off a frenzy. Marjorie, who was making copies for her sociology professor, dropped what she was doing, and in the confusion she flung open the front door in an effort to escape in case there was a real fire. As she tried to escape, she slid on the oiled plastic, fell, and broke her coccyx. She was hospitalized for a long while, and at one point in time, her recovery looked gloomy. Speculation was that she may never walk again, but the university provided her with the best doctors and physical therapists, and she recovered satisfactorily.

School officials begged for calm. "Tone down the rhetoric. Stop the hate. Violence toward anyone, especially females, will not be tolerated. If this asinine and barbaric behavior continues, we will have no alternative but to permanently suspend the campaign and assign someone to the position."

Denville Linzi denounced the attack and denied knowledge of any involvement by any of his supporters or surrogates. To this day, no one was held accountable except the university, which was sued by Marjorie's parents, Maisie and Edgar Baruke. To save face, the Linzi family reimbursed the university for what they'd paid out to the Baruke family. Perhaps they hoped that Denville would automatically be given the position.

The campaign was temporarily suspended for a while, and all debates were canceled. When these activities resumed, Ionnia's focused on women's issues. She focused on violence against women and the inequities meted out to female students who were paying the same rate of tuition as male students, yet when they graduated and obtained employment in similar capacities, their salaries were less than their male counterparts. "Women need to be protected," Ionnia stressed. She led an extensive campaign to have educational institutions either lower their tuition rates for females or to have employers offer comparable salaries—equal work for equal pay. She had her platform, and this was just the beginning of a movement to advocate for women's protection from an unjust society monopolized by men.

Ionnia's message was heard loud and clear, both near and far. Female advocacy groups that had intervened jumped on the bandwagon and lobbied the universities and labor unions to take appropriate action. Rallies were held throughout Puca Luca. News media were inundated with petitions. Some people, especially men, blamed sixteen-year-old Ionnia for the uprising. Others lauded her for opening their eyes to the inequalities of the labor force and the education system. Her opponent had a difficult time debating the issue and was labeled a male chauvinist. The business establishments belonging to his parents were picketed, and female employees had a lot of stories to tell. The Linzies set an example by being the first employer to rectify the situation with equal pay for men and women.

The campaign came to an end, and Ionnia was elected student council president of the University of Krepston. She was the youngest in the institution's history to hold that position, which she held until she graduated.

Although Denville didn't win the coveted position, he became an advocate for change within the business industry. Not long afterward, a national law was passed bridging the gap between male and female salaries, and the law was named after Ionnia: the I Dunn-Ryte Legislation. Trade union representatives made sure that the changes were implemented, and in some cases, employers were compelled to retroactively compensate female employees. Also, in some instances where resistance was met, the tertiary institutions from where these female students graduated were asked to reimburse them a portion of their tuition fees.

The Linzi Corporation received the Company of the Year award for setting an example in upholding the new law. It created and supported high levels of professional accomplishments for its women employees. With the disappearance of salary inequality, women were encouraged to excel in the company and forge a path of leadership for other women to emulate. They were promoted to positions that had been always held by men. They had Ionnia to thank for this. She accomplished what the powerful labor unions could not do. "You have done right," they would say.

Fifty-Two

Roger and Tourmaline, who had been dating steadily for some time, were madly in love with each other and were now ready to tie the knot. Roger formally proposed at a New Year's Eve ball shortly before midnight, and they both agreed on a May wedding. When Roger broke the news to his mother, she at once contacted Crystal Vernetti, the area's most renowned wedding planner, to make the wedding dress with Loretty's assistance and directions. The guest list included close friends, relatives, and coworkers of the couple. The pair became husband and wife on a beautiful spring afternoon on the small island of French Reef, with Opal the maid of honor, Chad the best man, and Ionnia and Jade as attendants.

As the guests and some members of the wedding party began arriving for the four o'clock ceremony at the Eastern Methodist Church, an unforecasted shower of rain came down, but it lasted for only ten minutes.

"This is a sign of good luck," said Murdell Kiffin, who was assuming the role as mother of the bride. "Old wives' tales have it that the couple will have a long life and as many children as the raindrops."

Everyone burst out laughing. Murdell spoke highly of Tourmaline as if she were her own daughter. She was as proud as a peacock and wore a square-topped light gray hat with yellow feathers and a calf-length soft gray silk dress with a light velvety yellow scarf.

Twyleith and Priscilla got a chance to catch up where they'd left off, when they'd met at the airport in San Clewert some time ago. Then Priscilla started to complain. "I can't believe that I was not asked to play the role that is given to Murdell." She was also upset that her girls were not included in the wedding party.

Twyleith reminded her that she didn't speak kind words about Tourmaline. "You are lucky you got invited. You should thank Murdell, who begged Tourmaline to include you. Your rejection and punishment are self-inflicted. Are there any regrets in the way you treat my niece-in-law?"

No one could forget the day when Tourmaline had been around eight years old and had attended the Orange Blossom County fair with her aunt and cousins. An old friend of Priscilla's had approached her and the children and asked, "Who are these little ones?" Pointing to her biological children, Priscilla had said, "These are mine." Then she'd looked at Tourmaline and said, "This is the spare."

As the women continued talking, Priscilla's daughters joined them, and the conversation changed.

Inside the church, the nervous Roger sweated profusely. What was going through his mind? Was he thinking that his fiancée would not show up? He was given words of encouragement by Jonas Kiffin, Bishop Ryte, Chad, Loretty, other members of the family, and well-wishers. While they waited anxiously for the arrival of the bride, some of the little children complained of being hungry, and others took a catnap. A few parents slipped outside in the rain, which had now downgraded to a drizzle, and went to get a few sandwiches from a nearby deli. No one wanted to miss the happy occasion, so when they looked down the road and saw the limousine approaching, they hurried back to the church.

Tourmaline and her party sat in the vehicle until the rain ceased and a rainbow became visible across the now cloudless sky. She emerged from the vehicle wearing the most beautiful gown one had ever seen. It was a satin A-lined dress embellished with beads along the V-neck line. It had a train around six feet long, and Opal and Ionnia tried their utmost to prevent it from getting soiled.

"My future daughter-in-law looks like an angel. All she needs is a pair of wings," Loretty said with a broad smile.

The bridal party reached the steps of the church, and Jonas Kiffin made an elegant bow, proudly took Tourmaline's arm, and walked her down the aisle on the red carpet to the music of "Here Comes the Bride." Roger couldn't wait for Jonas to bring Tourmaline to him, so he took a few steps forward and relieved Jonas of his duty. The three flower girls who were assigned to sprinkle carnations and roses on the carpet did a very good job, and the photographers captured the moment as the couple glided their way through the variegated petals toward the altar. The task of ring bearer was entrusted to Lupert Thurnston, the grandson of Murdell's older sister, and when it was time for him to walk up the aisle and hand the rings to the minister, he got halfway and then made a run from whence he came. He ran straight in the arms of Ionnia's cousin, Thalia, and her husband, Fenton Locksley, who had been late getting to the church. Fenton, who could easily be mistaken for one of the groomsmen, gently took Lupert's hands, walked him back to his position, and stood close to him to prevent a recurrence of what had just happened.

The congregation was extremely elated when the officiating minister charged them to hold the couple accountable for keeping the marriage together. Twyleith turned around and looked at Priscilla, who hung her head and was almost at the point of tears, knowing that she couldn't keep her own marriage together yet was to be held accountable if her niece's marriage should fail.

The reception was held in the Platinum Ballroom of the Southern Creations Hotel. It was the perfect setting with polished marble floors and triangular vases on the tables and the walls that held a single stem of carnations and a sprig of jasmine, Tourmaline's favorite flowers.

No detail was overlooked. The perfect meal was served, prepared by one of the country's famous executive chefs, Muzzy Asheed, who had been featured in almost every culinary magazine and had won most of the region's coveted awards. The emcee for the occasion was one of the nation's best entertainers, Manuel Upton, who was popularly known as Dr. Man-U. He selected the perfect song for the first dance, and Roger and his bride took to the floor, which indicated that they had been practicing for a long time. Dr. Leroy Boot gave a memorable toast to the bride and those responsible for her upbringing, and Darrel Bundle toasted the groom and his family.

The dinner, the first dance, and the speeches and toasts were completed. Next, it was time for the tossing of the bridal bouquet and the garter, and all the single attendees took their places. The bouquet was caught by Roger's cousin, Polly McEarth, and the garter was caught by Cordell.

The cutting of the cake by the bride and groom created much excitement, and it was followed by Roger first feeding a small piece to his wife. When it was time for Tourmaline to feed her husband, she gave him such a big piece that he could hardly close his mouth. The wedding photographers caught it from every angle.

"Ladies and gentlemen, the dance floor is now open to everyone," Dr. Man-U announced. Then came the evening's bid surprise: Kingsley Muggerdon emerged from nowhere, took Loretty by the arm, and led her on the dance floor.

"I wasn't going to miss this opportunity," he said. When they finished dancing, Kyle and Tyrone were the first to ask their mother who her mysterious dance partner was. She tried her best to explain, but when Kingsley saw how much she was blushing, he took over. When he identified himself as a Muggerdon, both boys looked at each other and smiled. While the inquiry, interrogation, and explaining were taking place, the newlyweds made a dash for their waiting limousine, but they were unable to move because Kingsley had blocked them in. This was deliberate because he used the opportunity to present the couple with a generous monetary gift.

The couple honeymooned for two weeks in the neighboring island of Ludwick, and then it was back to work as usual. Roger went back to the Locksley group of companies as a human resource manager, and Tourmaline was transferred to the Whickam County General Hospital as a nurse supervisor. It took a while getting used to her new name, Quane, but she did not object when others who knew her continued to refer to her as Nurse Brandstalk. Two months after her employment at Whickam County General, her father, Armand Brandstalk, was admitted to the hospital, suffering from a number of health issues. This was a man who had abandoned his children following the death of his first wife, and he'd caused much harm to his second wife, Doreen, and their children. When she could no longer endure his treatment, Doreen took the children and left. Her final decision came about when another woman with whom Armand was having an affair called her around two o'clock one Sunday morning to come get her husband out of her bed because he had had a heart attack. Doreen made arrangements to have him taken to the nearest hospital, where he spent a considerable amount of time. He had other medical issues that required him to see different medical specialists, so he was transferred to Whickam County General Hospital. His health continued to deteriorate rapidly, and the doctors were unable to identify the causes of his additional problems. Those who believed in witchcraft and the supernatural commented, "This is truly the work of the devil, and retribution for treating his family the way he did." Others dismissed this as an affliction by the hand of God.

While Armand was hospitalized, the marital dwelling was bull-dozed by the Department of Local Government. His home and other buildings were seized through a system known as imminent domain, and this area was earmarked for a parking lot for a nearby sports complex. Doreen and her children were now living with her mother, and she wasn't concerned where Armand would live if he got out of hospital. She visited him once, and as she confessed, the visit was to see how close he was to dying. She kept the children away from him, and he never asked about them. Doreen was determined to raise them by herself. She also held on to the proceeds of the property to help support and educate her children.

While at the hospital, Armand drifted in and out of consciousness. During one period of lucidity, he overheard one student nurse consulting with Nurse Brandstalk regarding the patient in the other bed in his room. At another conscious moment later that evening, he rang the buzzer and requested to see Nurse Brandstalk. Tourmaline asked another nurse to accompany her to the room. When they got there, Armand said to her, "I am so proud of you." Looking in the other nurse's direction, he cleared his throat and said, "I am lucky to be in the same hospital where my daughter works. I know she will see to it that I get the best care possible."

One million memories rose from the past and pulled at every nerve in Tourmaline's body. The flames of hate flickered at her heart. She looked at her father with disgust, held his hand, and whispered in his ear while she pretended to fluff his pillows, "I don't know you, and you don't know me either. Remember the letter you sent me? May you rot in hell. And if you attempt to say anything to anyone, it will be my word against yours." With that said, she pulled the covers over his shoulders—something that he'd never done for her when he'd left her to freeze to death on the church steps. She turned to the nurse who was with her and said, "This patient is hallucinating, and we are definitely not related. I will be making a referral for him to be transferred to the psychiatric facility across the road."

After Tourmaline got off work that night, she discussed the day's incidents with Roger. With deep empathy for his wife, he took her in his arms and asked, "How does it make you feel, being around a man like that?"

"I want a way out of this hospital. Other people may believe him, and as long as he is a patient in the hospital where I work, I am obligated to see that he gets adequate care per the ethical principles of the nursing profession. I can't do it. I need a transfer. I can't risk losing my license over that man. I struggled too hard to be where I am."

"I love you and will support any decision that you make," Roger assured his wife.

The following day, Tourmaline made contact with the chief physician in charge of the hospital and requested time off to rest because of problems with her pregnancy. She applied for six weeks' leave of absence, which was granted without hesitation. She did not care whether this Armand Brandstalk died an agonizing death or lived in pain for the rest of his life.

During Tourmaline's absence, Armand Brandstalk was discharged from the hospital with nowhere to go. The shock of losing his home, his property, his money, and his family sent him over the edge. At first he was admitted to the psychiatric facility across the road, but when his health began to deteriorate more, he was sent to an indigent home whose funding was made available through charitable and religious organizations. But due to the number of indigent and uninsured who were admitted each month, there came a time when funds were inadequate to provide the level of care that all the residents required. The Health Ministry did not want to be shamed and ridiculed if this becomes another Ward R, so legislation was passed to make funding available. Armand Brandstalk spent the rest of his life as a pauper and died without apologizing to his daughter and the rest of his family for his treatment toward them.

Tourmaline maintained a good relationship with her maternal siblings, Opal and Jade. Her cousins Jessica and Arlene Dutte relied on her for career guidance because they were in and out of permanent employment. They were so spoilt that they paid little attention to their careers. Tourmaline had a special love for the Kiffins' children, especially the last one, Fern. After a while, Doreen's children got to meet her, and they too expressed their love for her. She never discussed with them the letter that Doreen had written to her, but she left a copy in a spot where it wasn't difficult for anyone to find it—and if they had, no one talked about it. At a later date, Doreen talked about it and almost overdosed on remorse.

Ionnia looked up to Tourmaline as a big sister and received good advice from her. She would babysit for her whenever she had the time, and she loved to be with her nephew, whom she had the privilege of naming Joel.

Fifty-Three

Being a valedictorian seemed to have become a trend in Ionnia's life. She had done it already, and she was about to do it again. It came as no surprise because she'd been preparing for this role from the very first day she'd set foot on the grounds of the University of Krepston. She hoped that she would be selected by the committee, which was made up of faculty members and a few members of the board of governors. All along, she hoped that a more democratic approach would be implemented to replace the old system of selection, which favored students whose parents made big contributions to the institution. She didn't want preferential treatment because everyone was aware that the Rytes also made huge personal annual contributions. Fellow students were asked to submit nominations, and soon her dreams were realized. She won over a pool of six students including Elore Twitney, who behaved as if the whole world revolved around her and she was entitled to something.

Although the others accepted this in good strides and congratulated Ionnia, Elore took this personally, lapsed into a period of depression, and became socially withdrawn. "How will I explain this to my parents? I am not accustomed to being passed over. I am not accustomed to failing," Elore lamented. She was an only child and was used to getting everything she asked for. Therefore she did not possess the coping skills to handle what she considered failure when things didn't go her way.

"Snap out of it," Icene Flemmington, one of the contestants, said to Elore. "You are not entitled to anything. Do you think Moses brought your name down on a stone tablet from Mount Sinai? Someone had to win, and this does not mean that you should give up. It simply means that you should try harder. And as the saying goes, 'Catch a bear before you sell its skin.'" It was rumored that Elore had given her parents the impression that she was chosen to be the valedictorian, and her mother had already written her speech.

"I have tried hard enough, and there may be nothing more to live for. I feel like jumping off a bridge."

"Wow. Let me know when you will be doing that. I have never witnessed a suicide before. And make sure you do it in your birthday suit." Icene's tone came across as insensitive and deriding.

She was reprimanded by the debate coach. "Do you know that if you encourage her to commit suicide, and she carries it out, you could be charged and held responsible for her death?"

Ionnia used Elore's situation and reaction as the theme of her valedictory speech. "To succeed is to have failed." She cited nineteenth-century American film director George Cukor, who once said, "You can't have success unless you can accept failure." She mentioned the many occasions in her life when she could have given up but didn't. Ionnia recalled an experience she'd had in fifth grade during the start of a science invention, when the teacher had begun by telling them that they were not going to achieve success in the first or second attempts, and if they were not willing to use that as a yardstick for success, they shouldn't bother to waste their time. They'd all thought of backing down, but then he'd encouraged them by citing examples of trial and error by famous inventors, telling them that failure gave one the opportunity to try a new approach, and that failure was nature's plan to prepare someone for great responsibilities. "Failure does not mean that you will never succeed in what you do.

It is simply an indication that things may take a little longer to get to that level where you are satisfied," she said.

Ionnia had strong words for people who were used to getting the kind of feedback that everything they do was great, even when it was not. "We are setting up these people for permanent disappointments," she said. "If these people should suddenly be faced with a difficult challenge, they just wouldn't know what to do, and then they look at themselves as inferior compared to other people."

Ionnia was in the spotlight for a full half hour, quoting many famous people. In her concluding remarks, she urged the graduates and other members of the audience to never think of themselves as too proud to fail. She assured them that the ability to handle failure was a sign of maturity, because one couldn't have success until one accepted failure. It was necessary for her to remind them that each person's idea or concept of failure was different from anyone else's.

Ionnia received a standing ovation that lasted for nearly three minutes. She had fond memories of the unprepared and unrehearsed musical performance at Cordell's recognition function in Trevine. The only difference this time was that she was not presented with a bouquet of flowers but with plaques, honor awards, and certificates. She was proud of herself. If her father was alive, maybe he wouldn't call her a mistake. As far as her grandfather was concerned, she planned to send him pictures of the graduation, but she didn't care what he did with them.

Loretty was too moved for words, but other family members lavished Ionnia with words of praise. What happened the following day was something no one was expecting. Ionnia's picture was on the front page of one of the major print media in Puca Luca with the headline "Star Power."

With college behind her, Ionnia wasted no time in following upon her appointments for a full-time job. She applied to various lucrative companies and was offered positions with MUJALI, the Locksley Group, and Zeme Industries. She ruled out the first two because her mother worked with MUJALI and her brother was an employer of the Locksley Group. She had already performed a work study and an internship with Zeme Industries, and during that period, the owner's wife, Beatrice, the co-owner of the company, had acted as a mentor to her. One of the highlights of Ionnia's interaction with the company was the time Beatrice Zeme took her to a Chamber of Commerce function, where she was a guest speaker. Beatrice was motivated and inspiring, and she left an indelible mark on this young lady. Beatrice insisted that Ionnia read financial magazines and the financial pages of the daily newspapers, and Ionnia followed her advice. Victor Zeme was right, and his advice seemed to work for many of those who had achieved success.

For several months, Ionnia received responses from different companies begging her to share her talents with them. When she scrutinized the various responses and offers, she concluded that the salary and perks were more enticing at Zeme's, and she saw more opportunities for upward movement.

Her first paid job with Zeme's Industries was as a marketer and sales representative, and she was paid handsomely. They did not make the mistake of paying her less than her male counterparts. Her first assignment was selling advertising space to big media houses and small community newspapers. She was very successful at this. Shortly afterward, she was appointed managing editor for one of Zeme's Fashion Magazines, *Stitches*. Ionnia felt gratified, empowered, and satisfied. "I will work as hard as I can to achieve the success for which I yearn, so that young women will emulate me."

At the start of her career at Zeme Industries, Ionnia was advanced four weeks' salary so that she could rent her own flat in a respectable neighborhood. This was the first time she'd been given this amount of money. She rented a two-bedroom apartment from Reuben Ernakki, an architect, developer, and entrepreneur. He was the uncle to her friend Penelope, and she trusted him to find her a house to purchase later. He came through for her and found her a three-bed, three-bath in an adjoining complex at a reasonable price. Home ownership marked another milestone in Ionnia's life, and she felt very proud. She remembered what her aunt Arthel had once told her: "If you are going to embrace singlehood, by a certain age you have to own a car, a house, and a profession." She had the house and the profession, and she did not feel the need to own a car because she was privileged to drive one of the company's cars and use it for her own personal purposes.

Ionnia liked the idea of being single, and she hoped that she would not experience the social stigma of getting to that magic age and not being married. "What has getting a husband done to enhance some women's lives?" A number of women came to mind, one of whom Ionnia had recently met. Kerline Dash was a millwright's daughter who had become Ionnia's new best friend. She had the misfortune of having been married and divorced twice. There was no car and no house, and judging by her various trips to different doctors, it would be safe to assume that marriage was hazardous to her health.

Her parents were outraged that she was not able to make her marriage work. "What is wrong with you? Why you are unable to hold on to a man?" her mother asked.

"Because I refuse to put up with their bullshit. The next time, instead of leaving, I will try to remember my wedding day and these three words: aisle, alter, hymn. Does that satisfy you, Mother?"

Knowing what she did about Kerline and other unfortunate women who suffered under the hands of men, it was no wonder Ionnia ignored the unpleasant existence of marriage. She was aware that she might be called derogatory names such as old maid and cat lady, but she didn't care.

Ionnia and Kerline first met at Chad's office. The young lady, who revealed that she had recognized Ionnia from the newspaper, was unemployed at the time. Ionnia remembered Roger telling her that a position for an assistant financial consultant was available within his company, so she asked him to arrange an interview for her new friend. Kerline, who had a degree in economics, prepared a rather impressive resume and got the job after being interviewed by three of the top executives of the company. "I don't know how to thank you," she said to Ionnia.

"No need to at this time," she replied. "If we are going to remain friends, there are certain things you should know about me. One of them is that I want the best for my friends, as I want for myself. I am not expecting anything in return except that you make the best use of opportunities that are afforded to you." Blessed with sharp business acumen, Ionnia taught her friend the art of keeping a good job, managing her resources, saving money, and living within her means. She considered herself a proud achiever and enjoyed talking about the less fortunate days when things were hard to come by. "Just live and learn," she told Kerline. Then she asked her a question the woman wasn't expecting; "When was the last time you were happy and healthy?"

"Before I married one of those tyrants, and since I divorced the last one," Kerline said.

With a unique understanding of what it felt like to be in need, one of Ionnia's pledges was to share whatever she had with others, especially those who were willing to show appreciation. When her longtime friend Ibrau Kraun contacted her and begged her to let his cousin Aireen stay with her for a while, she agreed without hesitation. Aireen was a shy, introverted eighteen-year-old, but when she saw how down-to-earth Ionnia was, she opened up to her. She was the product of a marriage that had been broken up when she was around ten years old. Her mother was distraught and broke and was not in any position to raise her two children; Aireen was the younger daughter, and Sally was the older one. Aireen lived with her father for a while, but when his girlfriend resented her, she went to live with her mother, Aldith, who had begun to get her life back together. While Aireen was off at boarding school and college, Aldith remarried because, according to her, she was not able to live without a man. The marriage started out with each person thinking that either one had met his or her soul mate. But then her husband, Cecil, turned into a different person. He beat Aldith almost every day for no apparent reason, or for the simplest reason, until she was forced to run away and seek refuge with one of her friends, Stephanie Osgrovel. Cecil found out where his wife was staying, went there one early morning, broke the door down, and shot everyone in the house, including Stephanie's four-year-old daughter, Charmaine.

Aireen had one year left to complete her studies in atmospheric science, but she did not bother to return to college because she was in so much pain over the loss of her mother. She wanted to live with her cousin Ibrau. Then he thought of his childhood friend, who would be the perfect role model for Airee. Ionnia mentored the teenager and encouraged her to return to school as soon as possible. However, one of Aireen's major setbacks was public speaking. She disclosed to Ionnia how much she had prepared for a presentation. She had practiced in front of her peers, but when the moment came for her to speak in the presence of strangers, she froze and broke down in tears. "It seems so easy for you," she said to Ionnia. "I don't know how you do it." Ionnia introduced her to Iris Depping, and Aireen had some weekend sessions with her for six months.

On their way back from charm school one weekend, the young ladies decided to attend the annual pantomime in the huge auditorium at Independence Village. "If we are able to get tickets at this late stage, I think we will be in for a treat," Ionnia told her friend. After succeeding in their effort to get the last two tickets, they were escorted to their seats by one of the ushers. While seated, Ionnia felt a slight tap on her shoulder coming from someone behind them, and when she turned around, she was staring in the eyes of her friend Ibrau.

"Imagine meeting you here," she said.

"I was planning to come see you both afterward, and to thank you in person for helping out a relative in need." Ibrau was seated beside a very plump and robust female who wore a pair of dark blue gloves. Before anyone could ask Aireen if they were together, Ibrau introduced his female companion to both of them as Merle. Ionnia did not recognize the young lady, and she didn't know whether she recognized her prior to hearing her name, or whether she was the same person caught in Mr. Giddeon's trap. Both were civil to each other and behaved as well-brought-up young ladies.

The cast of characters for the pantomime was introduced, and Ionnia focused her attention on the stage rather than being reminded of her schoolmate Merlette. She told herself that if this were the same person, she would not tell Ibrau about the incident at Mr. Giddeon's shop. She saw that he was happy, and therefore she was happy for him too.

The afternoon's occasion concluded, and all four people ended up at a very nice restaurant, where they would be having dinner together. When the young lady pulled her gloves from her hands, Ionnia couldn't refrain from staring. She reached across the table and shook hands, making the introduction formal. She hoped to make a distinction between the real fingers from the prosthetic ones. It turned out that this wasn't the Merlette she'd known from Redwood Vale. This Merle was the owner of a well-established private school in Trevine. Merle reached out to Aireen, and since then their relationship had been a very positive one. Ibrau and Ionnia got to meet more often and catch up on the lost years. He had continued his career as a chef and was doing well for himself.

Fifty-Four

The owner of Zeme Industries, Ryland Zeme, was a bald-headed man in his late fifties. He had established businesses in different locations in Puca Luca and around the world. Ryland had grown up in abject poverty but had managed to turn the situation around to become one of the most powerful and wealthy men on earth. The story of his life was produced in a television documentary titled *From Tatters to Tux.*

Ryland's father, Elrick Zeme, a sheep farmer and butcher, hailed from a small farming community called Black Forrest, situated in Gravadee County. He spent much of his time going from place to place and buying goats and sheep. He was also a wool trader who specialized in quality products, which he sold to renowned wool merchants near and far. But the one thing for which he would always be remembered was his interest in witchcraft and the occult.

Elrick's brother, Lathan, was responsible for the sheep shearing, preparation, and packaging of the wool, which they would sell to the only factory in Puca Luca or take to Stechion Bay for export.

When Elrick Zeme met Ryland's mother, seventeen-year-old Deslean Bingham, in Willow Creek, he was mesmerized by her beauty. "I wasn't aware that there were such beautiful young ladies around here," was his first comments. She was beautiful, all right, but she was poor, vulnerable, and not very well educated. It could be said that men took advantage of her, but her parents turned a blind eye because they would benefit from the gifts she would receive from these individuals. Elrick struck up a conversation with Deslean by questioning her about other people who had animals for sale in the area.

"The only one I know is a sheep farmer, Manley Banderson, but he lives around three miles away from here in a place called Blue Hole Junction."

"How do you know?"

"I know his son."

"Is he your boyfriend?" Elrick asked.

"No, sir. We went to school together."

"Can you ride with me to find Mr. Banderson?"

Deslean was a little hesitant at first, but the sweet-talking Elrick convinced her that he would take her there and back before her parents started to miss her. He kept his word and quickly brought her back home. He was very grateful for Deslean's assistance, gave her a few dollars, and pledged to give her more the next time he was in the area. She felt she could trust him.

Elrick visited Willow Creek once every two weeks and would bring foodstuff and other gifts for Deslean and her parents. She would sneak away with him for an hour or two each time, and he would tell her how much he loved her. No one else had shown her this type of attention before, but when she told him that she was pregnant, his reaction was not exactly enthusiastic. He started staying away for longer periods of time. It baffled Deslean why he treated her that way, especially in a time when she needed him most.

Deslean gave birth to a baby boy, whom she named Ryland, and Elrick did not deny he was the father. He retrieved his Polaroid camera from his vehicle and snapped a couple of pictures. He supported Deslean and the baby for the first two months, and then he asked her to allow him to take the child. "He will be raised under better circumstances than those which he will be subjected to at your home."

Deslean's parents would not hear of this. "Ryland is our first grandchild, and we want to be around for him with whatever resources we have," they told him.

When Ryland was about three months old, his father made an unsuccessful attempt to kidnap him. The villagers set up a road block, snatched the child away from him, and were about to beat him senseless. "Do you want us to eviscerate or behead him?" someone asked Lindon Bingham.

"No, just blindfold him and take him away. But make sure you get all the money he has on him."

"You will regret this, all of you," Elrick said.

"Yes, and if you were to report this, you would be charged with custodial interference. You can't even be sure the child is yours."

That was the last time Elrick Zeme was seen or heard from in that area of Puca Luca. No one knew whether he was dead or alive, and his witchcraft had no effect on anyone.

It hadn't rained in Willow Creek and the surrounding areas for a long period of time, and the Binghams and other farmers struggled for an existence. They lost most of their animals and agricultural crops. When Deslean's financial conditions became severe and she could not adequately care for her son, her father asked Brenton McHerring, the young man in the village who delivered telegrams for the post office, to ask around if anyone knew from whom Elrick Zeme was now buying animals. Brenton could not identify anyone who had placed eyes on this man, but he'd found out from his colleague in Wilson County that Elrick had fathered another son by the name of Kevin. This was one time when the Binghams wished they hadn't told Elrick to stay away. They could certainly use his money. Deslean took her child and sought odd jobs in Smack-a-Boom, about fifty miles away from home.

Then additional tragedy struck Willow Creek. A furious fire swept through the village overnight, and most of the dwellings and the residents of the community were burned to cinders. The Binghams were among the dead.

Deslean Bingham had been moving from place to place with the little boy because she was called a disgrace by some of her family members and others in the community for having a child out of wedlock, especially with someone the likes of Elrick Zeme. Little Rye, as he was called, never had a chance to settle down in any one place and attend school, and therefore he missed out on an early education. In order to survive, Deslean slept with anyone and everyone who could give her a few dollars to put food on the table or give her old clothes for the boy. Sometimes these were so tattered and torn that Rye could hardly determine in which opening to put his legs and arms. Some of the men were in her age group, some were younger, and some were much older than her. The young child was a witness to most of this. She suffered physical and mental abuse at the hands of some of these men, but she moved on to the next as soon as she considered herself healed of her physical and emotional wounds. That healing didn't take long.

The young mother did household work for a few people and was allowed to stay in detached quarters reserved for maids and helpers. Rye was afraid to fall asleep at nights in some of these rat-infested places. He had heard stories of rats nibbling on children's toes while they slept, and he didn't want that to happen to him. While he was awake, he listened to the sounds of the rats gnawing at the scant furniture and scurrying all over the place, knocking over pots and pans. He also didn't want the rats to fall in the jug of water his mother had on the small table, so one night he crept out of the corner of the bed and covered the container with an old pillowcase.

As soon as Deslean got thrown out for bringing boyfriends to the premises, she moved on with her little boy to another village. Rye saw and heard much more than he needed to see and hear at this stage of his life. His mother encouraged him to steal, and she punished him when he didn't do it. He developed a skillful way of doing this without being caught. One time, he stole a harmonica and taught himself to play this instrument. The villagers paid him to play for them, and at times they would give him food and clothes for him and his mother.

Rye was a big boy for his age and had always thought of running away from home. He had heard about his brother Kevin and wanted to be with him, but he didn't know where to find him. He yearned for a sibling with whom to play marbles and fly kites. With his thinking came the preparations. He realized that he could not walk barefooted for any long distance, so he collected some pieces of old tires and made a pair of slippers (zapatto), which he hid behind a large stone in the yard. This was the straw that broke the camel's back. One Saturday night when his mother put him to bed, she waited till she thought he was asleep. Then she went out as usual on her regular schedule and returned with one of her male conquests. A misunderstanding developed between Deslean and the man she brought home, and it escalated into a brawl. From the argument they were having, it seemed as though Deslean had taken this man's money and then refused to do what sexual activity he demanded.

The brawl woke Rye from his sleep. He peered through the keyhole, saw the man's hands around his mother's throat, and heard her begging, "Please, Sidney, don't hurt me. I have a son who depends on me."

Rye could never forget those hands because they contained extra digits located near the pinkie fingers. (This condition was known as hexadactyly.) He contemplated whether to break the door down and hit this twelve-fingered monster with the nearest available object, but he decided against it when Sydney released Deslean, pushed her to the floor, and left. He couldn't live this kind of life anymore. After all had quieted down, he put his harmonica in his pocket and slipped outside. He strapped the slippers on and walked for miles, guided by the light of a full moon until, he came to a farm shed where two ewes, one ram, and two little lambs were sleeping. Ryland took one look at the menacing ram with its huge horns and instantly decided that he was not afraid of him, so he pushed the ram away and tried to get some sleep in its straw bed. The bed felt warm and comfortable, much better than the one at home. In the corner of the shed was a small container, which he suspected was used to collect milk from the mother sheep. The boy tried to fall asleep while literally counting sheep and perfecting his next move.

Dawn broke, and Rye was awakened by the crowing of roosters and the sounds of Sunday morning church bells echoing in the morning's silence. He grabbed an aluminum bucket from the corner of the hut and milked the two mother sheep. This was fun for him. He drank some of the milk and then placed the container with the remainder of the milk on the shelf on the opposite side of the doorway. He disappeared before anyone could find out what was going on. To date, the owners never found out the identity of the mysterious being who'd milked their sheep.

Ryland's next stop was in a sugarcane field. Because it was Sunday, there were no workers cutting cane, but there were several bundles of cane placed at strategic locations, ready to be trucked away on Monday. He broke pieces of sugarcane, squeezed some juice in his mouth, and swallowed as much as he could. Then he made a loud belch. This intake of sugar reenergized him, and he was ready to move again, all along wondering whether his mother had begun to miss him. He looked back as far as he could and didn't see anyone coming after him. He picked berries and ate. He climbed walnut trees and filled his pockets with the fruit. When he alighted, he cracked them with stones and ate until his belly full. Life on the run fascinated him. When he grew tired, he found a comfortable spot under a cashew tree, played his harmonica, and drifted off to sleep.

The sun had begun to set, and as the boy's thoughts raced about a more comfortable place than an animal shed to lay his head, he saw smoke a distance away. Rye walked toward the area and noticed a small dwelling. He was familiar with people cooking on wood fires, and as he imagined someone preparing supper, he started to salivate. He walked a little faster in that direction. In the yard, he picked up a handful of marbles, and that gave him the feeling that boys, perhaps of his age group, resided there. A lady with two containers of food exited a tiny outdoor kitchen and headed toward the main dwelling a few feet away. He positioned himself where she could see him, and he approached her shyly. When she first saw him, she gave him the look like that of a washerwoman looking down at a bundle of dirty clothes. The lady looked menacing and mean, but beneath this appearance, it turned out that she was a kind, considerate, and protective person. This is an instance when one should not judge a book by its cover.

While looking down at the boy with the marbles in his hands, the woman assumed that he was one of her sons' friends who had come over to play with them.

"It's too late to play with Fitzroy and Egbert," she said, referring to her adopted sons. "You must return home right away." She was as blunt as a hammer.

"I am not here to play, miss …"

"Call me Miss Jean; everyone does. But my real name is Imogene Kopper."

"I don't have a home Miss Jean," he said pitifully. "Can I please stay with you and Fitzroy and Egbert tonight, ma'am? And maybe tomorrow they can help me find my brother, Kevin."

Miss Jean dared not argue with him because she instantly felt the same obligation to help this boy just like when she'd taken in the other two. "Come inside, and we will talk. If I can find your parents and your brother, I will notify them that you are here. But it's late now. We will do that tomorrow."

"Thanks, ma'am."

The young lad with his torn, smelly clothes instantly fell in love with this family, and stepped inside as briskly as a flea. He met the two boys, and when they heard his name, Fitzroy snickered and said, "If you are Rye, then I'm Barley." He pointed to his brother Egbert. "And surely he must be Oats."

From that day onward, the three boys—Fitzroy O'Rigby, Egbert Digginboss, and Ryland Zeme—were known as Barley, Oats, and

Rye. Ryland never disclosed his correct name to Jean and the boys, and he doubted that she would take steps to find out anything about him. He made up stories about his real family and never mentioned his brother again once he became aware how much this new family cared about him.

"Look at those hands," Miss Jean said. "Did you kill something?" His hands were stained with blood from the crushed corpses of hundreds of mosquitoes. Without hesitation, Miss Jean took him to the back of the house, filled a large tub with water, and insisted that he take a badly needed bath. Then she gave him some clothes outgrown by one of her sons. The boy was given some food, which he gobbled down. It was now bedtime, and she reached for an old mattress that had been leaning against a wall, placed it on the floor beside her bed, and said to Rye, "This is your bed for the night. Make yourself comfortable." To the other boys, she said, "Tomorrow, you will get to know this little lad better, and we can all try to find his parents." He thanked them and showed his appreciation by playing a well-known folk song on his harmonica.

Rye did not sleep soundly, and when he did, he had nightmares. Apart from being tired and sore, the slightest sounds he heard reminded him of the footsteps of men entering his mother's residence. He couldn't forget the altercation the previous night between Sidney Blender and his mother. Other incidents of abuse on his mother played over and over in his head. He then drifted off to sleep thinking how much he hated having to play doctor and bodyguard to his mother. Even though Rye loved his mother, he definitely did not want to go back, and he wondered whether she missed him.

Deslean definitely missed her son. She stopped asking around when she convinced herself that Elrick Zeme had finally succeeded in kidnapping him.

Miss Jean had various legitimate ways of earning a living, and she was happy for the extra help. She stayed up all night plaiting straw and completed nearly twenty-five yards, which was sold to women at a trading post on the other side of the lake who used it to make hats, placemats, and baskets. During the days, she made castor oil from castor beans that she had picked from nearby properties. These would have gone to waste because the owners of the properties either didn't know the value of this commodity or couldn't be bothered. The boys helped out as much as they could under supervision. When not supervised, they put their little-boys' tricks into motion by not completing the tasks according to instructions.

Monday morning came, and Fitzroy and Egbert were ready for school, but Rye refused to go with them. Not wanting to leave this little stranger alone, Miss Jean had no other choice but to take him with her to the market. By doing so, she would get an opportunity to start her efforts in finding his relatives.

"We can either ride the old mule down the long dirt road to the market, or we can take my dug-out canoe and go down the lake and across the river," Miss Jean said to the little boy. Rye was excited and chose the latter. The two of them loaded up the canoe with the various items she had for sale. Rye had fun assisting Miss Jean with the rowing of the canoe, and he enjoyed it when she praised him for his efforts. "It seems you have a knowledge of boats and the water, like my other two boys."

The marketplace was a busy one, and Rye looked around to see whether any woman looked like his mother. Miss Jean taught the boy how to negotiate a sale, collect money, and make change. He was much smarter than most people thought he was. He was a fast learner and was very street-smart, but he didn't know how to read or write.

"It's a smart little lad you have here, Jean," one customer observed. Turning to Rye, she asked, "What's your name, son?"

Rye pretended not to hear and ran off to join some boys who were flying kites behind the building. They stole fruits from some of the vendors and then hid behind one of the small latrines while they filled their little stomachs. He much preferred this to going to school, but he knew that Miss Jean would insist that he attend school the rest of the week. He saw how much value she placed on education.

In order for the boy to be registered in school, it was necessary for him to provide them with his correct name and birth date but because he did not want to be found, he made up the name Zimmie Ryland. When Miss Jean finally enrolled him in school, the other children made fun of him. The teacher lavished praises on the other students whenever they completed their work correctly. They frequently called Rye Big Boy and Dunce. He was always getting into fights, and on rare occasions Barley and Oats came to his rescue. He became frustrated with school and begged Miss Jean to take him with her every Monday to the market. During the week, while Barley and Oats paid attention to their schoolwork, Rye made kites and go-carts from scrap material he had gathered from different places, and he would sell these at the market. His entrepreneurship began early. The kids loved his kites, and the designs were unusual. He now had a third nickname: Designer Boy. Rye loved this new name. He saved his money because he had a plan. He may have been a dunce academically, but if he was going to be one for the rest of his life, he sure was going to die a rich one. He learned self-worth and economic security at an early age.

Rye stayed with Jean and the boys till he was nearly nine years old, accompanying her to the market on Mondays and going to school when he did not pretend to be sick. Jean solicited donations in the form of khaki school uniforms from some of her acquaintances and customers. The boys were exposed to the Bible, and because of the distance to the Baptist church, she opted to become their Sunday schoolteacher and choirmaster. On Sundays, she pulled out her portable podium from under her bed, seated the boys on a four-foot-long bench, and started Sunday school. Barley, Oats, and Rye were the only members of the congregation and were expected to participate fully. Miss Jean had the boys memorize the Ten Commandments, and they would repeat these Sunday after Sunday. Other Bible passages were of equal importance. Although Rye didn't attend school as regularly as his brothers and could not read as well as they could, he had a very good memory, and he certainly knew how to entertain them with his harmonica. Miss Jean gave them small incentives for their efforts.

Another Monday, another busy day at the market, and Jean and the new addition to her family were getting a lot of attention. A gentleman who identified himself as Lathan Zeme claimed he was the boy's uncle and would be willing to take him if Miss Jean would let him do so. Miss Jean was very skeptical of this individual and decided to conduct her own investigations. She had learned a lot of investigating tactics while employed as a housekeeper for Vinnie Digginboss. She had also learned to treat everyone with suspicion. She gathered as much information as possible about the Zeme family and posed some interesting questions to Lathan the next time they met. Lathan was prepared for Imogene's interrogations. It turned out that he was telling the truth, especially when he produced a photograph of Rye when he was a baby. Lathan Zeme, who had a wife and a stable home, had raised three children of whom he was proud. He was the proud owner the famous tailor shop in Logby Run, Zeme's Seams.

Imogene agonized over the fact that her family was going to be broken up, but she was happy that Ryland would be with a two-parent family. He needed a father figure. However, she didn't simply hand him over to Lathan. "Can I take him back tonight to say goodbye to the other boys?" she asked Lathan.

When the news was broken to them, they didn't know whether to cry or be happy for him. This was the first time they learned his real name.

"We are going to miss you," his brothers told him. "You have taught us survival tricks that certainly will come in handy if and when the need arises for us to defend ourselves."

"I will always remember your kindness," he said to the boys. To Egbert he said, "I will not forget your haircut, which made your head look like the shape of a bicycle seat."

"Be nice, boys," Miss Jean said.

"And what will you remember me by?" Fitzroy asked.

"Your brain. I am sure people will be curious when I tell them that my brother's brain is on his shoulder."

"We will always remember you by those sweet melodies. Sunday school will not be the same without you," they told Rye.

Fifty-Five

Uncle Lathan and his wife, Esmine (affectionately known as Essie), had been empty nesters. Now, they planned to raise the boy the same way they had their three children, Logan, Phaye, and Valerie, who were now grown, had very good jobs, and had established lives for themselves in different areas of Puca Luca. People would come up to Lathan and ask whether the boy was his grandchild, and when he said that Ryland wasn't, before he could say anything else, he was asked if it was his child out of wedlock. "None of your damned business," he would tell them.

Lathan planned to send his nephew to one of the best schools in the area, but he was soon to discover that Ryland hated school and would throw temper tantrums or fake an illness each morning—and when he did go to school, he mixed up letters and sounds and wrote numbers backward or upside down. However, Ryland had a photographic memory, was very artistic, and was good at spelling. He would give the answer to the most difficult mathematics problem while others struggled to work it out with pencil and paper. The principal met with Lathan and recommended that Ryland be sent to a special school for learning-disabled children. It was heartbreaking for Uncle Lathan because the only school he knew that would provide that type of special education was sixty miles away. He suspected that

Rye had vision problems, so he had the boy's eyes examined. It wasn't until his teenage years that finally a name was put to Rye's disability, dyslexia, and he was able to receive the proper help and academic instructions.

Ryland's life with his uncle was exciting, and he hoped he would not have to move before he reached adulthood. He never asked about his brother, Kevin, or any of his other relatives in case they would want to take him away. He was quite comfortable where he was, and he did his best to please his uncle, who was a very strict disciplinarian. Uncle Lathan took his nephew almost everywhere he went. He taught him many things and reinforced such issues as the value of earning one's own money honestly and the many benefits of saving it. Rye had a few dollars of his own, which he'd earned from selling kites and go-carts. Young boys would enter kite-flying contests and go-cart racing contests, and Rye would be given small trophies and verbal recognition whenever they won. Sometimes he would be compensated in cash. He made his own piggy bank, deposited every penny he got in it, and put it in a secure place in the house. Aunt Essie encouraged him to open an account at the bank, and she would find ways of helping him earn extra money. He loved her like a mother. He loved Miss Jean, but his love for Essie was different.

Then tragedy struck. Aunt Essie was gored by the horns of one of their sheep, and she did not get better.

After Essie's death, Logan and his wife, Laura, wanted to take Ryland, but his uncle wouldn't hear of it. "I need the company, and Ryland is a valuable help to my tailoring establishment." Rye took customers' measurements, sewed buttons on garments, ironed the clothes, and delivered them to the customers. At times he would draw sketches of garments, and he observed as his uncle followed these guidelines unquestionably. Lathan had to be away some weekends to purchase quality material for the business, and he would take his nephew with him. Sometimes he couldn't take him along, but he trusted the young man to be on his own, with the neighbors keeping an extra eye on him. One weekend when Lathan had planned to go on his regular trips to buy material for his business, Rye complained about not feeling well, so Lathan left him at home and asked Delores Darrighan, one of the neighbors, to look in on him. She gave the boy something to eat, stayed with him for a while, and then made sure he locked the door behind her.

Not long after Delores left, Rye slipped out of the house unnoticed and went with two bigger boys to an adjoining town, where a mini fair and circus were in progress. Several boys were competing in different events and winning cash and other prizes. Rye wanted to get in on the action but hadn't yet figured out how he would participate. He always wanted to do something different. He wandered around the fairgrounds, found a seat beside some men who were smoking their cigars and pipes and spitting as far as they could. As strange and nauseating as this activity appeared to be, the men were having a jolly good time. Ryland thought for a moment and got the men and with his friends to organize a spitting contest. This sounded gross at first, but the organizers agreed. The cash prize was very enticing, but the spitting distance was set at ten feet. They probably did that to discourage the younger boys from participating, but that did not deter Ryland Zeme.

After all the participants had their turn, the first prize in the men's section went to one man whose spit fell eight feet. The farthest spitting distance in the boys' category was six feet, and this was achieved by Darren Wick. But Ryland hadn't had his chance yet, Now it was his turn. He grabbed a cigar from one of the men, took a long puff, and took his place at the starting line. He fixed his eyes on the finished line, cleared his throat, and appeared to be concentrating. Suddenly, he let out a loud *ptoo,* and out came a huge, gelatinous glob of spit that passed the ten-foot mark and hit a tin can nearby. It made such a loud noise that everyone thought the boy had lost a tooth. There was silence, and then after careful observation, Ryland was declared the winner of all categories.

The crowd erupted with uncontrollable cheers. He was lifted up on top of the stage and presented with his cash prize, which was more than he'd expected. In addition, almost everyone started giving him whatever change they could find in their pockets. He was approached by one of the circus managers to consider being a member of the circus. He thought about it but knew his uncle wouldn't hear of it. Ryland went home with more money than he had ever seen in his life, and all of which he'd made honestly.

When Uncle Lathan returned and learned that Rye had feigned an illness in order to sneak out of the house, he chastised him and told him of the consequences if he were to do it again. However, Lathan was impressed with the amount of money his nephew had made honestly, and he made sure the boy hadn't stolen it. He was more convinced when he read the article in the circus entertainment magazine and saw his nephew's picture below the caption "Simply the Best." Uncle Lathan took him to the bank and let him deposit every penny in the account that Essie had encouraged him to open. But this time, Lathan added his name to the account, and he also added his nephew's name to his personal account. Like his uncle, Ryland Zeme knew the value of money, and he'd always dreamed of being rich. He had begun to set his eyes on the goal.

Ryland continued to receive treatment for his dyslexia, and he began not only liking school but loving it. His grades were good, and at sixteen he completed college and enrolled in the Trevine Polytechnic Institute to study architectural design. He became fascinated with the exhibits and displays put on by the female students in the home economics class, decided to join the class, and added fashion design to his schedule. He was the only male in the class, and the instructors were in awe of his sewing experience and his artistic ability. He would be the first to develop sketches and designs, and he'd assist the others in improving on theirs. He had a very imaginative mind.

During his second year at the institute, Ryland worked part-time with Blender's Dry Cleaning and specialized in alterations. The owner, Sidney Blender, had several of these establishments throughout Puca

Luca. When Ryland met Mr. Blender, he was surprised to see that Blender had two extra digits on his hands. When Rye learned what part of the country this man hailed from, he concluded that this could be the man who'd hurt his mother. Rye had a plan up his sleeves: sweet revenge.

Mr. Blender liked the young man's enthusiasm and his creativity, so he listened to his ideas and suggestions and implemented many of them. Sometimes Rye would completely redesign the garments that came in for alterations, and Blender and the customers were extremely pleased with the results. Blender's profit margins began to soar, and he increased Ryland's wages.

As time went by and Rye realized that he was almost indispensable, he concocted a scheme where he would earn extra money without Mr. Blender's knowledge. He was used to taking chances and relished the idea of not being caught. Furthermore, he was determined to hurt this man in retaliation for what he'd done to Rye's mother. There was this particular instance when a young woman, Althea Gardens, took a dress in to be altered. Ryland took the measurements and drew sketches of what the dress would look like once he redesigned it. Althea loved the new look and agreed to it. As soon as Althea left, Rye got to work. When he was finished with the dress, instead of contacting Althea to let her know that the dress was ready, he rented it to another young woman to wear to a graduation dinner. When Althea went to pick up her dress, it was not in the shop because it had not yet been returned by the renter. Rye told her, "It must have been mistakenly sent to another location. I promise to track this down and call you when it arrives." The dress was returned and dry-cleaned, and within a week the unsuspecting Althea picked it up.

"I apologize for the problem and will make sure it doesn't happen again," he told Althea, who in turn gave Rye a worthwhile tip for what she called his efficient handling of the matter. She went as far as to tell the manager about it, and Rye was given an Employee of the Month award.

When Rye realized that he had gotten away with his misdeeds so easily, he made this activity one of his regular means of earning extra cash. But eventually his luck ran out.

Rye's closest friend, Garnett Crockett, paid a visit to the establishment and told him, "I have an invitation to take my fiancée, Prudence, to the annual law enforcement dinner and dance. I am looking for a very exquisite formal wear." He looked around and spotted one of the most beautiful expensive silk dresses on which he has ever laid eyes. "Oh, my goodness. All eyes will be on my Prudence if she wears something like this to the function. Can I borrow this? I will give you whatever you ask."

Rye couldn't resist the generous offer because he knew of Garnett's financial worth. As predicted, all eyes were on her when she walked into the ballroom. Loud gasps were heard coming from the elite crowd. They probably wondered how she could afford this stunningly expensive silk gown. Compared to other women in the community, Prudence could be described as a plain Jane.

The owner of the gown, Thelma Noah, who was the same size as Prudence, couldn't take her eyes off her knowing her socioeconomic status. Her chance of confronting her came when Prudence left the table to go to the ladies' room. Thelma followed her with a glass of red wine in hand. As she looked at the gown, she told herself, "This could be a counterfeit." But on examining it more closely, she recognized some special features and concluded that this was her one-of-a-kind, custom-made gown that she had left at Blender's Dry Cleaners. Thelma showed remarkable restraint when she said to Prudence, "I must confess that I envy you tonight. Where did you get this exquisite gown?"

Prudence did not hesitate to tell Thelma about the rental agreement. Then she looked her straight in the eye, gave a sarcastic smile, and said, "Poor, unsuspecting snob."

This angered Thelma, and she could not control herself any longer. She splashed the red wine all over Prudence. Before Prudence could react, Thelma held on to the spaghetti straps and ripped them from her shoulders.

Someone inside the ladies' room covered Prudence with a shawl while her attacker was whisked away to join her husband, Daniel, but not before Thelma revealed to everyone who would listen that Prudence had stolen her dress.

Ryland's friendship with Garnett came to an end, and so did his employment with Blender's Dry Cleaning. Perhaps he should have remembered a Malayan Proverb, "Don't think there aren't any crocodiles, just because the water is calm." This incident caused Blender to lose a lot of customers, and he was forced to close some of his locations.

The revenge was so sweet that Ryland could almost taste it. He felt that he couldn't leave Blender's Dry Cleaning without confronting him about what he'd done to his mother several years ago. Blender couldn't remember the specific incident, but Rye kept telling him things to jog his memory. Blender knew that Deslean had had a son, but he hadn't met him.

"I have regretted most of my actions during those early years, and I'm sorry that your mother was one of my victims. I wish I could right these wrongs. But please forgive me, and remember that your mother was partly to blame."

"She may have taken you money and not provide the required services, but that didn't give you the right to beat her up," Rye said. Picking up a pair of scissors, he continued, "I could use these to detach these extra fingers from your hands. Do you think it would hurt?"

Fifty-Six

Young Ryland Zeme felt a sense of pride that he was finally going to graduate from the Polytechnic Institute. The excitement and anxiety mounted, and he hoped that nothing would emerge to threaten this important event in his life considering his struggles to get to this point. However, one cannot predict the works of the Almighty, so two weeks before Rye was ready to graduate, uncle Lathan was called to his heavenly home. He was struck by lightning one Friday afternoon during heavy rains and an electrical storm. The young man was devastated, to say the least. This was his only relative who had witnessed his day-to-day achievements, and his graduation would have been a sweet reward.

The renowned tailor was sitting around his sewing machine and trying to complete a rush job on a tuxedo for a young man by the name of Stanley Gladwin, who was to be a member of a wedding party the following day. The fierce storm developed, sending blinding strikes of lightning straight through a grapefruit tree by the side window. The resulting fire burned it to cinders and then entered the house, hitting the sewing machine before Lathan knew what was happening. Uncle Lathan believed in signs and omens, and just two weeks prior, he had told Rye about the constant howling of his neighbor's dogs, which everyone predicted was a sure sign of death.

But Lathan did not suspect that he would be the one to make this prediction come true.

Uncle Lathan was not found till the Saturday morning, when Stanley came to pick up his tuxedo. He knocked on the front door and got no response. He thought Lathan had gone to the butcher shop as usual, as did many people on Saturday morning, so he sat on a big stone under an avocado tree in the front yard and waited. Stanley waited for more than an hour when he saw Melvina Kursock passing by with her week's supply of meat in a small bamboo basket.

"Hey, Melvina, did you leave Mr. Lathan at the butcher shop?"

"No, and I even heard Mr. Glenn getting concerned as to why he hadn't been there yet."

It was widely known that Lathan suffered from hypertension and would sometimes not take his medications. He would end up with headaches and not be seen or heard from for days. Stanley and Melvina decided to go toward the back of the house and take a peek through the window of Lathan Zeme's residence. When they saw the burned tree and the blackened walls, they broke down the door, and what they saw terrified them.

Lathan was still sitting around the sewing machine, looking like a piece of rag. The moisture was sucked from his body, the hair on his head was burned off, and his raw scalp was visible. His dentures were knocked to the floor a few yards in the hallway. Melvina ran and screamed so loudly that most of the neighbors heard and came over. Her packages beef, pork, and chicken were scattered all over the place, but she didn't care about that now.

Rye was contacted, and so was the rest of the family. A week later, Lathan was laid to rest in the family plot beside his wife, Essie. Rye was left alone again. Everyone whom he loved had disappeared from his life. There was one family with whom he decided to make contact: Miss Jean and the boys. However, he was out of luck. He learned from someone at the market that Miss Jean had been stung by bees while harvesting castor beans, and she'd died from anaphylactic shock. Egbert and Fitzroy were away in college, and they had not kept in touch with Rye. His grandparents had died, he had not heard anything from his mother, and to this date he has not found anyone by the name of Kevin Zeme.

By this time, Rye had graduated from the Polytechnic Institute and was ready to be on his own. Uncle Lathan had made a will after his wife had died, and he'd bequeathed the business, his money, and his property to Ryland. Phaye and Valerie had no problem with their father's decision. "Our cousin deserves it. He was there for Daddy when we weren't."

Logan disagreed with his father's dying wish and insisted that Rye share the profits of the business with him. Logon went behind the young man's back and attempted to withdraw Rye's savings from the bank, but he almost got arrested when the bank manager proved to him that the money was separate and apart from Lathan's account. Furthermore, Lathan's account listed Ryland on it and no one else.

Ryland heard about Logan's plan and came up with a plan to defeat and embarrass his cousin. He contacted Clarence McWilloughby, a prominent businessman, member of the Puca Luca Manufacturers Association, and member of the Chamber of Commerce. McWilloughby was widely known as a man who willingly lent money to people who wished to upgrade their businesses. Rye had him write a letter to Logan informing him that Lathan owed him a large sum of money, and he'd have to repossess some of the equipment if someone didn't pay up. He also went on to tell Logan that he may have to get a court order to freeze the account.

Logan backed off and let Clarence have his way. Clarence took charge of everything that Lathan owned and later returned it to Ryland. Soon thereafter, Ryland Zeme rented space in the town of River Glades and established his own tailoring establishment. He kept the name **Zeme's Seams,** and as time went by, he sold Uncle Lathan's property and bought the new premises. He remodeled and expanded the shop, and then he added dry cleaning to the business. Now he was competing with the mighty Sidney Blender, and that made him as proud as a peacock.

Ryland seemed to be no match for the existing competitors, but he was very aggressive on changing this. He purchased three old cars from the junkyard of the police department and had his friend work on them to make them drivable. He gave one of the cars to his foreman, Tyrone Gober, whose assignment was to pick up and drop off dry cleaning for his customers. Rye also became a consultant in interior decorating for a popular chain of furniture stores, and his exhibitions of women's and men's clothing at high-end department stores were the talk of the town. He was the first designer to cater to people of uneven size. He matched their size sixteen tops with their size ten bottoms, or their size twenty bottoms with their size fourteen tops.

Overnight success came Ryland's way like a speeding arrow, and he made lots of money. He found himself being able to hire several employees and was now a responsible taxpayer. If only his parents, Miss Jean, and his brothers could see him now. He joined the Puca Luca Chamber of Commerce and wrote articles for the monthly fashion magazine, *Stitches,* which was owned by Clarence McWilloughby and edited by his daughter, Sarah.

Ryland Zeme was street smart, and it was already proven that he had a way of earning money both traditionally and unconventionally. Some people would describe his schemes as dishonest, unethical, immoral, and illegal, but he didn't care. He was making a name for himself, and if he wanted to get out of trouble, he knew the right people. He was probably one of the few people on the island of Puca Luca who invested in other people's lawsuits. He first thought of this when one of his employees was involved in a motor vehicle accident and had no money to hire a lawyer. He bargained with the employee that he would pay the retainer and whatever funds were needed up front, making him sign documents promising to give him 50 percent of the settlement. However, if no settlement was received, the individual would have to pay him back the money he paid to the lawyer. Rye made lots of money this way until one dissatisfied person exposed him. The ethical, moral, and legal aspects of this activity were questioned. He was never charged with anything but decided it was time to discontinue this activity before something worse happened. Besides, he had other schemes in the works. Other people who had started this activity had the fear of God put in them when they learned that the government had gotten involved and passed a law to make it illegal.

Ryland bought his first new car, a black convertible Mercedes Benz, and began dating Sarah McWilloughby. He was the envy of several young men who had tried to date her and had failed. He loved the horse races at Quigland Park, and on Saturdays he would take Sarah with him. He betted heavily and always won handsomely, and the losers thought he had inside information.

Rye would organize fashion parades during the intermissions. Models vied for his attention and would do anything to be identified with the Zeme line of clothing. Puca Luca socialites and VIPs proudly strutted in clothes made by this new designer who had emerged on the scene like an erupting volcano.

One Saturday, Sarah was unable to attend the races with Ryland because she said she didn't feel comfortable with him flirting around with other women. At the end of the seventh race, the weather turned ugly, and the remaining three races had to be canceled. The dark clouds hovered overhead, and thought most patrons decided to go home, some opted to stay and socialize.

As Rye mingled with the crowd, he noticed one of the loveliest ladies he had ever seen. When she smiled back at him, he said, "Did the sun just come out, or did you just smile?" He extended his hand and introduced himself, "I'm Ryland Zeme, and my friends call me Rye."

"I know who you are. I'm Beatrice Inkst, and I'm pleased to meet you."

"Are you some lucky man's wife?"

"Not yet."

They took an instant liking to each other, and Ryland Zeme wasted no time in proving himself more worthy of Beatrice Inkst's company, love, and attention. They set a date, and the rest was history.

Fifty-Seven

"Behind every successful man is a successful woman," they say, and as time went by, Ryland's wife, Beatrice, could be described as the powerhouse propelling this successful man and his empire. She was the daughter of a prominent thoroughbred racehorse breeder and owner, Bertram Inkst, and at an early age she became a savvy businesswoman. After graduating with various degrees in business from the prestigious University of Casselton, she helped transform her father's breeding industry into mega companies. In that area of Puca Luca, not many women ventured further than high school, so Beatrice was viewed in a different light. She was revered and worshipped by the progressives, but she was accused by others of trying to do a man's job.

Beatrice's brother, Wendell, who was the favorite of their parents, never displayed the level of interest in the company that Beatrice did. His acquaintances and his father's employees saw him as a snob. He treated the stable hands, exercisers, jockeys, and others with disdain, describing them as simple and indifferent. He studied law at the same law school as Ansel McEarth, and he became a famous defense attorney for the rich and famous. He always maintained that the burden of proof was with the prosecution, and many times he never called a single witness. Whenever he rested his case, even the presiding judge expressed consternation. The weight of his case was always in his opening and closing arguments, and he never lost a case.

Wendell's wife and son were injured in a plane crash. He donated blood in case his son needed it, but the boy died the day he was to receive the transfusion. He asked that the blood be kept in the blood bank for any family member who needed that type. His wife died a few hours after his son, and Wendell never recovered from the loss. Within six months, he developed a mysterious illness and had to be sent him away for treatment. His father, Bertram Inkst, had a close friend who was a medical researcher and diagnostician at a teaching hospital out of the area, and Bertram was optimistic that if anyone could help his son, this friend along and his associates could.

Two months after Wendell was admitted to this institution, he disappeared, never to be heard from again. The Inkst family blamed the hospital for its lack of supervision and hired Ansel McEarth to investigate the disappearance of Wendell, but all efforts ended in futility. Wendell Inkst was declared dead after two years, and a memorial service was held. The family wrestled with coming up with an inscription on his tombstone, and the most appropriate one was, "The Defense Rests."

Wendell Inkst's perceived death must have broken his parents' heart because they made an exit from this world six months after, and their deaths were ruled a murder-suicide. Bertram Inkst shot his wife while she slept and then turned the gun on himself. He made sure he changed his will and left the entire fortune of the Inkst business to Beatrice.

But Beatrice could smell some trouble brewing. An injunction was filed in the Whickam County Resident Magistrates Court against the Inkst estate by attorney Fiffie Saddler on behalf of someone by the name of Curtis Bedwin, who claimed he was the illegitimate child of Wendell Inkst. Curtis was the son of Glovene Bedwin, née Hatford, a former household helper with the Inkst family. They both wanted to block Beatrice from inheriting everything that Betram Inkst and his wife owned, which they had willed to their only surviving child. Glovene saw an opportunity to avenge the Inkst family for what had happened when she'd been accused of stealing chemicals from them and giving them to Ethel Twipple.

When the pair heard of the new will made by Bertram Inkst leaving everything to Beatrice, they alleged that this must be fraudulent and insisted that the contents of the first will should be honored. By honoring the first will, 50 percent of the inheritance would be Wendell's, which Curtis could inherit if he could prove that he was in fact a member of the Inkst family.

Beatrice was represented by Ansel McEarth, who had left the law firm and established his own practice. His wife, Christine, a forensic scientist, was responsible for performing the paternity test. At first it seemed that they had run into a roadblock for samples, but Beatrice remembered the blood Wendell had given and that hadn't been used at the hospital. They contacted the blood bank, and sure enough, the blood was still in storage. This was handed over to Christine.

Curtis was reluctant to submit samples for testing but would be found in contempt of court if he didn't do so.

Fiffie Saddler approached Beatrice and said, "We could avoid the financial embarrassment and settle out of court." She almost sounded convincing when she added, "I'm sure you are aware that we can produce witnesses who can verify that your brother carried on a clandestine affair with my client." Fiffie Saddler loved to try intimidation tactics on the opposing side.

However, Beatrice Inkst was one woman with whom this would definitely not produce the effect Saddler had hoped for. Beatrice and her attorney preferred to wait for the test results.

When the result of the paternity test was read in court by Judge Jonas Darrighan, it revealed that Curtis had not a drop of Inkst blood running through his veins. The curious crowd in the gallery looked at the pair and shouted, "Liar, opportunist, thief!"

Curtis went as pale as a sheet. Tears streamed in torrents from Glovene's eyes as she pleaded with her attorney to beg the judge to be lenient with them. She turned to Beatrice, and with her hands clasped in a prayerful manner, she said, "We are very sorry, Miss B. Please show some mercy and do not send us to prison."

Beatrice looked at them in disgust and said, "I can't stand the sight of you. Get away from me. To me, you are like insects I would not bring myself to crush because it would soil the soles of my shoes."

After Fiffie Saddler finished pleading for leniency for Glovene and Curtis, Judge Darrighan asked if they had anything to say before he imposed sentence on them for extortion. Instead of shutting up, Curtis Bedwin went off on a tirade. He turned to the judge and asked, "Where is the justice here?" He ranted on and on. "Look at how many politicians and law enforcement personnel have squeezed the lifeblood from the ordinary people, and yet they are living normal lives."

The judge pounded his gavel and addressed Curtis. "If you continue this, I will find you in contempt."

But Curtis continued. "As far as I see, there is nothing much to be gained by following the straight and narrow. There's nothing wrong in taking from the wealthy. Honesty leads to poverty."

The judge became as angry as a wasp and reprimanded Saddler for not controlling her clients. He sentenced Curtis and Glovene to two years in prison. Glovene was ordered to reveal the true paternity of her child. It turned out that he was fathered by the notorious Harry Quane.

This case was Fiffie Saddler's last one for the next two years because she was suspended by the Puca Luca Bar Association for misconduct involving financial irregularities unrelated to this case. One of the complaints charged that Ms. Saddler concealed funds from a client for whom she had secured a large out-of-court settlement. Records showed that she had invested the money for herself while telling the client all along that the other party had not yet agreed to the settlement. She had to hand over the money and the interest that had accrued on it.

On another occasion, Ms. Saddler got a loan from a witness in a high-profile case in return for the promise of light questioning during cross-examination. But her method of cross-examination had nothing light about it—it was merciless.

"You heartless, thieving, bitch," he shouted from the witness stand. "You promised to go easy on me. What happened to all the money I paid you?"

Fifty-Eight

Loretty was dedicated to her work and would sometimes put in more hours than were expected of her. One afternoon she was working late by herself, trying to complete some paperwork for one of the MUJALI projects. She was so absorbed in what she was doing that when she heard a knock on the door, she was startled. Not taking any chances, she moved toward that direction with a pair of scissors in her hand. She had heard of stories where staff members at other institutions assaulted or raped female workers, and she didn't want this to happen to her. She had defended herself against one bully before, and she was prepared to do it again. When she remembered why she was at Blovingworth Mental Hospital, she let go of the weapon. "Who is it?" she called out.

"It's me, Brains."

Fitzroy O'Rigby, alias Brains, was getting better thanks to the experimental drug treatment program in which he was participating. He was properly monitored and took his medications, and his progress was remarkable. How good it was to see him in civilian clothes rather than hospital garb. He was wearing a pair of khaki pants, a blue shirt, a pair of newly polished black shoes, and a black felt hat. He looked like a security guard. The staff had begun to trust him and have him run errands for them. He took a special liking to Loretty and would tell her what he could remember about his life, which he would not reveal to anyone else except his psychiatrist. She would always listen respectfully to what he had to say.

"Hi, Brains. What brings you here?"

He handed her a note from Kittie, the manager's secretary. "Please come to the office. It's urgent," the note said. At first she thought of Kingsley Muggerdon, and immediately her face brightened up. She smoothed her dress, ran her fingers through her hair, and dabbed some lipstick on her lips. Fitzroy helped her lock up the Kinglore Center, and they walked toward the office. On their way, he mentioned three words twice: barley, oats, and rye. Loretty never asked him what was his fascination with those three grains, and he never elaborated. She assumed that in the past, he had worked at a brewery.

When she got to the office, she looked around, but there was no Kingsley in sight. Then Kittie Lawfries handed her the phone, and she felt certain that he was at the other end of the line. Kittie understood the need for privacy, so she ushered Loretty into a nearby room. She sat down in an armchair and began to unravel the knots in her stomach. "Hello?" she said nervously.

The voice that answered her was not Kingsley Muggerdon's. It was her attorney, Boysie Vernetti. "Can you come over to my office tomorrow so that we can plan strategies for your trial?"

"Has a date been set?" Loretty asked.

"We are looking at two weeks from today," Boysie told her.

"Okay. That means I have time to request a leave of absence."

"Fine. I already spoke to management, and they have no problem giving you time off till the trial ends. I also spoke to your psychiatrist, who has given the all-clear following your last evaluation."

It was a bittersweet moment for Loretty to hear that a date was set for her trial. She had longed for this date to arrive. She wanted closure. It had been two years since there had been a trial, and that first one had ended with a hung jury. Her attorney had argued that her mental condition was too fragile to have another trial so soon after that. During that period, the prosecution team, headed by Forrest

Gatsworthy, asked for a change of venue for the second trial, but the judge denied the request.

The thought of going to prison scared Loretty, and she couldn't sleep. She found herself folding her dirty laundry and putting it away in her dresser drawers. She realized what she was doing and questioned whether she was ready for this. She made herself a cup of tea and went to bed. When she finally fell asleep, she had nightmares. She tried to scream, but no sound came out, or so she thought.

The following morning, Vivienne, who occupied an adjoining room to Loretty's, asked her, "What was the matter with you? Why you were screaming so loudly last night? I almost had to break down your room door and come in to see for myself whether something or someone was harming you."

A jury of nine women and three men was selected to decide Loretty's fate. The trial began, and Loretty's attorney put on a brilliant defense, chief of which were self-defense and battered women's syndrome (BWS). "How ludicrous," Boysie Vernetti said, "is the idea of bringing this case back to trial because a woman defended herself against a batterer? Do not punish her for a venial error." He submitted in evidence pictures of Loretty's head, where Lensley had plucked out a clump of her hair. He submitted hospital records of her bruises, lacerations, and black eyes over a period of time. He solicited testimonies from neighbors, friends, and relatives. He then asked the jurors, "Do you really want to send this woman to prison when she was already there for all these years?" Some people in the gallery, including Ionnia's brothers, fought back tears.

Pro-Loretty demonstrators lined the route to the courthouse, and their chants of "Free Loretty" could be heard as far as two miles away. Outside the courthouse were counterdemonstrations from individuals who wanted Loretty to be severely punished. This made Loretty think of the worst possible scenarios for the outcome of her case.

"God knows I don't want to end up like Totlyn Lamb." Totlyn

was a lady who was battered and abused by her husband, and one day when he beat her mercilessly, she looked at him and said, "When you are finished, let me know." He apparently took a break, which was an indication that he had finished. Now it was her turn, and the unexpected happened. She used whatever tools were at her disposal and hit him on every part of his body. When he fell to the ground, she stomped on his balls. She continued beating him until he was dead. She was sent to prison for life but had her sentence reduced to twenty-five years after groups advocating for battered women intervened on her behalf, citing self-defense. Now the case was being looked at, and there was a possibility that Totlyn would be released with her sentence overturned.

There had been nonstop discussions on radio and television talk shows each day with opinions about what should happen to battered women who defended themselves against abusive spouses. The men were not left out of these discussions. One particular talk show host, who called herself Dr. L. Mae, blamed women for what had been happening to them. She continuously tried to convince them that if they were more loyal to their husbands, they would not be abused. She wrote several books beseeching women to revere their mates, and she requested that the men purchase these books as gifts for their spouses. While Dr. Mae's program and her books empowered the men, women's organizations did their best to shut her up. The organization RAW, which was jointly represented by Clover Fishley and Cislyn Tottenberry, continued their advocacy for what they called the frail, defenseless, and stupid. Ionnia put in guest appearances at several of the RAW conferences and promised the women that one day, they would have a safe place to go to where their abusive spouses would be forbidden to set foot, adding that as long as the women believed in themselves, they would be free.

The day of reckoning finally came when the verdict was reached, and Loretty Quane sat nervously in the courtroom. She looked at the crowd in the balcony and knew that most of the people supported her and didn't want to see her punished. Her confidence was reassured. She was not astonished that they would stare at her, but she realized that this event affected a lot of women, and if she were to be set free, this would set a precedence.

Her attorney encouraged her to remain calm and appear confident and optimistic. "Try to impress public opinion. Look at them and show them that this is not the face of a guilty woman," he said. "Show them that is a woman whose cup was full and had run over, and the time had come for the pouring to stop."

The judge retired to his chambers for five minutes while the jurors continued to deliberate, and everyone waited in suspense. Loretty reached in her purse for her hairbrush and brushed her hair with such artful strokes that some interpreted this as mocking the Quane relatives. She raised herself from her seat, smoothed her dress, and repositioned herself in a queenlike posture. Loretty was beginning to feel confident that the verdict would be in her favor, and she would be able to enjoy the life of freedom for which she yearned.

"She is mocking us," Ethel Twipple shouted.

The judge reentered the courtroom and took his seat. "Order!" he demanded, and he pounded his gavel so loudly that it caused Loretty to almost slump under the table, as if she were reliving some of the incidents that had caused her to be there in the first place.

Ionnia arrived late at the courthouse, and as she rushed toward the elevator, she saw a familiar figure: Emily Brank. This case almost ended in another mistrial because Emily was accused of flirting with one of the jurors and had to be removed from inside the courtroom. Ionnia wanted to hate Emily, but immediately a quote from seventeenth-century French poet Alphonse Daudet's came to mind. "Hatred is the anger of the weak." Ionnia also reminded herself of how strong a woman she had become, so all she did was smile at Emily, hold her head high, and take her seat. She entered the courtroom just as the bailiff handed the judge the verdict. The jurors took their seats and avoided looking at Loretty Quane.

There was silence and apprehension as the judge looked at the foreperson and asked, "Have you reached a verdict?"

"Yes, Your Honor."

Vernetti hugged Loretty, who she glanced at her children and then at Cecilia Delpheney, a television reporter to whom Loretty had promised an interview whichever way the verdict went.

"How say you?" the judge asked.

"We find the defendant …"

The short pause seemed like an eternity. The suspense cut through Loretty like a knife. She looked around again at her children, who looked at her with reassurance that everything would be all right.

"Not guilty," the jury foreman said.

A burst of jubilation erupted in the courtroom. Some women in the gallery clapped and cheered, and once again the judge pounded his gavel and asked the bailiff to restore order in the courtroom. Loretty wept tears of joy on her attorney's shoulder. He held her tightly as if still protecting her from harm. Her children ran to her and hugged her.

Lensley Quane's family members shook their heads. His mother gritted her teeth and wagged her finger at Loretty, and she made obscene gestures at Ionnia. Order was restored in the courtroom, and the judge thanked the jurors for their services then announced the adjournment.

Reporters from various media houses scuttled toward the doorway like vultures trying to consume a carcass. They began shoving their microphones in the faces of the jurors, the attorneys, the spectators, Loretty's children, and finally Loretty herself.

Ionnia was determined to shield her mother from more spotlights, so she stepped forward and declared, "I want to make a statement, and I will not answer any questions afterward." The energy of the dozens of supporting fans propelled her along, and the glitz of flashbulbs from all the cameras went off like fireworks. "My mother should not be treated like a criminal, and as you may be aware, the only crimes she committed were loving her husband and giving birth to a daughter."

She encouraged women who had had similar experiences to continue the fight and stop the way they allowed men to treat them. "I want to let you know that there's got to be a way to stop feeling powerless. There is a way to feel hopeful, and this is the time to wear strong emotional body armor to ward off the bullies in your life. I don't know when this is going to happen, but I have visions that one day, there will be a place where women will be safe from harm. Thank you."

While Ionnia addressed the crowd, Loretty secretly slipped back to a quiet area to give Cecilia the exclusive interview. Representatives from BONDAGE and RAW had their own opinions about the situation and gave an interview to Magda Ponce of *The Trumpet*. Loretty's trial was the lead story on the evening news and the newspapers the following day.

Other reporters interviewed some of the spectators who had opposing views of the verdict. Neolene Duffles from Channel 3 TV News pointed her microphone at one man who apparently was anxious to get some publicity. Obviously, he was an avid listener to Dr. L. Mae's show. As the wind whipped up the few strands of hair on his head, he said with a frown, "I think the jurors got it wrong. That woman should be held responsible. One can't chop up a man like a piece of dead meat and think it is okay to do so." From his rantings, excessive gesticulations, and obvious empathy and support for Lensley Quane, one could easily assume that he himself was a spouse abuser of some sort.

He was now the main focus of attention, and Neola asked the obvious question. "Have you ever abused your spouse?"

This question caught him off guard, and he snapped at her, "I was accused of doing something eight years ago, but there was not enough evidence to convict me of anything. I was on some type of medication at that time that caused me to do things of which I was not aware. I'm off these drugs now, and I'm a changed man. I couldn't hurt a fly."

Obviously, that was more than anyone wanted to hear.

"But did you beat her?" Neola pressed. She suspected that he was withholding something.

He must have sensed that this would start the bleeding of an eight-year-old wound in case his ex-wife happened to be watching the news later on. "I have no further comments," he shouted angrily as he shoved away the microphone. He disappeared in the crowd before Neola got the chance to ask another follow-up question.

He must have regretted this fifteen minutes of fame.

"That's a changed man, all right," the reporter said as she beckoned to her photographer and producer to stop the recording.

Neola approached a woman this time and asked, "Do you think justice was served today?"

"Oh, yes. Loretty did a good job of dispatching that no-good son of a bitch to the bowels of hell."

"So you do believe in the saying 'An eye for an eye and a tooth for a tooth'?"

The woman smiled and said, "If that were to happen every time one of those men put their hands on us, there would be a lot of blind, toothless men walking around."

The following day, Ionnia received calls from influential people who were curious as to her plans to help women beyond the involvement of BONDAGE and RAW. "There are already various established women's movements championing the cause of battered and abused women, so what would be different this time? What are your plans to save these women from their own powerlessness and stupidity? A person can only do to you what you allow them to do."

Ionnia accepted a part-time position as an advice columnist for a national newspaper, and she advocated more strongly for women. The letters of complaints and concerns from battered, abused, jilted, and neglected women piled up week after week. Ionnia answered them in a very straightforward manner. The newspaper circulation peaked to a new level, advertisers vied for spots, and their businesses prospered. Some businesses donated a portion of their profits to the women's movement.

Although women adored Ionnia for her advocacy, husbands and boyfriends saw her as a threat. She was accused of breaking up marriages and brainwashing vulnerable women. She was called all kinds of names and received several threats, but she never stopped her crusade to help women. She became an icon.

Men began to fear for their lives, as some of the women had the guts to threaten to render them immobile if the men ever laid hands on them or were caught cheating.

Fifty-Nine

"How would you like to be a part of the BRTV 9 family?" the station manager from Buek Ridge asked in the message he left for Ionnia. "We can offer you what our competition would find difficult to match. It's an offer you won't be able to refuse, no matter how hard you try."

There was a callback number, and Ionnia weighed her options, knowing that she had to make a decision between her full-time job at Zeme Enterprises, writing her column for the newspaper, and hosting a television show. The latter was the opportunity she had anticipated and about which she had dreamed. She would be in people's living rooms and bedrooms, and they'd discuss her around their kitchen tables. By accepting this offer, her message would generate discussions among different demographic groups.

"A trip to Buek Ridge wouldn't hurt," she told herself. "I have heard so much about the place, and I have never been there. Moreover, I would like to see the station and negotiate my contract in person. But at this time, I could only accept a weekend position." She made a call and set up a meeting. Her brother Chad arranged to take her to Buek Ridge in a twin-engine Cessna, which he would rent from Andy Vorgeston, who owned a private aerodrome off Stanton Road. Ionnia had completely overcome her fear of flying through bibliotherapy and other methods of psychotherapy. By going in a private plane with her brother, she would have a better opportunity to view unoccupied parcels of land that she could possibly acquire and develop so that one day when funds become available, she would realize her dreams and accomplish her mission of finding a safe place for abused women and children.

On Saturday morning at around eight o'clock, Ionnia met her brother Chad at Andy's place. Andy was a very interesting individual. He was a stocky, no-nonsense fellow in his late fifties with thick eyebrows. He spoke with a thick foreign accent. In addition to the number of small planes that Vorgeston owned and rented, he also owned a fleet of banner planes that advertisers used almost every weekend. Vorgeston was a flight instructor at one of the most prestigious flight-training schools on the island of Puca Luca. He taught Chad to fly small, twin-engine planes and helicopters, and among his long list of other students was Captain Lynval Clifford, whom he'd taught to fly large commercial airplanes.

As Chad and Andy finished exchanging greetings, their attention became focused on the weather report, which was at this time being broadcast over the radio and a nine-inch television set. The meteorologist predicted that there would be heavy thunderstorms in Sassawhackia, Buek Ridge, and Hampstead within the next two hours, so Chad quickly completed the paperwork, handed it to Andy, and hoped to lift off and get to Buek Ridge before the weather got ugly.

Either the meteorological office made the wrong predictions, or the media personnel read the wrong report, because all of a sudden the clouds got dark and the morning sky lit up with fierce, blinding flashes of lightning. One would think one was in a stadium when the lightning lit up the reception area of Andy Vorgeston's business place. The thunder roared like a freight train. It was a scary moment.

Andy Vorgeston shuffled toward his office and shouted, "Can't they get it right? They said in the next two hours." He cursed under his breath in a language no one else could understand.

The violent flashes of lightning came in quick succession, and Ionnia hid in a nearby closet until it ended. Inside the small closet, she competed for space with newspapers, old and new airplane parts, and dozens of boxes with nuts and bolts. It was a miracle she was not electrocuted with all that metal around her, but luckily she found a small tire and placed it around her neck. She sweated profusely due to fear and the lack of ventilation in the closet. Ionnia groped around for something to dry her face, and in the process she found earplugs on one of the shelves, which she placed in her ears to drown out the effects of the deafening peal of thunder that caused the place to reverberate just like the earthquake that had shaken the area ten years ago. The window panes rattled at each frightening peal of thunder, and the beams that supported the old ceiling creaked musically. This kind of storm was expected at this time of year, but not this serious, intense, and frightening.

When all the rattling and tumbling subsided, Ionnia embarrassingly emerged from the closet. Everyone drank coffee prepared by Andy's wife, Emily, and Ionnia contemplated going on the journey to Buek Ridge. Emily calmed her down and assured her that whatever was to happen would happen. Then the subject of conversation changed, and they talked briefly about Sharonique, who was employed as a sociology professor at the University of Trevine.

Andy and Chad talked mostly about airplanes. "When will you be ready to begin flight training for larger planes?" Andy asked.

"I'm satisfied with small planes and helicopters," Chad assured Andy.

"I could give you a discount."

"I won't be needing it."

"You never know. You or someone in your family may own a jet or two someday.

Darkness now enveloped the area where Chad and Ionnia would be heading, and a monstrous tornado moved ominously across the morning sky.

"I cannot imagine what destruction will follow. I've read about this type of weather occurring in other parts of the world, and the devastating aftereffect, but I hate to imagine that the same thing could happen here," Chad said.

"Religious believers uphold their beliefs that the Lord is at work," Ionnia added. "Our trip seems to be on hold for now, and nobody is to blame."

"Let's kill some time till the storm is over." Chad suggested. "Wait here."

Chad retrieved his car from the parking lot behind Andy's establishment, and the pair headed in the opposite direction, where there were a few clouds in the skies and where the sun occasionally peeked through. They were going to pay their mom a surprise visit at Crystal Vernetti's bridal shop. She still held her full-time job at Blovingworth, and she worked at Crystal's on the weekends. When Chad and Ionnia arrived at Vern's Bridal, the store was busy with young and middle-aged prospective brides, as well as mothers helping their daughters to make decisions.

"I'm thinking of changing my mind about getting married," Ionnia overheard one young woman, Verona Ainsley, telling her mother, Zelma.

Ionnia made mental notes as the young lady tearfully explained how badly her fiancé treated her and added that she did not wish to go through with the wedding. "Do you know how many times he threatened to kill me?" she asked her mother.

"But, sweetheart, he hasn't." Pointing at her daughter, Zelma said, "Here's living proof: you are standing right here in front of me. Things will change once he marries you." With that said, she hugged her and then proceeded to pick out one of the most gorgeous white dresses in the store. But the conversation was not over. Zelma Ainsley never stopped talking. "Young ladies are supposed to get married and have children. You don't have a career, so this is the right thing to do. Don't let me hear about this anymore," she warned her daughter.

"What will I tell my friends, all of whom are very excited to see you walk down the aisle?"

Zelma, a Whickam County socialite, was more concerned with what people would say if her daughter did not get married rather than the quality of the marriage and the subsequent treatment by the husband. The worst thing would be if her daughter remained single.

"I have a feeling that you just want to get rid of me, Mother, and that it doesn't really matter on whom you unload me. I hate you. I'd rather be dead than marry that son of a bitch. You can have him if you want to." Without looking back, Verona stormed out of the store and right in the path of an oncoming car. She was tossed several feet up in the air before landing on the hood of the car as it made contact with the walls of the bridal shop. Verona rolled off the car and onto the ground, where one of the front wheels of the car came to a stop just a few inches from her as the driver tried to back out of the shop.

The loud thud, the screeching of brakes, the violent impact of the car as it made contact with building, and the sound of a screaming woman caused everyone to rush outside, dropping heaps of bridal gowns on the floor.

What a deadly coincidence. The driver of the car was none other than Verona Ainsley's fiancé, Gerald Archibald. He was on his way to pick her up for an appointment with the minister at the Methodist church where they were to be married within a few months. Verona lay on the ground motionless while her blood ran down the sidewalk.

Everyone in the bridal shop had his or her own comments about the accident, and people recalled the conversation between mother and daughter.

Gerald was unhurt. He eased his body out of the wreckage and bent over Verona as she lay bleeding on the ground. He got to her just as Chad was assessing the extent of her injuries and began administering aid with improvised equipment.

"Get away from my fiancé!" Gerald shouted as Chad leaned over the partially lifeless figure. He spoke condescendingly to Chad and even tried to push him away from Verona, acting as though he cared.

"I'm a doctor," Chad said as he looked up at Gerald pleadingly.

Gerald said nothing else, but he bent over and pulled the engagement ring off Verona's finger.

As Ionnia watched Chad spring in action to save a life, her own mortality came into focus. She felt as proud as a peacock. *There goes my hero,* she said to herself.

Someone inside the store had called in the emergency, and the ambulance arrived at the scene while Chad was still with the injured girl. The police also arrived and began taking statements. Zelma Ainsley sobbed and held tightly to the arms of her future son-in-law. She regretted the earlier discussion with her daughter but said nothing about it. "I know you didn't mean to hurt her," she said to him. Turning to one of the medical personnel who was lifting Verona in the ambulance, Zelma asked, "Is going to live?"

Verona was transferred to the nearest hospital but succumbed to her injuries two days later. She was buried in the wedding dress that had been picked out by her mother at Vern's Bridal. Her funeral was held at the same church where she would have been married, and her bridesmaids were her pallbearers. One of the young ladies who shared the same birthday with Verona wanted to opt out because there was an unproven claim that it was a bad omen to be a pallbearer with someone born under the same zodiac sign, but because of their relationship, which went way back, she ignored what the seers and clairvoyants predicted.

The grieving Zelma now placed all the blame for her daughter's death on Gerald, despite the fact that the investigations showed it was an accident that couldn't have been avoided. They both played the blame game for a while. By this time, Gerald had heard about the exchange between Verona and her mother inside Crystal's establishment, and he blamed Zelma for had had happened to his fiancée.

It wasn't long after Verona's tragic death that everyone learned about Gerald's other girlfriend, Elaine O'Rigby in Hampstead, who was five months pregnant at the time. Shortly after Verona was laid to rest, Gerald proposed to Elaine with the engagement ring he'd yanked off his late fiancée's finger. She probably had no idea that this was Verona's ring, or maybe she simply didn't care. She had all she wanted: the much-sought-after Gerald Archibald.

Sixty

The bridal shop had to be closed for regular business for the rest of the day, and it would remain that way until someone's insurance company agreed to fix the damaged structure.

"Mom, let's go grab a bite to eat," Chad suggested. "There isn't anything much that can be accomplished after this."

"What a day," Ionnia said.

"The nearest restaurant around here is the Paradise Diner, and it won't open till 4:00 p.m. We could all have some of my lunch, which I carried with me," Loretty told her children.

"Thanks, Mom, but I think we will to go to the Rexington Café at the Harborhead Marina," Chad replied.

"I am not dressed for the occasion," Loretty protested.

"Don't worry, Momma. You look okay," Ionnia chimed in. "Just go powder your nose."

"Does it look as shiny as Rudolph's?" she asked, and all three got a good laugh.

Loretty left with her firstborn and her baby girl to have lunch at the most talked-about seafood restaurant on that side of Puca Luca. There were many people of significance in the restaurant: politicians, millionaires, expatriates, reporters, photographers, health professionals, and people in law enforcement. The trio blended in well.

"My favorite doctor," Deidre Kempton said in a delighted manner as they entered the restaurant. Chad knew her and her brother from high school. He had not kept in touch, but Deidre had kept up on his achievements. She'd had a crush on him back then and was more than delighted to see him again. "Let me find you a very comfortable seat by the window, where you can watch the activities below."

"No preferential treatment now," Chad said to Deidre. "If it bears any semblance of that, I'm sure your patrons will notice." As she ushered them to their seats, Chad discovered that Deidre was the owner of the place.

The two people whom everyone watched were the famous choreographer Jasmine Tou and her companion, the popular pollster who correctly predicted election results, Melvin Billhadow (affectionately known to his friends as Billy). Melvin was also the owner of several small and medium vessels that plied between islands either with passengers or with mail, and it was no surprise that he had his own private yacht anchored in the marina.

Everything about Jasmine was unique, and Ionnia recognized the dress she wore as one that bore the Zeme label. Jasmine was extremely elegant and graceful, especially when she danced with Melvin to the music of the thirteen-piece orchestra conducted by Luke Brackleigh, one of Dorothy Book's former students and also the ex-boyfriend of Dorothy's daughter Ordrette. Melvin's eyes roamed the room, probably to get the approval of the diners or to make some other man jealous.

People removed themselves from the dance floor and allowed the pair to enjoy themselves. Photojournalists had a field day and tried to capture every angle. Surely these and other pictures would appeared in the society pages of most newspapers in days to come.

Loretty, Chad, and Ionnia had a lot to talk about. These two children were extra special to Loretty. Chad expressed concern that neither his mother nor his sister was currently dating anyone. They asked why he hadn't found someone with whom to settle down. They knew of the relationship with Crystal's daughter, Heather, which had ended suddenly when Chad had told her that he wasn't ready to marry her. Heather ended up marrying Dale Gatsworthy, and that marriage lasted for a little over two years. Ionnia teased Chad about Deidre. "I saw how you two looked at each other earlier on." Chad just smiled as if he had something up his sleeves.

Loretty sat there absorbed in her thoughts, smiling and probably thinking about Kingsley Muggerdon. She hadn't told her children anything. "Oh, well," she said as she let out a sigh. "We can't predict relationships, and sometimes when you think it's over, it has just begun."

Chad kept quizzing his sister about her love life until she finally opened up and told them of a relationship that she'd had shortly after she'd started working for Zeme Industries, but it didn't last long.

"Who was this, sis?"

"Michael Brackette."

"The Michael Brackette who operates one of the largest high-end department stores in the Burning Wheel Mall?"

"Yes, that one. What do you know about him?"

Before Chad had a chance to answer, Loretty asked, "So what happened? How did you let him slip through your fingers?"

"Mom, all that glitters is not gold. We had lunch once, and then he told me in no uncertain terms that if he were to leave his business place to have lunch with me again, I would have to pay for the installation of surveillance cameras in his establishment."

Loretty was flabbergasted, and her appetite took a sharp decline. "The nerve of this creep!" she exclaimed in a distressed but concerned tone.

Chad had his piece to say too. "You did the right thing by breaking off that relationship. I know that many men think that women owe them a favor when they take them out. Sis, you owe no one any obligation. Furthermore, did you know that he was married?"

"How did you know that?"

"Let's just say I hear a lot that goes on, especially at the barber shop."

Loretty looked at her daughter inquisitively.

"I know what you want to ask me, Mother, and the answer is no, I didn't know."

Before they could finish their meal, the greatest surprise of the day was about to unfold. Melvin Billhadow was weaving in and out of tables and making his way in their direction. At first they thought that he was going to request a special song for Jasmine. When he stopped by their table, held out his hands, and asked Ionnia to dance, she was shocked but felt special. As she hesitated, Melvin looked inquiringly at Chad, who nodded his head and gave his approval. Loretty smiled contentedly and winked at her daughter, as if to say, "Good catch."

Melvin did approach the band and request a special song, and while they danced, he stared seductively in Ionnia's eyes.

Ionnia avoided Billy's eyes and said to herself, *I can read your mind. Whatever you are thinking of will not work.*

They danced for another five minutes, and when he brought her back to her seat, he thanked her and said, "Perhaps we can do this again another time?"

Ionnia smiled and politely said, "Sure."

If she had any intention of doing that, she certainly would be doing her homework. Melvin formally introduced himself to Chad and Loretty, and he and Ionnia exchanged business cards.

At around 4:00 p.m., Ionnia and her brother returned to Andy's place and canceled the trip to Buek Ridge. "We will be back in a day or two," Chad told Andy.

The storm was over, but after looking up at the sky, one could have easily come to a conclusion that the annual air show was in progress because aircraft were carrying local and regional politicians, and news crews and rescue crews, observing the carnage brought on by the tornado. During the course of the day, almost twenty inches of rain had fallen in Hampstead and Sassawhackia. Homes and business places were blown. Hundreds of people were injured, killed, washed away by the raging waters, hit by flying debris, buried under rubble, or electrocuted. These two places resembled a war zone, but Sassawhackia was the hardest hit. The last time something like this had occurred in Puca Luca was eighty years prior, in the town of Stechion Bay.

This seaport town was once referred to as the wickedest town in Puca Luca. Some called it the modern-day Nineveh. It had a reputation for lawlessness, sorcery, prostitution, and all manner of illegal activities under the sun. Girls who were taken from their families as payment for debts by men like Cyril Dulvert, Sam Muggerdon, and others were taken to this area. It had the country's largest deepwater pier and was the main seaport for imports and exports. The loading and unloading of ships with lumber, sugar cane, and other produce was done once per week. The central sorting office for mail was located in this town, and mail boats came and went every other day. It was almost impossible at times to differentiate between the legal and the illegal activities. But a great tornado leveled the area, and Puca Luca's economy came to a halt.

"Oh, my God," Chad and Ionnia said simultaneously as they watched news reports of the devastation on the small television set inside the waiting room at Vorgeston's. Additional reports on television later that day showed furniture, bathroom, and kitchen equipment scattered several miles away from their original destinations. Automobiles were stacked on top of each other. Dead bodies from a small cemetery were strewn all over the area, some of which got stuck in trees that had withstood the storm. The floodwaters had quickly risen close to rooftops, and people with small boats volunteered to rescue the occupants of Sassawhackia, but the downed power lines made this task more arduous than anticipated. A few victims who had climbed to the top of damaged homes and held on to debris were rescued by helicopters. The Puca Luca military, along with Whickam County

Emergency Management, sent in amphibious vehicles to rescue victims, and residents who had been away during the thunderstorm were warned to stay away.

It was later learned that the passenger train from Trevine to Buek Ridge was derailed in the snake-infested area of Hampstead by the rising waters from the raging tornado, and it would be a miracle if anyone survived. Most of them were on their way back to their homes in Sassawhackia. When it became possible for the search-and-rescue team to go in, they did find survivors and immediately took them to various hospitals near and far. When those who survived the derailment were subsequently released from the hospital, they learned that they had no homes to which to return. This caused them to experience bouts of depression, and they had to be readmitted. When they were well enough, they were put in emergency shelters in different areas of Whickam County, and it was like starting all over again.

Puca Luca's Emergency Management had a huge job on its hands. Food, water, and shelter had to be provided for the displaced people who'd had everything taken away from them. The area had to be cleaned up, and the dead bodies had to be reinterred. It took three weeks before the water receded. In the following days and weeks, those people who survived struggled amid the stench and the wreckage to find anything of importance. A curfew was imposed while the emergency crew dealt with the situation, trying to get these communities back to normal, but this would be no simple feat.

While the authorities implemented measures to rebuild the infrastructure, the most difficult task was to recapture the snakes that had been washed out of the lagoon at Hampstead. Experts were called in, and as a result, many of the reptiles were caught and killed, but there was no way of knowing how many more were on the run, so members of the rescue team had to exercise extreme caution in their approach. Another problem that they had to deal with was the emergence of swarms of mosquitoes, as well as the stench from the dead bodies of human beings and animals.

The outpouring of donations from all over Puca Luca and elsewhere, from both private citizens and government agencies, was overwhelming. So too was the number of volunteers who donated their time. It was heartwarming to see how united the citizens were in times of disaster. Some homes and business places were either uninsured or underinsured, and the owners welcomed any help they could get.

While the citizens struggled to regain normality in their lives, many licensed and unlicensed contractors devised unscrupulous means to capitalize on their misfortune and the rebuilding process as a whole. Some families' trust in humanity was shattered when they were conned out of their life's savings. But they had faith in law enforcement, and the arrests were fast and furious.

Sixty-One

Ionnia chose to wait until Monday morning before making another attempt to go to Buek Ridge. Beatrice had no problem giving her the entire week off. "I have seen the passion with which you advocate for battered women, and you have my unwavering support," she told Ionnia. "If there is anything else I can do, please let me know."

Chad, who was nearing the end of his well-deserved vacation, met his sister at Andy's, and this time the weather was in their favor. Her friend Kerline had dropped her off and would be picking her up on her return. Chad flew over small cays and large ones, over occupied and unoccupied islands, and over mountains, rivers, and lakes. Ionnia was fascinated by the physical features of the region. This was the first time she had flown over this area of Puca Luca.

As they neared Buek Ridge, Ionnia noticed fire coming from a small, uninhabited cay in the middle of the Buek River. Nearby fields of grass were incinerated. Ionnia turned to Chad, and asked, "Who would set that place on fire in the middle of nowhere?"

"God," he replied, referring to the electrical storm which had accompanied the tornado two days before. As he read her facial expression, he added, "No more destruction by water He promised, remember?" He pointed to the rainbow in the sky. "He promised to burn our you-know-what with fire and brimstone."

"Chad, stop the blaspheming."

"I am not blaspheming. Did you not read the story of Noah and the flood in the book of Genesis?"

"Those were the days, but I have a gut feeling that the destruction of the earth, if any, will not be caused by this type of fire," she said.

"What else would it be?"

"Nukes. Atomic energy."

"That's even worse."

Ionnia was met at the Buek Ridge airport by Becky O'Bannon, the news editor of BRTV9, who took her to the Sandy Port Hotel, where she would stay for the few days. A room would be reserved for her there on weekends if she took the job. Ionnia was pleased with the accommodation at the hotel. She changed into one if her pin-striped suits and headed to the station with Becky. On their way Becky briefed her on almost everything she needed to know. All that was left was for her to meet the staff and familiarize herself with the equipment. Her negotiations went well, and she accepted a weekend position, a three-hour show on Saturday and Sunday.

When she was introduced to the staff, most of them seemed comfortable with the new appointment, but Courtney Shackleworth, who had held those time slots for a long time, was not happy. She was given an option to either accept a different time slot or be transferred to another station in another position. She wanted neither, so she resigned. As luck would have it, a position for editor became available with *The Speaker's Choice*, the most widely read tabloid newspaper in Buek Ridge. Courtney applied and was hired. This was her chance to enact revenge on BRTV9 and the person who'd taken her job.

Chad had to get back to his job. "Sis, call me when you are ready. I'll come back for you if you need me to, or I can ask one of my friends to come and get you."

"Go back and get acquainted with Deidre. I want to experience another way to travel. I have already gone by road, by air, and by rail. This time I want to travel on water."

"Then I will ask my friend Melton Juveng if he can do me the favor. You know him, don't you?" Chad spoke as though he wanted to hook her up with this person, but she was not willing to go this route.

"I appreciate your concern, and I accept all the help you have given me. Don't worry so much; I'm a big girl now. I can take the regular ferry that transports passengers to and from the islands, or maybe I can take one of the mail boats."

"Here is an employee of the largest group of companies on this side of heaven, and she's going to ride the ferry or the mail boat. Girl, you need your own yacht."

"I don't forget where I'm from, Chad. I'm still me. I want to remain as humble as possible."

The following day, Ionnia decided to pay a surprise visit to Roxanne Milwinkle, who was very happy to see her. She congratulated her on her new gig at the television station. "If you should ever need anything while you are here, please don't hesitate to ask. As a matter of fact, I know just how I can help. You will stay with me those weekends that you are on the island." Ionnia was about to say that she didn't want to impose on her, but she was stopped by an insistent Roxanne. "I won't hear of it. I know what you are thinking, but the past is dead and buried."

It felt awkward and weird that after all these years and what had transpired at Dartsdam Elementary, this former teacher should welcome her and extend this hospitality to Ionnia.

"Thank you," Ionnia said. "The station has already paid for my accommodation at the hotel, but we can go out for lunch."

After a few days of intense orientation and much sightseeing, Ionnia was ready to return to her full-time job. She looked up Melvin Billhadow's number. He owned a fifty-two-foot luxury yacht anchored in the marina.

"Hi, Billy, this is …" There was silence for a moment, and Ionnia thought she had lost contact. "Hello? This is Ionnia."

"I know who it is; I recognize your voice. I have been thinking about you ever since we met." Then he quoted Lord Alfred Tennyson. "'If I had a flower every time I thought of you I could walk through my garden forever.'"

He couldn't see her reaction and hoped her voice wouldn't give her away when she said pleasingly, "I will get straight to the point. Can you take me back to Stanton in your lovely yacht?" This was a big, scary chance she was taking.

He didn't hesitate. "It would be my pleasure. When would you want to go?"

"Next week Tuesday at around ten o'clock."

"That's a date. Ten o'clock on Tuesday it will be. I can't wait to see you again. Where are you staying?"

A surprise preceded his arrival. A bouquet of twelve of the most beautiful yellow roses was delivered to Ionnia's hotel room. This was the first time someone had sent her flowers, and she didn't know what to think about whether or not she was special. Was this the way Billy treated all women? Ionnia wondered. *He didn't have to do this. It would be all right if he had given them to me on the ship.*

Just then, she heard another knock on the door. She looked through the peephole and saw a man in uniform. "Can I help you?" she asked as she opened the door.

"Miss Dunn-Ryte?"

"Yes."

"Mr. Billy has asked me to pick you up. I'm his limo driver."

"And where is Mr. Billy?"

"He is waiting in the limo, ma'am."

Billy was the perfect gentleman. He was a member of the famous Keltrock Bay Yacht Club and was qualified to captain his own yacht, but he preferred not to do so on this occasion. He hired one of Puca Luca's most competent boat captains to go with them. He wanted to show Ionnia every nook and cranny of the vessel and also ensure that she enjoyed every moment of her trip.

"I am surely ecstatic to be given this opportunity," he told her.

"There's no one out there who would object?" Ionnia inquired.

"Certainly not," Billy said emphatically.

Ionnia was skeptical, and she was sure would be looking around for photographs or other evidence of a female companion.

Billy showed her the many medals and trophies he'd received from participating in various regattas and yacht races. Ionnia was impressed with the marble fixtures, the drapes, the carpet, and the clocks on the walls. She was in awe as he showed her the piano in the living room. She couldn't resist the urge to play a few notes.

"Do you mind?"

"Not at all, go ahead."

When Ionnia was finished, he kissed her on the forehead and said, "That was awesome."

The tour of the vessel continued. Melvin pointed to a chest with his gun collection of various makes, models, and sizes. Ionnia's heart raced to a frightening level. She made her way outside, leaned against the rails, and watched the white-capped waves lapping against the side of the ship. Then there were sudden jerky movements and she thought she was going to topple over. She became nauseous and dizzy.

Melvin noticed. "Are you okay?"

"Just a little motion sickness," she managed to mumble.

He gently said, "Sit right here while I get you something. I have the right remedy for motion sickness. And don't hang your head down—keep looking toward the horizon."

While Melvin was gone, Ionnia's thoughts raced back to the gun collection, and she said to herself, *Could this be him?* She had read in the newspapers several years ago about a man who had taken a woman out on his yacht, and she had accidently fallen overboard. When the body was plucked from the water it was discovered that she had a gunshot wound to her head. Ionnia felt sicker at the thought. Was

Melvin going to harm her or take advantage of her in some way? In her head, she rehearsed her survival skills that she'd learned at Barry's gym. Her real purpose was not yet realized, and she had to do everything possible to ensure its fulfillment.

Melvin returned with a pill and water in one hand and a glass of brandy in the other. He kneeled down beside her and said, "Pick your choice."

"Thank you very much, but I'd rather suck on a piece of ginger. Do you have any?"

He didn't want to leave her alone again, so he called out to one of the deck hands, "Hurry down to the galley and get me some ginger."

"Right away, sir."

The young man, who was in his early twenties, took off in a manner as if he had heard the voice of God, and was back in less than two minutes with pieces of ginger root wrapped in a blue and white napkin with the initials "M. B." in the corner. Ionnia sucked on the ginger and was back to her old self shortly thereafter. By this time, calmness had returned to the waters, and they continued on the rest of the journey, which was pleasant and uneventful.

She learned a lot about Melvin but did not disclose much of her personal life to him even though he pressed her. Whenever he asked, she would say, "You will know all there is to know, in due course." She thanked him for bringing her home safely. He kissed her on the hand while he asked his attendant to take care of her luggage.

Ionnia could hardly wait to get home and tell her friend Kerline about the trip. She expected to see her at the Black Cay Pier at the Harborhead Marina upon her arrival. The pier was bustling with hundreds of people arriving and departing on various ferries to different islands, and others got on and off private carriers. Not a cloud was in the sky to obscure the brightness of the midafternoon sun. From the deck of the yacht, Ionnia could see Kerline waving to her in the crowd. But when she got closer to her, it appeared that she wasn't paying her any attention. That was because her eyes were focused on someone else.

"Well, well. Isn't that Margaret Hickles? I thought she was still in prison."

"I am not familiar with that name," Ionnia said. "Who is she? Why are you so surprised to see her, and why was she sent to prison?"

"I'll tell you on the way."

Kerline took Ionnia's luggage from the attendant and tipped him. As they made their way toward the car, she handed Ionnia the keys.

"I prefer if you drive," Ionnia said to her friend, but was that a mistake. They took their seats, and as Kerline backed out of the parking space, Ionnia shouted, "Watch out!" Kerline had steered the car too close to some pedestrians.

"Sorry, I got distracted. I'll be more focused."

"That Margaret character must mean something to you. Was she responsible for the breakup of any of your marriages?"

"No, but she did something worse than that to Maxine Brank, a friend of mine. She took advantage of the poor girl to the point where Maxine almost got thrown overboard one of these ferries and fed to the fishes."

"You mean the Maxine Brank whose husband owned a company that designed costumes for the circus?"

"She was the wardrobe consultant, and when her husband died, she inherited a hefty sum of money."

"So, what did Margaret do to her?"

"She plotted with her lover to con her out of the money. That's why she is popularly known as Connie."

"How was she able to accomplish this?"

"By trying to be a matchmaker. She claimed that one of her cousins had been a widower for a while, and it would be good if he and Maxine were to get together."

"What's wrong with that?"

"What's wrong is that Connie and her co-conspirator, whom she referred as cousin, were lovers."

"Kerline, we are almost home, and I have not heard the whole story. Will you fast-forward, please?"

"He proposed to Maxine, convinced her to put his name on almost everything that she owned, and took her on a cruise around the islands where he and Connie plotted to throw her overboard."

"But it didn't happen, right?"

"No, thank God. Someone who overheard the final plans alerted Maxine. If they had succeeded in killing Maxine, they would have done so for nothing."

"How so?"

"Maxine was smart enough not to put that man's name on anything. It turned out she tricked him into believing that she had already included his name on the documents, but what she gave him were fake ones."

There was a moment of silence as the car moved slowly toward the intersection with the red light. As they waited for the light to change, Kerline sneezed, and the car inched forward, almost hitting the one in front of her. She slammed on the brakes. Another near miss.

"Pull over when you can. I'll take it from here," Ionnia said to Kerline in a friendly voice. She knew that her friend loved to drink vodka, and she wasn't sure whether Kerline had drunk a few before hitting the road. Ionnia didn't want to offend her by asking.

The quick exchange of seats took place just as the green light came on. "Now, tell me about Billy boy," Kerline said to Ionnia as if she expected something intimate had occurred on the vessel.

"He was a perfect gentleman, and I had a good time."

"Are you telling me that nothing will develop into a relationship?"

"No. And moreover, I don't think I can trust anyone. I'm too happy being free."

"So are you going to spend the rest of your life being single?"

"What's wrong with that?" Ionnia asked. She was about to comment on her friend's two failed marriages, but instead of hurting Kerline's feelings, she calmly and respectfully said, "The decision with whom to spend the rest of your life should not be made lightly. As a matter of fact, people who decide to get married should enter into a five-year contract, and after the five years are up, if the couple feels like renewing the contract, then they should do so. If the marriage is not worth renewing, then they should go their separate ways."

Kerline changed the subject and asked, "Have you ever had sex?"

Ionnia was surprised that Kerline would ask her such an intimate question. They both laughed, and then she gave her an answer. "I did it once, didn't like it, and never did it again."

"Who was he? Do I know him? Was it that bad?"

Ionnia sighed. "I don't think you know him His name is Ralph Blender. And before you ask the follow-up question, let me tell you where we met. It was on a stormy day while I was on one of the company's overseas trips. I was at the airport, waiting in line to have my documents stamped by the immigration officer. When I got to the front of the line, he took my travel documents, looked up from over the top of his glasses, and beckoned to one of his assistants. While I watched him confiscate my documents, I could hear him when he whispered, "Take this lady to that room over there." It was one of those rooms where they interrogate people whose documents were questionable."

"What was going through your mind?"

"Everything bad. But then again, I knew that my documents were in order. This was not my first time overseas, however this was my first time alone."

"From what I'm hearing, I know you were scared."

"I felt like I was being punished, and the horrible memories of my childhood emerged. I started counting to a million. My thoughts went back to those moments in my young life when I curled up in a corner with my thumb stuffed in my mouth after hearing my father trying to sell me to one of his friends."

"That must have been a very traumatic moment, but let's not relive it. What happened? Get to the point."

"When I entered the room, I was more impressed and relaxed, rather than scared. The carpet felt like it was around three inches thick, the furniture was of expensive mahogany, and the smell of freshly brewed coffee permeated the entire room. In a gentlemanly fashion, the assistant offered me a seat. As he exited, he almost bumped into Ralph, who entered with a broad grin on his face. I swore that if he touched me inappropriately, I would grab the coffee pot and empty the contents in his face."

"But you didn't have to do that."

"No. Either he must have read the expression on my face, or he had good intentions."

"And it was the latter?" Kerline asked

"Yes, and when he told the assistant not to close the door, I no longer felt scared or threatened. He introduced himself, handed me my documents, and took a seat across the room from me. He let me feel at ease, and then he told me that the reason he asked to see me was to get to know more about me. It turned out that he knew my aunt Arthel."

"Get to the juicy part. Did he date your aunt?"

"Not from what he said. She had other love interests. He invited me out, and we had a relationship for a short while."

"I imagine you are the one who broke it off?"

"No, he was transferred to another location, and he told me he didn't believe in long-distance relationships."

They got to Kerline's destination, and before Ionnia dropped her off, they made arrangements to have dinner together. Kerline said, "Don't forget to bring your roommate, and don't forget to let Billy know that you got home safely."

Sixty-Two

Back at work from a very successful trip, Ionnia discussed her part-time work with Beatrice. "You have our support, and I can't stress it enough: we have confidence in you and pray that one day, your dreams will come through and you can build your rescue mission for those unfortunate women. I wish we had more people like you."

Ionnia had a surprise for the Zemes. While in Buek Ridge, she'd contracted with proprietors of large companies and small establishments to sell them advertisement spots that would be published in the company's magazine, *Stitches*. This included a one-page ad from Billy. To some of these struggling business owners, this was the break they had been waiting for. Ionnia negotiated with them future discounts, and they also could pay for the ads in installments. "If anyone asks from where I learned my aggressiveness, I will tell them I learned it from Mrs. Zeme, coupled with Aunt Gert's words about the art of negotiating."

Beatrice managed her father's company for many years before selling it to Morgan Dent, but she remained a consultant for the new owners for a long time. She was also the sole beneficiary of her brother's personal wealth. The Zemes had no children, so they devoted most of their time to the business and to their philanthropic endeavors. When Ionnia joined the business, they realized her potential and

knew that she could be trusted, so they started to take much-needed
vacations and leave her in charge of certain aspects of the operations
of Zeme Enterprise.

"I think we made a very good choice when we hired you,"
Beatrice said to her young employee. "I can see much of myself
in you."

Ryland had no problem with his wife's decision, but the men in
the company were jealous of Ionnia. They argued that one of them
should have been promoted from within. They grumbled about se-
niority versus youth, and one senior general manager resigned in
protest. He had appalling, abhorrent, sickening things to say about
women, and Ionnia pledged that she would address some of these
behaviors at the next meeting of RAW.

"I had no idea that this is the way he thinks about women,"
Beatrice lamented. "Had I known, I would have fired him long time
ago. No wonder he is not married. I shudder to think how he would
treat his companion."

Ryland Zeme constantly complained of headaches, but he dismissed
it as mere exhaustion from work. He would take over-the-counter
pain medications and postpone appointments to see his doctor. Before
he had a chance to finally keep an appointment his wife Beatrice had
made for him, he collapsed at a business convention and had to be
hospitalized. He was diagnosed with a brain tumor and immediately
underwent surgery. For the last four months before his death, he had
bouts of unquestionable lucidity, a strong voice, and an insatiable
appetite. However, his involvement with the company was significantly curtailed. He had twenty-four-hour nursing care at an upscale
rehabilitation facility. When Ionnia was not engaged in her work
and other activities, she visited Mr. Zeme and gave him updates on
the business. He got the chance to get to know her better and ask
her about the people who'd made an impact in her life. When she
mentioned Professor Digginboss, he stopped talking as if to recollect
his thoughts.

"Is his first name Egbert?"

"Yes, sir. Do you know him?"

"If there is no other person by that name, then I think he is one of the brothers I spoke about in my documentary. He was the one we called Oats."

"You bear no resemblance to him."

He ignored that comment and went on to say, "If you can get in touch with him, I would like to ask him about our other brother, Fitzroy, the one known as Brains, or Barley. And of course, you know me as Rye."

This piqued Ionnia's interest, but without asking any more questions, she said, "Mr. Zeme, you need to rest." Ionnia had a new project, and she pledged to have this completed before old Zeme departed this world. She had heard her mother talk about Fitzroy and the three grains he'd kept mentioning. *So these were names of people? Am I the best hope to reunite the trio known as Barley, Oats, and Rye?*

First, she got in touch with Professor Digginboss. After identifying herself, she said, "I think I may have stumbled across some information that may prove very invaluable to you."

"Have you found out who tampered with my boat?"

"No, sir."

"Well, then, it must be one of those unsolved scientific mysteries."

She wanted to keep Dr. Digginboss in suspense a little longer. "One-third has to do with scientific research."

"Go on."

"Can you accompany me to Blovingworth Mental Hospital one day?"

"It so happens that I will be there to attend the annual conference of the Puca Luca Association of Research Scientists within the next two weeks."

"Great. And I am sure you will be impressed by some of the recent developments. I will see you there. A young lady whom I had the pleasure of mentoring will be a part of the atmospheric science exhibit. Will you please give her some feedback for me?"

"Sure. I'm looking forward to seeing you."

Ionnia had arranged with her mother to have Fitzroy assist her with certain chores and make sure she had photographs of him, both then and now. When Dr. Digginboss finished his first day at the conference, Ionnia met him in the lobby and invited him to meet her mother. "How was your first day?" she asked.

"The highlight of today's session focused on one particular drug company that produced an experimental drug that is currently being tested on patients at this very hospital. The data presented, if correct, were very impressive."

During the five-minute walk to the Kinglore Center, Ionnia and her former teacher learned some very interesting information from each other. He asked her about work, and she told him about her boss and how ill he was. Dr. Digginboss had the same response as when she had mentioned his name to Ryland Zeme. "I have to see him as soon as I get back. I hope he can hang around that long. Did he ever mention Barley, Oats, and Rye?"

"Yes, sir, but he never seemed to be able to find either of you."

The front windows to the Kinglore Center opened, and Loretty saw her visitors as they came around the corner. They were about to knock on the door, but they didn't have to do so because Loretty swung the door wide open and greeted them both. They walked inside and sat down on the leather couch in the waiting room, where Fitzroy was putting labels on boxes of clothing. "Say hello to my daughter and the professor," Loretty said to the man who seemed to be enjoying his job.

When Fitzroy turned around, he first shook Ionnia's hand and then extended it to the male standing in front of him. Both were oblivious to the other's real identity. "Call me Brains," he said, and he unbuttoned his shirt to expose the brain-shaped nevus on his shoulder.

Egbert was speechless.

"Did I do something to scare you, sir?"

When Egbert recovered from the shock, he held Fitzroy close to him and said, "Barley, Oats, and Rye."

Fitzroy grinned. "What do you know about us?"

The women looked at each other, smiled, and excused themselves, but before they left the room, Dr. Digginboss asked Loretty, "How long has he been working here?"

"This is one of the medical experiments," Ionnia whispered, and she handed him the photographs. Dr. Digginboss viewed the before and after pictures, and then he hugged his brother and said, "I'm sorry."

Fitzroy was able to hold a coherent conversation with his brother, and they both cried when he mentioned some of the circumstances that had caused him to be institutionalized.

"Oh, God, I'm sorry," Egbert kept saying. "Don't say anything else. We will talk about that another time. Rye needs to hear this too, and we should make this happen before his condition deteriorates."

Barley, Oats, and Rye got together while Rye was still lucid. "I can die happy now, thanks to my little detective and her mother," Ryland Zeme said. "I am going to establish a trust fund for Fitzroy. Egbert, you will be in charge of it. I am also giving you my yacht, which is currently on dry dock at Userus Bushwackle's shipyard."

"We did not come here for handouts," Oats said firmly.

"I don't want to hear any objections," the dying man said. "And if you will allow me to continue, that cabin I have up in the mountains in Cornwell goes to the both of you. Beatrice will have no problem with my decision. Keep in touch with her, and she will give you the name of my attorney, who will ensure you get the titles."

"Well, what can I say?" Barley said. "I'm sorry I let you guys down. I should not have been so weak."

"Don't talk about it now," Oats begged him.

"One last thing I need you to do for me," Rye muttered between heavy breathing.

"Anything. Just say the word."

"See if you can find my paternal half brother, Kevin."

Not long after the reunion, Ryland Zeme passed away in his sleep just as his wife and the nursed decided to leave the room to organize his medication for the following week. Egbert was able to find Kevin, but not before Ryland's death. Kevin and his son, Victor, attended the funeral, and Ionnia had another opportunity to talk to Victor Zeme and his wife, Mavis.

"Imagine meeting you again. You have grown into a beautiful young lady. Congratulations on your achievements."

"Thanks. I followed your advice."

Kevin was doing well for himself and did not expect anything from his brother's estate.

Ryland Zeme was laid to rest in a custom-made mausoleum with so much gold, it was unbelievable. A space was reserved next to him for his wife.

Once again, Beatrice was totally in charge of another mega company. She proved her tenacity and resilience to lead. As time went by and she observed how well Ionnia managed some of the overseas holdings, she promoted the younger again and gave her substantial bonuses. She was aware that other companies aggressively sought after Ionnia, but Beatrice was not going to let her go under any circumstances. Beatrice had no problem with Ionnia taking time off for personal commitments or to speak at various women's conferences. "Opportunity knocks once," she told her.

Ionnia made frequent trips to the different Zeme establishments in Puca Luca and overseas. Sometimes she was accompanied by Beatrice Zeme, and sometimes she went alone.

Two years after the death of her husband, Beatrice Zeme developed cervical cancer, and while she battled her illness, she appointed the company's lawyer, Melvin Grunt, as executor of the estate. She died shortly afterward. Two months after her death, Melvin summoned Ionnia to his office. He welcomed her with a firm handshake and a smile that would melt a hundred-pound block of ice in less than five minutes. Ionnia didn't know what to make of this gesture, and she remained standing until Mr. Grunt observed her uneasiness.

"You need to sit down to hear this."

"Please, sir, I am willing to relinquish my post, if that's what Miss Beatrice wanted."

"You will be doing no such thing, young lady. Beatrice rewrote her will, and I have taken care of all the legalities. She has left the entire fortune of $650 million cash to you, along with the homes, the jets, and the several companies all over the world. Everything, and I mean everything. I will continue to be the company's lawyer, if you will allow me."

Ionnia was a little puzzled at first. It seemed so surreal. "If I am hearing you correctly? Please allow me some time to process all this. Could this really be happening to me?"

"Congratulations," he said as he smiled and again offered his hands to the young lady, who appeared to be in a daze. "We will be meeting again—soon, I hope."

This was the longest day of her life. The whole thing seemed stranger than fiction, but when she was presented with the documents, the reality hit her like a ton of bricks. She had dreamed of being rich, but she couldn't imagine that it would be so soon and in this manner. Later, when Ionnia broke the news to her family, her mother and brothers were also stunned but extremely happy for her.

The first couple of weeks passed by without anything exciting in Ionnia's life, but as word got out about her inheritance, to her annoyance, hundreds of letters arrived from relatives, organizations, and others whom she didn't even know. All the letters had one common theme: people requesting monetary assistance for everything—food, house, transportation. Beggars came out of nowhere like mice in a cheese factory. Some of those who had made fun of her in the past now came crawling like centipedes. She had tried to keep her home address private, but they somehow found out. Not all the correspondence came to her personal address; a lot went to the office.

Some of Ionnia's distant relatives desperately tried to get in on some of the action. She was besieged with requests in several of the letters explaining how much they needed money, stating that their lives would be much better if Ionnia shared her newfound wealth with them, and how additional blessings would abound if she spread the wealth. She had never heard of some of the names, and she called her mother and two of her aunts for verification. It turned out that some of the names were fake; the people were not related to her.

Uncle Lennie wrote to his niece and asked her for money to purchase a new bus. Her uncle Harry wanted money to purchase modern, computerized equipment for his mechanic shop. Curtis Bedwin, who'd changed his name to Quane and referred to her as his cousin, also put in his request for money.

Ionnia spent countless hours going through the many letters from people who were honest enough to say that they weren't related but needed help. Some requested assistance for their schools, their churches, and other nonprofit organizations. When they did not receive any assistance, they described Ionnia as "The new millionaire joining the ranks of the others trying to suck the lifeblood from the common folks." No one asked for work. Aireen's help sorting the letters proved invaluable, and each morning, Ionnia would sit down to have breakfast and rummage through the pile of letters and postcards that Aireen had placed on the table, sorted in two groups: those that were typewritten, and those that were handwritten.

"It would be nice to help the homeless, the hungry, and all the drunks in the world, but I'd rather spend money on creating employment for the many hundreds of people who need to work. Most of all, I want to help the many hundreds of abused women out there. Many of them need someone to knock some sense in their heads for putting up with the femicidal maniacs with whom they chose to align themselves. Now, my rescue mission is a priority rather than an option, and this money will definitely make it a reality."

Ionnia had gone from a poor girl whose only means of transport was an old jackass to a wealthy woman with corporate jets at her disposal. She laughed. "From a jackass to a jet. This lie would make nice a title for a song, a poem, or a book." She remembered a promise made by Timothy Inkst at Cordell's award ceremony in Trevine, put on by the Jockey Club of Quigland Park. Maybe she should take up his offer, make a recording, and donate the proceeds to BONDAGE and RAW.

Sixty-Three

As the new owner of the Zeme Group of Companies, Ionnia had a monumental task of ensuring that the different companies continued to be run efficiently, or even better. She made a unilateral decision to make some new changes. First, when she called a meeting of the general managers of all the companies to discuss the implementation of these changes, she was faced with a rather awkward situation. When she entered the conference room, it appeared as a shock to some of the general managers that this young woman was now totally in charge and that they answered to her. Resentment and envy were written all over their faces.

Dale Humbrick was one of those who was very vocal in his resentment toward Ionnia. "This must be a mistake," he said as he looked at her with disappointed eyes.

"I apologize," one of the senior managers said to her.

"That's okay. That's what my father said too, but I survived then, and I will survive now. I just hope the men will act their age and not their shoe size, and realize that women can compete in a man's world." She was not about to let this lukewarm reception deter her. Neither was she going to allow herself to be bullied—she'd had enough in her life. She had an obligation to make sure that all aspects of the company would continue to thrive successfully. This was not just for her appearance but for the many women whose lives depended on her. She thought of Epictetus, a fifth-century Greek philosopher who once said, "Know you not that a good man does nothing for appearance sake, but for the sake of having done right."

It was as clear as day that many of the employees would be resistant to change. They were most fearful about losing their status in the company should the changes be implemented. Ionnia had no intention of terminating anyone, but she gave them the option of resigning if they felt uncomfortable having her as their boss. She assured them that they had nothing to fear once they learned how to cope with the level and pace of imminent change. She handed out a survey for them to identify where changes could be implemented, and for them to make suggestions. The new boss realized that she had to exhibit a lot of patience with her employees, and the quote of twentieth-century American businessman Arnold Glasgow came to mind: "You get a chicken by hatching the egg, not by smashing it open." Ionnia thought of the immense responsibilities that faced her at Zeme Enterprises, but she came prepared as one who was competent and highly efficient in carrying out her responsibilities. She was the new employer of nearly a thousand workers in different parts of the world, and she had to prove herself worthy of walking in the founder's shoes. At one time, she found herself saying, "I am little scared. This transition from a mistake to a millionaire, and from employee to owner, is overwhelming."

She had reviewed the company's vision and mission statements, made a few additions, and distributed these to the board members for approval. Her interaction with the group this time was both inspiring and motivational. They realized that this was a situation with which they had to live.

Ionnia's next assignment was to meet with the company's blue-collar workers, so she decided to pay a visit to one of her factories. The reception was totally different. This group of workers welcomed her with open arms. Many employees were familiar with her name, and some had already met with her when she and Beatrice had visited on different occasions. Many of them had been with the company a long time and were now ready to retire. One such employee, Stanley Tarp, had joined the company as a sewing machine repair technician at the age of seventeen. He had taught other young men the trade and was now the chief equipment supervisor. He had a hearing problem that had gradually gotten worse over the years due to the noise of the machines in the factory. He was the first one Ionnia convinced to retire, and he was given a hefty severance packet. He then worked part-time with one of the community technical training centers, teaching young men and women to become sewing machine repair technicians. His hearing problems were addressed and adequately taken care of through the Employee Injury Fund.

Keeping the workers happy was one of Ionnia's top priorities. She had heard from them how some of the bosses behaved like bullies and treated them like slaves, and they were intimidated and afraid to report this to Ryland Zeme. They had no trade union to represent them. Ionnia vowed to change that. She was aware that this type of bullying, if allowed to continue, would result in low productivity caused by stress, absences, phobia, and other physical and emotional problems. She introduced a system to modify and rearrange the company. She created new types of job descriptions and tasks, introduced new workplace practices, and offered workers shorter working days and early retirement. Employees who went the extra mile to complete a task were given points to redeem for extra days off. Employees attended monthly improvement training sessions and were recipients of scholarships for themselves and their children. She also gave them the option to become unionized.

Ionnia made changes to the Employee Injury Fund and brought in Sharonique Vorgetson to head the employee benefit program, which was aimed at providing support for a safe working environment and proper equipment maintenance. She lavished tangible and intangible rewards on her employees. They were given bonuses, commissions, promotions, gift cards, plaques, and Employee of the Month status. Best of all, their opinions were valued. They were given individual cards on which to submit their views regarding how to improve the company and themselves. Ionnia took motivation and satisfaction to new heights.

Ionnia continued the rounds. The next meeting was with the models and the magazine staff, and she had no qualms about it: these were her pet projects. What she discovered was startling. There were scam agencies out there that took advantage of the young women, promising them modeling jobs and giving them false hopes. They paid the girls whatever they wanted to give them, but most times they never secured jobs for them. Ionnia established her own modeling company and recruited her friend Nickie as casting director. Ordinary girls with potentials but who were unable to have strings pulled were selected and sent to Iris Depping for training.

Ionnia gave her apartment to Aireen and took up residence at the Zeme mansion. The first thing that appealed to her was the baby grand piano in the exquisite living room. Her eyes lit up like a new penny, and she made a few athletic strides along the polished wooden floor. It was smooth sailing because there were no broken pieces of board or holes in them, like what she'd grown up with in Dartsdam. The sheet music was open to "Amazing Grace," but as she touched the keys, all she could hear was "Across the Bridge."

The house stood at an elevation where she could get a good view of the vast expanse of the compound. When she was done playing, she walked over to the French windows and shocked herself with the vast expanse of real estate she now owned. She found herself pleasurably absorbed in this unfamiliar milieu. Here was a brand-new world opened up to this once underprivileged girl—a world with such opulence that she was only partially prepared to handle it. Then she was awakened from the afternoon's reverie by a voice in her head that kept saying, "Get used to it."

Ionnia enjoyed everything that life had thrust upon her, and she would show everyone how selfless she was.

She was soon to learn that nothing lasts forever. The vulture was at it again. Fiffie Saddler sued Ionnia and Zeme Industries on behalf of a group of environmentalists, who claimed they suffered mysterious health issues due to chemicals from the wool factory in Bardell. While Fiffie sought compensation for the plaintiffs, she also advocated for the closure of the factory.

She had brought the fight to the wrong person. Zeme's lawyers proved her allegations as nothing but frivolous. She thought that the lawsuit was going to be a piece of cake, but she didn't have the means to hire the expert medical witnesses. When the complainants were tested, they were all in good health.

Sixty-Four

"Every time I close my eyes, I can see that burning piece of real estate," Ionnia said. "I know there is a message somewhere in it, and I am already imagining myself owning that island. How would I acquire and develop it? So many questions and not many answers. But where there's a will, there's bound to be a way."

The more thought Ionnia gave to the acquisition of this property, the more ideas flooded her mind, and the more determined she was. "I must have it. This would be the ideal place to erect a community, a safe haven on behalf of battered and abused women. There is only one way of finding out. I hope I can get some answers."

Ionnia set up a meeting with Crossdale Archer, the mayor of Buek Ridge, and presented a proposal. "I would like to attend the next meeting of the Zoning and Development Committee regarding the possibility of purchasing a particular piece of vacant property."

"And which piece is that? I am not aware of any new listing."

"The piece that caught fire during the thunderstorm."

Mayor Archer laughed so hard, one would think he was have an epileptic seizure. After he recovered, he shook Ionnia's hands and said, "Check with my secretary, Zenaida Berden, regarding date and time of the next committee meeting, and I will make sure this gets on the agenda," he said sarcastically with another chuckle.

Land sale was the second item on the meeting's agenda, and all the members expressed an interest in hearing what Ionnia had in mind. The members looked at each other, listened, and shook their heads in disbelief. "Have you thought of the imbecility of such a conception?" another committee member asked. "Trying to develop this property is like threading a needle wearing a baseball glove."

"No bank would lend you money to buy this worthless piece of land. And then what would you put up as collateral?" Harold Zacklyn, the deputy mayor, asked.

"Does this worthless piece of land have a name?" she asked politely.

"Sulfur Cay," Mayor Archer replied.

"I don't think I will need to borrow any money from the bank to purchase Sulfur Cay," Ionnia said as she looked him straight in the eye. "And moreover, there is nothing worthless in this world—you simply have to unearth the beauty within."

"Then you want it for nothing?"

"If that were possible, I would be extremely happy, but I think I am in a position to make a very generous offer. And by the way, I plan to rename it the Isle of Hope, reachable via the most awesome bridge one will ever lay eyes on."

Booming laughter reverberated throughout the meeting room, and after they settled down, Hefton Plink, a land reclamation specialist who owned a construction company on Whelksfield Street and Cashmair Boulevard, shouted, "Give your money to charity."

Mayor Archer turned to Ionnia and said, "This is a dream that you will soon wake out of. Therefore we may come to an agreement to simply give it to you and watch you make a fool of yourself. This is a monumental task. Why would you not want to vacant areas somewhere else, instead of tackling this obstacle?"

She assured them that she had no intention of abandoning the idea of reclaiming and developing the land she had her eyes on. She was determined. She quoted a twentieth-century writer, Charles Swindle, who once said, "We are faced with a series of great opportunities brilliantly disguised as impossible situations."

After a lengthy discussion and many suggestions, the men realized that they were not going to be able to convince Ionnia to give up. "Many developers have tried to do something with this piece of land in previous years, and they have had to give up either because of frustration or a lack of resources. Miss Dunn-Ryte, you too shall fail," Mayor Archer said.

At that point, she reflected on the valedictory speech that she had made about failure, but she said nothing. She felt motivated.

When it was time for Commissioner Bradley Meekely to speak, he said, "It is rumored that one developer encountered evil spirits on the property, and since that time, no one else has dared discuss its development."

Their tactics did not deter Ionnia. Instead, she stared each one in the eyes and asked, "Can you tell me why the spirits scared him away? Did he want to turn the place into another Stechion Bay?" Ionnia asked another question that nobody wanted to hear. "Is it really true that Sulfur Cay was a worthless piece of property, or was it that the spirits resented the proposed development by men?"

The mayor jumped to his feet, threw his hands in the air, and angrily shouted, "So now we have a sexist piece of real estate? You know what? You can have the property. Let's see what will happen when the spirits rise up against the female of the species."

"One last fool," someone grumbled, and no one knew whether he was talking about Ionnia or Mayor Archer.

Archer pretended not to hear and said, "I will have the necessary paperwork drawn up, and an attorney will have a look before you sign it. I'm sure he or she will talk you out of this joke."

"Thank you," Ionnia said, smiling. She rose to leave. She felt like the luckiest person in the world. "If only Mrs. Zeme were alive to see my dreams come true. Miracles will happen across the bridge."

"If you run out of cash, don't expect us to use taxpayers' money to bail you out," Lyle Rutherford, a civil engineer with the city, said angrily. "I have additional documentations that I can make available to you so that you could prove for yourself that this is indeed a worthless piece of land."

Ionnia glanced out of the corner of her eyes and saw Commissioner Bradley Meekley whispering to Clara Maysfield, who was recording the minutes of the meeting. When Clara looked up and smiled at him, Ionnia couldn't help but wonder what they were they plotting. Ionnia asked herself, *Could this be a conspiracy to sabotage my plans?* She gave it no further thought but thanked the committee again and walked proudly away. Things had begun to fall into place.

That night, she dreamed that she was picking up cans by the bamboo clump that was close to the little hut where she'd been born. Did that mean she was going to lose all her money and go back to being poor? She told her mother about the dream, adding that this was the first time she'd had doubts about the proposed project.

"I am not a psychiatrist, but what I think that means is that you can do it," her mother assured her. "Get used to saying *I can.*"

Ionnia felt reassured and knew in her gut that something was about to happen. She sure did not want any negative thoughts to short-circuit it. She would prove the skeptics wrong. She would make sure her dreams become a reality, and everyone would watch the miracles as they happened. Women needed her, and she was not about to fail them. They would battle the spirits together.

Ionnia continued to champion the cause of battered and neglected women. So impressive was her work that she was asked to temporarily head the Bureau of Women's Affairs in Buek Ridge until a permanent replacement could be found. They were depending on her to make recommendations to the legislative body in Trevine.

Ionnia immersed herself in research about land reclamation and the many companies that were proficient in performing this operation. Bids were invited, and dozens were submitted. Ionnia selected Nollis, Olverwood, and Mumford Engineering Company (NOMENCO), an all-female company headed by Celena Nollis, the stepdaughter of Lillian Finlaw. This company was to explore the possibilities of erecting a whole new city on the island.

Celena, a famous architectural engineer, had won many medals and awards for her original concepts in urban design. Her firm was featured in several magazines, including *Association of Puca Luca Architects.*

Ionnia was criticized by prominent businessmen who had a bias toward successful businesswomen. Men had dominated the business world for a long time, and with the emergence of women competing successfully in a man's world, the men were petrified. They decried what they called the feminization of the male-dominated workforce, and after learning that bids weren't accepted from the male-owned companies, the tensions between rebellious lawmakers and the female population escalated. Many men still held on to the idea that women should be housewives and mothers and not professionals. One elected representative had the nerve to tell female constituents, "Stick to what you know best, such as nursing, teaching, and above all motherhood."

The NOMENCO reports were positive. The first phase of project involved construction of the bridge connecting the proposed development on Isle of Hope to the existing island of Buek Ridge. Some people jeered and called it Nowhere Bridge. Ionnia had not envisaged or anticipated the magnitude of the resistance that followed, and it wasn't just the elected representatives who opposed the idea. The more they resisted, the more she endeavored to proceed with the project. Ionnia's opinion was that one side had to give up, and it certainly wasn't going to be hers. Using the tug-of-war analogy, she asked, "Who breaks the rope: the one who pulls, or the one who holds on to it?"

There were massive protests among some of the residents of Buek Ridge when they learned that they would be displaced and would have to relocate to another side of town due to the new airport runway that had to be constructed. The disgruntled and irate residents, especially the men, requested that the government stop the madness. They went as far as to sign petitions to recall Mayor Crossdale Archer and other elected representatives from office if this plan was implemented. After many meetings and demonstrations, some civil and some not-so-civil, an agreement was reached that the residents would be placed in hotels, following which they would be relocated to the newly redeveloped community of Sassawhackia. But many harbored negative thoughts about this particular place. Some said that it was cursed and that they feared the anger of the departed souls who had perished in the tornado.

One such person whose family would be affected by this relocation project was Ferdinand "Ferdie" Winchell. "Would someone please explain to me where we will find jobs in Sassawhackia?" he wrote to the mayor. "Would we have to ride the ferry every day to Buek Ridge to work in order to feed our families?"

It wasn't till that time that everyone became aware of how much money Ionnia had at her disposal. She made a commitment to establish a new Zeme factory on the island of Sassawhackia, and she pledged to assist the government with any socioeconomic issues that may arise. She met with Ferdinand Winchell and offered him the coveted job of factory manager, presenting a handsome package that he couldn't refuse: a free three-bedroom house, and lifetime tickets on ferries to Buek Ridge. Ferdie's wife, who was a teacher, was given the extra responsibility to form and oversee the new Sassawhackia Community Association. Here again, Sharonique was asked to play a role working alongside Mrs. Winchell.

Ionnia was still careful in answering the telephone, and she checked the messages on the answering machine. She panicked when she heard a male voice. She paused the recording, steadied herself, and knew eventually she had to take action, so she reluctantly hit the play button and listened to a rather polite greeting followed by a short message. The caller identified himself as Vernon Dudley. He owned a fleet of airships, which resembled blimps. "I know you are anxious to get up close and view your new property, so I am offering to fly you over the island at no cost."

Her suspicions heightened. "Why is he doing this? I can use my own plane." After pondering this for quite some time and discussing it with her public relations representative, she sent a reply to Vernon Dudley. He was sent the names of other people who would like to go along with her. Ionnia also tried hard to have him make a commitment as to the cost of this trip, but he insisted that he didn't want to be paid. This was the first time Ionnia was to fly over the property since she'd witnessed its burning while she and Chad had flown over it. Although the airship was equipped with expensive cameras to capture the most minute details, Ionnia made sure she took along her own photographer, Venton Rigger, just in case Dudley decided to sabotage the effort. She also had Dudley sign a contract to hand over all the pictures to her. Consuela Nye, the public relations person for NOMECO, and three other people would be on the trip.

Dudley appeared not to too pleased about Ionnia's request, but he reluctantly agreed. Just before they were ready to lift off, he offered the group alcoholic beverages, but one quick glance from Ionnia indicated that they should decline the offer.

"I don't think it's a good idea to drink and fly, Mr. Dudley," Venton said. "I need a steady hand with these cameras."

Dudley shook his head in a disappointing manner and told the group, "I have been doing this for many years. I've always had a drink before leaving, and I've never had a crash."

"So what you are telling us is that if you don't have a drink now, you will not be able to do a good job?" Consuela asked.

The trip lasted close to two hours after circling the isle a few times. Dudley had promised that he would hand over all the photographs to Consuela the following day, and he was kept under constant surveillance for fear he was acting on behalf of those who opposed Ionnia's efforts. One of Ionnia's classmates from the University of Krepston, Ron Tidley, who owned a private investigating company, was given the task to watch Dudley. What he discovered was that Dudley had planned to keep some of the pictures to sell to the local tabloid,

The Speaker's Choice. The editor, Courtney Shackleworth, who was Dudley's cousin, had a personal vendetta toward Ionnia and thought that if she ridiculed the proposed project, Ionnia would be deterred from continuing with it. It would have been no surprise to see Dudley and his cousin have lunch together, but when he handed her an envelope, Ron and his assistant made sure they captured the moment. Here in living color were pictures of Sulfur Cay.

When Consuela was informed about this situation, even before she spoke to Ionnia, she immediately contacted Vara Wick, the editor of a competing paper, *The Buek Ridge Echo.* "There is a conspiracy afoot, and we cannot wait to see what the outcome is going to be." Vara wasted no time in interviewing Ionnia and a lot of other people in order to publish a midweek version of her newspaper. Ionnia got a hold of Simeon, and she agreed to fly him out to meet her overnight. On the plane, she gave him a mental picture of the place where she was born because of abuse to her mother, as well as the proposed community of what would eventually be a refuge for abused women. By the time they landed, Simeon had the perfect sketches, and underneath he wrote, "From There to Here."

"Perfect," she said.

They rushed to the offices of the *Echo,* where Vara and her team were waiting. The story and the many pictures were the highlight of the paper. Most of the thirty-two pages of the paper hailed Ionnia as a champion for women's rights, and it offered her lots of encouragement in her effort to help battered and abused women. Courtney's story was killed. Ionnia thanked Dudley for the pictures and confronted him about his underhandedness. His scheme was exposed. He apologized profusely and begged that the situation be kept quiet because this would be bad for his business. Lucky for him, Ionnia had a conscience and didn't expose him or Courtney.

Ionnia worked diligently to get the project off the ground. She felt very good that people had started believing in her effort and would continue to do so. If not, then let the war begin.

Sixty-Five

People from all walks of life continued to seek Ionnia's attention, and the requests for her to give motivational speeches kept coming in. The tension had not completely eased when it came to retrieving messages from her phone's answering machine, so she handed over the task to her secretary, Genniveve Darrighan, who was an extraordinarily efficient person and who had something in common with Ionnia. She was tall and slender, like the reeds at the edge of the Buek River, and she took her work seriously. She tried her utmost not to let her boss receive any messages that would be upsetting to her.

This day in particular, the agile young lady came running into Ionnia's office with a handwritten note, and she could hardly contain her excitement. "Miss Dunn-Ryte, this sounds very urgent." She handed her the piece of paper and left as hurriedly as she'd entered.

When Ionnia unfolded the paper, she saw that the message was from someone by the name of Kenute Glenn. He was requesting to have lunch with her to discuss something very important. She remembered the name. Could this be the same person from Diamond Globe High School? He was one of those male students who had been suspended for having an inappropriate relationship with some of the underage girls from different elementary schools who took high school–level classes at the Diamond Globe campus.

"What on Earth could he want? I wasn't his type then. Maybe he wants a job."

Ms. Dunn-Ryte waited a few days before asking Genniveve to call Glenn. When Genniveve did, he told her, "I would rather speak to Miss Dunn-Ryte in person."

Ionnia reluctantly took the phone and told him to make it brief because she was busy. To her consternation, she discovered that Glenn was now interested in establishing a relationship with her. He may not be aware that this was the same Ionnia Quane from Dartsdam and Redwood Vale, and obviously he had not read Vara's article in the *Buek Ridge Echo*. Ionnia was very polite in accepting an invitation to dinner with Kenute two weeks from now, but she took no chances. Ron Tidley was again called upon. "Are you available for another assignment?"

"Any time you wish."

"Find out all you know about someone by the name of Kenute Glenn. I don't care how you get the information—just get it."

"I can't unearth what doesn't exist. The police department and some law firms use my services, and they have no complaints."

"Don't be so cocky, Mr. Archeologist." After they recovered from a hearty laugh, Ionnia continued. "Just remember, I don't care how much this costs."

"Under normal circumstances, I would ask for a percentage of my fee up front, but I can wait till I complete the job."

"Can you do it within a week?"

"Sure. I have a number of competent people on my staff."

One of the things that Ron discovered about Glenn was that he was envious of Ionnia and all other powerful, educated, independent, successful women. He was also one of those men known as LOW—living off women. He would pretend that he cared for his women, and after he gained her confidence, he would come up with some cockamamie story, ask her to advance him some cash for urgent business transactions, and promise that she would eventually be able to invest in his business enterprise. After he got the cash, he would disappear.

One would think he was the offspring of Mr. Arrineldie or other men who took advantage of women's vulnerability and generosity.

Ron taped a conversation between Glenn and Bertram Peoples in which he said about Ionnia, "That woman is gaining too much popularity. She is getting too rich and powerful, and she has to be stopped. She has to be brought down."

"How are you going to do that?" Bertram asked.

"Marry her and get her pregnant every year. Give her lots of kids. She won't have the time to concentrate on business. I will find a way to take most of what she has. See, I have the means and the motive. All I need now is the opportunity."

The worst was yet to come. What Ron discovered about Glenn was frightening. He had been in prison for five years on charges of disturbing a corpse, and for drug trafficking with intent to sell.

Some years ago Kenute Glenn coached basketball at a high school in Bregmar Creek, and when his mother died he did not attend the funeral. His team was competing in a major playoff that day, and he couldn't be absent. According to him, he didn't want to leave the team's future in the hands of the assistant coach. Kenute had a casket custom made for his mother and shipped to Redwood Vale. No one suspected that he had carefully cushioned the lining of the casket with cocaine. All his other siblings thought that this was a good gesture on his part, showered him with accolades, and accepted his excuse for not attending the funeral.

Glenn thought he would never be caught, but he was being watched. He lived an affluent lifestyle that was quite questionable because the salary he received as a coach could not have possibly maintained that lifestyle. Five days after his mother's funeral, Kenute went to the mausoleum to pay his last respects to her. He had made arrangements to sell cocaine to an undercover drug agent, Julian Ernakki, the brother of Jillian and Penelope Ernakki. Julian arrived fully wired. His code to the other cops would be, "Got It."

They opened the vault and gently pulled out the casket. Kenute opened it, tossed his mother on the floor, and started ripping apart the casket. As Kenute ripped the soft velvet lining of the expensive casket and saw his stash, he looked at his mother's corpse and said, "Thank you, Mother."

The mausoleum attendants looked on with disgust and in disbelief. They tried to stop Kenute Glenn, but their pleas went unheard. They even turned to Julian for help, but he knew that the game would soon be over and said nothing to the attendants. Kenute retrieved his stash, looked at Julian, and asked, "You have my money?"

"Got it," Julian replied, and he opened the briefcase, exposing to Kenute close to a quarter of a million dollars.

Kenute took hold of the briefcase, and his eyes lit up like a sunflower. He grinned, but the grin was short-lived. Suddenly, a dozen cops entered the mausoleum with guns drawn and cameras focused. They grabbed Kenute Glenn, cuffed him, and hauled him off to jail. It made the 6:00 p.m. news. The next day, the newspapers carried it as their front-page story. One headline read, "Dead Woman Caught with Cocaine." Another read, "Mother Conceals Drugs for Her Son."

The mausoleum attendants carefully retrieved Mrs. Glenn's body and tried to place her back where she belonged. Kenute's grieving father and siblings were notified, and to say that they were appalled was an understatement. The family arrived a few hours later with a new casket and had the remains removed to another site unknown to Kenute. He was estranged from his family after that day, and his father disinherited him in a new will.

For the crime, Kenute served five years in prison and was placed on ten years' probation. He held much disdain for the female judge who tried his case and sentenced him. He thought his sentence was too harsh. He gave up the names of several other persons with whom he was involved, and his probationary period was reduced by two years.

After receiving this nauseating information, Ionnia contemplated whether she should meet with this person. "He creeps me out, but when I'm finished with him, he may start to think of much-needed changes to his life."

She would meet with Glenn at the Dergalante, an upscale restaurant near the Buek Ridge airport. Ionnia had secured the services of bodyguards. Ron Tidley and one of his assistants, Duncan McDeel, positioned themselves inconspicuously in the restaurant in case Kenute Glenn attempted any inappropriate behavior. They were adequately armed with cameras, guns, and other tools, ready to defend one of the wealthiest and most powerful women on this side of heaven.

Ionnia walked in with her distinctive air of confidence, and the hostess directed her to the table where Glenn sat. He was preoccupied with the *Weekly Standard*, one of the daily newspapers in Buek Ridge, which carried at least two full pages of advertisements for Zeme Industries. Ionnia was as polite and sophisticated as ever. She was conservatively dressed, looked like a million dollars, and had an air that suggested she was not ready to be married and be pregnant once a year for the rest of her fertile years.

Kenute Glenn rose from his chair with a peculiar smile on his face, and he pretended like his intentions were genuine, but Ionnia knew that this was a façade. While she also faked a smile, she had control of her emotions. Glenn held a red rose in his left hand, extended his right hand to Ionnia, and said, "So glad you could come, Ms. Dunn-Ryte. Call me Ken."

"Thank you," she said politely while harboring feelings of disgust for this despicable specimen of a human being. Why was she having dinner with him? She began to feel nauseous just looking at him, but she wanted him to know exactly with whom he was dealing.

Ionnia did not immediately offer any hint that she knew who Kenute Glenn was, and it appeared that he was clueless as to her real identity. She listened to him exaggerate about himself, listing all the elite clubs to which he belonged and bragging about what a privileged life he'd led. He spoke about owning shares in METEX and the airlines, and he bragged about the size of his yacht anchored in a marina in Trevine. Ionnia appeared to be impressed, but she wasn't.

"Your mother raised you well. I am sure both of you are proud of each other."

The man who was sent to prison for disturbing his mother's corpse didn't want the conversation to go in the wrong direction, and at that point he said, "I've talked enough. Tell me something about you. Were you ever married?" Before she could respond, he continued. "I assume that's the reason for the hyphenated name?"

What she said next didn't seem to be what he wanted to hear. "There's no room for intimate affairs in my life."

Ionnia made mention of a recent article in a prestigious financial publication that Beatrice Zeme had given her. It referred to studies showing that successful career women made unsuccessful wives and mothers. The publication, she said, pointed out that "Successful career women are more likely to get divorced, more likely to be unfaithful, and are unlikely to bear children." "Don't you see the wisdom in staying away from people like us?" Ionnia asked him.

She also made reference to another newspaper article, which stated, "If you want to be happy, take a woman who is totally dependent on you. By so doing, your ego will be elevated, and you will not have anyone to compete with."

Glenn listened. This time he was the one who seemed somewhat impressed. "I'm speechless," he said. "And I can understand why a woman like you would play hard to get. But when you meet the right person, such as the one you are looking at, you will change your mind."

Throughout this, Ionnia remained calm, her disgust for Kenute Glenn was like a fire burning holes in her body. The meal was ordered, and as soon as it was served, Ionnia could wait no longer to make some revelation. "Do the names Ionnia Quane and Diamond Globe High School ring a bell?" she asked.

"Oh, yes." He laughed. "That skinny, silly-looking athlete. No boy was interested in her. She was not our type. And I bet wherever she is now, no man would waste his time trying to date her. I heard she tried to stir up trouble with the high school entrance exam, but some boys beat the hell out of her. All I could say was that they did a good job."

"Did they confess?"

"Not exactly," he said. "But Dutte's brother, Conrad, was a friend of mine, and he told me the whole story. Did you ever hear what has become of the girl?"

Ionnia looked him straight in the eye and said slowly, "You are looking at her."

Ken's expression changed. She could tell by his demeanor that he was thinking, *Where is an earthquake when I need one?*

She had not tasted a bite of her meal, and she had no intention of doing so. She told him the whole story and how her new name came about. She continued to jog his memory while trying to look him straight in his eyes, even though he made several attempts to bow his head, perhaps in shame. "I am sure you remember my friend Penelope?"

"No."

"Well, I don't think you could forget her brother, Julian Ernakki."

On hearing that name, Ken's fork stopped midair, his mouth opened wide, and he shifted uncomfortably in his chair. He appeared unable to breathe. One would think that Kenute Glenn had seen a ghost, that the food had stuck in his throat, or that he was having a stroke.

"Something wrong, Ken?" Ionnia asked in a tone that could possibly be mistaken for concern. She looked around at the other patrons. "Does anyone know how to perform the Heimlich maneuver?"

"I'm okay, Ms. Quane. No, sorry—Ms. Dunn-Ryte," he stuttered nervously, and he gave a slow, wicked grin.

Just then, Ron Tidley emerged with copies of the newspaper articles about Kenute Glenn, placed one in front of him, left some on the magazine stand, and invited all the patrons and employees to read it.

Ionnia still hadn't touched her lunch, but she offered to pay for both, and Ken did not object. Again the fake grin appeared on his face. Ionnia imagined that his face must have ached from this one, which seemed to last for almost two minutes. She tried hard to control her laughter. He sure looked pitiful and stupid. She looked at him disdainfully, placed the money on the table, and said, "Enjoy the rest of the meal. Choke on it and keep the change. And don't ever try to get in touch with me again. You are one despicable, disgusting human being." To all the people who looked on, she told them who she was and what Glenn's intentions were. "Take a good look at him, and keep your daughters and nieces away from him."

Kenute Glenn got up from his chair but sat down very quickly. He looked somewhat dazed, as if the floor was swaying under him. He tried to process everything Ionnia had just said. Had his feelings just received the greatest shock from which they would never recover? Or did nothing matter to this person with an inflated ego?

As she was about to take her exit, she looked back at Kenute Glenn and asked, "Does your probation officer know that you have traveled out of your range?"

Sixty-Six

Ionnia never flaunted her wealth, and so to those people who were oblivious that she was a nouveau riche, it was business as usual. They remained civil, courteous, and friendly to her. But it didn't take much longer for the word to get out, and then things changed when they discovered the real situation. At this point, more people vied for her attention, and she was in higher demand than ever before. She was invited to many dinner parties and other social events that were mostly attended by the rich and famous. She was one of the wealthy, beautiful, polished, and respected persons of eminence. She attended functions that Beatrice had attended and would have wanted her to attend.

The invitations and requests kept coming for Ionnia to speak to groups of people, address graduates in high school or college, or participate in inaugural celebrations of events. She remained committed to her church and women's groups. She was very self-disciplined and had the stamina to work almost twenty-four hours per day. She was dubbed a superwoman. And then there were her radio and television shows. In one of her television shows, *On the Edge,* she invited battered and abused women to monthly meetings at the HERS complex; if they couldn't get to that location, they should find the nearest chapter of either BONDAGE or RAW. She also invited women who were not able to call the show or put in an appearance somewhere to send in tapes about their sad experiences with members of the opposite sex, explaining what had now brought them to the edge. Both audiotapes and videotapes came in by the hundreds each day, and Ionnia spent a great deal of time listening to them and watching them. She had strong words for those individuals who thought that it was okay to stay with someone who cheated on them and physically abused them.

The latest invitation to Ionnia came from a member of one of the most powerful and distinguished families, Gus Muggerdon. His grandfather's plan had materialized regarding the establishment of an amusement park on the site where the Four Eyes Cave was discovered. The old man was not alive, but as promised, his heir would take over from where he'd left off. It wouldn't surprise anyone if Gus were to go to his grandfather's grave and say to him, "Aspirations achieved."

In his letter to Ionnia, Gus wrote, "I am aware of the events that led to the discovery, and I would be more than honored to involve you in the inaugural ceremony." The invitation also requested Ionnia to consider being one of the judges in the Junior Miss Whickam County beauty pageant to be held at that location that same day, and to have her models give a preview of her new labels by participating in the fashion parade.

Ionnia felt an incomprehensible sense of pride that Gus Muggerdon would consider her an integral part of this. *But after all, were it not for me, he wouldn't be aware of the gold mine on which he was sitting. This is a bittersweet moment, and nothing in the world will keep me away, only acts of nature.*

As promised, Muggerdon sent a private plane for her and the models, and limousines were at the airstrip to pick them up when they arrived at his private airstrip. On her arrival at the park, she was awestruck to see the unbelievable transformation of the property. She shed some tears when she remembered the events of many years ago. She tried to relive the moments when she'd run through the thicket to the cave, and she immediately asked to see what developments had taken place in that location.

Ionnia was escorted into the cave to the hotel and spa by Gus's wife's nephew, Daniel Wilberthon, an assistant editor for the *Mercurian Central*. The narrow passageway to the cave through which Ionnia had inched her way years ago was no more. A wide entranceway was now in place, and several steps were hewn out of the rocks, leading to the waterfall. She gazed long and hard at the area where the stone might have been and on which she had sat and thrown pebbles in the water that night. In the pristine stream below were two glass-bottomed boats that would take passengers to the other side, where they would have a perfect view of the Shafton River. At the far eastern side of the cave was a medium-sized structure, which Danny described as a miracle health resort and spa. Danny told her that water from the stream was piped into the building, and people with various ailments would take thirty-minute baths and recover from whatever physical and mental problems doctors were unable to diagnose and treat. Ionnia had been right years ago: the water in the cave contained healing components, and Muggerdon had kept it a secret all this time.

As Ionnia entered the building, she saw a familiar face: Lorna's sister Olive. Olive was in charge of the spa and was the number one physical therapist in Whickam County. Patients who were treated by her swore that they had received an additional miracle. She told Ionnia and Danny that there was a long waiting list, and as soon as the business was fully operational, this would be one of the most lucrative ones in Whickam County.

Ionnia looked at her watch. "Oh, my goodness. I have to get out of here. I'm one of the judges in the Miss Whickam Teen beauty contest."

As she turned around to exit the cave, Danny held her gently and led her out. While they were on their way, Ionnia told him of her past ordeal.

"I know everything," he said.

"So why didn't you say something?"

"This is your moment, and I didn't want to interrupt what you are feeling inside. I am a keen observer, and I watched your expressions as you tried to take responsibility for this. So, tell me, what exactly was going through your mind?"

"I have a feeling this is an interview for your paper, and that it was no coincidence having you escort me on the tour of the cave," Ionnia said to Danny, who neither denied nor admitted to her observation. They stopped at the entranceway, and waiting for them was Danny's camera crew. Ionnia explained to Danny how emotional this day was for her.

"I guess you can safely say that lemons have been made into lemonade," Danny said.

Following the tour, Ionnia wound her way through the crowd and headed toward the pavilion, where the contestants were already assembled. One close look at them, and Ionnia swore she had seen contestant number nine before, probably in a dream or in a past life. She believed in reincarnation and frequently listened to people telling stories of who and what they were in a previous life. She dismissed this and continued to proceed to the pavilion. As she passed one of the many concession stands, she overheard someone shouting menacingly to a frightened little girl, "If you think you are going to get away with eating my food and not paying the correct amount, you have a whipping coming to you."

She was familiar with a tone of voice and the nature of those words. The only good thing was that the person with whom she could associate this behavior was already dead. The man at the concession stand with that thunderous voice did not look anything like his voice. He looked more like a skeleton or a scarecrow; tall and bony with sunken eyes and a nose that looked like a parrot's beak. He pointed to the whip hanging on the wall, and Ionnia feared the worst. She quickly reached in her purse and handed the man some money. While she was waiting for her change, she heard a sound that terrified her more. One of the fiercest-looking bulldogs was gritting its teeth and looking straight at her.

"Keep the change," she said as she trembled and shook while trying to exit as quickly as possible. Memories of her past pulled at her heartstrings. This was supposed to be a happy occasion, but instead the day was filled with terrifying memories. Ionnia was convinced that these incidents had made her into a stronger and more resilient person. The little girl, who appeared to be between ten and twelve years of age, stood immobilized. Ionnia moved closer to her and held her hand.

As she wiped her tears and questioned her about her parents' whereabouts, there came a stern voice shouting from behind. "Leave my child alone! What did you do to her?"

Ionnia wasn't surprised to see Theresa Grantley, but it was what she looked like that made her want to comment. The pitifully disheveled Theresa had four other small children pulling at her red-and-white gingham skirt. She wore a multicolored blouse with puffed sleeves, and she had a blue scarf on her head. Ionnia's first instinct was to grab the scarf and wrap it tightly around her neck in retaliation for the hell she and her friends had put her through, but Ionnia decided against it. Instead, she composed herself and greeted this onetime bully with kind words. A woman in her position was expected to behave in a certain manner, and she wanted to live up to that expectation.

The little girl told her mother the whole story. "I'll pay you back," she said to Ionnia, and she began rummaging through a dilapidated purse with a broken latch to find money to repay the person who had saved her child from the wrath of the skeleton man. She felt ashamed that of all the people who should be standing in front of her showing no animosity toward her and her children, it was none other than Ionnia Quane, to whom she had done wrong at Dartsdam Elementary.

Ionnia could see that Theresa wanted to give an explanation, but before she could say anything, Ionnia said to her, "Let bygones be bygones, Theresa. Keep your money. I'm in a better position than you." Ionnia felt sorry for the woman, gave her one of her business cards, and asked her to keep in touch. Obviously, she would be needing help.

Before Ionnia proceeded to the pavilion, she was very curious to know more about Theresa and what she must be going through. She found out that Theresa Grantley, who was Emily Brank's niece, was now married to Blanford Felcopper, who had once been her aunt's boyfriend. Emily almost lost her mind when she realized that she was getting a taste of her own medicine. Theresa was no stranger to abuse, but she hung on to the so-called husband who was still seeing her aunt.

The brief exchange between Theresa and Ionnia ended just as Ionnia recognized her mother and some other members of her family in the huge crowd. They spoke as they moved closer toward the pavilion where the pageant was being held. Ionnia had never seen her mother this happy, and she bet it had something to do with Kingsley Muggerdon. She looked around, but he was not in attendance.

Ionnia kept thinking of contestant number nine and couldn't take her eyes off her. She was very beautiful and appeared extremely confident. If it turned out that this person was someone whom Ionnia knew, should she recuse herself from judging?

Ionnia took her seat along with the other five judges. In the first phase of the competition, the contestants in semiformal wear stepped forward one by one and introduced themselves. In less than two minutes, they would reveal their vital statistics, their current level of education, their career goals, and their hobbies.

Contestant number nine who wore the sash of Miss Morgan's Beach Hotel, came forward. "Hi, my name is Daisy, but most people call me Bubbles."

Someone in the crowd shouted, "Is it because you love bubble gum?"

She smiled and said, "No, it's because I love to blow bubbles."

Ionnia felt connected to Daisy, and her heart skipped a beat. She remained composed, telling herself that she would judge impartially and no one had to be made aware that she knew the young lady. She was sure other judges knew at least one of the girls, so she quickly dismissed the thought of withdrawing her services. Instead, she decided to concentrate on the business at hand. She could be fair. She could rule from her head and not from her heart.

Daisy spoke proudly of her educational achievements and of her goal, which was to enroll in one of the country's tertiary institutions to pursue a course in international studies. She said that during her spare time, she volunteered at shelters for runaway and orphaned children.

Daisy was no longer the frightened little girl on the train. She was a well-rounded teenager who was confident in herself and who would certainly be a role model for other young ladies. Ionnia thought, *Whoever is responsible for her did a good job.*

Before the second phase of the competition started, the Zeme models paraded around the stage, showing off their latest fashions. Ionnia did not participate in this section of the competition. She doubted whether she could do this impartially, so she spoke to the organizers, who called on someone who was once one of the country's top models, Cindy Wilberthon, to do the honors. Ionnia could see her family and friends in the crowd giving her the thumbs-up. She could also see marketing managers from prominent department stores making notes as to what pieces they would want in their stores.

The display of talent by the pageant participants was a highlight no one was prepared to miss. A few of the contestants sang, some played musical instruments, some read poetry, and other performed acrobatics. But when Daisy took the stage and started blowing the most beautiful bubbles in various shapes and colors, the crowd was mesmerized. They went wild with their applause. If one was viewing this display from afar, one could easily assume that this was a display of fireworks without the sound. No doubt Daisy scored the most points with the judges.

The speeches and ribbon cutting preceded the final phase of the competition. The keynote speaker was none other than Gus Muggerdon. *Times have really changed,* Ionnia said to herself. *Imagine sharing the same stage as a Muggerdon, and imagine my mother sharing bed with one.* Gus made her the center of attention, and she was sort of happy when the official introductions were over. However, she realized that this was something to which she would have to get accustomed.

Gus proved that he really had blood running through his veins, the likes of which couldn't be compared to that of his grandfather's generation. He was a decent man and one of good moral character who seemed eager to do justice to the descendants of those folks who were wronged by his ancestors. He made an announcement that not only would ordinary people find enjoyment on his property, but the first month's admission would be free. The roar that erupted from the crowd lasted for several minutes, and Gus seemed to enjoy the expressions of gratitude. He stood with a broad grin on his face and then held his hands up, lulling them into silence. They knew something else was coming. He also promised that when the free period was over, he would put aside a percentage of the admission receipts to establish a scholarship in Ionnia's name for poor children and the children of abused women.

Then it was the teenagers' time to parade across the stage in their formal wear, created by famous local and international designers. On a scale of one to five, most of them scored a 3.5 or a 4. Again Daisy stole the judges' heart, and she was given a perfect 5.

It wasn't a surprise to anyone that when the elimination began, Daisy was among the top six contestants, then the top three. Eventually there were only two girls on the stage: Daisy Crustanzie, who wore the sash of Miss Morgan's Beach Hotel, and April Karr-Nation, Miss Puca Luca Public Service Company.

As the suspense mounted, the two young ladies paraded across the stage and waved to the judges and the audience in a queenlike fashion.

This was followed by another fashion show, this time n garments from international designers. Finally, the moment arrived when the new Miss Whickam Teen would be chosen. The winner would receive a scholarship to the University of Trevine, as well as various cash prizes from different sponsors.

Ionnia hugged Daisy when her name was announced as the new Miss Whickam Teen, and she made a request to place the crown on Daisy's head while the reigning queen presented her with the bouquet of flowers. Up to this point, she had not revealed to anyone that she knew Daisy, but later that evening, she couldn't withhold it from her aunt Twyleith.

Other organizers of the pageant presented both girls with their various prizes, which included gift certificates to high-priced department stores and jewelry stores, tuition scholarships, and money in a bank account to be accessed on completion of college.

The parents of both girls were given the opportunity to pose for photographs with them. There was no sign of Cassandra Dutte; it was obvious she had no say in her daughter's upbringing. Daisy had been adopted from Naomi Felder by Jannis Crustanzie. Following the incident on the train, Naomi was found, but she was in no position to raise the child whom she said she was keeping as a favor for another woman. Ionnia wondered whether she was all right. Or had she made another attempt at her life and eventually succeeded?

The following day, the newspapers had the pictures of both the queen and the runner-up, and one headlines read, "Beautiful Flowers: Daisy and Carnation."

Sixty-Seven

Ionnia had little time to focus on her private life, but she didn't care at this time. She was busy running the I Dunn-Ryte Enterprises, which consisted of the various Zeme companies. She still had her weekend show, *On the Edge,* at BRTV9, and she continued to engage in her pet project of freeing women from femicidal maniacs. As a member of the Puca Luca Chamber of Commerce, she attended many luncheons and award ceremonies, which allowed her the opportunity to meet and mingle with other businesspeople. It was such an honor to be included in these people's companies. She was invited to one such luncheon on New Year's Eve, which was to be held in the grand ballroom of the Golden Crown Hotel and which was to be followed by the annual New Year's Eve ball later that evening.

Ionnia chose to go alone, even though she could have accepted one of the many invitations from her male acquaintances who expressed the pleasure of escorting her to this event. Sometimes all she wanted was a social companion, but most of her male acquaintances wanted more than that. Her first choice for this particular occasion would have been Melvin Billhadow, but he was out of town and therefore would not be back in time for the occasion.

Ionnia was seated at a corner table with other prominent dignitaries, including the chairperson of the Puca Luca fashion industry,

Hugh Mann. She had a good view of who was arriving with whom, and she felt like a news reporter or a gossip columnist for a tabloid newspaper. She caught herself. *This is not my job.* Among the list of reporters present was Jean Molby from the *Puca Luca Tattler*, who was making sure nothing was missed.

As the guests filed in, Ionnia's attention was so focused on Chester Saddler that she nearly missed the identity of the woman by his side. It was Prettiana Del Ayoren, the daughter of Victor Del Ayoren and his wife, Katherine, who were the owners of the largest sawmill and timber factory in the county. Prettiana's parents arrived later but did not sit with Saddler and their daughter. Unconfirmed reports were that they despised him because he was suspected of pushing his first wife, Pearline, out of a car and then backing the car over her and killing her, because she'd caught him cheating on her with her cousin and, according to him, had the nerve to confront him about it. Saddler pretended to be the grieving husband for a long time, always maintained that his wife's death was an accident, and he was never charged with anything.

Pearline was an only child from a wealthy family, and when her parents passed away a few years ago, she inherited everything they owned. When she died, all her inheritance was automatically left to her husband, Chester Saddler. He took possession of the parents' property, including the mansion by the beach where they had lived most of their lives, which he converted into a small guesthouse. He acquired other properties and operated a lucrative hospitality business, but despite his success, that stigma of being a murderer still hung over his head, and women were careful not to get too close to him. It got to a point where many described themselves as Saddlerphobic.

The Del Ayorens threatened their daughter, Prettiana, that they would disinherit her if she continued to see Chester Saddler, but she ignored them. It was as though Saddler had cast a spell on her, and rumor had it that his mother was famous for this kind of occult activity. Maybe she was related to Elrick Zeme, or he had taught her the art of necromancy.

When Prettiana took her seat, she sat as if waiting for someone to photograph her or paint her portrait. She wore expensive diamond earrings and necklace. She was young, wealthy, and elegant, but she vapid. Without the beauty, wealth, exquisite jewelry, and her parents' popularity, not many men of consequence would look at her. It must have been awkward for someone like her to be at this function among people of such caliber. It had been heard in social circles that she would handsomely reward men for accompanying her to different events. Saddler sat beside Prettiana like a proud peacock. He might even be a well-paid gigolo.

How ironic is it that Saddler and I should be having dinner at the same location? Ionnia's thoughts took her back in time to when he had spitefully withheld food from her and her brothers. Saddler's face brought back aching memories that Ionnia had put behind her, and she found it difficult to relive them at this time. This was like a nightmare. Ionnia tried hard not to show the emotions that had welled up inside of her. She felt a sudden tightness in her stomach, a lump in her throat, and an unexplainable pounding in her head. She felt faint, was sweating, and felt like that scared, hungry little girl from Dartsdam Elementary. She hoped no one noticed. She started some deep breathing, and the anxiety subsided. Ionnia had a vivid recollection of what Saddler had done to her.

Her brothers, along with other poor, underprivileged children, were the recipients of the school's free lunch program, and each day senior students were assigned to collect names and submit them to the nutrition staff in the kitchen. One cold December day, when Saddler was in charge of collecting the names, he intentionally left the Quanes' names off the list. He had a grouse against them because of lies his little sister had told him about Tyrone. The children, most of whom had no breakfast in the mornings, lined up and patiently waited their turn for their lunch trays. Everyone was served except for Ionnia and her brothers, who were left standing like children waiting for the arrival of Santa Claus.

A full five minutes had passed before the assistant canteen manager, Miss Nellie Wiggins, saw them standing there. Assuming that they had already gotten lunch, she asked them, "Are you waiting for something else?"

"My lunch, ma'am," Ionnia answered.

"Are you all together? Tell me your names."

"The last name is Quane," Roger chimed in.

"Your names are not on the list today," Miss Wiggins said disappointingly as she thumbed through the pages over and over.

Shocked and in disbelief, Ionnia's brothers went through the list line by line with Miss Wiggins, as if hoping for some miraculous appearance of their names.

"Let me see if there is anything left in the kitchen. Sometimes the staff has leftovers, which they take home for their dogs." She returned with a jug in her hand and some cups. "There was nothing else in the kitchen except this skimmed milk, and I was just about to stop Miss Myrtle from pouring it in the bowl for her cat."

Ionnia went back to class the rest of the afternoon without food. She pretended to be comfortable, but she was not. Her usual level of participation in class was lacking, and her teacher expressed concern and disappointment until she learned what had happened. Rain fell all afternoon, and Ionnia was kept at school later than usual. Her little stomach growled, and the consumption of the skimmed milk made matters worse. Finally, the rain ceased, the sun came out, and everyone made a run for it. On the way home, the rain started again. There was nowhere to stop and seek shelter, and even if there were, Ionnia was scared of doing so just in case she was attacked by other children.

When Ionnia got home, she looked like a hungry, drowned cat. Her mother fixed her and the boys some ketchup soup and some bread she had brought home from Felcopper's bakery, which she'd gotten in exchange for cleaning the facility. When she learned of the situation at school with the lunch, her heart sank. She was hurt and angry. Did anyone have a right to do this to her children?

"This is not fair. I'm a good person, and my children have never hurt anyone." Then she remembered the words of Dennis Wholey, a twentieth-century radio talk show host, who said, "Expecting the world to treat you fairly because you are a good person, is a little like expecting the bull not to attack the matador because he is a vegetarian."

Seated at the table with Ionnia was former police officer Sheila Bluggard, who owned a security company. When she saw the pain that Ionnia was trying to suppress, she asked her, "Do you need anything? Is it too warm in here?"

"I'm fine. It's that time of the month. Thanks for your concern."

They say that time heals all wounds, but if that were so, why are we told that the way to recognize and identify Jesus is by the nail prints in his hands? Why haven't Jesus's wounds disappeared? In this case, Ionnia's emotional scars had obviously not gone away.

Saddler must have recognized Ionnia's name from the guest list, and as he looked around the room, his roving eyes caught hers. She smiled and waved politely to him as if to say, "Are you looking for me? There is enough food here for everyone this time."

Saddler looked at Ionnia curiously and questioningly, and then he continued to drink his champagne in a manner that suggested if he were in a church, he would certainly go back for seconds at communion.

At the table next to Ionnia's were three other well-known couples whose businesses made the Chamber of Commerce's top 100 list. It became very obvious that one of the wives, Ashley Conorton, definitely didn't want to be there. She ate almost the entire time and seldom applauded when the guest speaker delivered the keynote address.

Ashley's husband, Russell, was in the transportation business and owned a fleet of taxis, limousines, and luxury tour buses. He flirted with any woman who was vulnerable enough to fall for his sweet talk. He had as many illegitimate children as he had vehicles.

Ionnia and Ashley met in the ladies' room after they had finished eating, just before the trophies and awards were to be handed out. Ionnia said to her, "I couldn't help but notice how uncomfortable you were at the table."

"Wouldn't you be uncomfortable if you were sitting beside the man from whom you've endured several years of hell?"

"Do you want to talk about it?"

"If we had the entire month," Ashley replied.

"Then summarize it."

Ionnia listened with rapt attention as Ashley told her how miserable her life had been, and still was. "When I met Russell, I was still living at my parents' home with four sisters and two brothers in a small, three-bedroom house. He introduced me to the good life, and not long afterward, I moved out of the crowded environment and into a four-bedroom house in Trevine while I continued to pursue my ambitions as a teacher."

Ashley dried her hands, opened her purse, and started to apply a thick layer of concealer and powder on her face to hide the physical scars left there by her husband. However, no amount of makeup could hide the emotional scars that lingered, unobserved by many.

Ionnia didn't take her eyes off Ashley. "Did you keep in touch with your family, or did he prohibit you from making contact?"

"Not at first. Two of my sisters; Rosa and Arlene, visited frequently, and I was oblivious of the fact that they were having an affair with Russell, who had become my fiancé."

"What did you do about it?"

"When I found out, I asked them not to come back to my house."

"Did you confront your fiancé?"

Ashley said, "I did."

"And what was his response?"

"He denied it—and slapped me so hard I was speechless. I almost stumbled and fell. While I was trying to regain my balance, I could hear him muttering something about spreading the love around, and how selfish I was to prohibit that."

"Why didn't you leave when you had the chance?"

"And go where? I couldn't afford to pay rent, and I couldn't go back home. I was totally dependent on him because he was helping to pay my tuition at the University of Trevine. However, he was very repentant and promised he wouldn't do it again."

"And you married him?" Ionnia asked.

"Yes."

"Why?"

"Because he asked me."

"I guess Mr. Conorton was not prepared to have any woman say no to him. But you need to remember this so you can pass it on to your daughters: you should never marry a man simply because he asked you. You are a beautiful woman, and I'm sure that there were many other men around who may have displayed an interest in you. Did he ask any of your sisters to marry him too?"

Ashley was caught off guard with this question, and there was a blank stare, as if she were putting some thought to it. Before she could answer, Ionnia asked her a question that she could answer, "Did your sisters come to your wedding?"

"I didn't invite them, but they came anyway, perhaps by invitation from Russell. And guess what? Both of them were pregnant at the time. Five months after my wedding, Rosa gave birth to a boy, and another month after that, Arlene had a girl."

"And were you suspicious that these were your husband's children?"

"Yes, I had my suspicions. But in order to keep peace in the family, I kept my mouth shut. When Russell asked me to assist in raising the children, knowing the struggles of the family, I couldn't say no. They were not to be blamed for anything."

"Did they know that Russell was their father?"

"I don't know, but they referred to him as Daddy. I thought nothing about it. My sisters were struggling, and he was there to lend a helping hand. That was the only father figure they knew."

"I don't know what to say, other than that you are an extraordinary woman."

The two women stopped talking when other women began visiting the rest room. Ashley beckoned Ionnia to two armchairs situated in a small sitting area, and they resumed the conversation.

Ashley said, "You must think I am strange, spilling my guts to a stranger, but I feel as if I have known you a long time. I am still bewildered that a man who was once kind, loving, and generous could turn out to be what he is."

Ionnia patted Ashley's hands and said, "Don't worry about it." She quoted a Zulu proverb: "'The most beautiful fig contains a worm.'" After thinking for a few seconds, Ionnia asked, "Do you still teach?"

"Yes, I have been teaching reading to children who were overlooked by other teachers and said that they would not be able to read and would not amount to anything. Those were the children who had moved from place to place with mothers who were victims of abuse. Well, I have had high success rates in most of the schools I teach. I also teach adult literacy classes at the community center."

Ionnia could not let go about Ashley's husband. "Did you eventually find out that Russell was the father of your niece and nephew?" she asked.

"Yes. He told his grandmother, who passed on the information to me in confidence while on her deathbed. She also told me that her grandson was living a lie."

"What else could there be?"

"That his real name was Anthony Veller."

"You are right: we don't have an entire month to hear about this part," Ionnia said. "I may sound like a broken record, but I am asking you again: why did you stay with this fraud? It must be really humiliating, loving someone who thinks so little of you."

"He threatened to kill me if I left. And trust me, he will find me wherever I go."

Ionnia gave her a business card and said, "Keep in touch. There is a better life out there, but you have to be willing to let go and seize the opportunity when it knocks." She cited Sujit Lalwani, a thirteenth-century Indian entrepreneur. "'The two toughest lessons to learn are Let Go, and Let's Go.' Very soon there will be a safe place to where you will be able to escape, and your husband will not be able to find you unless you want him to. And, if he tries, he will be in big trouble." As they walked back to the meeting room, Ionnia told her about her plans across the bridge.

Sixty-Eight

In record time, the construction of the bridge leading from Buek Ridge to Isle of Hope (formerly Sulfur Cay) was completed, and no one could deny that this work of art was a sight to behold. The engineering was unique, and the bridge bore no resemblance to any other in that hemisphere. NOMENCO did an incredible job, and as a result the company was nominated for an award by the Puca Luca Chamber of Commerce and featured in newspapers and architecture magazines, both locally and internationally.

Phase two of the project got underway, and Ionnia received immeasurable support through the kind generosity from the MUJALI group, which constructed a new marina to assist with the delivery of equipment and supplies so that the project could be completed without delay. She was successful in getting the company to sign a contract that entrance to Isle of Hope would no longer be accessible once construction ended; that the only entrance would be across the bridge. This piece of property, situated east of the island of Buek Ridge and surrounded by the Buek River, had been acquired and developed by Ionnia Dunn-Ryte, and it was appropriately named Isle of Hope. She said *Hope* stood for "Helping Other People Escape."

Heavy equipment of all shapes and sizes came to the island, and materials of every description were trucked to the site via the new bridge. Ionnia's longtime friend, Melvin Billhadow, contributed by transporting workers to and from the site free of cost. Before long, the property was cleared and reclaimed, with all required infrastructure put in place.

Within another eighteen months, phase three was launched, and when completed, it was the only topic of conversation for a long while. One of the first sections to be completed was the Hope Empowerment and Rehabilitation Services (HERS) complex. The other sections comprised of many different units that catered to the various needs of women. Such names included Hopeville Gardens, Hopeville Manors, Hopeful Meadows, and Hopeville Landings. Erection of homes, businesses, schools, medical facilities, a golf course, and the gamut of what made up a community was to be found on this three-and-a-half-mile-long and two-mile-wide stretch of once abandoned and unclaimed fen. It had now been refashioned and reshaped, and now it was fully resplendent with multi-million-dollar structures. One such structure was a five-star restaurant owned and operated by Ionnia's brother Kyle, and the head chef was her childhood friend Ibrau. The six-story tower, which was named Hopeville Towers, served as headquarters for Zeme Industries, which had been renamed I Dunn Ryte Industries. One floor was dedicated as a conference center for meetings and social activities, and it would be the future venue where the Ministry of Women's Affairs held its annual conferences and workshops. On top of the tower rested a helipad, which made it easily accessible and convenient for Ionnia and other executives to come and go with ease.

At first, Ionnia's project generated a barrage of comments and reactions from people from every stratum of society. People were shocked and awed by the magnitude of the investment, and they had their own suggestions and ideas as to who and what all that money could be spent on. As Ionnia's public relations machinery began to turn, people started to show optimism, and they became less wary of Ms. Dunn-Ryte's intentions. Before everyone became aware of who would be living on the island, a lot of them questioned Ionnia's motives, and their curiosity led them to ask whether any average person could afford to live there. They wondered whether the only acceptable alternative was to be a hired help. But as more and more educational workshops were held by BONDAGE and RAW, reality sunk in: the island was to be a refuge for many women who had been battered and abused physically, emotionally, and financially. Eventually, people saw that there was an urgency to protect women from their haters: men. Ionnia was hailed as a heroine, and people went as far as to nominate her for national awards and recognition.

At one of the award ceremonies, she stressed the need for women to be respected and sent a warning. "No longer should the country condone abuse, disrespect, and harassment in the home and in the workplace." She went on to issue a guilt-ridden statement. "Your silence is consent, and to be silent is to condone."

But there still remained the critics and the skeptics. Elvie Brownshoe was among a group of influential elite women who suffered in silence, viewed the whole thing as brainwashing, and took to the airwaves accusing Ionnia of breaking up marriages and relationships. It was dumbfounding that Elvie should hold those views based on her experience with her second husband, Alfred—and it was more disturbing that she was resistant to change. Elvie was treated like a slave or a hired help, depending on who the observer was. On Saturdays, when Alfred would give her the week's money to cover household expenses, he would give her a shopping list with an estimated cost of each item, and she dared not overspend by buying something more expensive. She had to produce the receipts and whatever change was leftover. One week she bought a personal feminine item, and Alfred went ballistic when he saw this on the list. He accused her of not knowing how hard he worked for his money, adding that she should learn to improvise. When Elvie pleaded with her husband, he reluctantly included that item on future lists. He would refer to her as "my little PITA." When his friends pressed him about the significance of that name, his response was, "Because she is a pain in the ass." He was not the only one with an alias. He was nicknamed Inspector Tightness.

Elvie's first husband, who was thirty years her junior, was a living, breathing parasite who'd married her because he thought she had inherited money from her grandmother. When she revealed that the money was left in a trust for her children, he did not believe her and tried to strangle the life out of her. Elvie pretended to be dead, so he left to report to the police that he had just killed his wife, but when they got there she was gone.

Were Elvie and her group afraid of living like independent women? Why didn't it trouble them to see how animalistic and wretched men were toward women? And didn't it trouble them that society knew their miserable circumstances and viewed them as victims? Was it because their self-esteem had eroded to the point where it appeared that they hadn't yet hit rock bottom? In his book *The Art of Worldly Wisdom*, Baltazar Gracian, a seventeenth-century Spanish Jesuit writer and philosopher, stated, "The best skill of cards is knowing when to discard."

Ionnia made a final flyover of the project to evaluate her achievement, and by the gleam in her eyes, one could see that she was pleased. She had never experienced such a sensation and felt like a kid in a candy store. She turned to those who had accompanied her and asked, "Have I done right?"

Nothing but positive comments came from each member of the group, and Ionnia's face flushed with satisfaction and the pleasure of knowing that her unselfish purpose in life was fulfilled. Its success was up to the people who would be benefitting from this. The idea that had once seemed farfetched has now a reality, and the miracles were coming through. The person who was once rejected was now a shining light in other people's lives. "I guess it wasn't a coincidence that I was always given the part of Rudolph the Red-Nosed Reindeer at most of my schools' Christmas concerts," she said. "You all know his story of rejection."

Ionnia was summoned to appear before a special session of the House of Representatives to defend the project across the bridge so that the government could consider whether or not such a project was worth funding in any way. If it was worth financing, they surely wanted to take credit. Ionnia accepted the invitation with much humility. She had expected to be grilled mercilessly by the male-dominated house for taking on such a monumental task, but she also hoped that they would see the importance of protecting women and would subsequently pass legislation dealing with this epidemic, and providing matching funds for some of the programs. While she prepared her presentation, a thought came to her. *This meeting should be held on my turf, on the Isle of Hope, across the bridge.*

When word got out that Ionnia wanted to change the venue, her haters, who were appalled at the thought that she and many others advocated for an end to the widespread abuse of women, criticized her endlessly and continued to hurl their insults. They said that she wanted to stay in her comfort zone because she was a wimp and afraid of the big dogs. But that did not bother Ionnia because she knew who she was and for what she stood. She knew her strength. The politicians debated this unprecedented approach to a parliamentary session but eventually acquiesced. They thought it was a brilliant idea so that they could have the opportunity to gain firsthand knowledge about every aspect of the facility on the island.

She asked permission to invite members of the Puca Luca Council of Churches and the deputy commissioners of police to the meeting. By doing so, these officials would be given the chance to tour the island, join the scheduled informal session and rally at the HERS complex, listen to some of the occupants tell their stories of years of abuse, see pictures of some who were no longer around, and view pictures of women who bore physical scars as a reminder of the bullies in their lives. "Ladies and gentlemen, it's all about these victims, and the Isle of Hope is their comfort zone."

When Ionnia and members of BONDAGE and RAW addressed the members of the God Squad, as the Council of Churches was known, one could hear a pin drop in the room. She gave them an unprecedented, severe scolding for not providing the proper education to the men in society that women should be loved, respected, and protected, as promised in their marriage vows. She reminded them of sections in the book of Genesis that talked about a beautiful world, one in which man's purpose was to worship his helpmate instead of unleashing his selfishness and hatred on her. The next question took them by surprise. "You men of God, how does it make you feel to marry the women and then bury them in a few months or years, knowing that your male counterparts contributed to their demise? Obviously it didn't faze you, because in most cases it was about money—hefty fees for weddings and burials." Ionnia went as far as to tell them that if the men in society continued treating women as they were doing, in the future their place in a woman's life might be replaced by robots. The sarcastic laughter that erupted from the men was soon replaced by cheers from the women, followed by the chorus from her favorite song, "Across the Bridge."

After the eruption subsided, Ionnia turned to the lawmen and expressed her disappointment that more of these batterers were not arrested and brought to justice. She asked the police commissioners, "Are you aware that on many occasions, your subordinates have refused to arrest abusers? Instead, they give them a slap on the wrist and tell them not to do it anymore." Then she asked them what they were going to do about their own adulterous members of the force who were alleged to have abused their spouses. She went on to say, "The world should be appalled at the levels of abuse meted out to women of all walks of life, some of whom suffer in silence. It is frightening how abuse has become an acceptable form of social behavior." She delivered a mandate to the churches to hold nationwide conferences and workshops to educate men as to how they should treat women. She urged the politicians to pass stricter laws that would serve as a deterrent to domestic violence. She urged the business executives to stop harassing women to consent to affairs in order to be promoted.

"We tried to fix the problem," Joyce Woodson, the member in charge of women's affairs, reported. "But we have run into roadblocks with the male-dominated House of Representatives. Whatever we did was just a Band-Aid. And, yes, we agree that the souls of the dead women must have been angered at the lack of reform needed to solve the problem. It's about time women begin to speak out about the workplace culture, unafraid of repercussions. I want you all to know that this problem of bullying, violence, and rape is close to my heart." Joyce also urged more women to consider running for political office, and she demanded that the prime minister and other parliamentarians nominate and place more women in cabinet positions, where they could advocate for the rights of women and children.

Ionnia couldn't help but notice how much this parliamentarian resembled Phyllis and Jonas Byroo. *Could she be the product of Lena Woodson's rape?* They would be working together, so sooner or later, Ionnia would know the truth.

A vote was taken regarding funding for the project, and a unanimous decision was reached by the lawmakers to set aside a percentage of the annual budget to subsidize some of the undertakings across the bridge. The lawmen pledged their support to do their utmost to prosecute male batterers to the full extent of the law. They also made it unequivocally clear that those law enforcement personnel who looked the other way could be held responsible for any harm that befell any of the women they failed to protect. The commissioner pledged to start in his own backyard, and he made reference to a number of policemen who physically abused their spouses; when the complaints were lodged against them, their supervisors did nothing. But things would change. These supervisors would be held responsible in the future.

The God Squad pledged their support to do their utmost to help men to be better husbands, boyfriends, and fathers. "It will not be an easy task to reach all the men in the society," the president of the

Puca Luca Council of Churches stated. "But it is worth a try." This was the beginning of the miracles.

Following the conclusion of the parliamentary session, an informal meeting commenced, with Ionnia telling the group how disgusted she was with the fathers who condoned the wrongdoings of their sons and shielded them from the law. "Such actions have led the young men to believe that there are no consequences for their actions." She went on to ask the men if they remembered the incident some years ago in Redwood Vale when three young boys attacked an innocent and helpless little girl, rubbed stinging nettle all over her, and broke her arm with a baseball bat as a way of preventing her from competing in an essay competition. At that time, parents, especially fathers, were aware of these boys' actions but did nothing about it. "Who among us is innocent? Raise your hand." Following a deadly silence that lasted for thirty seconds, every male raised his hand except the vice president of the Puca Luca Council of Churches, Bishop Ephraim Morette. It was obvious that she had struck a nerve, and Ionnia focused her eyes steadfastly on him. Morette sat clutching his chest as if he were having heart attack, and he sat there looking like a frightened animal that was about to go to the slaughterhouse, ready to give its last kick. The group looked at the bishop in wonderment and waited for him to raise his hand. He rose from his seat, and when he found his voice, he asked to address the group. No one was ready for what he had to say except Ionnia and Magda Ponce. The bishop confessed to his past behavior, expressed remorse, and immediately resigned his position as vice president of Puca Luca Council of Churches. Ionnia felt relieved that after all these years, someone had claimed responsibility. Bishop Morette said that he would like his son and the other two men to apologize and make restitution to the young lady, if they knew where she was. She shocked a number of people when she revealed her identity. She was no longer the skinny athlete or the poor, unwanted mistake. She was wealthy and beautiful, and most of all, she did well at championing the cause of women and their children. How did she remain so calm?

The major movements that had declared war against the bullying of women conducted a survey on this behavior, and the results were stunning. What was more alarming was the burden it put on the healthcare system. Joyce read a report that stated in the past year, approximately 15 percent of the budget from the Ministry of Health was spent on addressing physical and psychological problems relating to domestic violence. She promised to do all she could to put preventive measures in place to stop this epidemic. The media had enough material to work with, and it came as no surprise that one of the stories contributed to the downfall of George Morette, Jeffrey Dutte, and Gladstone Bibb. Bibb was married to Simone, who immediately filed for divorce. All three came crawling to Ionnia and offered their apologies.

Sixty-Nine

The prospective residents on the Isle of Hope, the battered and abused women, were allowed to stay for a minimum of two years. They were carefully screened by psychologists and women's groups so that there was an understanding that they would not be returning to the men who abused them. They were given time to think about the fact that none of these men would be allowed on the island and were not allowed to visit or have any contact or communication with the women, given what they'd been through. If and when they expressed their desire to visit their abusive spouses, they would not be allowed to return to the residence across the bridge. During their stay, mandatory counseling services were made available for them and their children. These included financial counseling, psychological counseling, vocational counseling, and self-reliance, self-assurance, self-defense, and self-esteem classes. There would also be mandatory follow-up with sessions at various chapters of BONDAGE or RAW, where crisis plans and strategies were in place to instill in the women and young girls how to set values and goals for success, beginning with respect for themselves.

The waiting list grew bigger every day, and Ionnia hired Lorna Tottenberry as director of eligibility. Lorna would work alongside the psychologists, women's groups, and the Department of Women's affairs.

Some children attended schools that were subsidized in part by the Puca Luca Department of Education and grants from various organizations that supported the abused and battered women's movements. There was also the I Dunn-Ryte scholarship made available by Gus Muggerdon, and others were bused to schools in Buek Ridge. In the evenings, the women who needed continuing education received it, and those who were ready to enter tertiary institutions were sent over to the mainland. They respected and appreciated the opportunity they were afforded to live a life free from fear and from abuse of all sorts. It was a life they had never known would arrive because of their own refusal to see the light, even though it was bright enough to blind them. This scenario could be summed up by what Franz Kafka, a twentieth-century German novelist and short story writer, once said: "If a man has his eyes bound, you can encourage him as much as you like, but if he continues to stare through the bandage the will never see anything." These women had removed the bandages and had begun to see. They also had respect for themselves. They held their heads up high and walked with pride and self-confidence. As each group of women left the island to start new lives on their own, the various media companies interviewed them. The women stressed unequivocally that they would be able to survive without a man—something they never knew that they could do. The happiness that they eventually experienced and the singlehood they now embrace gave them an overwhelming sense of pride. The sensation was overpowering. "Was this a dream?" they asked. "How happy we could have been all these years, were it not for love that had stolen our youth and independence."

One woman quoted William Shakespeare: "I had rather hear my dog bark at a crow than a man swears he loves me." She went on to say, "Thanks to my experience across the bridge, and to the awareness and miracles that emerged. And thanks to Ms. Dunn-Ryte, RAW,

and BONDAGE, who made women aware that they should not remain in their winter when their spring arrives."

Although she knew the truth and had inspired a lot of people,
Ionnia Dunn-Ryte kept asking herself, "Have I done right by these
women?" The answers were obvious in every nook and cranny of
Puca Luca. In almost every household, in every level of political life,
in every place of worship, and in every workplace, men had begun
to show more respect for women and promote them to well-deserved
positions based on their qualifications instead of promotions based on
how many times they slept with them.

The seed was planted, and what were once thought to be obstacles
and mistakes emerged in the full bloom of awareness known as the
miracles across the bridge.

About the Author

E. VALLIN SUEDE never let the scars of being labeled "different" and a "misfit" as a child deter her from earning a degree in elementary education, a bachelor's degree in psychology, a diploma in communications and a master's degree in counseling. Since then, she has used her acquired knowledge and experiences to promote selflessness, empathy, and inspiration. *Miracles across the Bridge* is her first book.

CPSIA information can be obtained
at www.ICGtesting.com
Printed in the USA
BVHW072323020320
573891BV00001B/2